RADICAL ELIMINATIONS

BY

MICHAEL J BENSON

TO OUR GRANDCHILDREN

VIKTORIA
ALDEN
EMILY
ALICE

CHAPTER 1

NEW YORK CITY

The two men looked powerful and mean as they walked along Spring Street on the edge of little Italy. They wore long black coats to protect them against the cold winter weather but, unlike other people around them who walked with their heads down to protect them from the wind, these men held their heads high. It wasn't a pride issue, in their line of work they had to be aware of their surroundings always, this was especially true today. They were enforcers for Don Caputo, a very powerful Godfather for the Cosa Nostra. The two enforcers were on their way to talk to a local store owner who had sent word to the Don that some criminal group had moved into the Don's territory. Whoever it was, they were also running a protection racket and they were specifically targeting the Don's clientele. The Don was becoming very frustrated as several people in the area were behind in their protection payments. Some store owners even refused to pay claiming they had already paid. The problem for these people was they didn't realize it wasn't the Don they had paid the protection money to. He'd dealt with the non-payers in the past in his usual fashion by use of violence and threats. He had to take care of this newcomer on his turf before it became common knowledge as it would embarrass him in front of the other families.

The store was very successful selling domestic products like mops, brushes, cleaning products, anything that the regular housewife or cleaning company needed. Several local businessmen bought their goods from the store mostly because they knew that it was under the Don's protection and so were they. This unwritten agreement between local businessmen had been going on for decades, they only bought products from business owners under the Don's protection.

One of the enforcers, Pauli as he was known to his friends, stepped into the store as the second enforcer stayed in the doorway blocking it. He wouldn't allow anyone into the store until the business was conducted.

The man behind the counter was known to the enforcer, he smiled at him, "I understand that you have some information that you want to share," he said.

For some reason the enforcer looked much bigger than usual to the store owner which didn't help as he was already visibly shaking.

"I don't know what you are talking about," he replied.

Pauli's many years of experience had told him that something was wrong he knew this man, why would he be shaking with fear? He'd never used violence or severe threats against him in the past he didn't have to, he always paid on time. As he watched the man he could see that he was moving his eyes as if looking over his shoulder. The man was trying to warn him that someone was in the rear of his store. It took all of Pauli's self-control not to look in the direction of the opening that led into the storage area at the back of the store. His right hand was in his coat pocket and it gripped the handle of his revolver a little tighter. He had to break the silence before the person in the back got suspicious.

"Are you telling me that I was given the wrong information and you don't have anything to tell me?" He deliberately stared straight into the man's eyes so as not to inadvertently look towards the rear of the store.

"Yes, I don't know what you are talking about," he replied nervously.

"I hope nobody is playing games with me, I'll see you Friday as usual." He turned and walked towards the door where his partner was still standing.

"See you then," the store keeper half shouted trying to sound normal.

Pauli walked out of the store and turned left closely followed by his partner.

In the store room at the back of the store, Mohammed could see and hear everything that was said between the two men. He knew that the big man suspected that something was wrong and it was exactly what he'd planned. He and Sammy, his number two, were ready by the door leading into the alley behind the store. Mohammed left the store quickly before the enforcers could see him. Sammy waited inside the store for the two mafia men to appear in the alley where it joined the street.

Pauli tried to walk as casually as possible and stopped just short of the alley leading down the side of the building.

"There's something wrong in there the guy was practically shitting himself, someone was in the back watching us I know it. We will go around to the back of the store where the delivery door is and sneak in. Watch yourself and keep your gun handy. I don't know who we might meet back there," he said to his partner.

They entered the alley just in time to see the back of a short fat man leaving the rear of the store.

"Let's follow him," said Pauli to his partner.

As he said it, the man turned around and saw them. He ran across the alley towards another alley which led down the back of more stores.

The two enforcers gave chase, glancing quickly at the door leading into the rear of the store. It was closed.

"Hey! You stop. I want to talk to you," Pauli shouted.

The man didn't wait. He kept running straight past a parked van and down the alley and out of sight.

The enforcers gave chase but paused as they entered the alley just in case the man had stopped and was lying in wait. They looked down the alley and saw him still running. They started to give chase again.

Mohammed was sitting in the rear of the van watching the two mafia men as they ran after Sammy. As they went around the van in pursuit of Sammy, he jumped out of the van through the two rear doors.

The enforcers heard the noise of the van doors behind them and turned to see what it was. They stopped in their tracks. Standing not twenty feet away was an Arab man with an AK47 in his hand.

Sammy also heard the doors of the van bang open and jumped into one of the many recessed doorways that led into the rear of the buildings from the alley. He pressed himself against the wall, knowing that there was about to be a hail of bullets flying down the alley.

"What's your game?" Pauli asked the man with the AK47.

Mohammed didn't say anything he just pulled the trigger on his weapon firing in the direction of the two enforcers.

Both enforcers tried to dive for cover at the same time, pulling out their revolvers as they did. They didn't stand a chance as the bullets from the AK47 tore into them.

Mohammed was pulling the trigger in quick short bursts to maximize his aim and keep control of the weapon as it spat out the hail of bullets. He watched with joy as the two big men scrambled to find a place to hide but there was nowhere to go. He saw them both hit the ground as the bullets met their targets, tearing through clothes and into flesh.

Pauli's partner of fifteen years died instantly as bullets hit his head neck and shoulders. Pauli lay on the ground, his body riddled with bullets. He saw his partner's lifeless eyes looking back at him. He could hear footsteps and knew that it was the Arab coming to finish him off. He tried to lift his revolver which he still had in a tight grip only to have it kicked out of his hand.

Mohammed was smiling as he walked towards the two men. He could see that one was still alive. The man was trying to move his hand. Mohammed saw the revolver and kicked it, knocking it out of his grasp, sending the gun clattering across the cobblestone alley.

Pauli looked up at the Arab, "Whoever you are, my boss will see that you are a dead man." He coughed as a pool of blood came out of his mouth.

Mohammed didn't say anything he just pointed the AK47 at Pauli's head and pulled the trigger. The bullets decimated the man's skull. Some of the bullets went straight through and ricocheted off the ground, bullets spinning out of control down the alley. Mohammed realized that this wasn't the smartest thing to do, being so close to the man. He turned and from a safer distance this time, he did the same to the second enforcer even though he was dead.

4

"Let's go," he shouted to Sammy who now came out from his hiding place.

They both climbed into the van and drove off slowly without a word between them.

CHAPTER 2

WASHINGTON, D.C.

Senator Gatts and Khurram Al Khan, the Pakistan Ambassador to the USA, shook hands and congratulated each other on the individual speeches they had just given to the listening crowd of supporters.

"Come, let us meet your faithful fans and shake their hands," said the Ambassador. The Senator smiled that well-known smile of his and made all the correct political noises as he stepped down from the stage.

Waiving to the crowd who were applauding him again, he turned to his assistant Brad, "We need to leave after I shake a few hands," he turned and gave another huge smile and a wave.

The hand shaking didn't last more than a minute when the Senator felt a hand on his shoulder.

"This way please Senator," Brad did his job and let everyone know that the show was over.

The Senator's driver stood next to the waiting limousine in a position where he could see the Senator. He was always nervous at this point as the Senator had a foul temper and expected the car to be exactly where he wanted it without any delay. He was the Senator's third driver in less than a year and needed the job to support his family. He saw the Senator walking in his direction away from the crowd. The driver quickly got into the vehicle and drove the forty yards to where he would meet the Senator and his aid Brad, at the sidewalk. He stopped the car and got out. He quickly stepped to the rear passenger door and held it open for the Senator. He held his head high and looked over the passenger door making sure he didn't make eye contact with the Senator. As always, the Senator didn't acknowledge the driver as he bent his six-foot three-inch frame down and got into the rear seat. Brad ran to the other side of the limousine and got into the back of the car and sat next to the Senator.

The Senator rolled down his window and gave a final wave and smile to the onlookers and supporters.

He closed the window as the vehicle moved away and turned to Brad, "Thank God that is over I cannot stand those people."

"I understand, but you need their support and there are over ten thousand of them in this area and they have contributed nearly half a million dollars towards your election campaign. They are relying on you to keep your word on easing the immigration laws for immigrants from countries that supported us during the Gulf war." He was cut off in mid-sentence.

"Yes, yes, I know, but do I really have to do any more of these types of events? I truly hate being around them, if I had my way they would all be deported. They can't even wear US style clothing they insist on wearing those outfits from where they come from. It looks like a fucking Halloween party out there. You know as well as I do that I won't support their request to assist in reforming the immigration laws. Can you imagine what would happen? They and others like them would flood this country by bringing in their hoards. They would be copulating everywhere with no regard for how this country would be able to support them and their children's, children." He was really losing control of his temper and his emotions and slapped his head against the back of the seat in a pout.

"If anyone heard you say that we wouldn't have a campaign or any support for that matter! You must stop making those statements you never know who may hear you. Loose lips sink ships and one day it will be the end of your career and mine, for that matter." Brad stared at the Senator's bright red face he could see he'd worked himself into a total frenzy. "You are almost guaranteed the position as US Under-Secretary of Defense for policy when the vote takes place next week. When you get it, one of your first duties will be to attend the Council on Foreign Relations meeting in New York in six weeks. As Under-Secretary of Defense, you will be required to attend a lot more events with those kinds of people, as you put it."

The Senator just ignored him as he gazed out of the window.

The driver knew that he had to keep quiet he'd heard what the Senator was saying, that famous temper came out but at least it wasn't aimed at him. He was a former taxi driver and had heard a lot over the years from his passengers but nothing like the Senator's rants. Not long after he started to work for the Senator, he requested to be sent on an advanced driver training course, which most of the other Senator's drivers had been on. It would give him a high level of security training and defensive driving techniques. The Senator blew his top when he approached him about it telling him if he didn't think he could do the job, then he should find another one. Brad stepped in that day and saved the driver from the Senator and explained that the Senator wouldn't waste money on the driver's needs. He never asked for another thing from the Senator after that. Had he have been allowed to go on the drivers' security course, he would have most probably noticed the white car that was following them with two men aboard. He continued to drive in silence and entered the ramp to access the freeway.

The white car tailing the Senator's vehicle belonged to the Pakistan Ambassador whom they had just left. The Ambassador and his driver Ramzi watched the Senator's car as it moved onto the freeway, the driver accelerated so that he wouldn't lose the Senator's car.

"I'll use my cell phone to call him he may not answer if he does not recognize the number." The Ambassador punched in the numbers for the Senator's cell phone and handed his phone to Ramzi.

The short silence between the Senator and Brad was broken by the ringing sound of the Senators cell phone.

"Who is this now?" he said in anger reaching into his jacket pocket.

"Please remain calm," said Brad.

The Senator didn't even check to see who was calling him as he answered the call, "Yes," he said in a frustrated voice.

"Look out of your window Senator." The man on the other end of the phone didn't say anymore.

"What, look out of the window what do you mean?" He was curt and rude as usual.

When the Senator repeated out loud what the caller had said Brad looked out of the window on his side of the car but there was just a high grass embankment. He sat forward in the seat and looked past the Senator to the other side of the car and saw a car on the outside of their vehicle traveling at the same speed.

The Senator looked at Brad as he leaned forward.

"There sir," he pointed at the white car as the driver's window was opening.

The Senator and Brad saw that it was Ramzi, the son of one of his major financial supporters and the Pakistan Ambassador.

He turned to Brad with a frown on his face, "I wonder what he wants?"

Brad put his hand on the Senator's shoulder and whispered, "Calm," into his ear.

He smiled and turned to look back at Ramzi as he spoke into the phone. "What can I do for you?" he said with false cheer in his voice.

Ramzi had been listening to everything that they had been saying in the car, as he had been for some months. He'd placed two listening devices in the Senator's car when it was left unattended in the parking garage at his office. Ramzi was highly skilled with electronic surveillance and could access almost any vehicle without being detected.

"You are a very dishonest man Senator and for this you must pay with your life." Ramzi said.

The Pakistan Ambassador waved and smiled at the Senator to get his attention.

The Senator could see that the Ambassador had a black box in his hand which had a red button on the top. Ramzi had deliberately made the red button on the box large so that the Senator couldn't miss seeing it.

"What's wrong?" asked Brad as he saw the expression on the Senator's face change.

Ramzi smiled at the Senator and Brad, holding the Ambassador's cell phone to his ear he said, "Goodbye." He turned the steering wheel, maneuvering his car away from the

Senator's vehicle and headed towards an off ramp to leave the freeway.

The Senator was puzzled at first as to what the Ambassador had in his hand. He looked closer.

"Stop the car, stop the car," shouted the Senator.

He realized that the Ambassador was holding some sort of trigger mechanism for a bomb.

"What is it?" asked Brad.

"He's got a detonator in his hand. He must have put a bomb in the car, stop the car," he screamed at the driver.

They were the last words spoken by the Senator and the last thing he would ever feel was total fear.

The Pakistan Ambassador had a smile on his face knowing that he was about to kill the one man that he detested more than any other. His hatred for the Senator wasn't just for taking many thousands of dollars from trusting Muslim businessmen but more importantly for misleading his Muslim community.

He was anxious to see what the explosives would do to the car and pressed the button a little too early.

The blast was immense, it was far greater than Ramzi and the Ambassador had anticipated. The Senator's vehicle erupted in a giant fireball as it jumped twelve feet into the air. It came crashing down onto the road, a mangled mass of metal engulfed in red hot flames. A second explosion occurred as the fuel in the gasoline tank ignited, another huge fireball spat into the sky above. Other drivers on the road braked and swerved to avoid the burning vehicle, causing several small accidents.

The shock wave from the car bomb hit the car driven by Ramzi with such force that it blew the vehicle off the road, causing it to crash head on into a concrete barrier. The air bag on Ramzi's side of the car failed to deploy on impact and he wasn't wearing a seat belt. Ramzi's body flew forward, smashing his head into the roof of the car where it joined the windshield putting a six-inch gash across his forehead. Blood immediately appeared from the many small lacerations to his face from the windshield as it shattered. His chest collided with the steering wheel, instantly breaking several ribs and bouncing his body back into the driver's seat. The Ambassador fared better in the crash as his air bag did deploy and unlike Ramzi, he was wearing his seat belt. His only injury would be a broken hand, ironically the one he used to press the detonator and a few bruises from the seat belt.

The Ambassador tried to make sense of what had happened as he sat back in the seat. He looked across at Ramzi. He could see that he was in a bad way blood was pouring out of his forehead. The front end of the car was curled up in front of him the radiator was now gushing clouds of steam and hot water. He said a quick thanks to Allah for sparing his life. He knew that he had to get away from the vehicle before the police arrived. He reached for the door and saw white powder on his hands. He pulled down the visor and looked into the mirror his face also had white powder on it. The deflated air bag was sitting in his lap. He knew that this is where the powder had come from. He quickly grabbed a bottle of water that was on the floor by his feet. He opened his door and crawled out of the car, his legs gave way under him as he tried to stand. He knelt on the damp grass gathering his composure as he got his bearings. He felt slightly light headed. He was now in survival mode and staggered to his feet and looked around. He could see people walking on the freeway looking into cars, checking on the occupants. The explosion had caused several accidents. There was a group of trees at the side of the road. He staggered towards them. Before anyone could see him, he needed to disappear. He didn't give a second thought to Ramzi or his condition, his aim was self-preservation. Ramzi would be taken care of later, if he survived.

Once he was deep into the trees out of sight, he took a moment to wash his hands and face with the bottle of water. He knew that the white powder would bring attention to him. He removed his jacket and shook it, getting as much of the white powder off as he could before he put it back on. He took a comb out of his jacket and pushed it through his hair as he tried to make himself look respectable. He frantically searched his jacket pockets for his cell phone and realized he'd given it to Ramzi.

He could hear voices in the distance towards the freeway. This made him refocus. He had to find a phone to call the Embassy to send a driver for him. He could now hear the familiar sounds of sirens from the emergency vehicles responding to the explosion. He staggered on through the trees. In the distance through the branches he could see a Wal-Mart store. He headed towards it. As he got to the tree line next to the Wal-Mart parking lot, he looked around at the vehicles in the parking lot and the people going to and from the store. After quickly assessing the area, he saw that all the people going in and out of the store were very casually dressed. He knew that he would stand out if he walked into Wal-Mart wearing a suit and tie. He stepped back into the trees a little further to give himself cover and took off his tie and jacket as he emptied the pockets of his jacket and tore the inside pocket of his suit jacket off. The pocket showed the name of the tailor who had made the suit and this could possibly lead investigators back to him if the jacket was found. He rolled the jacket into a ball and stuffed it into a thick patch of grass and weeds under a tree and put the tie and torn tailor's label into his trouser pocket. He slowly stepped forward to the edge of the tree line again. He now focused on a line of parked cars and pickups not more twenty yards from him. As he scanned the parking lot and the store building from the safety of the trees, he could see four surveillance cameras on the roof. He knew there would be more inside the store and that they would all be recording what they were seeing. He had to hide his face from the cameras somehow. A hat would be the perfect solution. He stayed in the cover of the trees as a pickup pulled into an empty parking space close to his position. He stepped back a little further into the trees and watched as the driver got out and walked towards the store. He considered stealing a vehicle but dismissed the thought almost immediately as this would ring alarm bells with the police when they investigated the explosion. Now was the time for him to move. He walked out from the trees in a crouched position, keeping the line of parked vehicles between him and the surveillance cameras. In the back window of one of the cars was a baseball cap, he checked to see if one of the doors was unlocked and it was. He quickly took the baseball cap and put it on his head, pulling it down a little at the front to help hide his face from the store cameras. From his crouched position, he gave one last scan of the area to make sure nobody had seen him, he was clear. In one move, he stood up with the car door open and closed it like he'd just got out of the car and confidently walked towards the store, keeping his head slightly bowed, another move to hide his face from the cameras.

The doors at the front of the store opened automatically as he approached them. A blast of cool air washed over him as he entered the store. An elderly lady in a Wal-Mart uniform greeted him and welcomed him to the store. He nodded at the lady without showing his face to acknowledge the welcoming greeter. He saw a sign to his left next to a McDonald's fast food restaurant for the restrooms. Thankfully, when he entered there wasn't anyone inside the restroom. He washed his face and hands again this time using the mirror to make sure that he didn't leave any telltale signs of the white powder from the air bag. As he washed his hands and face, he grimaced in pain several times, as the broken right hand was already starting to swell and was now very painful. He dried his face with the paper towels provided and was concentrating on his hands when a man walked into the rest room, he kept his head down. Out of the corner of his eye he could see the man was wearing a Wal-Mart employee waistcoat. The man went straight to the restroom cubicle and locked the door.

The Ambassador was sure the man didn't take any notice of him and took this as a good opportunity to find out where a pay phone was. He could hear the man undoing his trouser belt and then he saw the trousers resting on the man's shoes. He was sitting, no chance of him coming out now to help when he asked his question.

"Is there a pay phone around here?" he asked in a reasonable American accent.

"Yeah! Over at the gas station," the man in the cubicle replied.

He left without replying and walked straight over to the gas station in the parking lot. He called the Embassy and told his secretary where he was and instructed her to send his head of security to pick him up immediately. He told her about the wreck on the freeway and to pass this on to his head of security. By avoiding the freeway, he knew it would only be fifteen to twenty minutes before he was picked up.

A fire truck was the first emergency vehicle to reach the burning limousine. The firemen dutifully leapt from the truck and went about their business of putting out the fire. Two police vehicles arrived at the same time sirens blurring and flashing lights illuminated on the rack on the top of the cars. The scene was one of total confusion with the burning vehicle and several accidents it was hard to know where to start. One of the officers called for more assistance and paramedics, they were already on the way.

A second fire engine arrived with a paramedic team on board and they stopped next to the vehicle which Ramzi was in.

Paramedic Steve Matiss carried his bag containing his emergency medical kit over to the car and saw a man slumped over the steering wheel. He opened the car door and checked the man's neck for a pulse it was there but a little faint. He methodically checked the driver's neck and head, the gash on the forehead was still bleeding. He tried to rouse Ramzi but he got no response. He cleaned the wound and put a temporary dressing on it, which helped to stop the bleeding. By now, several police cars had arrived and officers were talking to several members of the public who were standing close to him. He overheard the conversations and they were all describing how the limousine blew up. This reminded him of some of the videos he'd seen in the military of car bombs. His patient was now groaning and starting to show signs that he was going to regain consciousness.

"Easy pal, you need to sit still you have a bad cut to your forehead." He placed his hands on Ramzi's shoulders to hold him still in the seat.

Ramzi felt himself coming around and could hear voices. As he tried to wake up he was starting to realize what had happened. He knew that he had to get out of the car and escape to safety. He didn't know it but he had a serious concussion and hairline fracture of the skull, he was in no condition to try to move.

"Got to get away," he mumbled without realizing it.

"You are not going anywhere until you see a doctor," said Steve.

"Nasty cut he has there," a voice said behind him.

Steve turned around and saw a police officer standing over him.

"Yes, it looks like he banged his head on the steering wheel," he replied.

"What is he saying?" said the officer.

"Oh! He keeps groaning and saying he has to get away."

The officer immediately took a further interest in the injured man and walked around to the passenger side of the vehicle. "Did you open this door?" he asked Steve.

"No, it was open when I got here, I thought that it must have sprung open with the impact," he replied.

"Yes, most probably," the officer said.

He peered into the car. As he looked around, he noticed a box on the floor by the front passenger seat. He bent down for a better look. There was a large red button attached.

Steve watched the police officer, something had his attention. The officer was reaching for the box on the floor.

"Wait, don't touch that," Steve shouted.

The officer froze. "Why?"

"I saw something like that when I was in the military it was used to detonate explosives."

They both looked at each other and then at the burning vehicle on the freeway.

"Christ, you may be right. The other drivers described the vehicle over there blowing up. I had better report this to dispatch they will want the Feds involved."

Steve watched the officer step away from the vehicle as he called police dispatch on his radio. After a short conversation, he returned to the vehicle.

"Do me a favor, don't let anyone near this car, I am going to get some crime scene tape from my unit."

"OK." He replied.

His patient was coming to again, he was groaning but his time he was incoherent. Steve saw the officer return and watched him tie one end of the familiar yellow crime scene tape to the front of the car. He walked around the vehicle making a large circle, using a couple of the trees as posts to tie the tape to.

Ramzi was eventually removed from the car and placed on to a stretcher. He was drifting in and out of consciousness unaware of his surroundings. Steve and the police officer placed him inside an ambulance and the officer got in with him.

"When the Feds or my supervisor arrive, tell them about the box in the car and let them know I am escorting this guy to the hospital, I'll let dispatch know on my radio," he said to Steve.

"Will do," he replied.

CHAPTER 3

LONDON, ENGLAND

As part of a new initiative to fight terrorism in the United Kingdom, the Prime Minister put together a highly secretive group of people from government and former military Special Forces. They would be known to each other as the Mask Committee. Their job was to recruit a handpicked team of police officers from various police forces around the UK. Each of the officers was selected for their expertise in firearms, investigations and individual special skills, they would become the Mask Team. After the officers were selected and agreed to the very secretive mission, they were sent to the SAS Special Forces base in Hereford for extensive training in counter terrorism. As part of the training, they were also educated on the techniques and tactics used by various terrorist organizations such as the IRA (Irish Republican Army), Baader Meinhof, PLO (Palestinian Liberation Organization) and various Muslim extremist groups. The Team excelled at Hereford training, not without first receiving many cuts, bruises and blisters. The blisters were mostly on their feet from the daily running regime while carrying an eighty-pound back pack.

As the Team was developing at Hereford, it became clear to the instructors that one of them was going to be the team leader, his name was John Strain.

Strain would eventually give all seven of the Mask Team members' nicknames. He'd already been given his own - Animal - which he wasn't called very often. Steve Jones was called 'Shadow' for his uncanny ability to keep surveillance on people without them knowing he was there, Matt Grantham was called 'Bulldog', basically because he had a head like one and was mean when agitated. Stan Cartwright was called 'Sleepy' because he could fall asleep with ease whenever he wanted. Jack Kay was called 'Lover Boy or L.B. for short, ALL the women loved him, Terry O'Neill was called 'Wheels', there isn't a vehicle he couldn't drive and nobody could outdrive him. On loan from British intelligence, whenever required, were George Barton and Chalky White. Both men were incredibly talented technical surveillance and computer specialists. Much of the equipment used by the Mask Team was made by them and not available to others.

On the last job, they performed the Team lost two of its members, Ian Thomas and Andy Hobson, who were killed in a terrorist bombing of a pub in Liverpool, England. The Team had been targeted by former members of the IRA, Brian Foy and Kevin Donnelly, after the deaths of Foy's sons and Donnelly's daughter at the hands of the Mask Team. After the bombing both sides realized they were puppets of government officials and joined forces to avenge the dead.

The British government's success in its fight against Terrorism didn't miss the attention of the US government. Nobody really understood how the British were becoming so successful but they had the attention of many governments that were victims to these fanatical organizations.

The US President had held very discreet talks with the PM on a recent visit to the UK and had requested that the PM consider the idea of his counter terrorism team operating in the US in the same secretive manner. The PM agreed to at least bring the team leader to Washington on his next official visit.

Strain cleared security at the military airfield South of London where he was to board the Prime Minister's private flight to Washington D.C. As protocol dictated, he arrived well before the PM and his staff so as not to delay the PM when he arrived. There were strict instructions left for him by the PM's security detail to board the aircraft as soon as he arrived and stay on board out of sight until the PM came on board.

Strain only had to wait thirty minutes until he saw the PM arrive, he was early. He watched as the PM left the safety of his car and walked up the steps to the plane closely followed by his head of security from Scotland Yard. Laura, the PM's personal assistant and one of the Downing Street PR suits were already entering the plane.

The PR suit was surprised to see Strain sitting on the plane. He'd seen him at Downing Street on a few occasions but didn't know what he did or why Strain was on the flight.

He whispered in Laura's ear, "What is he doing here?" nodding not so discreetly in Strain's direction.

Laura looked at Strain and turned to the PR suit, "Apparently, he is in training for a possible position on the PM's security detail," she replied.

"Oh!" he said quietly and took a seat, his curiosity satisfied.

When the PM told Laura that Strain was going to be on the trip to the USA she suggested that the PM's security detail be told that Strain was in training. She briefed the head of the PM's security detail and had given him the same message but warned him it was confidential. The head of security, as always, never questioned something that came direct from the PM. He thought that it was a good idea to have someone tested, as his tenure with the PM was due to end in six months.

Strain watched Laura closely. She was wearing a white blouse showing a hint of cleavage and a dark grey stripe skirt and jacket, very businesslike. The outfit hugged her very slim body. Strain admired her dedication. Keeping her body in such good shape wasn't easy with the hectic schedule she had working for the PM.

"Good morning," the PM said to the pilot and co-pilot as he entered the plane. He stood just inside the fuselage of the plane and took off his jacket. Laura quickly leaned forward and took it off him. "Thank you, Laura," he said.

"Morning, John," he said as he turned and saw Strain stand. "Sit down John, no need to stand. After we take off, please join me at the back I have some things to discuss you."

"Yes, sir," Strain replied and sat down again.

The flight to Washington D.C. felt a lot shorter than Strain had expected mainly due to the two-hour private meeting with the PM at the start of the journey. They talked about the deaths of the members of the Mask Team and everything else from whiskey to rugby, but nothing about the reason for the trip to the US.

When Strain returned to his seat after his meeting with the PM, Laura was sitting opposite him. They talked quietly, for how long Strain didn't know but he couldn't remember the last time he'd enjoyed the company of a woman so much.

They were an hour from Washington D.C. when Laura went to sit with the PM. They met for about thirty minutes with Laura scratching away on her note pad throughout the meeting. She walked back to where Strain was sitting, "He would like to talk to you before we arrive."

"Now?" asked Strain.

"Yes," she replied.

He walked to the back of the plane where the PM was sitting staring out of the window.

"You want to speak to me, sir?" he said.

"Yes, John, couple of things we need to go through before we arrive? Take a seat." he said as more of an order than a suggestion.

"Yes sir." Strain thought that the PM looked tense.

"I need to tell you about something that happened in the US this morning as we head to the airport. A US Senator named Gatts was killed when his car exploded on a freeway in D.C. He was a long friend of the President and a close confidant. The US authorities are obviously assuming that it was a bomb of some kind that had been placed on his car. The Senator's PA and driver were also killed in the explosion, thankfully none of them suffered."

"Has anyone claimed responsibility for it yet?" asked Strain.

"No not yet."

"Whoever it was may never come forward anyway but you will get the normal crack pots claiming they did it," Strain replied.

"Yes, I am sure you are right, when we arrive in D.C., I want you to stay on the plane until the media has left. We don't want the media to know you are here. Your assignment will be very dangerous, John, that's if you choose to accept it."

"May I ask what the job is?" He was extremely curious as to what was going on but he knew that it had to involve his team and their counter-terrorism specialty.

"It's similar to what you have been doing in the UK. We will discuss the full details with the US President in his office at the White House. I want you to know that whatever your decision is after the meeting, I will give it my full support."

"Sounds intriguing, sir," replied Strain.

"Yes, it may be, but it's not a simple task that you will be asked to perform. One thing to remember, there is no restriction on the resources that will be at your disposal. You can select whomever you want as your team and as many as you think you will need to complete the assignment in a timely fashion. Unofficially, you will have my support and the support of the President," he paused.

"And officially where do I stand?" Strain already knew where this was going.

"You and your team will be on your own. We will try to protect you as much as possible but both governments will denounce you if you are discovered."

"Well, you don't make it sound very appetizing sir. I will of course keep both governments out of the mix, if I accept the job." He smiled at the PM, knowing already that he would accept it.

"When the press has gone, a Secret Service Agent will meet you at the plane and take you to the White House. You will be staying in a hotel in the city, here are the details." He handed Strain a brown folder. "Please write down the details and give it back to me."

Strain read the contents of the folder, he didn't write anything. He memorized the name and address of the hotel he would be staying at the Westin Hotel, 1400 M Street NW. He handed the folder back.

"Thank you, I'll see you later at the White House. The secret service agent will be your only contact." He placed the folder into a shredder next to his seat and they both watched as the machine made a grinding sound as it ate the folder and its contents.

The British Ambassador to the US met the plane when it arrived at Washington along with a small group of greeters. Strain watched the ceremony from the window of the plane. He was surprised at how fast the hand shaking took place as the PM was famous for his long hand shaking sessions, always taking time to make people feel important. Something was troubling him and Strain knew that it had to do with the meeting with the President and what they were going to ask him and his team to do. The armored vehicles that were to take the PM and his staff to the White House were parked close to the plane. The doors of the cars were open with a security protection specialist at every vantage point to protect the PM.

Strain watched the security operations provided by the US government from inside the aircraft where people outside couldn't see him.

The Bureau of Diplomatic Security provides security for many dignitaries and heads of state visiting the USA every year. The Bureau is the law enforcement and security section of the US Department of State. Each year, it helps protect over 200 of these visiting dignitaries. With nearly 40,000 agents worldwide, it also provides security in foreign countries for a wide range of people including US Ambassadors, visiting US dignitaries and Embassies. The remit also includes security evaluation and protection of the US Embassy buildings, intelligence and other US government property.

After the PM, had left, the plane was moved to a secure hanger and the doors closed. An hour had passed when Strain saw a man in a long black coat walking towards the plane. He was stopped by the security personnel at the bottom of the stairs. He watched as a short exchange of words took place and when the man produced what was obviously his I.D., satisfied, the security officer allowed him on board.

Strain stayed in his seat when the man entered the cabin. He was six feet tall and by his stature, he obviously worked out.

"Mr. Strain?" he said.

"Yes, that's me," he replied.

"I am Special Agent Thorn I am to take you to the White House."

Strain stood and offered his hand to the agent. They shook hands both noticing that the other hand a strong firm grip, eye contact was never lost between them.

They took a short walk across a parking lot outside where there was a black Oldsmobile car.

"Please get in," said the agent.

Strain did as instructed and climbed into the front passenger seat.

"Mr. Strain I'll be your only point of contact during your stay here in D.C. If there is anything you need, anything at all, call this number." He handed over a piece of paper with a phone number written on it.

"My name is John by the way." He didn't like being called Mr."

"O.K., John," the agent smiled. "I also have a cell phone for you, when you switch it on the number appears. I have already programmed my number into it.

After your meeting with the President I'll take you to your hotel, your bags are already in the car."

Strain just realized that he had not thought about his bags. "I guess if you are to be my baby sitter I should know something about you. What is your job?"

"I work for the Secret Service." He didn't offer any more information.

"I was told that earlier, but what is it you do for them or am I not allowed to ask?"

"I work for the Presidential security detail I'm assigned to him. As we are asking questions, what is it you do?"

"I am in between assignments at present, just traveling with the PM. I not sure what he has in store for me."

"What do you do in England?"

Strain thought that the agent's accent was very strong especially when he said 'England'. "I am in the police."

"I guess that gives us something in common, what do you do in the police?" he asked.

"I am on a firearms support unit, you Americans call it S.W.A.T., I believe." He had to play down his real role in the police service.

The remainder of the drive was spent exchanging pleasantries and trying to get to know each other.

As they drove into the city, Strain started to recognize some of the famous landmarks. Everything was very clean and official looking, most of the buildings had been painted white or pale beige. As they drove up to the White House gates, he couldn't help but think that it looked a lot smaller than it did on television. The police officer on the gate checked both I.D.'s and cross checked on his clipboard that they were expected. Steel crash barriers that were blocking them from entering were lowered below the surface of the road and they were waved into the grounds. They didn't go to the front entrance but to a side door. Strain was a little disappointed, as he'd visualized walking in through the main doors. Another police officer checked their ID and then allowed them to enter the building. Strain followed the Agent to a small room where they would wait for only five minutes before being summoned to the President's office.

Inside the spacious office were the President and the PM, both stood as they walked into the room.

"Mr. President, let me introduce John Strain," said the Prime Minister.

"Pleased to meet you John," the President said.

"And you, sir," he replied.

"You already know Special Agent Thorn from the airport." The President said to the Prime Minister. "Sit down, gentlemen, please."

Strain realized that Thorn had stood inside the hanger at the airport the whole time.

"John, may I call you John?" the President asked.

"Yes, sir," he replied.

"As you have most probably heard, we have suffered some quite horrific terrorist attacks in recent months. We are doing all the usual things to investigate who is responsible but we keep running into brick walls. You have been very successful in the United Kingdom in tracing terrorists and bringing them to justice. I would like to ask you if you would be interested in helping form a similar team to the one you have in your home country. Of course, you would have all the assistance we could offer in the way of finance, equipment and manpower support that sort of thing. This will be no ordinary team John it will be highly sensitive and confidential. Prime Minister, maybe you should explain the rest, he is your man after all."

"Yes, John, we have had a great deal of success in the past using the usual conventional methods of fighting terrorism. You yourself told me some years ago, that we couldn't use the conventional ways anymore, we had to operate differently. Your recent success in the UK has caught the attention of the President. He and I have had a very frank and open discussion prior to you coming into the room. We discussed the terrorist attacks here in the US and back home." He was interrupted by the President.

"John, what he is trying to say is that we want you to go out and find the terrorists who are attacking our US homeland and kill the bastards." He realized that he'd interrupted the Prime Minister and immediately regretted it.

"Not very subtly put, Mr. President. John, you must understand that you and your team will be operating as independents and we will wash our hands of you if you are caught eliminating anyone. Keep it the same as the UK and I do not see why this wouldn't work, in other words, accidental deaths, or deaths that can be cleaned up before the press get to the bodies."

"I am afraid the Prime Minister is right that we will disown you as fast as we can if you are caught and by that, I mean by the press or other public body. We will obviously assist if there is an opportunity to do so without it involving either government."

Strain smelt political cover-up and self-preservation all around, he couldn't blame them.

"We do not expect your answer today, think about it for a day or two," for the first time ever The PM felt awkward in Strain's presence.

"I obviously have several questions but I need a couple answered now." Strain said.

"What are they, John?" replied the PM.

"You say that I'll be able to choose my own team. Does that include my present team members in the UK and who will help me source potential team members here in the US?" He got the feeling that Thorn was going to be a player in this.

"You can choose whomever you want from anywhere in the world, Thorn here will help you. You had better read a little about him first, after all it's only fair, as he has already read your dossier, here," replied the President passing Strain a thick folder marked, 'CONFIDENTIAL' in bold letters.

Strain took the folder and gave Thorn a sideways glance, he already knew about Strain's background?

"John, financing is not an issue, the treasure chest is open, so to speak." The PM said.

"I'll give you my answer today." Strain wanted to read the file on Thorn first but he knew that he would accept the assignment, he just hoped the old Mask Team would join him.

"The President is putting together a committee like the one we had in the UK. They are the top people in intelligence and security. They will be helping you and Thorn with some of the information they have gathered on various terrorist groups and sympathizers here in the US." The PM crossed his legs and let the President give the bad news to Strain and Thorn.

The President pressed the intercom on his desk phone, "Send them in now please."

Strain looked over at Thorn as if to say what's going on, Thorn shrugged his shoulders to indicate he knew nothing of this.

The door to the Oval office opened and in walked four people that Thorn didn't want to see.

The President stood, everyone else followed suit as he walked around his desk.

"Gentlemen let me introduce you to Butch Shattuck Director of the CIA, Randolph Atkins director of the FBI, Dan Pierro director of the NSA and finally Victor Corinth Director of the Secret Service and Thorn's boss. You all know the Prime Minister, this is Special Agent Thorn and the gentleman at the end is John Strain with the Prime Minister's Office. Please sit."

The President returned to his seat at the desk as everyone shook hands.

Strain and Thorn both watched the faces of the men who had just entered the room. It was obvious by the expressions on their faces that they didn't have a clue why they had been summoned to the Oval office.

The President cleared his throat as everyone sat down.

"What I am about to tell you stays in this in this room and you will understand why I am saying this in a moment. In the last year, we have seen some horrendous terrorist attacks on US soil. The UK has had more than its share of terrorist incidents over the years with Irish dissident groups and more recently Muslim extremists. The Prime Minister will tell you a little of how they have made great in-roads into fighting back against these groups."

"Some years ago, a committee was formed in the UK of a very small group of government officials. Some of the committee members held positions in the British government like the positions you gentlemen hold. Thiers included a former Special Forces commander. The committee was given the task to identify individual police officers with a certain set of skills from around the UK to form a specialist counter terrorism team. The team was formed with the remit to locate terrorists and their sympathizers and bring them to justice. The team operated under the radar without a safety net, they were alone if caught. After some time, it had become obvious that conventional policing methods wouldn't work in apprehending these terrorists. The team moved into a much darker modus operandi and became very unorthodox and brutal. This they did with my blessing and the support of the committee. No expense was spared in fitting them out with whatever they needed in weapons, technology, cars, planes etc. Once a month, the head of the team, Mr. Strain here reported back directly to me." The PM sat down indicating that the President should continue.

"Thank you." He now directed his words to the four Directors that had entered the room. "Gentlemen I have made the decision to formulate a similar committee here in the US. The four of you will be a position on the committee. If they accept I want Mr. Strain and his team to operate here on US soil with Mr. Thorn as the US member of the team."

The shock on the faces of the four Directors was plain to see.

Randolph Atkins was the first to jump up. "Mr. President, we can't have a foreign entity operating on US soil." He was stopped by the President raising his hands.

"After my meeting with the PM, I'll ask the four of you to come back in to discuss the matter. When you do come back in, keep one thing in mind, this is going to happen so have some positive ideas ready. Victor, your man Thorn here will now report direct to me and eventually the committee. He will, for the time being, have the equivalent rank as you and the security clearance to go with it. Thank you, you may all leave while the PM and I talk."

Strain and Thorn walked behind the four Directors as they left the Oval Office. Outside, Thorn quickly directed Strain down the hallway in the opposite direction to the four Directors.

"Thorn, over here we need to talk," said Victor Corinth.

"Sorry, under strict instructions from the President not to talk to any of you until you have met with him again," Thorn replied.

"Thorn," Corinth shouted again, only to be ignored.

The President waited until they all left the room before he spoke.

"Well, that went down like a rock in a pool." The President knew that they wouldn't like this.

"I think you have a lot of work on your hands with your Directors, I am somewhat concerned about how they will act."

"Don't worry, I'll have them all on board or they can resign, which none of them will, they like what they do too much." The President was very confident of this.

"John seems like a man who knows his business, very laid back." The President thought that he was in many ways like Agent Thorn.

"Yes, he is very good at what he does and will accept the job we are offering him."

"You are sure of that?" he asked.

"Yes, he will bring in his team members from the UK if they accept. Knowing some of them from their files and what they have already achieved, I would imagine that they will all join Strain. He will work well with your man Thorn, I get the feeling we are creating a monster putting them together." The PM was impressed with Thorn's experience and knew that Strain would be.

"Thorn is a bit of a loose cannon as we say over here, they will make a deadly team. I am going to one of our military firing ranges in the morning to review a new form of weapon, would you like to come along?" The President wanted to brag to the PM about the new military weaponry they were developing.

"No, I am sorry but I'll fly back to London early in the morning. Do you have time for dinner this evening and we can talk a little further about this joint operation?"

"Yes, why not, how about seven here?" the President replied.

"Good, we have a lot to discuss in the meantime, so let's move to my private quarters where it's more comfortable."

On the way to the private quarters, they walked past the room where Strain and Thorn were sitting talking.

"I'll talk to you later, John." The PM said in a slightly raised voice as he past the doorway.

"Yes, sir," Strain replied.

Thorn waited until the President and PM were out of sight before he closed the door.

"You want a coffee?" Thorn said trying to break the ice.

"No, but a whiskey would go down well," he replied.

"Ah! Yes, I believe Glenturret is your favorite." He walked to a cabinet next to the door.

"You have done your homework now I'll do my homework on you." He opened the file and started to read.

Strain had only read the first paragraph when a hand appeared in front of his face holding a glass containing what looked and smelt like whiskey.

"Glenturret straight up as we say over here, your Prime Minister brought it with him. I guess he thought that you may need a drink after hearing the proposal." He held his glass up as if to toast.

Strain touched his glass to Thorn's and took a sip of the whiskey, he knew straight away that it was an eighteen year old.

"Phew! This stuff is firewater," said Thorn after taking a rather large gulp.

"It's to be sipped and savored for it to be enjoyed." Strain said harshly.

They sat in silence for fifteen minutes as Strain read the file on Thorn. Strain was impressed. Thorn had a long distinguished military career the last three years of which were spent in Delta Force. He was a sniper, hand to hand combat instructor and explosives specialist. Strain put the file on the table next to his chair and walked over to the cabinet where the bottle of Glenturret was resting. Strain poured himself a healthy measure and the same was poured into Thorn's glass, he didn't ask him if he wanted another.

"So where do you come into the picture, Thorn, are you supposed to be my watch dog?" said Strain.

"No, not a watch dog a working partner. Look, I know we have gotten off on the wrong foot but I have my instructions as you have yours. It does not matter if you accept this or not, I am part of the package whoever takes it on."

"Then why are you not running the operation already, you certainly have the experience?" Strain was curious.

"There is a school of thought that thinks it's better to have a group of Brits with the kind of experience that is needed to run the operation. I do not care who runs it, I just want to get those responsible for the terrorist attacks and stop them from killing more innocent people."

"I guess you and I'll get on then." Strain smiled and extended his hand in friendship.

Thorn knew that Strain would take the job, he could see the excitement in his eyes. "I look forward to it also, where would you like to start?" asked Thorn.

"I suppose we should tell them that we are going to work together."

The whole day was spent reviewing copies of confidential files on the terrorist attacks that had taken place in the US and a stack of information on suspected terrorists and their supporters. The information had been collected from various government sources such as the National Security Agency (NSA), Central Intelligence Agency (CIA), Federal Bureau of Investigation (FBI), Department of Justice (DOJ) and numerous law enforcement departments around the USA. What Strain didn't know was that the President had ordered copies of the terrorism intelligence from the NSA, CIA, FBI and DOJ separately. He then gave the reports to Thorn who had the unusual opportunity to see intelligence that these agencies wouldn't share with each other, let alone Thorn.

Granted the agencies would share a certain amount of intelligence but they wouldn't share the game winning information, as they saw it. There was a lot of inter-agency mistrust. They wanted to catch the terrorists themselves and gain the glory for their own agency.

This lack of inter-agency information sharing and lack of trust had gone on for decades, not just in the USA but the United Kingdom also. The stubborn resistance to share highly confidential data with others agencies had caused many rifts within the US and UK governments. It is said by some that if the agencies of each other's countries had shared their intelligence that some terrorist attacks could have been avoided. The first attack on the World Trade Center, US Embassy attacks in Africa, Pan Am Flight 103 and London 7/7, the list goes on.

Could they be blamed for this? Not entirely, as history has shown there have been moles within governments and agencies before and intelligence leaks were their biggest fear. Leaks have caused chaos with government departments over the years and in some cases deaths.

Both men had now started a good working relationship, trust would take a little longer.

"This is an interesting report from New York. Two enforcers for a New York Mafia family were slaughtered in an alley after visiting a store that was under their protection. The store owner told the police that two Arabs were extorting money out of him and he sent word to the Don. Two of the Don's top enforcers showed up at the store and the owner said the two Arabs were lying in wait in the back. When the store owner gave one of the enforcers a sign that he wasn't alone, they left the store. It appears that when the enforcers left the store, they went around the back and were ambushed by the Arabs. Here are the photos of the scene in the alley where their bodies were found. Around the same time of the shooting, a block away a van was caught on one of the traffic cameras. The camera picked up the face of one of the men in the front seat. Through the facial recognition system at the CIA he has been identified as Mohammed Ali Ghahi." Thorn handed the photos to Strain.

"They went into total overkill on these two, there's not much left of this guy's head. They are either sending a message that they are taking over his turf or they just love to kill with extreme force. This does look like the kind of thing Mohammed would do, he is a blood thirsty bastard. If it isn't him, it's someone that has worked with him or has been trained by him. We had Intel in the UK that he fled to the US but we had nothing concrete." Strain slid the photos back across the table.

"Don Caputo has sworn revenge and it looks like New York is getting ready for a blood bath. He has to show strength and find those responsible quickly or he will lose face with the other families," replied Thorn.

"It doesn't really make sense that Mohammed would go up against the Mafia. He is into robberies, wire fraud, money laundering and some extortion from Arab business owners. This is not how he operates unless he has been convinced that there is a lot of money in it. He is crazy enough to do anything and shouldn't be under-estimated." Strain didn't want Mohammed to get away again, if it truly was him in the vehicle.

"The Don is under surveillance twenty-four seven by the FBI. If Mohammed tries something it will be done under the watchful eye of the FBI."

"There's possibly a way we could turn this to our advantage if we can get the support of the Don," Strain replied.

"Fuck me John there's no way that Don Caputo is going to work with us. The federal government has been trying to get him for years for racketeering."

"I am sure, but he won't expect a Brit to approach him with a business proposition." Strain already had a basis of a plan spinning around in his head.

"Well, you can't just walk into his restaurant and talk to him, that's for sure." Thorn could see that Strain was mulling over something in his head.

"No, but I just might be able to get someone I know who is former IRA to introduce me to him and we can go from there." Strain wasn't a hundred percent sure that the Irish contact would help.

"Certainly, worth a try, what is the plan?"

Strain went through the basics of what he was thinking about with Thorn, he knew it needed a lot more work.

While Strain and Thorn spent the remainder of the day reviewing the intelligence information on the terrorist attacks and those suspected of being involved, the President and the Prime Minister went about the more laborious task of discussing international affairs and cooperation.

Strain and Thorn were called into the Oval Office to meet with the President and PM to give them an update on how they would handle the task ahead.

"Sit down, gentlemen," the President said as they walked into the room.

They did as ordered and waited for the string of questions to start.

"Prime Minister, he is your man, I suppose you should start?" The President pointed to Strain, he wanted to hear what questions the PM would ask.

"I don't have any questions other than do you think you can perform the task at hand?" The PM's facial expression was blank.

"We have a lot more information to work through, sir, but we are both in agreement, we can do the job. We know it won't be easy but if we can operate as my team has in the past in the UK, we feel we can make a strong contribution in protecting

US soil." Strain replied, as he looked at Thorn for acknowledgment.

"Yes, sir, we are already working well together on evaluating the intelligence material you provided, Mr. President," Thorn replied.

"We will have a tremendous amount of work ahead but there is already a lot of good information on the table that gives us several places to start. Our first job is to identify the group or groups responsible for the recent attacks and if we can obtain more information from them. Mr. President, I know that the Prime Minister has briefed you on some of my team's operations in the UK and possibly on the methods we have used. There are parts of our work that are decidedly unpleasant for others and I won't discuss our methods with you. This is for your protection. I am confident that I can get the support of my team in the UK and with the expertise of your man Thorn here I know we can get results. The unknown part of this is of course is how long it will take, I can only assure you we won't move slowly."

"I can speak for my office and the people of the United States when I say that we need you to find these people and stop them. How you do this is up to you both and what happens to them is of no concern to me." The President sat back in his chair.

"We will, at some point if not already, come under the watchful eye of our government intelligence agencies here in the US. I know you will make it clear to them in your next meeting that they don't run background checks on any of the team. I would also ask that if we are being impeded by any of them that you, Mr. President make the order to call the dogs off and allow us to do our jobs." Thorn knew that after the meeting in the Oval office the four Directors were already researching who Strain was.

"I have already arranged for them to visit with me when you and the Prime Minister leave. They will all be told in no uncertain terms that they are to cooperate with you both and not to run operations behind your back to see what you are up to. If they step out of line, I'll take care of it."

The conversation between the four men went on for another thirty minutes as they mulled over the financial logistics and unofficial support for the operation.

The President knew that the meeting with the Directors of the FBI, CIA, NSA and Secret Service was going to be very difficult. The four men walked into his office just after the Prime Minister had left.

"Let's get down to business, sit down, please." He could tell by their faces that they had already discussed what they were going to say.

"If I can start?" said Atkins, head of the FBI.

"Well you can't, Randolph. I have had a very difficult time over the last two months thinking about this new task force. I have had many conversations with the British Prime Minister about his undercover team. They have had tremendous success in stopping terrorist acts and bringing those responsible to justice. As always, we are expected to play by certain rules and not infringe on civil liberties etcetera, well that is going to be put aside for a short time. If we continue to operate with handcuffs on, so to speak, we will only get further behind in stopping terrorism. We have always tried to play by the book and it doesn't work ninety percent of the time. I have made my decision, Mr. Thorn and Mr. Strain will operate a very secretive undercover team here in the United States. They will have all resources possible made available to them without obstruction or bias from your departments. Make your questions brief as I have to change for dinner with the PM." Here it comes he knew he'd opened the flood gates of criticism for the four Directors.

"Mr. President, we can't allow these people to run wild around the US like a pack of dogs doing whatever they like. There would be a public outcry if it got out that we are condoning the actions of a group of vigilantes," replied Randolph Atkins. He wanted them to report to him at the FBI.

"Anyone else before I reply?" asked the President.

Butch Shattuck's voice boomed out first, "Sir, while I see the merits of possibly having a group operating without certain strings being attached, I can't agree with this idea. Just because it worked in the UK it does not mean it will work here. We are a much larger nation geographically and in population. We have some of the best, if not the best, intelligence groups in the world. This team, if it has to operate, should be sourced from our own departments and military."

They all started to speak at once now and the President sat for a minute allowing them to blow off a little steam.

"Gentlemen please, you have to understand that while I truly believe that you all have the safety of the United States at heart you can't change my mind. I have already authorized funding and as you can tell selected the two men who are going to run the operation. I am not going to change my mind so I would suggest as I said earlier that you each come up with ways or information that may support this group. Mr. Thorn will be your point of contact and ANY questions he has will be answered truthfully."

The four Directors starting firing questions at the President, each trying to get their question in first. It was a pathetic scene for men of their rank and position.

"Enough, I have no time for this, arrange with my assistant a day and time when you can come in to see me individually. Thank you, I must get ready for my dinner engagement." The President stood and they all took the cue to leave.

That evening the President and PM had dinner together while Strain and Thorn went their separate ways.

The next morning the PM and Strain had a 6am breakfast meeting in the PM's hotel suite and at 7.30am they were wheels up on the return flight to the UK.

On the flight, back to the UK, they talked for a good portion of the flight about the job ahead and the unofficial cooperation that Strain would receive from the US government. Strain knew that the PM and President really meant money wasn't going to be an object when the PM told him that he would have a private jet at his disposal twenty-four hours a day, a Gulfstream IV with a seating capacity for twelve people.

After his lengthy meeting with the PM, Strain returned to his seat and without realizing it, drifted off to sleep for the last hour of the flight. Strain was abruptly shaken out of his slumber by the sound of the Captain's voice announcing that they had twenty minutes before touchdown. He looked down the plane and saw that the PM was still fast asleep. He wouldn't wake up until the plane landed and the noise of the wheels on the runway made him jump slightly.

As the plane taxied, Laura handed the PM a warm cloth so he could wipe his face and freshen up, she then gave one to Strain.

"Good sleep?" she said to Strain.

"Yes, thanks, don't even remember going off," he replied.

"You looked a little tired when we left Washington. Not surprising really, it was a busy couple of days if you add on the travel time and the meetings." She smiled at him.

"Yes, we didn't have any time for socializing, maybe next time." Strain couldn't believe what he'd just said.

"I would like that," she replied.

The PM watched the two of them, he didn't know what they were saying but he knew that their relationship would eventually go to the dating stage.

As the plane slowly rumbled into the high security hanger on the military airbase, the co-pilot walked into the main cabin with a sheet of paper in his hand, he gave it to the PM.

Strain watched the PM as he read what was on the paper, he saw a slight smile appear.

"John," the PM said, waiving Strain over to him.

Strain left his seat and joined the PM.

"Your associate in the US wants you to call as soon as possible. It would seem that there have been some new developments in the Senator Gatts incident."

"I'll call as soon as we clear the hanger, sir," he replied.

"John, be careful, but get this done quickly if you can. There is a lot riding on you and your team and we need results, I don't care how you get them, just get them." He gave Strain a concerned look.

"No pressure, then, sir," Strain replied with a huge smile.

"No, no pressure." The PM patted him on the shoulder.

The PM knew that the pressure on the team was going to be enormous but worse that they were in great danger. He mourned the loss of the two previous team members and appreciated that they had given their lives in the defense of their country. It didn't help when he thought of their families and how they were coping with the loss.

Strain called Thorn on a scrambled telephone from the military hanger.

"Missing me already?" Strain said when Thorn answered the phone.

"Yes, when can you return? The patient is slowly coming around and we need to act quickly" Thorn knew Strain would realize that he was talking about Ramzi.

"That's good news on the patient, I'll be there tomorrow," Strain replied.

"Call when you are leaving." Thorn turned the phone off.

Strain took the opportunity to call Alan Foy in Belfast, a former IRA member who had helped Strain in the UK against Mohammed. He'd also saved Strain's life, the conversation was short but he agreed to meet Strain later that day in Belfast.

Strain spent the rest of the day on the road visiting team members, explaining to them the job in the US. He wasn't surprised when they all accepted the job, but they were a little surprised that they had to leave in two days. Strain explained to each of them where they were to go and what hotels they would be booked into. The conversation with George and Chalky took a lot longer as they had to discuss what equipment they needed in the US. There was some technical equipment they each wanted to bring, more personalized items, the rest they would rely on Strain's contact to locate for them.

Chalky White and George Barton accepted without hesitation, the thought of going to America was enough for both of them. They also relished the thought of showing the Americans up when it came to technology. They had developed their own intelligence and surveillance equipment that they didn't even share with the British Government. These specific items of equipment were for the use of the team only and eventually would be passed on to the government for further development. At present, there wasn't anything like it being used by any British or US government agency that they knew of.

Strain knew that most of the team would join him in the United States, the question was how they would cope with being away from their families. In the UK, they would be away from them for a week to ten days at the most, in the US it could be a couple of months. This wasn't good if they had a family emergency, in the past they had been just a few hours away.

CHAPTER 4

NORTHERN IRELAND

The Gulfstream only took forty minutes to reach Belfast airport. Once it landed, the plane taxied to the FBO hanger and office building where Strain was to meet Foy. Strain told the pilots that he wouldn't be long and to wait for him for the return to London. He looked around as he left the aircraft, old habits and self-preservation setting in. As he entered the FBO building, he was met by a young man around twenty years old.

"I have a car waiting for you," he said to Strain without introduction.

"The meeting was supposed to be here," he replied.

"A slight change of plan," the young man walked outside to the car.

Strain didn't like this but he'd to go along with the change of plan if he was to get an introduction to the Don in New York.

As Strain followed the young man outside, he could see two men standing by a car. One of the men frisked Strain very thoroughly and told him to get into the back of the car. The two men then got into the back seat, with one either side of Strain.

As they drove off, one of the men in the back seat produced a black hood and put it on Strain's head. Strain didn't say anything he knew that if Foy wanted him dead he would have already been killed at the airport.

In the darkness of the hood, Strain tried count how many turns there were and how long it was between each one. Fifteen minutes later, the car stopped and the hood was taken off his head.

It took Strain a few seconds for his eyes to adjust to the light as he was helped out of the car. They were inside an auto repair shop, one of most probably hundreds in the Belfast area.

"In there," one of the men said pointing towards an old office in the corner.

Waiting inside the office was Alan Foy, "Close the door," he said to Strain.

"Thanks for meeting me." Strain put his hand out for Foy to shake it, he didn't.

"What is it you want Mr. Strain," Foy still had some deep desire in him to kill Strain for the death of his sons.

"I need someone with contacts in New York City that can get me in to see Don Caputo. I have heard over the years that there are certain Irish connections that might be able to arrange it."

"Why do you want to meet him?" Foy asked.

"I believe that Mohammed Ali Ghahi is operating in the US and he is responsible for the murder of two of the Don's enforcers. I want to meet the Don to see if he is willing to use his extensive resources to help locate Mohammed and his colleagues."

"Why should I help you, why shouldn't I just kill you now?"

"I don't know why you shouldn't kill me, but you are the only person I know that could make the introduction to the Don. I know your Irish contacts in New York are very powerful and the Don will listen to them. He may not trust them, but when they tell him they can arrange a meeting with someone who can help kill those that killed his enforcers, he will want to meet me."

"So, you are working over there now? You are an interesting man, Mr. Strain. If this meeting could be arranged, what is in it for me?" Foy wasn't necessarily interested in money but more in the possibility of future favors.

"Name your price and I'll see what I can do to accommodate you." Strain had no idea what he was going to ask for.

"First, one hundred thousand pounds in a Swiss bank account of my choosing. Second, there are three Irish men convicted of terrorism sitting in mainland jails, I want them transferred to Northern Ireland." He handed Strain a piece of paper with three names on it.

"So, I am expected to give you money that will fund the IRA?" Strain replied.

"No, you will support the widows and children of loyal Irishmen who have been murdered by British soldiers and their Irish traitors." Foy's eyes were cold as he stared at Strain.

"Fair enough, the money I can arrange, the movement of the prisoners is not possible," Strain replied.

"Then you have wasted both of our times, you will be taken back to the airport, goodbye." Foy didn't move he waited for a response from Strain.

Strain knew his bluff wasn't going to work but he'd to try even if it was just to agitate Foy a little.

"If I can arrange the prisoner move, it may take several weeks to happen, I need the meeting with the Don within a week. I'll make some calls in the morning, if they agree to the prisoners being moved, you only have my word that it will happen."

Foy thought about it for a minute, not taking his eyes off Strain for a second.

"Make your calls and transfer the money to this account as soon as the banks open in the morning. The money is non-refundable even if I am unable to arrange the meeting. I'll hold up my end Mr. Strain, you do the same your end and no surprises please."

"I'll call you as soon as I hear about the prisoner transfer request." Strain turned and left the office.

The trip back to the airport was the same as the one going out, head cover and all. Within ten minutes of arriving at the airport, Strain's plane was taking off for London.

CHAPTER 5

CALIFORNIA

General Bart Carey held the high-powered binoculars to his eyes, training them on the weapons test grounds in the distance. Several hundred yards away from his position in the protected bunker was a line of five old army vehicles. Three of these vehicles were troop carriers and two Jeeps they were today's targets for the weapons test.

Carey was a veteran of the Vietnam War with four tours under his belt. The last two tours he'd spent most of his time behind enemy lines, locating their positions and reporting them back to his intelligence command center. He enjoyed the solitude of the jungle but the thing he loved most was watching the enemy positions being obliterated by the napalm bombs dropped by US aircraft. His career spanned 27 years and at the age of 50, he felt like he could still perform with the best of his marines. He detested his new position although it was a promotion he knew that watching weapons testing and reporting back to the bureaucrats and military headquarters wasn't his idea of being a soldier. But today he was a little excited to test the new automatically controlled sniper mount on the weapons system.

Equally exciting was the fact that the President of the United States, the Commander in Chief, would be observing. Carey didn't want any problems or failures to occur in front of the President. The rest of the dignitaries attending, he couldn't care less about. One quick test was about to take place before the arrival of the President just to satisfy Carey's thirst for perfection.

"We are ready, sir," a voice said behind him.

"Proceed," was all Carey said.

He heard the muffled sound of gun fire outside of the bunker a split second after which he saw the troop carrier at the front of the line of test vehicles rock with the impact of the bullets. Pieces of metal, glass and dust flew into the air.

Although it was only a three second burst of six shots, Carey enjoyed the sight and sounds and was amazed at how accurate the strikes were on the vehicle.

Lowering the binoculars, he turned to Captain Smart next to him, "looks pretty impressive, Gary," he said.

"Yes, sir," he replied.

Gary Smart had been with Carey for two years as his administrator and detested the range and any sound of gunfire he preferred the sound of the computer room. Smart was instrumental in designing the software package for the computer system that operated the weapon control base. He was very nervous, as this was the first time the system was being tested in front of the military brass and the President. The radio resting on the box in front of him announced the arrival of the President. He turned around and through the window at the rear of the bunker he could see a dust cloud approaching about a quarter of a mile away. He looked up and saw Carey watching the dust cloud from the approaching vehicles.

"Here is the audience, Gary," he said.

"Yes, sir," he replied.

Unlike General Carey, he was looking forward to the test as it gave him the opportunity to show them all how good his software was. He followed Carey out of the bunker and into the hot California sun where a small detachment of marines stood to attention awaiting the arrival of the dignitaries. Carey looked to his right and left checking that the marines were all in position and staying alert, as always, they were true professionals and knew their duties. He checked the tree lines in the distance and several other positions that surrounded the area where the dignitaries' vehicles would stop. Hidden out of sight to all but the trained observer and in some cases even to Carey's eagle eye were Special Forces operatives providing security for the President. Carey knew that the Secret Service protected the President but this was his domain and as far as he was concerned, the President and attending generals where his responsibility. The line of vehicles approached and out of the center of the line three vehicles broke away from formation and drove straight towards Carey's position at the foot of the bunker.

The remainder of the convoy was directed by two marines to a makeshift parking area that had been roped off especially for the occasion. The three vehicles stopped some twenty feet from Carey and as they did, the secret service detail sprang into action and took their positions around the presidential vehicle. Carey approached the President's vehicle just as he was exiting and snapped to attention, giving the President the perfect salute. The President returned the salute with a loose looking wave of his hand to the forehead. Had this been one of Carey's marines, he would have had a dressing down and would have performed 20 laps of the parade square in full fatigues holding his rifle above his head for such a sloppy salute.

"Hello, Bart, ready for the show," the President said.

"Yes, Mr. President, we are ready when you are."

"Let's not waste any more of your time then."

The President walked up the steps into the bunker, followed by Carey. They were joined by four high powered generals and one military press officer. The rest of the observers were sent to the bunkers further down the line.

"Binoculars, sir," Carey said as he handed them over.

The President placed the strap over his head and let the binoculars rest around his neck.

Carey described the scene in front of them, using a microphone which transmitted through speakers to all the bunkers.

"Good Morning Mr. President and distinguished guests, this morning we will be demonstrating to you several rifles attached to a computer intelligent mounting. As you can see outside, behind the sandbags we have four marines who will switch out the weapons to be used on the control base. The actual firing of the weapon will be controlled from a computer in the bunker where I am standing. The first weapon to be tested will be a GAU-19, I guess you would call it a modern Gatling gun. The target will be the front and rear sections of the leading vehicle in the distance to your left. The second weapon to be tested will be a 50-caliber sniper rifle with specific targets on all five vehicles. These specific targets are marked with a red dot.

Questions on the system today will be answered when the demonstration is completed."

Carey wasted no time he wanted to get this over with he picked up the radio and pressed the transmit button, "We will test fire in five seconds." This was said for the benefit of the marines stationed behind the sandbags with the weapons system.

The President and the other observers looked through the binoculars focusing their attention on the targets.

"Proceed with the test, Gary," he said. Gary was at the computer more excited than he'd ever been in his life. He had hold of the joystick. On the computer, he could see the vehicles and the targets as if he was looking through a telescopic sight. Using the joystick, he zoomed in on the front of the lead vehicle and fired two short bursts of ammunition by pressing the red button on the joystick. Next, he swung the joystick across to his right which sighted the weapons system targeting the rear of the lead vehicle. He repeated the double burst of fire.

"Repeat that process on the wheels of all the vehicles" ordered Carey.

Smart proceeded without question and fired on the remaining four vehicles. Carey picked up the radio and ordered the marines to change weapons.

As this took a few minutes the President turned to Carey and said, "That seems rather impressive at that distance."

"Yes, sir and with the sniper rifle the distances, wind and all other calculations are automatically calculated by the computer. The weapon base does not move even a fraction due to the hydraulic system in the frame. You will see how important this is as we proceed with the second weapon to be demonstrated." He watched as the President and generals talked amongst themselves about what they had just seen.

"Ready when you are sir," said a voice over the radio. It was the marines that had loaded and mounted the 50-caliber sniper rifle.

General Carey politely interrupted the President and generals and informed them that the demonstration was about to continue. The 50-caliber weapon was much more powerful than the GAU-19 and the distinctive boom as it was fired could be heard clearly in the bunker as the shock wave soaked into the concrete walls. The first vehicle was hit on the target areas marked with incredible accuracy. For the final part of the sniper rifle demonstration Carey ordered Smart to concentrate on the engine area of the last vehicle in line. The first round hit the vehicle with such force it blew the engine to pieces throwing parts of it into the air.

"Mr. President, would you like to fire on the last vehicle?" said Carey.

"Yes, if you think I can. Let's hope I hit the target." He laughed looking at the generals.

"I guarantee you won't miss, sir," replied Carey.

"Captain Smart will show you how to operate the weapon from this computer and how to fire when ready."

Smart pushed his chair back and stood to attention, "Please sit in the seat, sir," he said.

The President sat in the chair and stared at the computer screen where he could clearly see the five vehicles that he'd been watching through the binoculars.

"The whole system is operated here from the computer we can use various methods of communicating with the weapons base which in turn fires whichever weapon is attached to it at that time. At present, we are communicating through a wireless transmitter and receiver. In front of you is a joystick such as you would find on any child's computer game. The joystick operates the movement of the camera mounted to the weapon base which in turn communicates through software to the weapons base unit and tells it in which direction to move. The base unit can turn the weapon 360 degrees which can fire downwards at an angle of 20 degrees or upwards at an angle of 90 degrees. The joystick has been modified so that you can zoom in and zoom out on the target with the camera which operates through a telescopic system. Once you locate the position on the target, you press this button on the back of the joy stick and the computer will lock onto that part of the target. Wind speeds, atmospheric conditions, distance between the weapon and the target and size of target are all input into the system. No matter where you aim on the target, the computer will adjust the firing position of the

weapon to compensate for all these factors and many more."
Smart gave a quick demonstration on the joystick controls which
the President quickly picked up.

"O.K. sir, fire when you are ready," said Smart.

The President operated the joystick and zoom controls,
deliberately choosing a position just off the target, he pressed the
red firing button on the top of the joystick and within a split
second the computer compensated and chose the center of the
target and fired a single round.

"That is impressive young man. I deliberately chose to be
off target after confirming the target and the dam thing ignored
me and fired on my original target sighting. You really have
something here Carey," he said.

"Yes, sir, Smart will quickly demonstrate the rapid firing
of the sniper rifle," replied Carey.

Smart went about his business, targeting all five vehicles
raking them with a massive amount of high velocity bullets.
Everyone watched as the vehicles were torn apart, they were
practically unrecognizable when he'd finished.

Carey was back on the microphone, "That completes the
GAU-19 demonstration, we have one additional test to show the
true accuracy and capability of this weapons control system. I
would like you all to focus on the television monitors above your
heads. As you can see there is a range of hills in the distance the
first hill is 1.2 miles away we will now zoom in on the hill in
order that you can see the target."

On the television monitors, they could see the cross-hairs
of a rifle scope as it slowly zoomed in on the hill in the distance.
Within five seconds, they could see the image of what appeared
to be three people sitting about ten feet apart on the side of the
hill.

"As I said, the distance between the weapons control
system, which has been re-mounted with the 50-caliber sniper
rifle and the three targets that you can see, is 1.2 miles. While I
have been talking, Captain Smart has recalculated the system to
recognize the sniper rifle and we are ready to fire. Please watch
the targets from left to right."

They all heard the 50-caliber rifle being fired outside of the bunker. The shots only had half a second between each one. The three targets burst into a cloud of dust, one after another.

"Those three targets were locked into the computer and the system was set to automatic fire. This again shows how diversified the system is once the target is located and the system locks on to it, the attached weapon can be fired automatically at any time. The final beauty about this system and the software designed by Captain Smart is that the weapons system can be placed anywhere in the world, waiting to receive information on its target. The weapon can then be controlled via computer by the operator from anywhere else in the world.

CHAPTER 6

WASHINGTON D.C., HOSPITAL CENTER

Ramzi had been in the hospital for four days and had shown only slight signs of regaining consciousness. His parents had not left his room other than to get food, drink and use the bathroom.

Agent Trey Field was an eighteen-year veteran of the FBI and had been serving on the counter terrorism unit for almost a year. He had spent the best part of the last four days at the hospital. When he first arrived, he asked the parents questions about their son and his friends, why was he in that area of the city? The usual questions an investigator would ask. They wouldn't cooperate, stating that they would help when their son regained consciousness. Fields asked them how they came to find out about their son's accident and they said someone called them, they assumed it was the police. The truth was the Pakistan Embassy had called them and told them where he was and not to talk to anyone about their son. They were also told that at least one of them should stay by their son's bed until he regained consciousness and the attorney spoke to him.

Fields knew that their story about who had called them was bullshit as he had their home and cell phone records. Their home phone showed that they had received a call from the Pakistan Embassy three hours after the accident. Since then he'd also found out that their son was on a list with the Secret Service as a driver for the Pakistan Ambassador. Fields knew something was wrong and could already smell the stench of diplomatic immunity being thrown in his face.

On the first day, a high-powered attorney showed up at the hospital and was directed to Fields.

"Are you the agent in charge here?" he asked.

Fields was six feet two inches tall and this little man in front of him was five feet four and forty pounds' overweight. He was wearing a black pin striped suit, white shirt and purple tie.

Fields knew that the suit cost more than his month's salary and this little man most probably had several more the same.

"Yes, I am the agent in charge," he replied.

"Here is my card I'll be representing Ramzi Binalshibh my name is Ali Omarzai and nobody is to talk to my client unless I am present."

"He has been unconscious for the last four days so how could he ask for an attorney to represent him?" He knew the answer but he didn't like this little man.

"His family called me, I am their attorney and they asked me to represent him. What is your name? I would like to see some identification."

The agent reached inside his jacket pocket and took out his I.D. and showed it to the attorney.

"Ah! It says your name is Field I suppose that makes you a field agent." He laughed out loud at his own joke. He saw a uniformed police officer standing by a glass door leading into the private room, the walls to the room were also glass and he could see Ramzi.

"How original I haven't heard that one before," said Fields in his most sarcastic voice.

"Just a little joke, you know something to lighten the mood, help you and I get along." He was still being sarcastic.

Over the next three days, the same aggravating attorney or one of his lackeys showed up at the hospital several times. Through the thin glass of the room, the policeman on duty could hear the attorneys continually counseling the parents not to talk to the police, FBI or anyone else without them being present. They were also told in no uncertain terms to call the attorney's office as soon as their son showed any signs of waking up.

Ramzi had drifted in and out of consciousness most of the fourth day. It was late in the evening when he made the first real signs of coming to when he opened his eyes and said, "Mother." He smiled at her and his father.

"Be still, my son," said his mother.

"I'll call Mr. Omarzai," said his father.

Ramzi's mother sat crying as she held her son's hand and stroked his face with her free hand.

"Speak only to us and Mr. Omarzai, my son," said his father.

Ramzi nodded his head acknowledging that he heard what they had said and drifted back to sleep.

The policeman outside the room heard them talking and saw Ramzi had his eyes open, he immediately called agent Fields.

Fields arrived at the hospital room and went in.

"I believe your son has regained consciousness," he said to the parents.

"Yes," his mother said with delight and without thinking.

"You can't speak to my son without his attorney," his father said harshly.

"I am not asking to interview him I am just pleased to see that he is improving." Fields was trying to show some compassion in the hope of gaining a little of their trust.

The door to the room opened behind Fields, he had a sick feeling he knew who had just walked in.

"Good evening, Agent Fields," said Omarzai.

"Evening," he replied.

"I hope you are not trying to interview my client without me present?" he said.

"No, I heard that he was improving and I was just asking how he was." Fields gritted his teeth.

Ramzi was waking up again, "Where am I?" he said in a weak voice.

"Ah! My client calls can you please leave us alone," said Omarzai, pointing to the door for Fields to leave.

"Young master Ramzi, you do not look very well. For the record, you are not to talk to anyone especially the police about what happened unless I am present, do you understand?" he smiled at Ramzi.

He nodded and gave a very weak "Yes." He didn't really know what he was saying as he drifted back into unconsciousness.

"I have several questions for you, sir and…" the attorney stopped Fields.

"My client is in no fit state to talk to anyone now. The family has requested their own physician to attend to him and give them a diagnosis of his injuries. Until my client is seen by the family physician and until he says that he is fit to be interviewed nobody is to talk to him, is that clear Agent Fields?" He looked at the agent with an air of confidence that comes with many years of experience as an attorney.

"Yes, but we would like to interview him as soon as possible people have lost their lives and we believe that your client may be able to assist us in our investigation." He knew that if he aggravated this man any more it would only put further barriers up between them.

Ramzi's health improved during the night, to the point where he was sitting up in bed the next morning holding a conversation with his parents. Omarzai, his attorney, arrived at 8.30am after his parents had called to tell him their son was fully conscious.

Again, Omarzai had arrived before Fields and was already in the room with Ramzi when he got there.

"How long has he been in there?" Fields said to the policeman on duty outside the room.

"About ten minutes, they have been talking so quietly I can't hear much of what they are saying and they are speaking in a foreign language anyway."

Fields could just about hear them and knew they had to be speaking in their native language. He tapped on the glass door and waved Omarzai towards him, he could see he wasn't pleased.

Omarzai opened the door blocking entry into the room with his body, "Mr. Ramzi hasn't seen his physician yet and for the record, he has diplomatic immunity so you won't be able to interview him." He closed the door before Fields could say anything.

Fields almost exploded with frustration, he saw that one coming. Diplomatic immunity only convinced him that Ramzi was involved in the explosion.

Back in the room with the door closed, Omarzai saw the surprise on the faces of the parents and Ramzi.

Omarzai continued in their native language, "Yes, you heard correctly you are now under diplomatic immunity. The Ambassador was going to tell you last week that you had been promoted to the Pakistan secret service. You are still his driver and this is his way of letting you know that he values you greatly. You should be proud of your son he has worked very hard for this position."

"Really, I am in the diplomatic police now?" he couldn't believe it.

"Yes, as I said you were already given this status a week ago, but with the Ambassador's schedule he has not had time to do it officially." Omarzai lied through his teeth, but was very good at it.

"Yes, he has been busy with the Senator's campaign." Ramzi gave a smile to Omarzai.

"Can I ask you to leave us alone while we discuss some diplomatic business and paper signing for his new promotion?"

Omarzai wanted the parents out of the room before he talked to Ramzi about the incident.

"Yes," the father said and they left the room.

"You are not to say a word to anyone, do you understand?" said Omarzai.

"Yes, I know what to do they won't get anything from me, when can I leave this place?" Ramzi replied.

"Soon we will take care of you for your loyalty. I must leave when your parents return. Here is your new passport with a diplomatic stamp in it as you will see this passport was issued more than a week ago. The American law enforcement people can't talk to you once you show them this. I'll tell them on the way out but they still try to get information out of you, do not say anything. You have to protect the Pakistani government, me and YOUR parents." Omarzai put a lot of emphasis on the parent's comment.

Ramzi knew that it was a veiled threat but he had no intention of talking so the threat was wasted on him. He watched Omarzai leaving the room and fully intended to discuss the threat with the Ambassador when he got the opportunity.

Fields was still standing outside the room when the parents left and he could hear some discussion going on between Ramzi and his attorney. He knew that they weren't going to get any information out of Ramzi now. He would have to find another way of proving he was involved in the Senator's death. He saw Omarzai hand something to Ramzi and after a short conversation Omarzai left the room.

"OK, he looks conscious enough for me to interview him now," Fields said to Omarzai as he came out of the room.

"He has diplomatic immunity." He enjoyed saying this to the Agent and watched the startled reaction in his eyes.

"That's suddenly convenient. Why didn't you mention this before?" Fields was furious.
Omarzai stepped right up to Fields and put his face a few inches from Fields'.

"Agent, I am directing you to keep all of your policemen and other agents away from my client. If anyone of you ignores my very clear instruction, you will be creating a diplomatic incident which I know your President does not want. We are making great progress in our bi-lateral talks, something that is way above your pay grade, as you Americans say. The Pakistan Ambassador is informing the head of your department of my client's diplomatic status as we speak. Stay out of the room, Agent." Omarzai gave a big smile and walked away, only to stop after a few feet. "One other thing, you can remove your security we will be providing our own."

"He is a possible witness to a terrorist bombing and murder of a Senator, we need to talk to him he may be in danger." Thorn couldn't believe what he was hearing.

"We will interview him in good time and give you a written statement of what he remembers of the incident, if he remembers anything at all. Now again remove your men." This time Omarzai continued walking until he got to a man that was standing at the end of the corridor.

Fields watched Omarzai and knew he could do nothing as he walked off and stopped to talk to the man. He knew that this had to be the security Omarzai was talking about. He stood and watched as the man walked over to him.

"I am here to provide protection for Mr. Ramzi, thank you for your help you can leave now." He stepped past Fields and walked into the room where Ramzi was and closed the door.

What Fields didn't know the security guard was Khalfan Ghailani, he'd worked with the Ambassador for many years. He had interrogated, tortured and murdered many people over the years for the Ambassador.

After a short conversation with his supervisor on the cell phone, Fields dismissed the police officer and left the hospital. On the way to his car he felt stripped of all his authority and capability to act. Omarzai had done a good job on him. He knew Ramzi was involved and was sure that Omarzai had a hand in it also, even if it was just protecting the terrorist, he felt had to do something. He sat in his car for fifteen minutes before driving to a pay phone and made a call to a trusted friend, Thorn.

CHAPTER 7

LONDON, ENGLAND

Strain woke up refreshed after an undisturbed six-hour sleep. The meeting in Belfast the night before had gone as well as could be expected. After brewing a pot of tea, he was on the phone to arrange the money transfer and making calls about the prisoners' transfer.

Strain was pleased with the way the conversations had gone about the prisoners. It looked very promising. The PM was the first call he made and he promised to assist in the process. The prisoners were all young men who had been convicted of supporting and harboring wanted IRA terrorists. There was no evidence of them being involved in bombings or killings. The background check of the three prisoners revealed that two of them were nephews of Foy. The other was the grandson of a former senior IRA official who was in very poor health and wasn't expected to live six months. The reason for the prisoner exchange was clear Foy wanted them closer to home so that family members could visit them in prison without travelling to the mainland.

Strain called Foy's contact and quickly got a call back from Foy.

"I received the first delivery," Foy said when Strain answered the phone.

"Good, I'll know about the second delivery within hours, it looks promising."

"I'll start things my end and will arrange the meeting when the confirmation of the other delivery is complete."

"I hope to get a confirmation of the transfer but don't forget it may take weeks to actually happen," Strain replied.

Foy listened, but didn't say anything before he ended the call.

It had been two hours since Strain had gotten out of bed and arrived at the private hanger at the airport. He had achieved a lot in those two hours and was pleased with the work so far.

He boarded the plane and gave the pilot and copilot a handshake before taking his seat for departure.

The plane was registered out of Switzerland and all costs would eventually go back to the US through inter-government support funds. Four former air force pilots had been handpicked for the Gulfstream two from the UK and USA, all with experience in clandestine services. If any one of the government agencies tried to background the pilots, an invisible electronic notification would go direct to the attention of the President and PM through the intelligence agencies and then their personal assistants.

Strain sat in the back of the plane and looked down at the row of seats. The seating on the plane was set out for fourteen passengers, he felt guilty being the only passenger on board.

Strain's plane arrived seven hours later at Washington Dulles airport and taxied to the fixed base operator's building or FBO as it was commonly known. An FBO is a commercial aviation business that is granted the rights to operate on airport property by the airport authorities.

As Strain sat on the plane waiting for customs and immigration to show, he saw Thorn boarding.

"OK, let's go," said Thorn as he stuck his head inside the plane.

Strain picked up his duffle bag and backpack and thanked the pilots on the way out.

Thorn was standing by an SUV, "Put your bags in the back," he said.

Strain did as he was told and got into the vehicle.

"Good to have you back, John," Thorn fired up the engine and started to drive.

"Good to see you again, but what's going on for you to bring me back so quickly?" Strain wasn't complaining he was just curious.

"We are safe to talk in here, but let's just be certain and not discuss this until we arrive at the house." Thorn was taking Strain to a safe house that he was going to use.

Strain knew from Thorn's file that he was an avid baseball fan. "So, you like baseball?"

"Yes, the finest sport there is," he replied.

"So, do you have a league like English football?" Strain was building up to his ultimate teaser question.

"You mean soccer, don't you?" Thorn smiled.

"No football, that's why we play it with our feet," said Strain.

"OK I guess you guys got the name first. There are two leagues, the National league and the American league." Thorn replied.

"In the UK, the football team with the most points at the end of the season is the league champions. If you have two leagues, does that mean you have two champions?" Strain already knew the answer.

"Yes, but the champion from each league goes on to play in the World Series against each other. They play the best of seven games and obviously the first to win four games is the World Series champion." Thorn replied.

The trap was laid. "So, if it's called the World Series why is it that only American team's get to play?" Strain was starting to enjoy this.

"Well, that's just the way it has always been."

"So why don't you guys invite other countries to play in this World Series." Strain was prodding further.

"Because we came up with the concept and it has always been between the American League and the National League. It doesn't really matter anyway as we have the best baseball teams in the world and other nations wouldn't stand a chance." Thorn replied.

"Interesting, I thought that the World Series idea came from Spalding, the sports equipment folks. Their idea was to include other nations back in 1904 when the Reach Guide reported on the first official World's Series. It wasn't until the

1930's that they and Spalding dropped the S off the end of World's after a merger changing it to the World Series."

"You bastard," Thorn said as he took a playful swing at Strain.

"You don't know how much I enjoyed that," said Strain.

"OK, I owe you one you did your homework, son of a bitch you got me good."

Both men laughed and continued the banter until they reached the safe house.

Strain's phone made a noise alerting him that he had a text, he checked it.

"What is it?" asked Thorn.

"Looks like I have a meeting with the Don in the morning."

"That was quick," replied Thorn.

"Well, I did press hard for it to happen soon," Strain replied.

At the safe house, Thorn parked the vehicle in the underground parking garage. The safe house was a mid-terrace three story building with two bedrooms and a small kitchen.

"Make yourself at home John," Thorn said as he walked to the kitchen counter.

"Nice place, clean, I presume." Strain was referring to the security and not cleanliness.

"Yes, here and welcome back." He handed Strain a large Glenturret whiskey.

"Excellent, now what is this all about?" he replied.

"You know about the bombing of Senators Gatts' vehicle."

"Yes, he was a close friend of the President," replied Strain.

"Correct. Well, we have a new development. There was a vehicle relatively close to the senator's car when it was blown up and it crashed because of the blast. The car was the Pakistan Ambassador's." Thorn took a sip of the whiskey.

"No shit. He has to be involved," said Strain.

"Well, it looks like he could be, as his driver was in the car when it crashed. The front passenger door was open but no sign of a passenger. In addition, when the paramedics and police responded, they found a trigger mechanism on the floor of the vehicle. The Pakistan Ambassador has not been available for questioning, not that we would get far as he would plead diplomatic immunity. His driver was unconscious for several days and only recovered consciousness properly yesterday. As you can imagine, he has been provided with a high-class lawyer to act on his and his family's behalf. Here is the twist, the lawyer went to the hospital room yesterday and handed his now client a new passport. I am sure you can guess what stamp he has in it?" Thorn took another sip of the whisky he was starting to get a taste for it.

"He has been made a diplomat," Strain replied.

"Yes, what's worse is we can't interview the mother and father as they have disappeared. This whole thing stinks, they have tied our hands completely, or so they think."

"What have you got in mind?" asked Strain.

"Well, the attorney dismissed the security detail that was protecting his client. He stated that they would take care of his security, even though they didn't think it was needed. I have a feeling that after he leaves hospital he won't live long. As you know they have a way of making people disappear, like his parents, who they will think are a danger to them, another drink?" said Thorn picking up the whiskey bottle.

"Sure, do they have security with him now?" asked Strain, holding his glass up for Thorn to refill it.

"Yes, one man in his room nobody else around, I have a man at the hospital with eyes on the room."

Thorn had one of his men dressed as a hospital worker walk into the room to empty the trash can. The security guard gave him minimal attention after he checked that he was wearing a hospital I.D. badge. When he placed a new box of tissues on the bedside cabinet, the security guard gave the box a cursory check. Hidden in the cardboard of the box was the smallest of cameras, you would have to tear the cardboard apart to find it.

"We have got to get in there and interview him," said Strain.

"I agree. Let's head over there and see if there's a way around the security guy. I have a small bag of tricks we can take with us." Thorn picked up a brown bag that was sat on the table.

Both men finished what whiskey was left in their glasses and went straight to the hospital.

Thorn and Strain arrived at the hospital and went to a white van in the parking lot with hospital authority markings on it. Thorn tapped on the rear doors twice and stepped back, the doors opened and both men got in.

No introductions were made inside the van as Thorn and Strain looked at four TV monitors.

"What do we have here?" asked Thorn.

"I put one camera in the room and three other cameras in place. One at the front entrance, one on the stairwell closest to the room and one in the corridor that leads to his room," replied the camera operator.

"Good pictures on all four, any voice on the one in the room?" Thorn knew this was too much to expect.

"No, the camera and microphone was too big for the tissue box." He handed them both a plan of the hospital floor where Ramzi's room was showing the layout of the hospital rooms and stairwells.

"Is that the food cart in the corridor?" asked Strain.

"Certainly, looks like it," the camera operator replied.

Strain realized Thorn was rummaging in his bag for something.

"Stay here, I'll be right back," said Thorn as he got out of the van.

Strain didn't know what Thorn had planned but something had come to mind. He watched the monitors but didn't see Thorn enter the hospital.

Thorn made his way straight to the north side of the building where there was a staff entrance. He saw a nurse going in and followed her just as the door was about to close. He made his way down the corridor to the fire stairwell on the opposite corner to where Ramzi's room was. Once on the floor, he saw the meal cart being wheeled along to one of the multiple occupancy wards.

Strain and the camera operator watched the monitors with interest as they could now see Thorn, they were curious to see what he was up to.

Thorn saw a well-read newspaper on a chair in the corridor and picked it up as the meal lady came out for more food trays. He waited until she went back inside the ward and quickly scanned down the food racks holding the trays. There it was a label on two trays with Ramzi's room number on it. One tray had a plastic container with fruit juice in it and a small bowl of Jell-O. The second tray had a bowl of soup, a sandwich and a cookie. This had to be for the security guy.

Thorn looked around, there were no staff about and he couldn't be seen from Ramzi's room. He had to work fast before the food lady came out again. Five seconds later he was on his way towards the fire escape.

Just before he reached the fire escape door a hospital staff member came out of a room to his right he casually looked inside as he walked. Thorn could see shelves full of laundry and some white coats on hangers.

Strain heard two knocks on the van door he looked at one of the monitors he could see Thorn outside.

Thorn climbed into the back of the van. "Have they had their food delivered?" he asked.

"She is just going in the room now," replied Strain.

They all watched as the nurse took both trays of food into the room, she put one on a portable table over Ramzi's bed and one next to the security man on a cabinet.

"When we leave the van, I want you to collect your cameras, except the one in his room I'll get that one. None of this is recorded, is it?" Thorn asked his surveillance tech.

"No, you said not to," the surveillance tech replied.

"Good. Once you have the cameras take the van back to the safe house and you can head home."

They sat and watched as Ramzi pushed away his tray and lay back with his eyes closed. The security guard was reading something and completely ignoring the food.

"Come on, eat the dam food," said Thorn under his breath.

As if he'd heard him, the security guard picked up the bowl of soup and peeled back the cling film. He bent forward and sniffed at the bowl, gave it a stir with the spoon and sniffed again. He put the soup down and picked up the sandwich, opening it up to see the contents.

"What the fuck, do you think you are you some kind of food critic?" Thorn said out loud. "Eat something, eat."

Now the security guard put the sandwich down and picked up the bowl of soup again. Five minutes later, the security guard had finished the soup but not before he'd put it down and picked it up several times.

"Christ, he took his sweet time eating that," said Thorn.

"How long do we wait?" Strain knew he'd put something in the food.

"Twenty to thirty minutes' tops, we need to move, let's go." Thorn picked up his bag.

"Take care," said the camera operator.

Strain followed Thorn into the hospital through the same employee entrance he'd used earlier. They stopped at the bottom of the fire exit stairwell.

Thorn took out two radios and ear pieces and gave one to Strain. It only took them a minute to set them up and feed the push to talk button down the inside of their shirt sleeves. The ear buds were put in place and the wire to the radio went over the ear and down the back of the shirt.

"OK, here is what we do. I have put a heavy-duty laxative in the security guard's soup and sandwich. Ramzi's room shares the bathroom with the room next door and when the other patient uses it they lock Ramzi's door from the inside so they are not disturbed. You go into the restroom from the other room and lock it from the inside. The nearest restroom is all the way down the corridor almost to the far side of the building. It will take him a minute to walk to it and then of course he will have a problem getting off the porcelain." Thorn paused when he heard voices on the other side of the stairwell door as people walked past.

"I got it," Strain replied.

"As we come out of the stairwell, there is a door on the left, hopefully nobody is around and we can go straight in. It's a laundry room and they have white coats which we can use to blend in a little." Thorn put his ear to the door and couldn't hear anything he opened it and entered the hospital floor.

They were lucky there wasn't anyone in the laundry room and they were soon walking down the hospital corridor wearing white coats.

"Give me a minute and I'll make my way to the fire stairwell on the far side of the building. This way I won't have to walk past Ramzi's room and can enter the patient room next door without being seen."

"OK, let me know when you are in place," Thorn replied.

As he walked down the corridor towards the stairwell he'd just come out of, Strain picked up a clipboard and stethoscope that was in a box at a vacant nurse's station. He went down one level and walked into the hospital corridor making his way to the opposite stairwell.

It only took Strain four minutes and he was in the patient's room. "OK I am in position," said Strain on the radio.

As Strain entered the room, he pulled the sheets back on the bed and roughed the pillow up a little to make it look like someone was using the bed. He then went into the restroom and locked the doors on both sides.

The security guard heard the door lock click on the restroom door and got up out of his chair. He tried to turn the handle but it was locked.

"Who's in there?" he said.

Strain heard the security guard and started to make it sound like he was throwing up.

"It will be the patient in the next room, we have to share the toilet," said Ramzi without even opening his eyes.

The security guard walked to the next room and looked through the glass he could see the ruffled bed sheets. He walked back to Ramzi's room to hear the noise of whoever it was in the restroom throwing up again.

Thorn was in another empty bedroom down the corridor and had a good view of Ramzi's room. He closed the curtains in the room so that he couldn't be seen and watched Ramzi's room through a gap in the curtain.

"He is getting out of the chair moving out of the room towards your position, he has stopped now heading back to Ramzi's room." Thorn said into the radio not knowing that Strain was faking throwing up.

They had been in position for fifteen minutes when Thorn saw the security guard stand up holding his stomach.

"He's on his feet heading towards the restroom."

Strain heard Thorn and once again started to fake throwing up.

Ramzi was fast asleep when the security guard stood up holding his stomach. He felt the stomach pain getting worse and had the sudden urge to go to the toilet.

He stepped towards the restroom only to hear the patient from the other room throwing up. He sat down again hoping that the pain would go away but it suddenly got worse. He did a quick check of Ramzi who was in a deep sleep, he had to make it to the toilet. He quickly walked out of the room and down the corridor towards one of the larger wards. A nurse came out just as he was passing.

"Where are the restrooms?" he asked not so politely.

"Down the corridor to the end, turn left and they are at the end on your left," she replied.

He walked as fast as he could without losing the content of his bowels.

Thorn could hear him asking for directions and left the room as the nurse went back on the ward.

"Heading your way," he said to Strain on the radio.

Strain unlocked both doors in the restroom and quietly opened the door leading into Ramzi's room just as Thorn was entering from the corridor.

Neither man said anything as Thorn opened his bag. He took out a recording device and two syringes containing liquid, he placed them all on the bedside table.

"Close that curtain," he pointed to a curtain that gave anyone in the corridor a view of them in the room.

Strain closed it just as Thorn was injecting liquid into Ramzi's intravenous line.

"What's in that?" whispered Strain.

"A cocktail of Sodium Amytal, Ativan and Sodium Pentothal, specially designed for situations like this." Thorn gently woke Ramzi.

He was already feeling the effects of the cocktail as it surged through his veins into his brain.

"Mr. Ramzi how are you feeling?" asked Thorn as he turned on the recording device.

"I am feeling very relaxed, but a little sleepy doctor," he replied.

His drowsiness helped them as he couldn't focus properly and saw the white coats immediately thinking they were doctors.

"How did you get injured?" asked Thorn.

"My car was in a crash I think, I'm not sure."

"Who was in the car with you?" asked Strain.

"My Ambassador is he OK?" he was fighting the drowsiness.

"Do you mean Khurram Al Khan, the Pakistan Ambassador?" asked Thorn.

"Yes, where is he? I need to speak to him."

"He is fine. He will be here in a couple of minutes. He wanted us to check your condition before he came in to see you. He is very concerned about you." Thorn knew they had to move this question session along.

Strain went to the window and watched the corridor in case the security guard came back.

"The Ambassador told me about the bomb on the Senator's car. You have done a great service for us." Thorn hoped he would answer as he knew that he would soon go into a deep sleep.

"You are one of us?" Ramzi asked as he tried to focus on Thorn's face.

"Yes, and we will win this war against the dogs like Gatts. Who had the honor of pressing the remote control for the bomb?"

Ramzi was mentally fighting with himself but couldn't resist answering the questions, "The Ambassador."

"Did he put the bomb on the car or was that your good work?" Thorn only had a few more questions.

"I did and the bugs."

"You put listening devices in the car, who helped you?" Thorn looked to Strain for assurance that the security guard wasn't coming back.

"I am going down the corridor," Strain said.

Thorn carried on asking questions, "Who is in your team?"

Ramzi was starting to realize that something was wrong. Why was the doctor asking him these questions? His brain was fogged and he was drifting back to sleep when he felt a sting on his face.

Thorn gave Ramzi a couple of solid slaps to the face to keep him awake.

"Who are you?" asked Ramzi in a doped voice.

Strain was halfway down the main corridor to the restrooms when he saw the security guard heading towards him. Strain turned and walked quickly back towards Thorn.

"He is on his way back and he is not taking his time," he said into the radio.

"Roger that, see you downstairs at the staff entrance," Thorn replied.

Thorn picked up the second syringe that he'd put on the bedside table and injected the liquid into Ramzi's IV just like he had with the first. He turned off the recording device and put it in the bag with both syringes. He then opened the curtains that Strain had closed and looked into the corridor, there was nobody around, he quickly left the room and went to the stairwell. As Thorn closed the stairwell door, the security guard came around the corner of the corridor. He picked up the pace as he got closer to Ramzi's room and could see through the glass he was still asleep, he could relax. It would take him several visits to the toilet before his stomach started to relax, he was grateful that the other patient wasn't occupying the adjoining restroom anymore.

Thorn and Strain went to his car and headed towards the safe house.

"How did it go?" asked Strain.

"Bloody fantastic considering. The recorder is in the bag on the back seat if you want to listen to it?"

"Do I ever," replied Strain who was already reaching for the bag.

They sat in silence as Strain played back the recording.

"I don't think Ramzi will be alive much longer but I think we can speed his death up a little," said Thorn.

"I think you're right especially when he wakes up and realizes that he has been interrogated."

"He won't remember much, if anything, of the interview. Right before I left I put a good dose of Rohypnol in his IV line."

"The Ambassador is up to his neck in this shit," said Strain.

"Yes, and I guarantee he will be quietly shipped out of the country if he gets wind that someone knows," Thorn replied.

"Well, right now we are the only ones that do know and we can keep this to ourselves until we need to use the recording." Strain relished the thought of getting the Ambassador locked up for his part but he knew it would never happen.

"Your right and I know just the person to play this to when the time comes, the President. He was very close to Gatts, they were old friends and his death has hit the President hard. Don't worry, John, the Ambassador won't go unpunished for this, not if we have anything to do about it." Thorn meant every word.

The security guard was in the toilet when he heard Ramzi begin talking. He quickly pulled his pants up and went into the room. There wasn't anyone there Ramzi was mumbling something in his sleep. The guard got close to him and listened to what he was saying.

"Bomb, bomb," Ramzi said.

The guard listened for a couple of minutes to Ramzi he said bomb again twice and mumbled something about the

Ambassador. He had to tell Omarzai straight away, he dialed his number on his cell phone.

"Our man is talking in his sleep," he said when Omarzai answered.

"Is he saying anything of interest?" Omarzai knew not to say too much over the phone as you didn't know who was listening.

"Yes, he is mentioning our client and what they were doing together."

"Have you left him at any time?" he asked.

"No." He lied because he knew that he would be killed if they found out he left the room.

"Good, I'll call you back soon."

The security guard was cursing his bad luck and the bad hospital food that gave him diarrhea.

Omarzai called the Pakistan Ambassador, "There is a problem."

"What is it?" he asked.

"Our colleague is delirious and his condition is not good. He's keeping the guard awake talking in his sleep," Omarzai replied.

"Was he doing that before?" The Ambassador was pacing up and down in his bedroom.

"He started about ten minutes ago, he's talking about what led up to his accident."

"I hope he stops soon, this is not good for his health. Tell the security guard to finish and go home, he won't be needed anymore. Call me back when he goes home."

"I will," Omarzai replied.

The Ambassador hung up the phone and kicked the bed in anger.

The security guard kept a close ear to Ramzi. He only mumbled once more and it was unintelligible. His cell phone rang.

"Hello."

"Is he still doing it?" asked Omarzai.

"Yes," the guard replied.

"Then finish your work and go home for some rest, you won't be needed again." Omarzai had told the guard before he got to the hospital that if he was given this instruction then he was to kill Ramzi.

"I understand, I'll call you when I leave," the guard replied.

Both men finished the call.

The security guard closed all the curtains in the room and walked over to Ramzi. He calmly pulled one of the pillows out from under his head and placed it on his face. Ramzi started to wake up as his body was being deprived of oxygen.

The security guard pressed down hard on the pillow using his upper body to prevent Ramzi from thrashing too much. It took over a minute before he was comfortable that Ramzi was dead. He placed the pillow back under Ramzi's head and opened the curtains. He made the call to Omarzai.

"I am leaving for home," he said when Omarzai answered.

"You have finished work then?" asked Omarzai.

"Yes, there's nothing else to do here," he replied.

"I'll let the client know, goodbye."

The conversation between Omarzai and the Ambassador was one way, "The work is finished."

CHAPTER 8

ATLANTIC CITY

Atlantic City was everything that Mohammed hated about the United States, the lights, the gambling, drink and sex everything was to excess and he hated it. He was dressed just like any other punter in the city with his drab brown pants and golf shirt, he blended in perfectly. As he walked towards the Trump Plaza hotel, he was scanning everything around him, always on guard. To perform counter surveillance in this city was very difficult as there were so many people buzzing around. The doorman opened the door of the hotel, welcoming him to the hotel. He smiled at the doorman, letting him know that he'd heard him. In his mind, the man on the door was no more than a robot trained to perform a duty and smile. Inside, the hotel lobby was very grand with more lights, floral decorations and glitter. The reception and concierge desks were very busy with people checking into the hotel and guests that were leaving. He slowly walked towards one corner of the lobby where there was a comfortable looking bench. From the bench, he would be able to observe the lobby, its entrances, exits and elevators. He stopped at a table on the way and poured himself a complimentary coffee provided by the hotel and picked up a newspaper that a previous customer had left. He sat to enjoy the coffee and continue his observations in between reading the newspaper. His routine of scanning a room no matter where he was or who he was with was his own personal paranoia.

He sat thinking about the young men he'd trained. He had not seen them since their last training exercise. He was very proud of the training he'd provided them and how they had all progressed. He knew that they were all ready for the task ahead and very capable of performing their required lethal duties without hesitation. It had been six years since some of the trainees had moved out of the camp in Southern Morocco. He had monitored their progress over the years at the other camps that they had attended to maintain and hone their skills. They had all infiltrated the US with ease. They established themselves in the Universities that they attended and in the social community in which they revolved. Nobody would suspect them of being terrorists. They were just students that never got into trouble or brought unwanted attention to themselves. Twelve young men all in their early twenties, not one looked Arabic, some would even be mistaken for a Hispanic, a deliberate decision by Mohammed. Each man was ready to fight and die if necessary for the Jihad issued by Mohammed against the US and its supporters. Every one of them had a high level of skill in explosives, weapons, electronics and driving. All of them had been handpicked by Mohammed for this reason. His older soldiers kept him informed of the day to day activity of the new recruits and if any one of them brought undue attention to themselves, he would take care of it personally.

This would be the first-time Mohammed had called the older members together to meet in one place on US soil. Each one of them thought that they were going to a private one on one meeting, but they didn't know who it was to be with. As far as they were concerned, it was just another one of their periodic contact meetings. This was the first meeting of its kind for all of them.

The older soldiers all had their own businesses and all were very successful. They enjoyed the high life that American business offered and they prospered as a result. The money to set up the companies was provided by Mohammed, his share was seventy per cent of the profits. He hadn't cared what they did with their thirty per cent, until now.

This hotel meeting was arranged by Mohammed's most trusted soldier, Samir al Bahrani, Sammy to his friends. All the room reservations would be in his company name, Computer Parts US. He was known by the hotel staff as a frequent visitor and often booked several rooms for meetings that he was holding, a perfect cover for this group.

Sammy always arrived at the hotel in a limousine and sat inside the vehicle waiting for the driver to open the door. He enjoyed this part of his life being pampered by others and he gave little in return as they were all servants to him. The door opened and he got out slowly, wanting people to notice him. He was only five feet six inches tall, with black graying hair that sat high on his head. His large round stomach hung over his trouser belt, showing that he didn't walk away from many meals hungry. He smiled at the driver and nodded at the hotel doorman as he put a large cigar into his mouth. He loved the night life of Atlantic City especially the gambling and prostitutes he had an addiction to both. He always booked himself into a suite and on this occasion, had booked a connecting suite for Mohammed.

"Hello, Peter," he said to the doorman, one of the few people that Sammy liked, mainly because he had the phone numbers for the best-looking prostitutes.

"Good to see you again, sir," he replied.

Sammy entered the hotel looking very businesslike in his dark blue suit and blue tie.

It had been over a year since he'd seen Mohammed and he was looking forward to meeting him again and bragging about how good the business was doing.

Mohammed had a second cup of coffee on the table in front of him. He had observed several people in the thirty minutes that he'd been sitting in the hotel lobby. As always, he was looking for something that was out of place and he'd found it. He was becoming more uncomfortable about two men sitting on a seat across the lobby from him, he could tell that they were performing surveillance. He had been watching them closely for some time and saw that they were giving the occasional discreet hand signal to another man standing by the elevators.

They had to be police or FBI and he wasn't in a good position where he was sitting in the lobby, he had to move he was sure that they were watching him. He could feel his nine-millimeter handgun resting in the small of his back. He felt confident that he could certainly take two of the men out when they approached him. He decided to try to make a move towards the main lobby doors, if he got outside he had more of a chance to escape.

His attention was drawn to the elevators when he heard the distinctive ping announcing that an elevator had arrived. He watched as the double doors of an elevator opened and a group of woman spilled out into the lobby. They were heading towards the main lobby exit, all chattering away, busy in their own little world. Their path would take them between him and the policemen. He calmly stood up and drank the remains of the coffee in the cup and placed it back on the table and started to walk. There was another ping from the elevator bank and he looked in the direction of the noise. Four large black men exited an elevator, all wearing long black leather coats and sunglasses, they would provide more cover for him.

Mohammed looked back towards the group of women they were now in a good position to block the way of the police. Stay calm, he told himself as he approached the group. Then, without warning, the policemen jumped up and drew guns out from under their coats. Two of the women at the back of the group did the same. They were all shouting the same thing, "Police. Get down on the floor."

Two more men appeared as if from nowhere, they also had weapons drawn shouting the same orders, except none of them were pointing at Mohammed. They were all aiming at the black men who had just left the elevator. Things started to get a little confusing for some of the hotel guests in the lobby as they started to scream in fear. Not knowing what to do, the other women crowded together for safety and ran for the front doors of the hotel. A plain clothes policeman walked slowly towards the four men, intimidating them with his gun and repeated the order to get down on the floor as they glared back at him.

Mohammed moved slowly towards the group of women and pretended to be in shock at what was happening, like the rest of the hotel guests. He was just relieved that they weren't after him. He never took his eyes off the black men, one in particular concerned him as he recognized the wild look in his eyes, he was high on drugs.

"Fuck you," the black man shouted and reached under his coat.

A chorus of shouts came from the policemen they were all shouting, "Stop, don't move, armed police."

The black man took no notice and started to pull a gun out from under his coat. A volley of shots was fired by all the policemen.

The man staggered backwards as the rounds from the policemen's weapons hit his bullet proof vest. He smiled as he started to raise an AK47 from under his coat, his finger was already on the trigger. Two bullets hit him in the throat and one in the face, his index finger squeezed the trigger on the AK47 firing bullets into the floor as he fell backwards, by the time his body hit the floor he was dead.

The screams from the hotel guests became deafening as the remaining black men put their arms up shouting, "Don't shoot." This was followed very quickly by them lying on the floor face down.

Mohammed was now close to the group of women as they were all being ushered outside by police officers. He followed, cowering like the rest of them, pretending to be scared. He saw Sammy trying to enter the hotel, but he was being pushed back outside by the group of women exiting.

Sammy had heard the gunfire from outside as he approached the hotel doors. He froze temporarily, thinking that Mohammed had been discovered by the FBI. Before he knew what to do, he saw Mohammed in amongst a group of women who were storming out of the hotel. He thought it looked funny as he watched Mohammed being jostled by the group of heavy set women. They saw each other and Sammy gave Mohammed a quick nod of the head to follow him. Sammy didn't want to stand out from the rest of the hotel guests. He acted as if he was one of them in this situation and turned away from the hotel as if in fear and headed towards the parking lot.

Sammy waved at Mohammed to follow him as he walked to the road outside the front of the hotel. He crossed the road and entered a patisserie followed by Mohammed a short distance away. He sat at a table and waited the few seconds that it would take for Mohammed to catch up.

Sammy saw Mohammed enter as he sat at the table and raised his hand to catch his attention, a normal reaction for two people who had arranged to meet.

"Good to see you again," Mohammed said.

"And you, my friend," he replied.

They shook hands, resisting the temptation to hug and kiss each other on the cheek as they would normally do, this would be an obvious attention grabber.

"It looks busy outside there are a lot of police cars racing down the street," Mohammed said, just loud enough for the other patrons to hear as they were all looking at the police cars racing towards the hotel. This again was to help them blend in with the other people in the patisserie who were engrossed in what was happening at the hotel.

"Yes," he replied.

Sammy ordered two espressos from the waitress.

Sammy leaned forward to talk to Mohammed and in a very quiet voice asked, "What happened?"

"It looks like the police had a surveillance operation going on when a group of black men came out of the elevator. The next thing, there was a lot of shouting and gunfire."

"I thought that it was you when I heard the gunfire from outside the hotel." Sammy smiled.

"Thankfully it wasn't. What do you think they have done, these men?" asked Mohammed.

Sammy took a wild guess, "Most probably drug dealers. This town is full of them."

"I don't think we need to go back in the hotel yet." Mohammed wanted to keep out of the way of the police.

"I agree, we can go to my room later," he replied.

CHAPTER 9

NEW YORK

As Strain left the plane in Newark Airport, he was curious how the meeting with the Don would go. He just hoped that he would agree to help.

The Gulfstream was already proving to be invaluable, as he didn't have to go through the usual public security checks in the main airport terminal. Strain placed his sidearm into the belt holster and asked the pilots to be ready to leave in a couple of hours.

At the bottom of the steps of the plane was an athletic looking man in his late-twenties wearing a dark three quarter length coat.

"Mr. Strain, my name is Tony." He pushed out his hand and shook hands with Strain.

"Pleased to meet you," Strain replied.

"The car is this way."

They walked across the concrete aircraft stand to a black sedan that was parked by a chain link fence. There was another man in a black coat standing by the rear of the car holding a door open.

"In the back, please," said the man.

As Strain got into the back of the car, the man closed the door and then got into the driver's seat. Tony joined Strain in the back.

"My father sends his apologies for not being able to meet you here but he is waiting for us at one of our restaurants," said Tony.

"No problem."

"I have to ask are you armed?"

"Yes, I have a sidearm in my belt holster." Strain knew that this was going to be taken from him.

"Can I have it please? You will get it back when you return to the plane."

"Yes." Strain reached very slowly for the weapon so as not to spook him.

"Thank you," replied Tony, handing the gun to the driver.

They made small talk for the remainder of the drive to the Little Italy quarter of New York City.

"Not long now, about four blocks ahead," said Tony.

Strain was admiring the old buildings, trying to imagine what it was like in the old prohibition days. He could almost see the old gangsters in old Ford motor cars, some of them standing on the running boards holding Thompson machine guns.

The car stopped at a traffic light in heavy traffic as a line of vehicles turned across them, from a side road into the road they were travelling on.

Strain was looking at the vehicles when he saw a face he recognized, it was Ali Fahmi one of Mohammed's nephews. Ali Fahmi was suspected of many terrorist acts in Europe and the Middle East, mostly assassinations.

Tony saw the look on Strain's face, "What's up?"

"I am almost certain that the white car ahead has a known terrorist in it. His name is Ali Fahmi."

The light changed to green and they drove on. There were about five cars between them and the white car now, as they moved very slowly in the heavy traffic.

"Who is he?" asked Tony.

"He is an assassin for Mohammed Ali Ghahi, he is his nephew."

"What is he doing here?" asked Tony.

"I don't know, but I have the license plate and I can run it."

"We will turn left soon most of the traffic will stay on this main street. There isn't much down the side street we are going to turn into except a few local shops and restaurants. Maybe he is one of the people collecting payments from the store owners?" replied Tony.

"I don't see him doing that, he is very accomplished at what he does. Collections would be for the newer recruits that Mohammed could keep in fear."

"They are turning left," said the driver.

"That doesn't make sense there's nothing down here but...."

Strain cut in, "The restaurant does your father go there often?" asked Strain.

"Yeah! Most days for lunch, Oh! Fuck," Tony started to get out of the car, quickly followed by Strain.

"Give me the gun," Strain said to the driver as he got out.

The driver handed over the weapon without really thinking.

Tony was fast and already fifteen yards ahead of Strain as he ran down the sidewalk.

Strain stayed in the road, running between parked cars and vehicles driving along the road.

Tony suddenly stopped and jumped behind a parked van, he was watching the white car. Strain caught up and joined him on the other side of the van.

"Tony, if any of them get out of the car you go for the person nearest the restaurant, I'll take the second man.

"How do you know there will be two?' he asked.

"There were two in the front seat, the one in the back was Ali, let's go car to car for cover, go." Strain said.

Both moved from car to car on the sidewalk side of the vehicles. Strain didn't want the driver of the white car to see him in his wing mirror.

They stopped just thirty yards from the restaurant where the Don was supposed to be. The white car drove past slowly and turned right around the corner, out of sight.

"Is there a back entrance to the restaurant?" shouted Strain.

"Yes, a delivery door," replied Tony.

"Get your father out of there. I'll go around the back."

"Go down this alley turn first left it's the only door on that part of the building," replied Tony.

Both ran as fast as they could. Tony was in the restaurant in a flash.

"Pop, we gotta go quickly," Tony shouted as he ran into the restaurant. He was waiving his arm for his father to follow him.

His father stood up from the corner table, wondering what was going on when he realized his son was pointing his gun towards the rear of the restaurant. The Don had one of his trusted men with him providing protection and he was on his feet with his weapon drawn.

"Cover the front," said Tony to the man protecting the Don.

Strain saw the white car pulling up at the back of the restaurant two men were getting out, one was Ali but he didn't recognize the second man.

Strain had to move quickly to distract them. He stepped out into the road and fired two rounds at them.

Ali heard the shots and immediately ducked down behind the open car door, returning fire with his Uzi.

Strain ducked back into the alley for cover as a hail of bullets hit the wall where he'd just been.

Tony and the Don's bodyguard were walking him towards the front door when they heard the shots being fired in the back.

Tony turned towards the back of the store where the shots were coming from. There were only about twelve customers in the restaurant and they were all diving for the floor, except one. Tony saw the man raise an Uzi to shoot him, but he was too slow. Tony put two bullets into his head. The man fell like a stone, landing on top of the table behind him. He was dead.

Tony and the bodyguard quickly surveyed the room. Nobody else was standing they were all cowering under the tables.

"Behind the bar, Pops," he said to the Godfather.

Tony knew he couldn't risk going out of the front door now. He got his father in a safe place behind the bar. Two of the restaurant staff were holding shotguns to help protect the Don. Tony headed towards the back of the restaurant.

Strain heard the shots inside the restaurant and feared the worst. He stuck his head out into the road for a quick look and was amazed when he saw Ali coming towards him on the other side of the street. Strain knew his gun was no match for the Uzis and looked around for an advantage. Just behind him was a short steel ladder that led up to a window above, it was a fire escape. He went to climb the ladder and saw one of the bolts securing it to the wall sticking out. He took his heavy coat off and hung it on the bolt, then scurried up the ladder as fast as he could.

The second man with Ali went into the back of the restaurant as soon as he heard the gunfire from inside. He quietly opened the outer door and stepped inside where there was a storage area. Next to the boxes was a ladies and gents restroom, he slid past them towards another door with a small glass panel in it. He crept up to the door and peaked through the glass.

"Looking for me?" Tony was behind him. He fired three rounds into the man's head at close range. "Next time check the restroom asshole," he said to the dead man.

Strain was now on the flat part of the fire escape, ten feet up and standing next to an apartment window.

Ali had worked his way up the street with his Uzi fixed on the spot where Strain was standing. He was almost at the point where he would be exposed when he jumped forward to get a quick view of the alley. There was the man that shot at him he was standing against the wall he opened fire with two quick bursts from the Uzi.

Strain stayed still as Ali came into view. He saw him jump forward and start firing. Strain calmly stepped away from the apartment window and fired four shots at Ali. All of them met their target in the chest and stomach.

Ali felt the burning sting of the bullets as they bored into him. He dropped his weapon as he fell backwards, the last thing he saw was Strain on the fire escape, pointing his gun at him.

Tony heard the gunfire at the back of the restaurant he opened the back door quickly keeping himself out of the line of fire. A quick glance outside and he stepped out into the road, just as the white car was racing away. He let loose the remaining bullets in his weapon at the car.

Strain heard the car and the shots being fired as he was getting down from the fire escape. He was at the entrance of the alley when the car was passing, like Tony he emptied his weapon into the car. Tony and Strain both watched as the car swerved to the left and crashed into a brick wall. Both men had reloaded their weapons and approached the car, the driver was dead.

"Let's get your father to safety," said Strain.

The Don, Tony and Strain were four blocks away when the first police officers showed up.

The bodyguard drove Strain in his car to a private club where he would meet the Don. By the time they arrived, there was an army of men inside and out to protect the Don.

Strain made a call to Thorn and told him about the incident at the restaurant and he said he would take care of it with the cops. What he really meant was he would have the Feds send a cleaning crew to take care of the scene and the bodies. The press would get to know that it was a dispute between two brothers, a domestic situation.

Strain arrived at the club directly behind Tony, who stood by the door waiting for him.

"Inside," said Tony.

Strain stepped into the entrance of the club only to be thrown against the wall by one of the goons protecting the Don.

"Sorry, but we got to frisk you," said Tony.

"The gun is in my holster, left side."

"He's clean," said the goon after he took Strain's gun.

"Come on in, my Pops wants to meet you." Tony showed Strain into the club where there was a heavy smell of cigar smoke.

The Don was sucking on a huge cigar as he watched Strain walk towards him.

"Sit down, Mr. Strain," said the Don.

"Thank you," he replied.

Standing behind the Don where two huge men, several others were scattered around the room. The place looked like it had not seen daylight for many years and he could imagine that this was once a great speakeasy. Old wooden panels and a bar that had the cleanest glasses he'd ever seen glistened in the lights above them.

"My son tells me you were responsible for recognizing those rag heads that were trying to kill me."

"Yes, I recognized one of them," replied Strain.

"How did you know they were coming after me?"

"I didn't, we watched them in the car ahead of us and thought, where else are they going? Tony here got out of the car first and I followed, once the driver gave me my gun back. So really it was your son who made the first move."

"They killed two of my best men not so long ago. They made a big mistake then and they just made an even bigger one now. What is it you want from me?" replied the Don.

"Simple really I think these people are trying to increase terrorist activity here in the US. They are most probably planning bombings as we speak. They are getting low on funds these days due to various governments shutting down their illegal accounts. They are raising funds now through drugs, extortion, robberies and other criminal activity." A glass of wine was put in front of Strain by the barman.

"Salute," said the Don.

"Salute and thanks to your son. Tony has a serious pair of balls," replied Strain.

Everyone laughed at the same time, but no louder than the Don.

"You have a sense of humor that is good."

"I would like to ask a favor." Strain knew that the foiled attempt on the Don's life had just made his request a lot easier.

"What is it?" asked the Don.

"You have many contacts in the US, particularly with the unions and other work forces. I need to locate these people and find out where they are hiding or storing goods. There is a good chance that they are operating in a remote warehouse or very busy warehouse district or on a dock somewhere. They will try to blend in with other work forces, so this is why I say docks or warehouses. They wouldn't choose office buildings or store front locations where they would stand out, offices would be for a smaller operation. If you were to put the word out for your contacts to keep an eye out for any suspicious or unusual activity by Arab or Pakistani looking men, I would appreciate it. If you're able to obtain credible information on their location I can put them under surveillance. My team is dedicated and we will try to stop the terrorists who are killing innocent men, women and children. These people have no scruples and will kill anyone that gets in their way." Strain took a drink of his wine.

"OK, Mr. Strain I'll see what I can find out."

"Thank you, we need to talk in the future about the surveillance on you."

"Tony take him back to the airport or wherever he wants to go. We may meet again Mr. Strain, but I'll arrange the transportation if we do meet." The Don didn't trust him yet and didn't know if he was working for the Feds. He would call Foy and get a lot more background on Strain, especially after what happened today. He wanted to trust him, as he seemed genuine in his quest to find the terrorists.

CHAPTER 10

THE BRONX

Ehab lifted the explosive-laden vest that was lying on the table and held it up for his friend Idrees to put his arms into the sleeves.

"Here is your destiny," he said.

Idrees turned his back to him and slid his arms into the sleeves of the vest. Ehab let go of the vest and it rested on his friend's shoulders. Idrees knew that the vest was heavy because he'd handled it many times during his training and in preparation for this day. Somehow today the vest felt much heavier, a burden not only on his body but on his mind. He fastened the buttons and clasps on the front of the vest and looked up at the mirror in front of him. He looked at his reflection in the mirror and for the first time he suddenly realized what he was going to do. Now that the vest was on his body, he felt scared, a feeling that he wouldn't get rid of.

"OK, stop dreaming of your future glory. Help me with mine," said Ehab.

He looked across at his friend who was holding his own vest ready for him to try on. Idrees helped him put his vest on. How did Ehab remain so calm and relaxed, he couldn't understand it, Idrees felt nothing but terror and a sickness in his gut.

"We are ready," said Ehab.

"Are we doing the right thing?" Idrees said, as he questioned himself. He was starting to sweat.

"Yes, you know we are this is the day we have been waiting for, this is our destiny, our glorious moment." He had a wild look in his eyes that his friend had never seen before.

"I am nervous," he replied.

"Why wouldn't you be? You have twenty pounds of dynamite strapped to your chest." He laughed trying to make a joke of it.

"Are you concerned about this?" He needed reassurance from his friend.

"No, I am going to sit with Allah and receive my glory. You will be fine, don't worry."

"OK," he replied. He started to shake. The fear was really taking over him and Ehab could see it.

"I'll make coffee and we can relax after we take the photographs."

Ehab walked into the kitchen to put the coffee on and knew that he had to get courage for his friend from somewhere. He went back into the lounge with the digital camera in his hand. He mounted the camera on a tripod and hung a white sheet on the wall as a background for the photographs.

"Here are the head bands," he handed one to Idrees.

"You see nothing to worry about. Stand by the sheet so I can line up the photograph of us."

He set the tripod in the correct position and pressed the time delay on the camera. This would give him time to stand next to Idrees before the camera took the picture on the automatic timer. He took four photographs in all and put the chip from the camera in an envelope that he'd already addressed and stamped. They took off their vests and enjoyed the coffee. Idrees put his head phones on and listened to music, this always calmed him.

The coffee and music seemed to work on Idrees, but his hands were still shaking. He was thinking about his mother and father and three sisters. He hoped that they would understand why he'd committed suicide. He sat looking at the vest. It was revealing the sticks of dynamite sitting in the specially designed elongated pockets. They were surrounded by more pockets which had nails and ball bearings in them. Wires were looped from one stick to another and connected to the trigger mechanism that he would press to detonate his deadly device. There were so many wires he couldn't make out what they all meant.

Ehab called the mosque from the kitchen and asked for the Imam, his religious and spiritual leader.

"It's me," he said when the Imam answered the phone.

"Yes," he replied.

"Idrees is getting nervous I don't think that he will go through with it, I am worried."

"What makes you say this?" he asked.

"He is asking are we doing the right thing and acting very oddly."

"Sit with him and pray you will both find strength in prayer," he said.

"Thank you, God is great," he said in Arabic and returned to the lounge.

The Imam knew that this wasn't a good sign as they both had to be totally devoted to the cause. To have one of them back out now would be disastrous it would reduce the desired media impact and set back years of work, they had to succeed.

The Imam walked around for several minutes searching his mind for the right solution to the problem. There was only one, he needed to call Mohammed to tell him about the telephone conversation he had with Ehab.

CHAPTER 11

WASHINGTON D.C.

George and Chalky arrived at Washington Dulles airport and were whisked through the immigration and customs areas by special agents. Thorn was proving to be very useful. He'd arranged for them to be brought through the airport with VIP status. The usual questions by customs and immigration about why they were visiting the US and what they had with them didn't occur. Thorn had several people that he trusted in customs and immigration work the VIP line just for their arrival. They were taken to a private office within the secure area of the airport where they waited for their luggage.

"I wonder if we will always get this kind of treatment?" asked Chalky.

"I wouldn't bet on it," replied George.

"Pretty stern looking chaps in immigration they must remove their personality as part of the pre-qualification for the job. At least they smile at you in England." Chalky never did like authority anyway.

"We have some miserable bastards too. What is taking them so long?" George wanted to get out of the airport and see what it was really like on the streets of Washington D.C.

The office door opened and a man dressed in an airport security uniform stepped inside.

"Gentlemen, you are clear to go. Your bags are in the vehicle outside, follow me please."

Outside there was a large Grey passenger van with slightly tinted windows. The rear doors were wide open with another airport security guard standing by them.

"Can you check that we have all of your baggage please?" The guard was all business as he stepped to one side as they looked inside the van.

"Yeah, it's all there," said George after a quick bag count.

"Thank you, sir." The guard stepped forward closing and locking the rear doors to the van.

George and Chalky got into the van and drove towards the security gate, a short check of the paper work by another security guard and they were on the way to the hotel.

George and Chalky arrived at the Westin Grand Hotel without any problems and in no time, they were in their rooms. All the bags had been delivered to George's room.

He looked at the phone to see how he could dial Chalky's room direct, "Just dial the four numbers of the room, dummy," he said out loud to himself.

Chalky answered the phone, "Hello."

"The bags are here," was all George said and quickly hung up the phone.

They went through the bags together in George's room. One of the bags had a sizeable dent in it but this didn't bother either of them as they were designed to take a beating. All the cases also had a special digital combination lock that was very difficult for anyone to get into.

George punched in the security code numbers on the damaged bag until the red digital display appeared saying open. He opened the case and removed the specially shaped foam that protected the equipment. Neither of them could believe their eyes the directional microphone was severely damaged.

"How did that happen?" said Chalky.

George put his fingers to his lips to tell Chalky to keep quiet.

They quickly opened the other cases and found several other pieces of equipment had been damaged.

George picked up the note pad at the side of the bed and wrote something on it and showed it to George.

'We have to tell Strain straight away.' He indicated that they should leave the room. Chalky nodded as George picked up his cell phone. They headed straight for the fire stairwell and went inside. After a quick check to make sure that nobody was inside the stairwell, they talked very quietly.

"We will call John and tell him what has happened and then we go back and fix what we can. We need to sweep all of the rooms and check for listening devices and cameras in total silence." George was as angry as he'd ever been in his life, nobody had done this to him before.

He dialed Strain's cell phone number.

"Hello," Strain answered the call.

"John, we are here, but there is a problem." George said.

"What kind of problem?" he asked.

"Some of our equipment was damaged and we will need to repair what we can or find some new stuff," he replied.

"Do what you can for now I'll see you in about three hours." Strain knew that they were going to have a few problems along the way, but not this soon.

George and Chalky returned to the room and started to repair what they could. It took them two hours to repair most of the equipment that was damaged. Whoever had done this didn't know what parts to damage to cause a major problem. Everything but the directional microphone was repairable.

They meticulously swept both of their bedrooms and found a total of fourteen listening devices but no cameras.

"George, can you put this in the bathroom for me?" asked Chalky.

"Sure."

Chalky handed George a small black box that he hid inside the air conditioning vent in the bathroom. Chalky did the same in the vent in the main bedroom area, far enough inside that if anyone came back to check the vent they wouldn't see it. The box sent out a continuous high frequency signal that messed up any receiving devices that might be in the room. This little gadget was one of Chalky's brainstorms and although experimental, it had proved invaluable in the past. They would place these devices in all the team members' rooms after they had swept them for listening bugs and cameras.

CHAPTER 12

          Steve Jones (Shadow) and Matt Grantham (Bulldog)
arrived an hour and thirty minutes after George and Chalky.
They were also met by Thorn's connections and avoided the
usual immigration and customs channels. Terry O'Neill
(Wheels), Jack Kay (L.B.) and Stan Cartwright (Sleepy) would
arrive on the flight from Manchester two hours later and would
receive the same special treatment from Thorn's people. As far
as the US Government authorities were concerned, this team of
men had never entered the country and didn't exist. Bulldog and
Shadow were to get a taxi to the city at Strain's request he
wanted to see if they would be under surveillance. Wheels, L.B.
and Sleepy would do the same when they arrived.
          Bulldog and Shadow were escorted by one of the
customs men into the public area of the airport through a side
door that was used by airport staff only.
          "That was easy," said Bulldog, as they walked through
the airport.
          Like most international airports, there were people
everywhere some were running, some walking and some just
looking at signs like they were totally lost.
          "Taxis," Shadow said, pointing at a sign hanging from
the ceiling.
          "Right, let's go," replied Bulldog.
          Outside there was a long line of people waiting for a taxi.
At the front of the line, was a tall man in a uniform who was
talking to someone on a radio. It wasn't long before they
realized that he was calling the taxi dispatcher to send more
taxis.
          "The taxis must be at a staging area away from the
terminal like we have at Heathrow. He loves the power he has
with that radio, he is in charge, or at least he thinks he is," said
Bulldog.
          "There are two others up there helping him. Trust the
Yanks to make a big deal out of something as simple as getting a

taxi." Shadow didn't have a great deal of time for Americans, as the only ones he'd met were on vacation in the UK. Most of those he'd met or rather heard were very loud and brusque with no patience whatsoever.

As they reached the front of the line there were no taxis left. The man in uniform was on the radio again.

"A cab will be here in a moment, Sir," he said.

"OK," replied Shadow.

Almost immediately, a cab approached from the far end of the terminal building.

The cab stopped next to them the man in uniform said, "Enjoy your stay."

"Thanks, we will," Bulldog replied.

The driver got out of the car and opened the trunk. They traveled light and only had one suitcase each which they placed in the trunk. The driver closed it and returned to the driver's seat.

Shadow and Bulldog sat together in the rear of the cab.

"Where are you going?" asked the driver.

"Westin Grand downtown," replied Shadow.

Shadow tapped Bulldog on the side of the leg and pointed to the driver where he couldn't see what he was doing, he gave the thumbs down sign to Bulldog, he nodded his head, he got the message he also didn't trust the driver.

"You here on business?" the driver asked looking at them in his rear-view mirror.

"No, holiday," Bulldog replied.

"This is a great city, welcome to the United States of America," he replied proudly.

"Thanks," said Bulldog.

"Hey, if you guys need a taxi to get you around the sights, I am also a registered tour guide. I know all the historical sites and all the fun places to visit, if you know what I mean. Here is my business card." He handed a card back to Bulldog.

They knew what he meant, but the last thing they wanted was to get involved with ladies of the night. Besides, they felt that he had a more intimate knowledge of the inside of US government buildings.

"Thanks," Bulldog said as he took the business card.

The driver continued his chatter, "You guys ever been to the US before?"

"No," was the short reply from Shadow.

"We have some of the best restaurants in the US here in D.C., I can recommend some if you want." He was pressing them for business.

"No, thanks, we are the adventurous kind," replied Shadow.

"I can really help you." The driver wasn't going to give up easily.

"No, thanks again," said Bulldog curtly.

The driver didn't speak again until they arrived at the hotel.

"Here we are," he said as he stopped the car on the drive at the front of the hotel.

The door next to Bulldog opened almost as soon as the taxi stopped, a doorman in a very smart uniform had opened it. "Welcome to the Westin, gentlemen," he said standing to one side to let Bulldog out.

"Thanks," he replied.

The driver was out of the car and had already opened the trunk remotely. Shadow was quick to pull both suitcases out of the vehicle. "You can pay for the cab," he said to Bulldog.

"Thanks," he replied with a sneer.

"Can I assist you with your bags, sir," the doorman reached for the cases to take them out of Shadow's hands.

Shadow pulled away and said, "No, thanks, we travel light."

"Certainly, sir," the doorman replied stepping aside to allow them to enter the hotel.

The large circular lobby was very modern and as the hotel name stated, it was grand. Large wooden columns made the reception desk stand out. In the center of the room was a very thick high quality carpet which had small circular tables and chairs placed on it for use by hotel patrons. The receptionist was ready to welcome them she played her corporate role well and quickly had them checked in and on the way to their rooms.

As they got into the elevator, Shadow leaned over to Bulldog and whispered, "When you get to your room ask to be moved, make up some excuse that you don't like the room, I'll do the same. Let's meet in the lobby in thirty minutes."

Bulldog nodded.

They both experienced a little resistance from the receptionist about changing rooms. She was very hesitant and totally different to the smiling face that had checked them in. They eventually got their way.

Both men checked out each room thoroughly looking for listening devices, they didn't find any. They both knew that just because they didn't find any didn't mean that they didn't exist, so they would have George and Chalky sweep the rooms. They would find any bugs or cameras remove them and run interference for any bugs they may not have found.

CHAPTER 13

CALIFORNIA

Sgt. Douglas Matthews waited by the line of army vehicles, expecting the call to go onto the firing range to load the military's latest secret weapon on his truck for it to be delivered back to the base.

His duties on three previous occasions when the weapon system went to the test grounds were security and transportation. Matthews had become disillusioned with the US military and government after his service in Iraq during 'Desert Storm'. He'd been home from Iraq only six months when he had converted fully to Islam. His interest in Islam developed when he was serving in Kuwait, where part of his duties to liaise with the local people on the outskirts of Kuwait City. His remit was to offer support to Iraqi families who had become victims of Saddam Hussein's regime and been made homeless by the Iraqi army.

It was on one of these liaison duties that he met twenty year old Numa, an Iraqi refugee. Her father and grandfather had been tortured by the Iraqi secret police and the whole family fled to Kuwait. Unfortunately, the invasion of Kuwait by Saddam's forces took place two months after they had fled to Kuwait.

Matthews had learnt to speak reasonable Arabic during his tour of duty and spoke to her family almost daily. Numa was becoming too modern for the women of the family and her fascination for anything European or American caused many family arguments. A couple of months after Matthews and Numa met, he told her that he'd fallen in love with her and wanted her to marry him and return to America with him. Numa knew that this wouldn't be acceptable to her family but agreed anyway on the understanding that he didn't tell her family, not until she was ready. A week later, she would lose her virginity to him when she admitted she loved him also, her fate was now sealed with her family if they found out.

Numa and Matthews always met at their secret location away from the prying eyes of the military and her family. He told her that he was going to be shipped back to the US in a few weeks and he was going to speak to the Chaplin and his commanding officer to see if they could get married in Kuwait. He hoped that this would mean that she could return with him or closely behind him. Numa was ecstatic and couldn't control her emotion she had to tell someone and she did, her best friend Badil. Unfortunately, her best friend couldn't be trusted and she went straight to Numa's mother and told her the full story, including the fact that she had lost her virginity. This news threw disgrace on the family and their daughter Numa the family couldn't let this news become public. Even though it didn't become public knowledge, Numa's father, brothers and uncles felt the stain of shame on their family was too much for the family. The men of the family dragged her out of her bed early one morning and took her to a house that had been bombed during the initial US insertion. In this partly demolished home, she was thrown down onto the rubble of the house and stoned to death by the male members of her family.

Sadly, Numa wasn't the first or last woman or girl to be killed by family members in order to save the family honor. Honor killings had gone on for hundreds of years without the watchful eye of the western world. Even in today's modern world, honor killings are still an everyday part of life, not just in Muslim countries but in the US, Canada and Europe. These ancient, strong barbaric ways migrated with the families into their new western homes.

Matthews eventually found out from Badil that Numa had died but she wouldn't reveal to him how. He took her death terribly and tried to see the family many times to find out how she had died. The continued visits and questions by Matthews forced the family to move to another town in fear that the news of their daughter's affair with the soldier would become public.

Matthews went into an emotional downward spiral, shunning contact with his army colleagues, eventually suffering deep depression. He couldn't confide in his army pals, as they would have mocked and humiliated him for falling in love with an Iraqi woman. It became obvious to all that met him that something was very wrong. His commanding officer tried to help Matthews, but he denied anything was wrong and he was eventually shipped home by the military.

Back in the US, he resumed normal duties and came out of the medical assessment with flying colors, it was all put down to the stress of war by the doctors.

Matthews wrote to Badil several times requesting that she send the enclosed letter to Numa's family. In one of his letters, he confided in her that he'd converted to Islam and even told her which mosque he attended. Neither the family nor her best friend ever returned his letters.

He became very isolated over the coming year and didn't reveal to the military or his army pals that he'd converted to Islam. He was devout in his following of the faith and studied the Koran as often as he could. He enjoyed his new-found religion and made several friends at the mosque, he couldn't tell them that he was in the military or they would shun him and possibly even ban him from the mosque.

One friend that he met at the mosque was Musaad Al-Saeed. He was what he called a more modern Muslim as he enjoyed a lot of Western things in life that some would say is not the way of Islam. One such enjoyment of Musaad and his brothers was street luge. Matthews thought that they were mad after he saw them race for the first time down a very steep California hill. He was fascinated how they managed to lay down on a very skinny board on wheels and race down a hill without any brakes. Musaad and his brothers were very good at the sport and had many trophies to their names. They had not yet convinced him to become a pilot, that is what they called the riders, but he was an avid spectator. He was even starting to understand some of the street luge 'speak'. Like most of the spectators, he enjoyed the speeds at which the pilots traveled down the hills. He also enjoyed when they would crash into the hay bales at the side of the road. These makeshift crash barriers would be hit so hard at times that they would be dislodged by the impact. Crashing into the hay bales didn't deter some of the pilots and if they could rejoin the race they would. They all looked more like motor cycle racers than someone on an elongated version of a skate board. Crash helmets, leather body suits and gloves were standard equipment to protect the pilots.

He would eventually trust Musaad with his secret about his military career and he wouldn't see him again for a long time. This revelation caused him to be cast aside by Musaad and his brothers Fadi and Ghaazi.

CHAPTER 14

WASHINGTON D.C.

As planned, Shadow and Bulldog met in the hotel lobby but not before they had put the "do not disturb" sign on the hotel door and laid a couple of traps to see if someone entered the room while they were out. With the "do not disturb" sign on the door, they knew that a hotel employee wouldn't enter the room.

With the strong feeling that they were being watched, they decided to put those feelings to the test. The best way to do this was take a walk around the streets of D.C. and see who, if anyone, was keeping them under surveillance.

"Are you ready for a walk?" Shadow said to Bulldog, as they walked into the lobby.

"Yeah, let's go," he replied.

The sun was shining outside it was a pleasant sixty degrees.

"I thought that this place was supposed to be cold," said Shadow.

"Nice enough right now,'" replied Bulldog.

The hotel was on a street corner, they stood for a moment to get their bearings.

"Let's go this way," said Shadow, crossing the road.

They both said very little as they enjoyed the local scenery and made observations on things around them as they walked. After several blocks, they heard music coming from a bar.

"Fancy a beer?" asked Bulldog.

"Best thing you've said all day," replied Shadow.

It was a typical bar they could have even been in one of the new trendy places in London it was so generic. There was very little smoke and that appeared to be the only difference to London bars which would also be smokeless before too long. A waitress walked past them.

MICHAEL J BENSON

"Take a seat I'll be right with you," she said with a huge smile.

"Wow, we don't have ladies like that in our pub," said Bulldog.

"Because there are people like you in there," Shadow, quickly replied.

"Ha! Ha! Very funny, sit down." Bulldog pointed to a table in the corner that had a speaker above it. Jazz music was coming out of the speaker that he didn't recognize.

As they sat down, the waitress appeared again.

"Can I get you gentlemen something to drink," she asked.

"I am sorry you must be talking to someone else, as we have never been called gentlemen before," said Bulldog.

"I love your accent where are you from?"

"England," Bulldog replied.

"Can we have two of your finest draught beers please," Shadow jumped in quick to spoil Bulldog's fun.

"Right away, sir," she smiled.

"Bloody hell, Shadow, I was in there," said Bulldog with a wry smile.

"Sure, you were, that young lady would eat you for lunch," he replied.

"Fine by me," he said laughing.

The beers arrived along with a bar menu. The waitress leaned forward deliberately taking her time to allow Bulldog to get an eyeful of her very large breasts.

"Is there anything else I get for you?" she asked.

"No, thanks," replied Shadow.

They both watched as she walked away in her tight-fitting waitress outfit. A good marketing tool to bring the customers into the bar, once inside they would stay a little longer than they expected.

"She knows how to swing those hips," said Bulldog.

"She does and I bet she earns three times more than us in tips alone." Shadow watched her stop to welcome three men that had just entered the bar.

From their position at the table, they could see the whole of the bar and the street outside.

Shadow leaned towards Bulldog. "Don't you think that it was strange that all of the taxi drivers at the airport were Indian or Pakistani when we waited in line and then as we get to the front of the line the next two drivers were white Americans?"

"Yeah and ours was very kind to give us his business card," replied Bulldog.

"I get the feeling we are being monitored wherever we go. I thought that we were supposed to be here under cover."

Shadow was watching the three men who had just walked into the bar. He could see that all three were looking into the giant mirror at the back of the bar. Their heads were all at the same angle, a slight turn to the left, they were watching him and Bulldog.

"What do you think is going on?" Bulldog was also paying attention to the same three men.

"Not sure," replied Shadow.

Shadow had turned his attention to a car that was parked across the street with a female in the driver's seat. Behind her vehicle was another with what looked like an elderly lady in the driver's seat.

Bulldog continued to talk quietly, "Strain won't be very happy if the Yanks are watching our every move. We can't operate here if our cover is already blown."

"Well, we have company across the street," said Shadow, as he watched the two cars.

"Where, in the cars?" asked Bulldog.

"Yeah, I think the young blond is watching the bar, this should be interesting there's a traffic warden working her way along the line of parked cars."

They both watched as the traffic warden walked up to the vehicle with the old lady in it. He tapped on the window to get the driver's attention and bent down. It looked like a conversation was taking place, within seconds the car drove away.

The traffic warden moved on to the car with the blonde inside, he did the same thing and tapped on the window. Another conversation, a little longer this time, but the traffic warden didn't make the driver move, he walked on leaving the car where it was.

"Thought so, who would the traffic warden not be able to move?" Shadow said.

"We know the answer to that one," replied Bulldog.

"Well, let's drink our beer and give them some exercise," said Shadow.

Bulldog gave a huge smile, as he liked to give others the run around.

"I guess we will have those three at the bar following us as well,' said Bulldog.

"The more the merrier." Shadow was going to enjoy this as much as Bulldog.

With a long walk ahead of them, they visited the restroom, paid the waitress and made their way to the door.

The three men who had walked in after them were still sitting at the bar. Shadow noticed that the one closest to them was watching them out of the corner of his eye. He knew something wasn't right. The man stuck his foot out, catching Bulldog's foot as he walked past causing him to trip. As he stumbled forward, he managed to prevent himself from falling by grabbing the back of the stool the second man was sitting on. Shadow watched it happening like it was in slow motion. As Bulldog grabbed the stool for balance, the second man's beer was knocked out of his hand spilling beer over the bar.

Bulldog didn't see the foot stick out and cursed himself as he tripped on it he knew a set up was coming. As he grabbed the back of the stool to steady himself he picked up a small stool that was next to a table. He could see the feet of the third man as he stepped in front of him. Bulldog took a blow to the back of his head as he stood up, it didn't slow him down. He lifted the stool fast, smashing it into the man's head, knocking him unconscious.

Shadow saw that these people meant business and didn't hesitate, he plunged his right fist into the left kidney area of the man that had tripped Bulldog. The pain was evident in the man's face as he grimaced in agony. Shadow wasn't finished he immediately came across with his left hand in a sweeping motion catching him in the stomach. Another fast blow with the right hand to the side of his head and he went down.

Bulldog spun around and saw the second man throwing a punch at his head. He ducked quickly and swung his left arm over the man's outstretched arm and wrapped his arm around his assailants locking it straight against the elbow. With his right hand, he hit him three times to the side of the head with his elbow. He unlocked the arm and the man fell to the floor joining his associates.

They both could hear the commotion from the bar staff around them and didn't wait to answer questions they quickly left. In the street, they walked slowly so as not to bring attention to themselves just in case the police showed up.

"Who do you think they were?" asked Shadow.

"Don't know, don't care, they lost, we won." Bulldog was still furious for falling for one of the oldest tricks in the book.

"Well, our lady in the car has got out and is walking towards the bar," said Shadow.

"Good. I hope one of them is her boyfriend." They both laughed.

For an hour and a half, they, led the surveillance team on a merry chase in and out of stores, museums and finally a coffee shop, where they decided it was time to lose them.

They entered the coffee shop which was very busy. They saw a table in the corner near to a sign indicating the restrooms.

"You get the coffee and I'll sit at the table," said Shadow.

"OK. Black or latte?" replied Bulldog.

"A medium latte," Shadow watched as a man and woman walked in behind them, it was the same team that had been following them.

They sat at the table for twenty minutes, slowly enjoying the coffee and talking about the city and some of the places they had just visited. No particular subject, just general boring tourist stuff for anyone listening.

"Shall we go?" said Shadow.

"Yes, but I need the toilet first. This coffee is going straight through me," Bulldog stood up and walked towards the restrooms.

There was a long dark corridor leading towards the restrooms which couldn't be seen from the coffee shop sitting area. As he went into the restroom, he noticed a fire exit sign above the door at the end of the corridor.

He turned left, pushing open the men's restroom door. Once inside, he quickly checked that there wasn't anyone inside the cubicles, he was alone. Above the urinals on the end wall, were two long windows, too small for him or Shadow to climb through.

He went back into the corridor it was clear so he decided to check out the fire exit door. As he quickly walked towards the door, he couldn't see any signs saying that it was alarmed. To the right of the fire exit door was a small alcove that he'd not seen before. Set back about four feet was another door with a glass panel in the center. He could see a small kitchen through the glass panel and a man he assumed was an employee, dressed in jeans, a black shirt with a white apron wrapped around him was wrapping a sandwich in clear plastic wrap. The man stopped what he was doing and walked towards the door, as he fumbled in his jeans pocket. Bulldog turned and hurried away from the door hoping that the employee didn't see him. Just as he got level with the men's restroom door, the employee came out of the kitchen and turned right, immediately pushing open the fire exit door.

Bulldog watched, the man he didn't even look in his direction he had a cigarette and a packet of matches in his right hand he was obviously heading outside for a quick smoke. As the fire exit door opened, sunlight flooded in from outside, washing the corridor walls with a yellow light. Bulldog shaded his eyes slightly and saw that there was a road outside he also saw a large industrial size trash dumpster. No alarm on the door and a large dumpster so there must be access outside for vehicles and that means other streets for them to make a quick exit, excellent thought Bulldog.

He made his way back into the coffee bar area where Shadow was patiently waiting at the table.

Bulldog turned his chair slightly so that when he sat down his peripheral vision would pick up the corridor leading to the restrooms. He didn't have to wait long until the corridor was again briefly filled with bright daylight, the employee had finished his cigarette. He smiled at Shadow and put the coffee cup up to his mouth as if he was taking a drink and spoke quietly to Shadow, "There's a fire exit door past the restrooms meet you outside in one minute."

Shadow waited a few seconds as if he didn't hear Bulldog, then casually got up from the table and headed towards the restrooms. Ten seconds later he was outside in the alley.

At the end of the room, Bulldog could see that the man and woman had followed them inside. There was a blind spot at the end of the display cabinet by the cash register that Bulldog could use to his advantage. He stood up and took three steps towards the cash register just as a very large man was paying for his order. He stood by the man's side as if waiting to ask the cashier something. Bulldog moved back half a step to let the man and woman watching him see that he was still there. He then stepped forward and made his move he was down the corridor and out into the alley before they even knew he was gone.

Shadow was standing to the side of the dumpster outside keeping out of sight of the road when Bulldog appeared.

"Give me a hand with this," Shadow said as he started to wheel the dumpster towards the coffee bar door. It moved surprisingly easily on the big wheels as they pushed it hard against the door blocking anyone from coming out. Shadow wedged a big wad of folded cardboard under one of the wheels.

"This way," said Shadow as he ran off down a narrow side street.

They easily lost the people following them and eventually ended up back at the hotel.

CHAPTER 15

MICHIGAN

Hamed had worked his way through a huge number of gun shows in the Southern States of the US and Michigan over a two-year period. He had become a familiar face to some of the gun dealers, mostly those dealing in unusual weapons. He collected older firearms and knives so the false friendships he'd built with the dealers helped him quench his thirst for building his private collection. The friendships were false as he only needed to keep in touch with the dealers to find out who dealt in the illegal weapons trade. In the early days of attending the shows, he was often asked where he was from. Hamed had an answer already rehearsed and told the inquisitive that he was from the island of Cyprus. He enforced his story by telling people that he hadn't lived on the island since he was a teenager, as his father was Turkish and his mother Greek. He then went on to explain that his parents' mixed marriage was frowned upon by both the Greeks and Turks and his parents eventually left the island for fear of being killed. Most people accepted the explanation and didn't ask any more questions about his background.

Four of the dealers had trusted him enough over the two years to offer him the odd stolen or illegal weapon which he often bought from them. This brought him further into their trust and made them comfortable with him. He wasn't really interested in the small arms weapons he wanted the large caliber automatics.

On this day, he was in Gaylord, Michigan, at a very large show that he'd attended on three previous occasions. He had selected the dealer that he knew dealt in illegal automatic weapons and decided that it was time to test him out as it was only three weeks before the planned attack.

He paid his entrance fee at the door to the exhibition hall and wandered in with the rest of the crowd. Hamed spent some forty five minutes meandering around the exhibition hall, shaking a few hands and exchanging pleasantries. The hall was buzzing with chatter as people talked about the different kinds of weapons and exchanged war stories. The smell of gun oil and gun metal filled his nostrils as he edged his way towards his intended target. There he was Big Bill, a very round bellied man who had eaten more than his share of meals, some of the food still in his scraggy looking beard. He was wearing a pair of coveralls, a red undershirt and unpolished army boots, he really looked the part of a country boy.

Hamed walked towards him and gave him a big smile, "Big Bill, how are you?"

"Good, how are you today?" he inquired.

"I am in a buying mood, as you can see." He held up a grey canvas bag that obviously had some heavy items in it by the way the handle was straining.

"Yes and what did you buy?" Bill felt like he'd missed the jackpot when he saw the bag.

"Three nice knives and two handguns, you know how I like knives." He practically drooled at the thought of what was in his bag. "I have an excellent collection in my home now and these will just add to the quality."

Bill was even more curious now, "What do you have in your collection?" He asked.

Hamed leaned forward and gave a quick look over each shoulder to make sure that nobody was listening. Bill didn't realize it, but he instinctively leaned forward to listen.

"I have a very private collection in addition to my normal one, large caliber automatic weapons if you know what I mean," he said, as he stood up and winked.

"What are they?" he asked.

"Now you know I can't say what they are." He said in a lowered voice.

Another customer approached the table and Hamed pretended to look interested in a handgun. "How much is this monstrosity," he said pointing to a gun on the table.

Bill was taken back a little by the sudden change in his friend. "That is a nineteen sixty-nine Smith and Wesson in excellent condition." He picked up the gun, checked that it wasn't loaded and handed it to Hamed.

He inspected the gun and passed it back to Bill as the new customer looked on.

"You can take it off my hands for three hundred and eighty." He smiled at both of his customers, showing his yellow teeth through his beard.

"You are joking this isn't worth two hundred, what do you think? He said handing the gun to the new customer.

The new customer ignored Hamed and walked off to another table.

The big man leaned across the table, placing his giant fists in the middle as they took the full weight of his body. "You just scared away a potential customer of mine," he said angrily.

Hamed leaned forward again this time Bill stood his ground with his arms folded across his flabby chest.

"I'll make it up to you if you can get me a TEC-9," he replied.

A TEC-9 is a 9mm semiautomatic pistol which has a magazine capacity of 10-50 rounds, a powerful gun.

"Are you mad? I could lose my license if I even tried to get one of those they are banned."

"That is what makes them so attractive. What about a Colt AR-15?" He smiled as he saw the shocked look on Bill's face.

"I don't believe you even asked me to get such items, an Armalite Rifle? You are mad. Christ, I would go to prison." His face reddened as he became very agitated.

Hamed now knew that Bill did at least have access to these items as he wasn't protesting openly but very discreetly so nobody else would hear. "You are right, my friend. I apologize. I shouldn't have asked for a banned firearm. I'll pay you three hundred for that Smith and Wesson and not a penny more."

"Three fifty," he replied.

"Three twenty-five and that is my final offer. You are a thief but I was wrong to scare your customer away." He knew Bill would take his last offer.

"OK. But I get the feeling that you have done your own fair share of stealing in your time or do you call that business?" He showed off his yellow tombstone teeth again as he smiled. "I'll find a box for it."

"Everything is business these days. Bill. You know that." He watched as the big man placed the gun into a box.

"Here," Bill pushed the box across the table and saw that his client was counting out the cash from a large role of new one hundred dollar bills. "I should have charged you more," he said as he saw the new notes.

Hamed handed the money over and placed his new purchase into his cloth bag. He left Bill counting the money and moved to the next row of tables. He looked at his watch, only thirty minutes to the end of the show. He would spend the rest of the time browsing around the remainder of the gun tables. The announcement came over the loud speaker system that the show was closing and he joined a group of people as they walked out into the parking lot.

Outside, waiting in a car were Tony and Rudy Hoffman, two brothers that Hamed had used on several occasions as bodyguards. They were both very good at martial arts but were just a couple of bullies with little or no brains. Hamed liked this about them as they were easily controlled by him and his money.

He'd first met the Hoffman bothers outside Detroit Metro airport in Michigan. He'd been waiting at the car rental pickup point when his briefcase was picked up off the floor by an opportunist thief. Hamed was caught off guard by the man as he ran off with his property. He gave chase all the time shouting, "stop him, stop him." Hamed had no chance of catching him as the man reached the sliding glass doors leading into the airport. The Hoffman brothers were coming out of the doors as the thief tried to go in he ran straight into Rudy Hoffman. He fell backwards onto the floor, immediately jumped to his feet and attempted to push Rudy out of his way.

Rudy watched the man get to his feet quickly after he'd run into him and didn't like him trying to push him out of the way. "Don't push me, you little fuck," he said and pushed the man down again.

The thief was quickly up on his feet again and pulled out a knife from inside his jacket pocket and threatened Rudy with it.

Rudy and Tony couldn't believe what they were seeing. "Put that away or I'll shove it up your ass," said Rudy.

Fear and adrenaline pushed the thief into making a grave mistake by lunging at Rudy with the knife.

Tony stepped back as the blade came towards his stomach and blocked the man's arm out of the way. At the same time, he kicked the man's hand with his left foot and the knife flew harmlessly through the air, landing on the sidewalk.

This was when Hamed became very impressed at the speed of the two men as they rained down kicks and punches on the thief's head and body. The thief collapsed to the floor unconscious and Rudy spat on him.

Hamed stepped forward to pick up his brief case off the floor. The two brothers saw him in their peripheral vision and turned towards him in a defensive stance. Hamed put his hands up in a gesture of surrender. "I do not want trouble I am just picking up my briefcase he stole it," he said pointing to the unconscious body on the floor. He watched as they lowered their hands and relaxed a little.

"Yeah! Well he won't be stealing anything for a while," said Tony.

"My name is Hamed. I can't thank you enough for saving my briefcase." He pushed his hand forward for them to shake it.

Tony stepped forward and shook his hand saying, "I am Tony and this is my brother Rudy."

"Thank you again, scum like this shouldn't be on the street they should be in prison," replied Hamed.

"He made a mistake by running into us," Rudy smiled.

"Yes, he did." Hamed reached into his jacket pocket and took out a small pile of business cards and handed one to each brother. "This is my business card. If you would be interested in doing some bodyguard work, please call me. There are times when I need the services of gentlemen with your obvious talents."

Tony looked at the card all it had on it was the name Hamed and a telephone number. "When would you need our assistance?" he asked.

"Why don't you call me in a couple of days and we can work something out. The telephone number on the card is my cell phone." He picked up his briefcase and walked back to the car rental pickup point.

The brothers watched the man walk away and didn't know what to make of him. They would end up working for him for the next two years.

Today was just another job to them and they watched Hamed as he left the gun show and walked towards their car.

Hamed opened the car door and got into the back seat.

"What's happening?" asked Tony.

"I'll point a man out to you when he leaves the hall. I want you to follow him and find out where he unloads the contents of his trailer."

"What has this guy done?" asked Rudy.

"All you need to know is he has property of mine that I have paid for and now he is holding it until I pay him more money." He lied.

"We can persuade him to give you the property," said Rudy.

"Don't worry your work is just starting. Under no circumstance are you to approach him until I say so, understood?" Hamed knew exactly how to assert his authority on them they were like puppets dancing to the sound of his voice and the money in his hand.

"Yes, boss, we understand," said Tony.

"Drive over there to the far end of the rear parking lot by the trees, we will be able to see him leave the building from there." Hamed pointed in the direction that he wanted them to go.

Tony did as he was told he started the engine and drove to the spot indicated by Hamed.

There were several cars parked under the spruce trees so they didn't look out of place. Thirty-five minutes had passed when Hamed sat forward in the rear seat, "That's him, the big man with the long hair and beard."

"He is a walking mountain," said Rudy.

They all watched as the man was closely followed by a very overweight security guard.

"If you do not think that you can handle him tell me now and I'll find someone who can," Hamed replied.

"OK, don't get all twisted up about it, I only made a comment." Rudy was furious at the way in which Hamed treated them.

They sat watching as the big man pushed a wheeled dolly across the loading dock, it was laden with large wooden boxes and green military metal boxes.

"Call me when you find out where his storage place is and don't let him see you."

"We have two cars he won't even suspect anything," said Rudy.

"I'll be waiting at my hotel." Hamed got out of the car knowing that he'd upset the pair but he didn't care. He would take a casual drive to the town of Lewiston in North Michigan where he was staying at the luxury Garland Resort. This was his favorite hotel, built by a German family out of many hundreds of logs and surrounded by golf courses. He never told the Hoffman brothers where he stayed.

The brothers stayed quiet for a couple of minutes before Rudy broke the silence, "I hate that fucker at times."

"Yeah, so do I, but he pays us more money than anyone else. I am going to tell him that we want a raise if we are to strong arm this guy. That will shake him up a little," Tony replied.

"Yeah, we deserve more."

"Let's see what this guy has in his storage place when we find it and maybe we will have something more to negotiate with."

"OK," he replied.

Tony was getting a feeling that this was no ordinary job. "I'll drop you off at your car and you can park on the driveway of that motel across the street. When he leaves, you take the lead and I'll follow."

Tony dropped his brother off at his car. "Don't forget, you take the lead and I'll follow about thirty seconds behind you."

"OK, see you soon," he replied.

It only took Big Bill ten minutes to load the trailer attached to his truck and he was on his way home. He'd had a long day and was looking forward to relaxing with a drink. He was still agitated by Hamed's request for banned weapons and he didn't like the thought that Hamed knew he had them. When he drove out of the driveway from the convention hall onto the main road, he didn't see the car pull out of the motel parking lot.

Rudy saw the white trailer approaching the main road and turn right, he waited for it to disappear around the bend before he followed. It wasn't hard to keep the trailer in view, as the roads were mostly quiet two lane country highways with little or no traffic. This also made it difficult for him to remain discreet. Fortune was on Rudy's side when two cars turned onto the main road behind Bill's trailer, giving him some cover. Forty minutes had passed when, in the distance, he saw the red brake lights of the trailer come on, shortly followed by the right turn signal. The cars ahead of Rudy slowed down as he did and allowed the trailer to take up the center of the road as it negotiated the entrance to a dirt road in between some pine trees. At first, Rudy didn't like this and thought that he may have been seen by Bill, but then he saw how narrow the entrance was to the dirt road.

The trailer slowly disappeared from view and the cars ahead of him moved forward, he slowly followed. As he drove past the entrance to the dirt road, he could see signs on the trees saying private road and no trespassing. A short way down the road, the headlights of the truck were lighting up the trees on either side, making it look like a scene from a Hollywood horror movie.

As he picked up speed, he saw that Tony had caught up with him and was now following closely behind. He followed the road for a couple of miles looking for a place to pull in when he came to a cross road down the road a few hundred yards he saw a restaurant and drove to it.

Rudy saw the sign as he drove onto the parking lot advertising "Fish Fry Night." He did enjoy good food and he was very hungry.

Tony joined him as he got out of the car.

"It looked like he might live down that road. I don't think that it would be somewhere just for storage, too remote," said Tony.

"I agree. Let's give him some time to go to sleep and we can go back and see if he has some sort of storage building. We should give it a couple of hours." Rudy was thinking about the fish fry as the smell of cooking drifted past them from the kitchen.

"Good idea, do you want something to eat?" The smell was also getting to Tony.

"Yeah, I am starving and thirsty what about you?"

"I could eat something and it's your turn to pay," he replied.

"I always pay." He threw a couple of open handed chops to his brother's head, which were blocked the play fighting continued to the restaurant door.

Rudy opened the door for his brother and invited him in first, saying, "Watch your ass doesn't squeak as you walk in." He was making a reference to his brother being tight with his money.

Tony just smiled as he stopped to let two elderly ladies walk out. They had heard what Rudy said and walked off with their noses in the air in disapproval.

Rudy looked at his brother and said, "Oops."

They both entered the restaurant with huge smiles on their faces for the moment Tony had forgotten about his concerns over the job they were on.

The waitress was very slow serving them in the restaurant but it suited them as they were in no hurry. The fish fry was reasonable and it satisfied their hunger, they paid the bill and left.

"What do you want to do?" asked Rudy.

"Why don't you park your car across the street at that motel? We can go to where we saw the trailer turn off and snoop around you never know what we might find."

They didn't say much to each other on the drive back and it wasn't long before they found the entrance to the dirt road. Tony turned off the lights on the car and coasted into the entrance of the road, the sound of loose gravel and rock being crushed under the tires rose through the car. There was a small clearing in the trees about twenty yards inside the entrance where Tony parked the car.

"This is a good enough place to park we can follow the driveway and see where it leads us. Let's go," said Tony.

"OK, but make it quick, it's freezing." Rudy didn't like the cold weather, especially when he had to walk.

They put heavy coats on that they had on the rear seat of the car and gloves. The gravel was making a lot of noise under foot so they moved to the side of the road. That was worse as fallen tree branches snapped loudly underfoot, they moved back to the road. The going was slow as they tried not to make a noise. The fact that the trees didn't allow any moonlight to filter through to the road made it darker. After a quarter of a mile the trees were thinning out allowing the moonlight to light the path a little, they could now see twenty to thirty yards in front of themselves. Through the trees, they saw a faint light but couldn't make out where it was coming from, they pressed on until they made out the shape of a house.

"This must be his place," whispered Rudy.

Tony didn't say anything but waved his hand for his brother to follow him. A hundred yards later they could see a log cabin in a clearing in the trees, a light was on inside. They both crouched down behind a tree and made mental notes of what they were looking at. Either side of the porch at the front of the house was a kennel but no signs of any dogs. Next to the house was a huge barn, the roof and wall were made of steel siding. At the front of the barn were two doors ten feet tall and on the side, was a window.

Next to the barn was an old rusting pickup with flat tires parked next to it was the truck that had towed the trailer earlier.

Tony tapped Rudy on the arm and whispered, "The trailer must be in the barn, let's take a look."

They stepped out from behind the tree and headed towards the barn, keeping as low as possible in an attempt not to be seen. They stopped every few paces, checking the ground in front of them making sure that there wasn't anything in their way that they might stumble on. What they didn't know is that they were being watched closely.

They made straight for the window on the side of the barn, the watching eyes following them. The window was just low enough for them to see inside the barn. It was pitch dark inside the barn, but right next to the window they could see the shape of the trailer. Tony waved at his brother indicating that they leave. Rudy turned and tripped on a small stack of fire logs, knocking some of them over they both froze, waiting to see if anyone responded to the noise. They could feel their hearts pounding as their pulses picked up. There was silence they hadn't been heard. They made their way back across the driveway towards the trees. They were in the middle of the drive-in front of the house when the silence was broken by the sound of two dogs as they surged out of the kennels, barking and snarling.

Tony and Rudy were taken by total surprise by the dogs and instinctively ran for the trees. Bill had trained his Dobermans to stay quiet and still if anyone approached the house but, if they tried to leave without him standing there, they would attack and savage the individual.

The dogs were dragging chains behind them as they bolted after the two men, the chains rattling on the ground. The dogs ran out of chain and were stopped with a loud thud as they continued to bark and snarl frothing at the mouth.

Both men darted behind a tree to conceal themselves thinking that somebody would have heard the dogs and no doubt come out of the house.

A porch light came on. They watched as the front door to the cabin opened, it was Bill and he was carrying a pump action shotgun.

"Who's there?" he bellowed.

The dogs continued barking and snarling as Bill stepped off the porch and walked between the two chains. He stopped ten feet from the house.

"Who's there?" Bill repeated.

He pumped the shotgun, putting a shell in the chamber. He fired into the trees twice in rapid succession. Bark and branches rained down on the two brothers as they pressed themselves harder into the tree for protection.

He pumped the shotgun once more when a deer bolted out of the trees from behind Tony and Rudy. The deer ran across the drive and into the thick brush on the opposite side, closely followed by two more.

Bill cursed out loud at the dogs, "Damn you hounds, it's just a deer."

They ignored him and continued to bark at the trees. "Shut up" he yelled as he yanked at one of their chains. This worked they scurried back into the kennels still growling watching the trees.

Bill returned to the warmth of the log cabin and turned the porch light off.

Tony and Rudy waited several minutes in the dark before they ventured back down the dirt road to their car.

They got to the car safely. Tony opened the driver's door while Rudy got into the back.

"What are you doing back there?" Tony asked.

"I am going to lie down on the seat and raise my arm, that bastard got me in the shoulder and arm with his shotgun." The pain was increasing and he knew that he had to elevate the arm to help stop the bleeding.

"Christ, we need to get you to a doctor. I can see the blood coming through your coat sleeve."

"No, not a doctor he will report it to the police. Let's go back to that motel where we left the car and check the wounds, they may not be that bad." Rudy was starting to feel a little faint as he lay down, but he wasn't going to pass out in front of his brother. He hadn't been shot before and couldn't believe how much it hurt.

Tony didn't argue he knew his brother was right. He drove cautiously back to the motel as he didn't want to get stopped by the police with his brother lying on the back seat.

The man behind the reception desk was all business, he had no time for the niceties of saying hello or asking how somebody was enjoying their day. Tony watched him as he slowly swiped his credit card through the reader. He was more interested in watching the racing on the television, the volume was much too loud it made the cars sound like they were in the room with them. The man picked up his can of beer, guzzling down a large mouthful, dripping some of the beer down the front of his already stained white undershirt. The credit card machine started to make a noise and churned out a piece of paper the overweight scruffy fat man ignored it. Instead, he gave out a loud belch and wiped his mouth with his hairy forearm.

Tony had seen enough and leaned over the desk, ripping the paper out of the machine. He signed it and slammed it down on the desk, "Give me a room key," he said angrily.

The man leaned backwards in the chair and without taking his eyes off the television screen he took a key off a board next to him.

"Number seven," he muttered as he dropped the key on the desk.

Tony was trying to stay calm. "Is there a pharmacy open this late around here?"

"No, but you might get some headache tablets at the garage store down the street." Again, he didn't take his eyes off the screen.

Tony picked up the key to the room and returned to the car where his brother was waiting.

"Come on, let's get you sorted out," he said as he opened the door to the car.

"I didn't think we'd be doing this tonight," he replied.

"No, but we will have you fixed up in no time."

He left his brother lying on the bed in the hotel room with his arm elevated.

"I'll be back in a few minutes the local garage has a store, maybe they will have some bourbon."

"Bring a bottle back for you as well," Rudy replied.

Tony left the room without comment, eager to get the first aid supplies his brother needed.

When he returned to the hotel room, Rudy was fast asleep flat on his back snoring hard.

He gently woke him, as he didn't want him jumping suddenly, opening the wounds.

"You got back quick," he said sleepily.

"Yeah! I got lots of bandages and some stuff to clean the wounds. We should try to keep the wounds clean until we get back home and have a doctor remove the pellets."

"I had a good look at the wounds and the pellets are only just under the skin, at least most of them are. You need to dig them out, I do not want to chance one of them becoming infected."

"I don't want to do that Rudy, I don't have the right kind of knife or skill to do it." He didn't like the idea of digging into his brother's flesh.

"Look, it can't hurt any more than it does right now. Let me have a few shots of the bourbon, you did get some I hope?"

"Yes," Tony replied.

"Good you can get those pellets out easily and any you can't then we will get a doctor to remove them when we get home, OK?"

Tony still wasn't happy but agreed to do it. "OK let's get this over with."

He took the bottle of bourbon he'd bought at the store out of the bag and poured two very large measures, which they both drank. Rudy would have another three before his brother started to dig away at the wounds.

It took Tony twenty five minutes to get the pellets out of his brother, leaving only two that he could feel but not see under the skin. He cleaned the wounds with alcohol and dressed them.

"There, all done." Tony smiled at his brother.

"We need to tell the boss what has happened." Rudy was starting to feel the bourbon taking effect.

"I'll call him in the morning until then he can sweat it out."

The next morning Tony called Hamed from a pay phone at the gas station that he'd visited the previous evening and told him what had transpired. Tony was very surprised at his response, he sounded genuinely concerned and wanted to make sure that Rudy was taken care of by a doctor.

Tony returned to the hotel. "Well, you will never guess what he said to me when I told him that you had been shot."

"What, he said I was a stupid bastard?"

"No, he was really concerned and wanted you to be taken care of by a doctor. He even offered to pay the bill."

"So, he fucking should I got shot for him."

"He surprised me, Rudy. There is a lot more to this job than he is making out and I now think that we can demand a nice big bonus when this is finished." Tony knew that Hamed wouldn't like being asked for more money, but he owed them now.

CHAPTER 16

CALIFORNIA

Several days after he told Musaad about his military career, Matthews was at a local book store that specialized in religious books. He was thumbing through an old version of the Koran when Musaad walked into the store. When Musaad saw Matthews, he quickly turned around and left the store, closely followed by Matthews.

He called after him in the street, "Musaad, Musaad." He was ignoring him. He ran after him and grabbed him by the arm and turned him around to face him.

Musaad pulled his arm free and said, "Get off me." He had rage in his eyes.

"What have I done to you?" Matthews asked.

"You don't know what you have done. You must be as stupid as the rest of the military robots employed to kill innocent Muslims."

Matthews could see the hatred in his face, "I knew that I shouldn't have told you, but I felt that it was important."

"Important to whom your military intelligence?" Musaad was getting angrier.

"No, no for our friendship. You of all people must know that I mean nobody any harm. You have taught me more about Islam and its beliefs than anyone I know. I am not a mindless murderer. I helped a lot of Muslim families in Kuwait and some Iraqi exiles." He hoped that Musaad would listen.

"Next you will tell me that you are married to a Muslim." Musaad gave a sarcastic laugh and turned to walk away.

"No, but I would have been married by now to a beautiful Iraqi woman if she had not been murdered." He watched as Musaad stopped in his tracks.

He turned and glared at Matthews, about to tear into him when he saw genuine pain in his face. "You were going to marry an Iraqi woman?" He questioned what he'd heard.

MICHAEL J BENSON

"Yes, but I didn't have the chance or honor to marry her. She was so beautiful she didn't deserve to die that way." He found it very difficult to talk about her and his emotions started to take over as tears rolled down his face.

"I didn't know," replied Musaad.

"We kept our love a secret, we didn't tell anyone."

"Didn't her family know?"

"No, she knew that they would disapprove she wanted to choose the right moment to tell them." He remembered the exact conversation they had together, it seemed so recent."

"Who killed her?"

"They never found out, but if I ever do, I'll take my revenge on whoever it was. I'll torture them and make them suffer as she did, it will be a long and painful death." He meant every word.

"There must be some clue as to who did it?" Musaad pressed him for more information.

"There were rumors that it was American soldiers, but nobody was ever caught. I was shipped back to the US very quickly after her death so I didn't get the chance to find out if the rumors were true."

"I am sorry for your loss, but once again American soldiers' rape and abuse an Islamic woman and they get away with it. You wonder why I didn't want to talk to you after you told me you were a soldier, I spit on American soldiers." He followed his comment by spitting on the sidewalk.

"They were only rumors and not all soldiers are like this. We had a few that shamed the whole army because of their actions. But I have also grown to hate my own government and military." He knew that this was a terrible statement to make, but he now realized that he really did hate them both.

Musaad turned his back on him and started to walk away. Matthews grabbed his arm once again.

"I am sorry for what some soldiers have done in the war, but I am not a murderer or a rapist. You have to understand that if I had found Islam before I joined the military I wouldn't have become a soldier."

"I thought that once a US soldier always a US soldier?"

Matthews knew that he was referring to the Marines slogan but that didn't matter.

"Look. I leave the military in a few months. I would like us to become friends again, maybe we can do this when I leave?" He watched Musaad as he stared at the sidewalk he could tell that he was thinking of a response.

"I am troubled by you being a soldier and by the fact that you know in your heart that someone in the military killed your future wife and you have not done anything about it. This is not the way of the Islamic people we would avenge her death and regain her honor in doing so." He could see that his words hurt his old friend, but he didn't care.

Matthews felt every word dig deep into his heart. He knew that Musaad was right this time he was the one that turned and walked away.

He'd walked about three blocks, shedding tears and wiping them away as he remembered Numa. He was also thinking about what Musaad had said and hated himself for not investigating her murder properly, but he knew that the military would close ranks and he would never find out what really happened. He stopped at the curb, waiting for a gap in the traffic, so that he could cross the road. A car stopped directly in front of him blocking his path, the window on the front passenger door rolled down. He looked in at the driver, it was Musaad.

"Would you like a coffee?" Musaad asked.

"Yes," he replied and he got into the car.

Over coffee, Matthews told his old friend everything about his relationship with Numa and everything that he knew about her. He was relieved to be able to finally talk to someone about her, it felt like a weight had been lifted off his shoulders.

Musaad could see that Matthews had a strong genuine love for this woman and a huge hole had appeared in his friend's life. What he found more interesting was that he could see that the man really did want to get revenge for the rape and death of his beloved Numa. After two hours of a mostly one way conversation, they left the café and went to the mosque and prayed together. Musaad made a promise to his friend that he would try to find out through his contacts what really happened to Numa.

Several days had passed since their friendship had been renewed over coffee when Musaad called Matthews at his apartment.

"Are you going to prayer at the mosque on Friday?"

"Yes, I am, why do you ask?" He attended prayer most Fridays at the mosque, it just depended on what time he got away from the barracks.

"What time will you go? I need to talk to you."

"I'll be there for evening prayer, what is wrong?" He was curious as Musaad very rarely called him at home.

"Nothing, but I have some news from overseas." He knew that this would get his interest.

"What news?" asked Matthews.

"We can talk about it on Friday after prayer. I don't want to talk on the telephone."

"OK, I'll see you Friday." He couldn't help but think that Musaad had information on Numa's death or maybe he'd located her family. He only had two days to wait to find out.

When Friday came, Matthews looked all over the mosque but he couldn't find Musaad. He went through prayer and slowly made his way out with everybody else. He stopped outside and waited five minutes, but he still couldn't see his friend. He was about to give up when he heard a car horn sound in the road behind him. He ignored the horn at first, but when it sounded again he turned and there was Musaad sitting in his car.

As he walked towards the car, Musaad shouted. "Get in the car,"

Matthews quickly walked around the front of the car and got in the passenger side. "What have you got to tell me?" he asked as he got into the front of the car.

"In a minute," Musaad put the car into drive and drove off without saying anymore.

"What is it?" asked Matthews.

"Soon," he said.

They had traveled about a mile when Musaad turned the car into a side street and stopped next to a delicatessen store.

"OK, let me tell you what I have found out before we go inside for coffee." He turned slightly in the driver's seat to face his friend.

"Is it to do with Numa?" he asked.

"Yes, it is. When you told me about your love for her and hers for you, I couldn't believe it at first, but the more you talked the more I saw that you had a great deal of love for her. Then you told me how she had died, I wanted to help." He was interrupted by Matthews.

"How could you help she is already dead?" he replied.

"I know. I meant I wanted to help find out who had killed her."

"And did you?" asked Matthews.

"Well not exactly, not by name anyway. I have friends in Kuwait and they have a very good relationship with the Kuwaiti police. I told them the story of how Numa had died and asked them to try and find out what really happened. I didn't tell them about you and her, as that may have stopped them doing anything to help."

"Yes, you're right it would make things more difficult."

"Anyway, one of my contacts has a brother who is the head of criminal investigations in the area where Numa lived. It turns out that he'd investigated her death and he had evidence to show that it was indeed US soldiers that raped and killed her," said Musaad.

"Wait a minute, you said soldiers. You mean that there was more than one?" Matthews could feel his anger building again the thought of her being raped was bad enough, but by more than one person, this was too much.

"Yes, there was more than one." He paused as he watched Matthews face.

"Tell me their names," Matthews shouted as he punched the dashboard of the car.

"Wait, I told you that I didn't have any names," replied Musaad.

Matthews grabbed him by the shirt and pulled him towards him. "I want their names who are they?"

Musaad peeled his friend's fingers off his shirt. "I am not your enemy so do not handle me like one. I told you that I found out what happened to her not exactly who had raped and killed her." He straightened out the wrinkled shirt.

"Tell me what happened." Matthews had to know.

"It's too horrible. I don't think you should know what they did to her." He knew that Matthews would now want to hear how she died even more.

"I have to know what they did to her. How did she die? You have to tell me." He couldn't control his anger or the hatred building up inside for the people who had killed his beloved Numa.

"Are you sure? Because it's a terrible thing what happened to Numa," Musaad knew that he had Matthews hooked and he would be his to control from this point onward.

"Yes, I want to know. Leave nothing out," replied Matthews.

"I will, but you must remain calm. We can't bring attention to ourselves by you beating the car or grabbing me."

"Yes, just tell me." He was becoming frustrated and the need to know what happened was growing.

"OK, as I told you there was an investigation by the police after her body was found. During the investigation, a young boy admitted that he'd seen everything that had gone on. Apparently, he was in an abandoned house sleeping in a corner of the back room under some wood that he used as a hiding place. There was a wooden door on the house but no windows. He woke up to the sound of American voices by the door of the house. He could see the doorway and part of the front room through his wooden hideout. The soldiers scared him so he kept quiet and didn't move. The soldiers were talking to a woman, one of them was trying to talk Arabic but it was very bad. The soldier talking bad Arabic grabbed the woman by the arm and she screamed. Another soldier put his hand over her mouth and they dragged her into the house. A third soldier followed them inside and he closed the wooden door, that's when it happened." He stopped talking.

"When they raped her, you mean, those bastards." He was finding it difficult to control his temper. "How did they kill her?"

"I do not like telling all of this," said Musaad.

"I need to know." He had to get some sort of closure on her death.

"They made her perform oral sex with them and then took turns to rape and sodomize her. When they had finished, she crawled into a corner and curled up like a terrified animal. The boy said that she was trying to cover herself with what was left of her torn clothes, I guess she was trying to save what little dignity she had left. They were laughing when one of the soldiers went over to her and urinated on her. He was saying things in English that the boy didn't understand."

"God, no, Numa," he cried out her name.

Musaad put his hand onto his friend's shoulder to console him. "You have to know that she was very brave, she didn't take this final insult."

"What did she do?" asked Matthews.

"She jumped up at the soldier and attacked him but she was no match for the strong man. She fought hard and bit him on the hand. The soldier knocked her down and hit her with the butt of his gun. The others joined in, kicking and hitting her with their guns. They left her to die, lying in his urine and her blood. I am sorry, but you said that you wanted to know."

Matthews wept quietly for almost five minutes, eventually regaining some of his composure. He wiped the tears off his face with his shirt sleeve.

"Did the police go to the military with this information?"

"Yes, they did and they said that they would perform their own investigation," replied Musaad.

"What did they find out?"

"Nothing, they said that they didn't believe that a US soldier was involved. My contact said that the US military covered it up."

"In other words, they closed ranks to protect their own, those bastards. All they care about is protecting themselves and their dirty little secrets." Matthews wanted revenge, but he knew that he would never find who did it.

"They must be punished, you will find out who did this to her." Musaad also knew that he wouldn't find out, but he said this for effect.

"You don't understand, when the army want something kept a secret or covered up they will use all of their power to do so."

"Then you must get back at the army for they are just as guilty as the soldiers that raped and murdered her. I'll help you," replied Musaad.

Matthews smiled at the loyalty of his friend, "Thank you, but you can't take on the might of the US Army."

"I do not mean the whole army, just a part of it. Do something to embarrass them, use one of their secrets to get back at them." He could see that Matthews was thinking about what he'd just said.

"I could. I am transporting something on a regular basis that would really piss them off if I dropped it off a cliff or something. You can't attack an army convoy they would shoot anyone that tried to steal the weapon." Matthews realized that he just divulged that the secret was a type of weapon, he didn't care.

"Can I ask what it is?" Musaad replied.

"It's a military secret." Matthews wanted to tell Musaad, just to show him that he trusted him.

"I understand, I am just curious as anyone would be, I am sorry if I offended you."

"You didn't offend me I trust you, you know that." He started to feel guilty after what Musaad had said. "Look, it's a kind of weapons system that allows you to use any kind of high powered rifle or large caliber weapon. You sit the weapon on a specially designed base that is connected to a computer. The key is that the weapon and base can be controlled from any location in the world through a computer. It operates just like a kid's computer game. You use a joy stick to move the weapon up, down or side to side and press the button to fire it. There is a camera on the front of the weapon which acts the same as a telescope on a sniper rifle. You can zoom in or out on the target and fire whenever you are ready, from the safety of the computer."

He realized that he'd already said too much and he didn't know why he was blurting this information out. He wasn't thinking straight.

Musaad got incredibly excited at what he'd just been told, but played it cool and claimed ignorance of weapons and the military.

"It all sounds very boring and technical, I'm sure that it's really exciting to those that understand that sort of thing. I have never had an interest in guns or the military, no offence to you," said Musaad.

"Oh! No offence taken."

"Maybe you should steal it and hide it from them for a few weeks. You could get some media attention and bring the murder into the public eye, which would force them to investigate her death properly. My two brothers know about the murder and we will help you avenge her death and bring those responsible to justice. You are a soldier you will think of a way for Numa's sake." He knew that this would stick in Matthews' memory.

Matthews liked the idea of getting the press involved and thought that it might be a way of forcing the army into holding a full investigation into Numa's death.

"I don't feel like a soldier." But he was starting to feel sorry for himself.

"Let's go inside and have a coffee." Musaad deliberately changed the subject.

"If you don't mind I'm just going to walk home, walking helps me think. We will have a coffee together soon."

"OK," Musaad replied and watched his friend get out of the car.

Musaad couldn't believe his luck, a weapons system that could be operated from anywhere in the world, he had to tell Mohammed.

CHAPTER 17

NEW YORK CITY

Strain took the Gulfstream to Newark airport in New York for his meeting with Don Caputo. As planned, when he came out of the security area, there was a very large man dressed in a long black coat holding the sign, "Mr. Malt."

Strain nodded to the man, acknowledging he was who the man was meeting. The man turned and walked away, followed by Strain. Neither man spoke until they were inside the car.

"Welcome to New York" he said in a very strong accent that Strain had only heard in the movies.

"Thanks."

"Sit back, it will take us some time to get there. There is a newspaper on the back seat, you should read it," he said as more of an order than a suggestion.

Strain picked up the newspaper that was folded in half. As he opened it he saw a post it note stuck to the front page written on it were the words, 'Being watched we'll change vehicles soon.'

Strain looked at the driver. "Interesting front page story," he said, acknowledging the note.

Thirty minutes had passed when they entered an industrial area with old looking warehouses lining the streets.

As the car approached one of the warehouses, its steel roller doors started to rise. The driver had obviously done this before and timed it perfectly, driving under the rising door into the warehouse. The door immediately closed behind them.

"Follow me," he said to Strain as he got out of the vehicle.

The driver opened the trunk with the key remote and Strain's suitcase was taken out by one of the men waiting for them.

Two men got into the car Strain had just left and drove out of the warehouse into the road on the opposite side of the warehouse from which they had entered.

The big man moved quickly through the warehouse into an adjacent building and up some stairs.

"The Feds will cover that street and feel very smug that they have seen us drive out of the warehouse. They will get a surprise in about thirty minutes when they realize they aren't the same two men." The big man chuckled as he picked up the pace.

Strain's eyes took everything in as he walked, wooden crates of all shapes and sizes lined the floor and walls of the warehouse. Upstairs, they walked along a steel walkway that seemed like it was a bridge or an adjoining conduit to another building. He was right. They had walked about fifty yards when they reached another warehouse. They went down more stairs to the warehouse floor where there was an eighteen-wheeler furniture mover's truck. The big man waved his hand at Strain as if to say keep up.

The rear doors of the truck were open and a steel ramp was leading into the rear of the truck from the floor. On the opposite side of the truck was a grey four door Lexus. The engine was running and there was someone in the driver's seat, the trunk was open.

The big man opened the front passenger door and indicated for Strain to get in. As he did, he saw his case going into the trunk which the big man closed.

Strain looked at the driver and found to his surprise a very attractive woman in her late twenties with long dark hair. She had very tight fitting top and tight pants that showed off her excellent physique.

"Put your seat belt on, you might need it," she smiled, exposing ultra-white teeth.

Strain did as he was told as the engine started.

The driver expertly drove the car up the steel ramp into the back of the furniture truck. The doors closed behind them, throwing them into complete darkness.

Strain sensed the truck start to move as the interior lights came on in the car. The driver turned on the radio and leaned towards Strain and smiled.

"Relax we'll be in here for a little while." She knew what she was doing, using her sex appeal to her advantage.

Strain thought she was going to kiss him at first and quickly realized what she was up to.

"O.K. to speak" he said.

"Sure, my name is Roxy," she lied.

"Well, I am sure you already know my name?" he replied.

"No, don't need to," she said confidently.

"What happens next?"

"You will soon see," she replied.

Another twenty minutes passed and Strain felt the eighteen-wheeler lurch to a stop. Almost immediately, the rear doors opened and Roxy started the car's engine. Five seconds later, they were going backwards down the steel ramps.

Strain could see another furniture truck behind them that looked the same as the one they had just driven out of. The two men from the warehouse very quickly pushed the steel ramps inside the rear of the truck where their car had just been and closed the doors. The furniture truck moved forward closely, followed by Roxy. She made a sudden left turn into a long narrow road, accelerating quickly to sixty miles an hour and equally quickly slowed down to enter another narrow road.

Strain looked back from where they had come and saw a box van had pulled across the road blocking it. These people are bloody good, thought Strain.

Within fifteen minutes, Strain was getting out of the car at Roxy's instruction and taking his case out of the trunk. The garage they had pulled into was very cold and damp. As Strain closed the trunk, Roxy drove out, leaving him standing there.

The garage door was obviously operated remotely as it closed as the car left. Again, Strain was in darkness for a few seconds when a faint light appeared in the corner by a door.

"This way," someone said.

Strain followed the figure through the door into a small storage room, where the light was coming from.

A short stocky man stood by a pile of wooden boxes.

"Close the door," he said.

Strain did as he was told. The man pulled one of the boxes away from the wall and lifted it so he didn't mark the wooden floor boards. On the wall was a metal ring. The man turned the metal ring and Strain heard something metallic move in the floor.

The man reached into a crack in the wall with his finger and pulled out a long metal pin. He inserted it into a hole in the floorboard by the corner of the wall and lifted the board, it was a trapdoor.

"Come on," he said, as he went down some stairs.

At the bottom of the stairs were a series of large open rooms with brick columns dividing them. The only light came from a flashlight that the big man held.

Strain knew they were in the foundation area of the buildings above. He recognized the damp smell and layout, it was the same as some of the old warehouse buildings back in Liverpool where he was born. They walked for at least a block and eventually came to another staircase.

Strain continued to follow as the man went up a flight of stairs and unbolted the door at the top. As he swung the door open, Strain could see the front of the door was loaded with cans of tomatoes on shelves.

"Inside," said the man, ushering Strain ahead of him.

Strain did as directed and found himself inside a pantry. The door slammed shut behind him. Strain turned, surprised, as he hadn't expected it. He was in a giant pantry full of cans of food, herbs, cured meats hanging on hooks and a variety of cooking implements. Straight in front of him was another door he opened it and found himself in a kitchen. The smell of tomato sauce cooking filled his nostrils and a hint of fresh brewed coffee.

Standing in the corner by an oven with his back to him was Don Caputo.

"Welcome Mr. Strain, coffee?" he turned with a coffee pot in his hand. Strain smiled, the man looked like something straight from a mafia movie. A large tomato-spattered apron hung around his sizeable waist, but his shirt was perfectly crisp and white.

'Yes, please," he replied.

The Don poured some coffee into a mug on a long wooden table in the middle of the room.

Strain realized there was opera playing in the next room, it was Puccini's Tosca.

"Ah! You have heard this opera before?" The Don could see Strain was listening. "Puccini is a particular favorite of mine, I understand you like opera."

"Yes, I do. I don't understand most of it but I enjoy it all the same." The old man had done his homework.

"If you take your bag up the stairs in the hallway, you are in the first room on the left. By the time you come down, I'll have spaghetti and meatballs ready."

Strain said nothing and once again did as he was directed but he didn't have time to stay overnight, that news he had yet to break. The apartment was narrow. There were two rooms to the right both looked like lounges with TV's. On the left, he found the bedroom the Don was talking about and placed his bag on the bed. The bedroom was tastefully decorated with a small bathroom attached. Strain went straight downstairs without unpacking. As warned, there was a large bowl of steaming spaghetti and meatballs in a place setting next to where the Don was sitting. He was grinding fresh cheese onto his pasta.

"Fresh Parmigiano Reggiano," the Don said thrusting the cheese grater towards Strain.

"Yes, it wouldn't be the same without it," he replied.

"No, it wouldn't and you can't have pasta without wine." He poured a generous amount into the glass next to Strain's bowl, "Salute," the Don said, raising his glass.

"Salute," replied Strain.

They both tucked into the meal, Strain was amazed at how good the meatballs tasted the red wine complimented the meal perfectly.

"These meatballs are excellent," Strain said, as he cut into another.

"Grazie, my mother's recipe, it was passed down from her mother and so on through the family." The Don could see his guest was genuinely enjoying the meal.

Everyone enjoyed the Don's meatballs. Who was going to tell him that they didn't like them? More wine was poured and they ate the rest of the meal in silence.

Strain decided it was time to start the conversation, "I haven't eaten that much in a long time" he said.

"You need to eat pasta more often," the Don said, wiping tomato sauce from around his mouth.

"After that meal, I will," he replied.

"Bring your wine with you." The Don stood with his wine glass in his hand. He went straight into the pantry where Strain had arrived.

"This was put in during the prohibition days and it was never discovered by the Feds. My father, God bless his soul, used it for years. If you look at the shelves on each side, you will see that they are supported underneath by steel bars. If you bend down and reach under next to the bottom shelf at the left, you will feel the shelf support slide it to the left and pull hard."

Strain did as he was told. He heard the bolts on the door leading into the cellar slide open.

"Now, reach under the third shelf for the bolt on the right and do the same thing," the Don watched.

Strain again did as he was told, this time the bolts slid back in place locking the door inside of the cellar.

"Very simple, but certainly effective," said Strain.

"There, you now know how we get in and out of here. This is where we will meet in the future, if we meet again before this business with the Arabs is finished. I choose to trust you, Mr. Strain, especially after the incident in the restaurant."

"We should talk about your work here in New York. Come we need to refill our glasses." The Don ushered Strain back towards the kitchen.

Strain was quietly impressed with the safe house, especially the means of entering and leaving unobserved. In the kitchen, he picked up the bottle of wine and refilled their glasses. They sat in silence for a couple of minutes admiring the depth and quality of the wine it was Villa Antinori, a classic Italian red wine.

"You have a very interesting background Mr. Strain, the last few years are somewhat cloudy."

"Call me John," Strain replied.

"You can call me Tony. I was told you can be trusted by our Irish friends. I like them because they are like us in many ways, men of honor. I'll trust you because of what they say about you and I owe you a debt of honor." If it had not been for Strain, he knew there was a fair chance he would be dead now.

Strain knew that he was referring to the restaurant incident when he said he owed a debt of honor.

"You owe me nothing, besides it wasn't the best way to meet for the first time," replied Strain.

"True, I would have arranged a welcoming committee for them if I had known. Your Irish friend has sat in that very seat several times over the years and I trust him, as he has not given me a reason not to." He was referring to Alan Foy.

"You can trust me, my only interest is getting the terrorists," replied Strain.

"Yes, and I want to avenge the deaths of my two soldiers, who were murdered by that Arab," said the Don.

"Well, we can work on that once we know where the terrorists are and with a bit of luck, possibly run surveillance on them," replied Strain.

"Yes, it's good to have some luck on your side, but you are beginning to sound like one of those FBI men."

"I can assure you that I am not one of them and never will be." Strain decided to leave well enough alone, as he could see the man's frustration with the FBI.

"You will have time to talk to them because they won't die quickly. I want to be kept in the loop if you find information that may concern me or my family. By God, I'll enjoy spending time with those bastards when we catch them." The Don remained calm this was only business to him. He would squash those who stood in his way or tried to take his business.

"I am very happy to hear you will entertain them for a while," Strain smiled at the Don, trying to lighten things up a little.

"Entertain," the Don said out loud and let out a huge laugh which made his whole body shake. "You English know how to understate things, I like you Strain." The Don was already warming towards Strain, an effect he had on people.

"Well, I suppose that's true," Strain laughed.

"I hope to have a very important meeting with one of the Triad leaders here in New York. I am waiting to hear back from him to see if he will agree to meet me. These Arab devils have encroached on his turf by bringing drugs into the city and trying to sell them. I don't deal in drugs and never will. It's a nasty business. The triads love the stuff and the head of their organization knows all there is to know about the business and who is on the streets. He will be invaluable when it comes to finding who these Arabs are."

"I hope it's a fruitful meeting," replied Strain.

They sat talking for another hour, telling war stores and talking about New York and somehow the subject of the FBI came up. That was when the Don went from total calm to visible anger and frustration.

"The fucking FBI, they are ruining things for me. I had a very quiet life until they started to snoop around again. They will try and get me for tax evasion or something else just like they did with Capone. They can't get me for anything else, those bastards," his face was bright red with rage.

"I can have words with certain members of the US Government to get them to ease off. If we get those responsible for the death of your soldiers and other US citizens, I'll make sure that the President himself knows that you were crucial to the success of the operation." Strain waited for a response.

"You really think that the President would call off those dogs in the FBI for me?" the Don didn't believe this.

"Well, he could certainly make them back off on the tax evasion stuff, especially if we get information that leads to the terrorist masterminds being caught." Strain saw a slight smile appear on the Don's face.

"As long as he doesn't want them to live, I have a debt of honor to pay." The Don looked Strain straight in the eye.

"You will have the honor of your family restored, nobody will try to stop that," said Strain.

"You see, I do like you," the Don smiled again, the chubby cheeks on his reddened face bulging out.

"Oh, I didn't doubt for a second that you and I wouldn't get on," Strain raised his glass as if in a toast.

The two of them continued talking and putting the world to rights before Strain made his excuses and left for D.C.

CHAPTER 18

ATLANTIC CITY

Mohammed and Sammy watched the hotel from the coffee bar for almost an hour and then moved on to a restaurant for something to eat. They had to give the police time to complete their investigation and clear out of the hotel. Three hours had passed when they returned to the hotel, entering through the fitness center at the back of the hotel. There was an elevator next to the fitness center that went to the conference floor and then gave them access to the main bank of elevators. Sammy pressed the arrow indicating that they wanted to go up. They didn't have to wait long. As the elevator arrived, the doors opened and several people exited. They both stepped in and the doors closed behind them. Sammy dug his hand into his jacket pocket and pulled out a small paper envelope with a plastic card tucked inside.

"Here is your room key. Just slide the card in the mechanism next to the door handle, make sure that the arrow is pointing down." He handed the card to Mohammed. On the envelope, it showed that he was in room 1808.

The elevator stopped and the doors opened, on the 18th floor. On the wall in front of him, Mohammed saw the room numbers and arrows indicating which way the rooms were on the floor. Next to this was a sign stating that this was the executive floor. He went in the direction of the arrow and found room 1808. He slid the plastic card in the mechanism and a green light came on indicating that the door was now unlocked. He opened the door and entered quickly, followed by Sammy.

Mohammed couldn't believe the size of the room it was huge. In front of him was a sitting area with two sofas and a desk. A cabinet was on the wall opposite one sofa inside he could see a television, DVD and music system. Next to the television was a pair of double doors. Opened them revealing another room which had a king size bed inside. In the center of the bedroom wall was the entrance to the bathroom.

Mohammed became angry, "What is this?" he said to Sammy.

"This is your room, my friend. My room is next door through that door there," he pointed to a door in the sitting room area.

"I told you to be discreet and not to stand out this is too much."

Sammy walked over to him and held his friends arm, "This is where I always stay when I come here, it's normal to stay in rooms like this when you are on business." He could see Mohammed was very angry.

"This is not a normal room," he barked.

"In this hotel, it's normal as most of the rooms are suites. Ours are a little bigger than the others, but that is only to be expected. We won't stand out here my friend. This is a very busy hotel with lots of frequent business travelers."

"I hope so, for your sake," he said.

Sammy was getting angry now as he had wanted to impress his old friend with his generosity and hospitality but it had backfired. "Let's make a pot of coffee and relax before the others arrive," he said.

"Where are the others?" asked Mohammed.

"They will all gather in my room at exactly three o'clock this afternoon."

"Good, that gives me two hours to sleep," he replied.

Sammy watched as Mohammed walked to the bedroom and closed the doors behind him shutting him out.

Sammy muttered his disgust to himself and walked to his room.

Mohammed slept well for an hour and a half. As he slowly woke, he remembered Sammy mentioning coffee. He went to the lounge area and found a coffee pot next to the television. He set it up to brew coffee and took a shower.

After the shower, he put on a white dressing gown that was hanging behind the door in the bathroom. He returned to the sitting room and poured himself a coffee. He could see that

Sammy had done a good job of setting up the room as he could visit the others when they arrived by going through the connecting door and not having to go out into the hallway. He turned on the television and started to watch the news on CNN.

Sammy could hear the television in Mohammed's room and decided to visit him to see if he was in a better mood. He knocked on the connecting door and waited.

Mohammed heard the knock on the connecting door and shouted, "Come in."

Sammy opened the door and entered the room, "Did you have a good sleep?" he asked.

Mohammed smiled as he could see that Sammy was wearing an identical robe to his. "Yes, I did, coffee is over there," he said. He knew that his friend was feeling bad about his reaction to the choice of room but it wasn't all bad.

"They have good strong coffee here," Sammy said.

"It's good. You have done well with this hotel, Sammy, but I do not want the others to know that I am staying here, understood?"

"Yes, that is why I wanted us to have the connecting rooms," he replied.

Mohammed looked at Sammy as he sat on the sofa next to him. For the first time he realized that his friend had put on at least thirty pounds t. His stomach rose inside the bath robe, making it look like he had a giant ball underneath. He didn't like this as it showed that his old friend was becoming lazy and used to the American ways.

He patted Sammy on the stomach, "You have eaten one burger too many," he said with a smile.

"I am paying for being in business in America they expect you to take them out for lunch or dinner every time you have a meeting. The portions are huge and there is always desert pushed in front of you at the end of the meal. It's just like a beautiful woman, hard to resist," he replied with a huge smile.

"Yes, and I suppose you have had too many of those, also."

"You can never have too many women," he laughed.

"Call the others, tell them not to come." Mohammed again wasn't pleased with the high-profile hotel.

"But they are on the way they will be here soon," complained Sammy.

"Cancel them, except for Hamed he needs to be here."

"Yes." Sammy knew not to argue when Mohammed was in this kind of mood.

Hamed arrived at the hotel on time and went straight to the room number Sammy had texted him. He'd been to this hotel several times to meet Sammy and was excited that there was a chance of getting girls that night.

Sammy heard the knock on his door from Mohammed's room. He walked into his room and looked through the door viewer, it was Hamed.

"Quickly," he said as he opened the door to Hamed.

"What's wrong?" Hamed asked as he entered the room.

"Nothing, he is in the next room," Sammy whispered.

The greeting was quick when Hamed met Mohammed and they went straight to work.

"I have several questions about the business first, are we set for all of the meetings we have planned?"

"Yes. We will take care of the litigation case in court the meeting with the bank is set, it will be in two days and we have the joint venture in California arranged," replied Sammy.

"What about the meeting with the Houston-based company?" asked Mohammed.

"That is still on target," replied Hamed.

To anyone listening, it would sound like any other business meeting taking place in a hotel. What the listener wouldn't know is that they were arranging bombings and robberies.

"When can I see the arrangements for the bank?" asked Mohammed.

"Now," replied Hamed.

"Let's go through them," he replied.

They walked through the plans for an armored car robbery. If anyone was listening, they wouldn't know it was a robbery being planned.

Mohammed's cell phone vibrated on the table in front of him, he picked it up.

"Yes," he said.

"We have a problem with our juniors you need to come immediately," the man said on the phone.

Mohammed knew it had to be something bad. He said nothing and ended the call.

"We have to go there's a problem with the court case," said Mohammed.

Mohammed was boiling on the inside with anger, how could there be a problem now? He knew the caller. It was the Imam from the Mosque who told him that there was a problem with the suicide bombers.

"Hamed, you go on to the meeting in the North. We need the equipment urgently. We will take care of the court case problem," Mohammed said.

"Yes, but there are two things that you both need to know about before you leave there may be a problem with the bank. I have been talking to some friends and they say that Tony Caputo, the son of Don Caputo, is involved with the sister of one of our employees."

Hamed held up two photographs. One was a young woman by the name of Karida, the sister of Shaady one of the young men who was going to be on the armored car robbery. The other picture was of Tony Caputo, the son of Don Caputo whose enforcers Mohammed had killed.

"When did you find this out?" asked Mohammed.

"A few hours before I came here," replied Hamed.

"Have they been discussing the company business?" asked Sammy.

"I don't know but she is spending a lot of time with the boyfriend, it does not look good."

Hamed meant it didn't look good for their arrangements but also for a Muslim woman to bed this Italian man. The three of them assumed that she was having sex with Caputo, even if she wasn't.

"Sammy will go to them and ask them some questions," Mohammed replied.

"The sister and brother live together. They moved to this address recently." Hamed gave Sammy the address.

"You said two things," replied Mohammed.

"Yes, the second is good news our friend and business acquaintance Mr. Khan has been purchasing some art work from a Chinese artist. It so happens that the artist is the daughter of Jimmy Chu, a businessman here in New York. We have talked about trying to do business with him in the past."

Mohammed knew exactly who Hamed was talking about when he mentioned Jimmy Chu, he was the head of the local Chinese Mafia. Mr. Khan was the Pakistan Ambassador and a big supporter of Mohammed's cause.

"Why is he buying paintings?" Mohammed was curious.

"He is buying them for his office. When he went to the gallery, he didn't realize who her father was. Mr. Khan requested that his associate Khalfan be with him on the day that he picked up the artwork he'd purchased. Khalfan as you know is very good when communicating with people, unlike Khan, which is why he wanted him with him."

What he meant was that Khalfan had left some listening devices in the gallery and office.

"I must hear more about this gallery. I too may be interested in buying," Mohammed replied.

"Yes, I thought you would. I have arranged a meeting, here is the time tomorrow." He gave Mohammed a card from the gallery on the back was the time and date.

Hamed walked over to the entertainment system in the room and turned the radio on loud. Mohammed and Sammy gave him an odd look but knew what he was doing. He was drowning out any possibility of anyone listening.

He walked over to Mohammed and whispered in his ear, "Caputo and Chu will be at the meeting," he stood up and said, "Sorry I put the music on too loud."

"It's too loud, turn it down. You have done well as always." Mohammed frustrated and excited at the same time, first the possible problem with the court job and now this amazingly good news. He would have the opportunity to take out the Don and Chu at the same time.

"I'll talk to our employee and his sister. What about the boyfriend?" asked Sammy.

"Talk to them, but first see what she has to say. I have other business arrangements with the boyfriend and his father," replied Mohammed.

"I'll leave now for the North, as I have a long drive ahead," said Hamed. He was looking forward to the drive to Michigan, a place he'd become fond of. Hamed had worked hard for a long time, becoming a regular at certain gun shows. He'd developed a good working relationship with several the exhibitors.

"Keep in touch and drive with care," replied Sammy.

Mohammed and Sammy waited two minutes after Hamed had left.

"When you go to the brother and sister, make it clear to them that this won't happen again." Mohammed was telling Sammy to kill them.

"I will. We can still operate the bank contract without him," replied Sammy

"Good, I am going to test our employee in California before I send him on the main job," said Mohammed.

"Good, it's always good to be tested, just as we were when we started." Sammy smiled as memories went through his mind of his first test when he killed several NATO troops in a bus.

"If he does well, I'll send him on a business trip to the sunshine," Mohammed replied.

"Yes, we are getting close to that job. I have our other employee ready to join him when the time is right." Sammy was referring to Adel another recruit who was working on the cruise ships in the Hawaiian Islands.

"Do you have all of the company equipment he will need?" He was talking about the bags of explosives and timers.

"Yes, I'll deliver it personally when you say he is to go. I must leave now I have a lot to do." Sammy knew not to ask anything about the job that he was going to test the California employee on. He was, however, very curious as to when they were going to deliver the explosives to Adel, the longer the explosives were stored the more chance there was of them being found.

CHAPTER 19

CALIFORNIA

Matthews was sitting at his desk on the army base, looking out of the window, day dreaming. It had been a week since he had talked to Musaad about the remote-control weapons system. Their conversation was continuously running through his mind, particularly what Musaad said about stealing the weapons system and getting the press involved. He knew that the only way to steal it was when they were on the road to or from the test range. If they attacked the convoy, lives would be lost and he didn't want Musaad and his brothers or any of his military colleagues to lose their lives. How do you steal such a thing? He kept going over and over it in his head.

He didn't hear the two soldiers come into the office and they saw that he was deep in thought. They took the opportunity to surprise him and slammed a heavy book down onto his desk, this resulted in a very loud bang which startled Matthews so much that he jumped out of his chair.

"Fuck," he shouted as he jumped up turning around to see what had made the noise.

"Sorry, did we wake you up?" The two soldiers were roaring laughing.

"You ass holes! You could have given me a heart attack." He held his hand on his chest he could feel his heart pounding.

They continued laughing, "Sorry, but you were such an easy target. We came to tell you that we have received our orders to ship out. Our unit leaves for Kuwait again at the end of next week," Specialist Ealing said.

"Your unit only just came back didn't it?"

"Yeah, we left a few days before you. Kind of surprising, really, because we thought that we would be there for another three months. It happened very quickly and now we are going back, it's a waste of time if you ask me."

"We have to go back and kick some ass," said Ealing's partner, whom Matthews didn't recognize.

"You mean 'get' some ass," replied Ealing.

"Yeah, those rag head women love it when they get some of this big boy, I make them squeal." His partner was grabbing himself by the crotch and was thrusting it forward in a simulated sex act.

They gave each other a high five and slapped the palms of their hands together.

The anger in Matthews raged inside of him it was an instantaneous reaction to their comments. "Get out of my office," screamed Matthews.

"Fuck, what's wrong with you man? You upset because you're not going to get any of that good pussy?" Ealing and his partner laughed again and were about to give each other another high five when they saw Matthews' response.

He had lost total control of himself and rage and anger took over. He stormed around the desk charging both men in a football style tackle, he knocked them both to the ground. They crashed against the door, smashing the glass panel, broken glass rained down on them. Matthews was like a man possessed, punching each man as fast and as hard as he could.

Ealing and his partner tried to block the blows that were being thrown at them but several got through. Two soldiers walking down the hallway heard the breaking glass, as did Colonel Taggert who was sitting in his office. The soldiers watched the fight for a second then saw the Colonel leaving his office. They and stepped in, pulling Matthews off the men.

Matthews, felt they restraining him, pulling him off Ealing, he resisted. "Get off me, get the fuck off me," he shouted.

"The Colonel is coming," said one of the soldiers.

"What the hell is going on here?" the Colonel shouted.

Ealing and his partner jumped to their feet. All five soldiers now stood to attention in the Colonel's presence.

"Sergeant Matthews, what is going on here?"

"Sir, nothing, sir," he replied.

"Nothing? The door is in splinters and you two look like you need some medical attention." The Colonel didn't mind some high spiritedness in his men, but this wasn't high spirits it was much worse.

"Ealing, what have you got to say for yourself?" He saw blood trickling down the side of the soldier's mouth, there was going to be a large bruise around his eye.

"Sir, just a little unarmed combat training, sir," he replied.

"A likely story, get out of here. Not you Matthews my office now," said the Colonel through gritted teeth.

"Sir, yes, sir," they all replied.

The Colonel turned and headed back to his office, closely followed by a still very angry Matthews.

They entered his office and Matthews stood to attention in front of the desk.

The Colonel stared at him, "At ease, man, sit down." He pointed to the chair in front of the desk.

"Sir, I'll stay standing, sir," he replied.

"You will sit down when I tell you to," the Colonel said angrily.

Matthews did as he was told this time, he was still so angry that he didn't care what the colonel was going to say or do.

"What is wrong with you? You have been acting weird ever since you came back from Kuwait?"

"Nothing is wrong with me, sir," he replied.

"Look, I am trying to help you, man. Something triggered that brawl out there and you can tell me what is wrong and I'll help or you can continue to be obstructive. If you do not talk to me, I can't help you. This is all off the record for the next couple of minutes." He truly wanted to help and was concerned that his sergeant was suffering from stress after his recent duty in Kuwait.

"Sir, I have nothing to say sir." Matthews wasn't thinking straight his total focus was on Ealing and on what he'd said. He wanted to get to him again.

"Last chance, what is going on?"

Matthews didn't reply.

"You leave me no choice. You will report to the camp doctor in the morning and have a full medical evaluation and stress test. I leave for Washington tomorrow. I'll be back in two weeks I'll review the report then. In the interim, you will be transferred to the supply warehouse as early as next week. I'll fill the paperwork out before I leave. You're dismissed."

"Sir, yes sir." He stood, saluted and marched out of the office completely oblivious to the salute returned by the Colonel.

Matthews sat in his office for the rest of the day, getting angrier and angrier with Ealing and his partner. He kept hearing Numa's voice in his head she was crying for help, screaming in pain. He put his hands over his ears many times and pressed them as if he was trying to squeeze her cries out. He thought about what they had said, 'getting some ass and making them squeal'. He played it over and over in his head. He convinced himself that they were responsible for Numa's death. It made sense to him they were in Kuwait at that time, stationed in the area where she lived, they were shipped back suddenly. It all fitted into place. He would get them back somehow. Musaad was right they must pay. He must regain Numa's honor and the honor of her family.

It had gone dark outside when Matthews realized that everyone had left for the day it was six thirty. He locked his desk, turned the light off in his office and closed the door. As he went past the mail trays in the hallway, he checked the incoming tray out of habit. There wasn't anything for him. In the out tray, was a large manila envelope with the word, 'CONFIDENTIAL' in bold print across the top. The handwriting on the front was Colonel Taggert's. It suddenly came back to him that he was being reassigned he'd forgotten about it. He would be removed from organizing the transportation of the new weapons system. He took the envelope out of the tray and returned to his office, where he opened it. Inside were two sheets of paper, he removed them. One was his transfer to the warehouse and the other was the new assignment of the transportation detail. Not only was Matthews being transferred to the warehouse, the Colonel had restricted him to desk duty. Sergeant Wynn was taking his place as the supervisor of the transportation escort detail. He stared at the papers for several minutes wondering what to do. He made his mind up. He was going to figure out a way to hijack the weapons system, but he had to be on the detail. He placed the transfer papers and envelope into the shredder next to his desk and watched them get chewed up. Nobody knew about his transfer and the Colonel wasn't due back for two weeks.

He had to make sure that the Colonel hadn't talked to Wynn about his change of duties if he had he was screwed. He remembered that Wynn's wife was pregnant. He called him to see how she was doing. During the conversation, he found out that Wynn had not been told about the transfer as he was taking his wife to North Carolina in two days so that she could be with her mother when the baby came. He'd been given permission to spend four or five days with her before he returned to the base.

Matthews started to formulate a plan. It was simple, but he couldn't do it on his own he needed Musaad and his brothers. He switched his computer on and checked the schedule for the weapons testing. There were only two scheduled tests left for the month one was in three days, the other was the next week. He knew that if he was to act it had to be on the second run, as the first would be used as a training exercise.

He would give Musaad and his brothers the route that the truck would take so that they could become familiar with the road. He wasn't sure how he was going to hijack the truck, but he knew that he would come up with a plan.

CHAPTER **20**

WASHINGTON D.C.

Strain had contacted all the team members and asked them to meet him in the hotel lobby.

None of them spoke as they waited for Strain to arrive. He'd arranged for a minibus to be delivered to the hotel by a car hire company. He paid the manager a hundred dollars to have the driver wait with the vehicle until Strain came out.

"Let's go," he said and everyone followed him.

Outside in the parking lot was the vehicle and driver.

"Everyone aboard," he said. "Has anyone talked to you?" Strain asked the driver.

"No sir, I was told to park here and wait. Are you Mr. Osbourne?" he asked.

"That's me son and here is fifty dollars for your troubles."

The young man couldn't believe that he'd been tipped fifty dollars, he was delighted.

Strain drove quickly out of the parking lot, not giving a thought as to how the young man was going to get back to the office.

The team said nothing as Strain drove the vehicle. None of them trusted it not to be bugged. Strain drove at the posted speeds all the way to Dumfries, to a restaurant famous for its seafood. He watched the three cars following them as they switched places in the traffic to avoid being seen. They were very good, but as he didn't want them to lose him, they had an easy job.

"Here we are lads, time for some good seafood and a drink. Come on you hungry barstards get out," he ordered.

He added the extra r in bastard as did his grandfather, who always said that it wasn't really a cuss word when said this way. Nobody really challenged him as it was one of his many quirks.

"I wonder what the most expensive item is on the menu?" said George.

"I don't know, but I am sure that we will all order it," replied Chalky.

"Go on, push your luck and I'll order a basket of fries between the two of you," Strain replied, with a wink of an eye.

"It had better be a bloody big basket I'm starving," said Bulldog.

"You're always hungry," replied Shadow.

The table had been booked in advance and had a great view of the boat dock outside. They took their time enjoying the meal and had picked out at least two surveillance teams that had followed them into the restaurant. Shadow recognized the woman from the car outside the bar where they had their altercation.

They talked about their visit to the city, English football and several jokes were told. Strain paid for the meal with cash and suggested that they walk outside to look at the boats. They all dutifully followed, realizing that he was up to something.

Bulldog was a little slow getting up, as he watched the waitress walk between the tables. She was carrying a large tray of glasses which were full of iced water. He couldn't resist the opportunity to get one over on the team following them. He stood up quickly, at just the right moment, knocking the tray out of her hand. The glasses all fell onto one of the men sat at the table behind them. He let out a yell as the cold water covered him.

"Oh dear! I am so sorry I didn't see the young lady there. Are you ok?" he said, in the most insincere way possible.

"You idiot, you soaked me," the man replied.

The waitress was devastated and tried to wipe some of the water off his suit with her towel.

"Get off me," the man said.

"Come, come now, old chap, she is only trying to help." He was really enjoying this, as the rest of the team made their way to the dock outside.

The restaurant manager came running over, "Sir, I am sorry for this. I can give you some of our logo clothing to change into." He was ushering the waitress away.

Bulldog wasn't going to have the waitress take the blame. "Listen mate that was completely my fault. The waitress couldn't avoid it. I stood up at the wrong time, so don't blame her," he said firmly.

The manager got the message, "Please, get something to clean this up, would you?" he said nicely, giving her the chance to get away from the situation.

"Here is some money for the damage," Bulldog held out fifty dollars.

"No, sir, that isn't necessary it was an accident," the manager replied.

"OK, well, maybe you can have the money for the laundry bill," he said to the soaked man. Bulldog could see that he wanted to punch him but he couldn't.

"No thanks, as you said, it was an accident," the man replied with his teeth gritted.

"Well, I must go. You should really take the manager up on his offer of the restaurant logo clothes. They have some very nice shorts and 'T' shirts with crabs on them. I think you would suit crabs." He winked at the young lady with him and walked away.

She had to put her hand over her mouth to stop herself laughing.

Strain and the rest of the team were outside admiring the boats when Bulldog emerged from the restaurant with a huge grin on his face.

"Looks like he has had some fun," said George.

"You know Bulldog anything to agitate the enemy, who happen to be watching us from the restaurant window," replied Shadow.

The man with the wet clothes and his female partner were standing by the window, watching the group of men by the moorings.

"Well, they are not going far. I am going to try and dry myself off a little, using the hand drier in the restroom." He was still very angry but knew he couldn't do anything about it.

"OK," his partner replied. She watched Bulldog as he joined the rest of his friends, she couldn't help but like him.

Strain and the rest of the team were admiring a thirty-foot cabin cruiser that was moored at the dock.

"They are not going to like this, so let's make it quick. Chalky, you untie the boat at the front. George, get the back. The rest of you jump in when I do. Is everyone ready?" he asked.

They answered in unison, "Yes."

Chalky and George walked to either end of the boat and quickly untied the ropes as Strain gave the signal.

"Look lively you sea devils and board the vessel," Strain said in his best pirate voice.

The surveillance team watching Strain and his men couldn't believe it when they saw them getting into a boat.

"Oh shit," said one of the surveillance team watching Strain.

Strain fired up the engine on the boat, quickly moved it into the middle of the harbor and headed out to the Potomac River. The whole team burst out laughing as they watched the panic onshore. The observers were running back inside the restaurant one with a cell phone to his ear.

"Let's celebrate American style," Bulldog said holding his arm up high they started giving him high fives.

The laughter continued as Chalky gave his impersonation of the observers onshore, running up and down the short deck with his cell phone to his ear.

"Sorry sir, we fucked up they got onto a boat." He continued as if he was talking to someone on the other end of the phone.

George chirped in like he was the commanding officer on the other end of the phone. "Get after them! Don't let them out of your sight."

Chalky had the worst American accent it only made the whole thing funnier. "We don't have a boat with an engine sir, only a row boat because you are a cheap bastard."

"What! don't talk to me about being cheap, budget constraints, cut backs - you have no idea what I have to put up with. Adapt man overcome and get in your row boat." George was really finding it hard not to laugh as he watched the antics of Chalky.

"Yes sir, I'll get in the row boat, maybe next time we can have one with go-faster stripes." Chalky was now sitting on the deck of the boat pretending to row fast. He kept looking over his shoulder trying to see if he was catching up to his imaginary prey.

"Enough stop," said Shadow laughing.

"There are some cold beers below if anyone would like one. Pour me one out, Bulldog and give those two idiots one as well," Strain said pointing to George and Chalky.

"Right away, Captain," Shadow was below decks before anyone else had chance to make a move.

The whole team had tears of laughter running down their faces as the mood lightened. They had been in the boat for about an hour when Strain brought the boat to a stop.

"We're in thirty feet of water George throw the anchor over," he said.

"Make sure there's a rope on it," said Bulldog sarcastically.

George was really enjoying this as he loved boats and the camaraderie.

They all sat around the deck, some in chairs and some on the sides of the boat. Chalky had found the radio and turned it on. Rock music was playing that none of them recognized.

"Just in case we get company," said Chalky.

"Well we're supposed to be here on the unofficial invitation of the US President but it looks like the intelligence agencies are keeping a close eye on us. I talked to Thorn about it last night and he claims to know nothing about it. I am inclined to believe him as he didn't realize that he was being watched as well."

"How do you know he was being watched?" asked George.

"Because I arranged the meeting and I tailed him for a couple of hours before we met. He had a team watching his every move."

"Who the fuck was it? I presumed this guy was one of their top agents?" said Bulldog.

"He is but there's a leak somewhere and it's his job to find out where. I got the feeling he knew he was being followed. Look we are going to do what we came here for and nobody will stop us. There's evidence that those involved in the terrorist attacks here in the US are connected to the attacks in the UK. We know we didn't get everybody, I have a feeling that the brains behind the UK bombings are behind the attacks here in America. They are too similar in style."

"I agree, let's carry on and do what we all came here to do," said Shadow.

"Well, how do the rest of you feel?" Strain said.

"I for one have not come all this way for nothing," said Bulldog.

They all agreed in unison.

"I didn't think you would want to go home yet. Remember this address in East Harlem." Strain put a piece of paper next to the bag on the deck. It's in an apartment building which has been kindly provided for our stay in New York, with enough bedrooms for all of us. George and Chalky do your thing and sweep the place when you get there. Set up hidden cameras covering the front door and rear fire escape."

"You don't think this place is clean?" Chalky said.

"I do as the owner of the building is a new-found friend, the local Don." Strain knew this would get a reaction.

"Oh! Would it be Don Corleone of the Corleone family?" Bulldog said in his mimic of an Italian mafia voice.

"Close but not quite. Get things in place you two and see what you need to set up some counter-surveillance."

"Will do," replied George.

"You will all go on the Gulfstream together your destination will be Newark. You will be met at the airport by an Italian mobster-looking gentleman. He will split you up into four vehicles. The four vehicles will make it very difficult for anyone to keep observations on everyone.

"Well, at least we can give the bastards following us another lesson in counter- surveillance." laughed Shadow.

"The drivers will take you to the apartment but you will need to remember the address for the future. Once they drop us all off, they won't be working with us again. It may take a while to get to the apartment as they know that we may be under surveillance, they certainly are. They deal with this all the time as they are constantly watched by the FBI. They are very good at losing them.

"What do they know about us?" asked Bulldog

"They only know that you work with me and we are trying to track down Arab terrorists. They had two of their people killed by some Arabs a few weeks ago. I'll give all of you the full details in New York. Any questions before we leave?"

"None that can't wait until New York," said Bulldog.

"O.K. here." Strain picked up a bag that was next to him and threw it into the middle of the boat deck. There is an envelope for each of you in the bag with fifteen thousand in cash, use it wisely," he smiled.

"I'll need some new equipment anyway," said George.

"Thorn is supplying some top rate stuff, he'll bring it with him," replied Strain.

Bulldog opened the bag and took out a plain manila envelope and placed it into his jacket pocket the rest of the team all followed suit.

"Cash for everything lads no credit cards etc. etc.," Strain said. "I leave in the morning you all leave tonight on the Gulfstream."

"One question, do we stay put in the apartment in New York or are we free to go walkabout?" asked Shadow.

"No everyone stay put until I arrive in the morning. You won't arrive in New York until late tonight anyway and you should take the opportunity to get some sleep, I get the feeling we will all need it. The apartment has ample food, water, etc. to see us for a couple of days. I don't have to tell you to keep on your toes, this one has the makings of getting very messy."

Strain started the boat engines again as George went forward to the anchor.

CHAPTER 21

NEW YORK CITY

The information on suspected Arab terrorists was slow coming in. The Don was getting very frustrated. He decided to call in a few favors from members of the Unions and the crime families, one of whom was Jimmy Chu, a Chinese gang lord. The Don didn't relish visiting with Jimmy as the Chinese gang empire was eating up areas that had been predominantly Italian in the past. Nothing had yet led to serious bloodshed. It was time to make the phone call. He called the number, it was answered immediately. "Jimmy Chu," the Don barked down the phone.

"Who wants him?" a Chinese voice asked.

"Just tell him it's his favorite Italian," the Don replied.

The phone went quiet for about thirty seconds, he heard someone breathing on the other end of the line.

"Is this who I think it is?" said Jimmy Chu.

"Yes, it is, how you doing?" the Don asked, though he didn't care.

Jimmy ignored the question. "What do you want?" He was wasting no time talking to the Don.

"I want a meeting, I have something to discuss that would benefit both us," he replied.

"Would it have anything to do with you looking for the people that murdered your thugs." Jimmy didn't mince his words.

"Yes, it does, as always you know everything that goes on." The flattery wouldn't work.

"Where?" he asked.

The Don knew that Jimmy Chu wouldn't meet at his properties, the meeting place had to be neutral but safe. "How about that gallery?" the Don was referring to the art gallery owned by Jimmy's daughter.

"Tomorrow at ten," Jimmy said and put the phone down.

The Don knew that Jimmy would have his son with him and possibly several others in hiding. To show his good faith, the Don took only his two most trusted and dangerous soldiers.

The Village area was scattered with all kinds of art studios, some traditional and some very extreme. The one thing the Don didn't like about the area was that it had a large gay community. He made no excuses for having a real dislike for them.

"Here we are in faggot land! Let's get this over with quickly before one of those lipstick-wearing excuses for a man tries to take you home with him, Benny," he was talking to his right-hand man.

In a very deep and slow voice, Benny said, "Geez, boss, don't even joke about that they make my skin crawl," and shuddered.

"Yeah, I can see them liking that ass of yours," joked Angelo.

"That ain't funny," he scowled at Angelo.

"Don't worry. We will keep them off your back, off your back, get it?" laughed the Don at his own joke.

"Come on, boss, don't say those things." Benny was a giant of a man six feet four and over three hundred pounds. He wasn't enjoying being the target of his boss's jokes.

"Oh, calm down, it's a joke. Here we are," said the Don as they approached the gallery.

There were two cars parked outside already. They recognized one as Jimmy Chu's.

"Stay with the car." The Don said to Pete, the driver.

Benny got out first, closely followed by the Don and Angelo.

Two small Chinese men stood either side of the gallery entrance. The Don ignored them and walked through the door, again closely followed by his minders.

The Don was surprised at the size of the main gallery as they walked in. A large painting hung down from the ceiling on wires, it was at least six feet square. He couldn't make out what it was supposed to be. It looked like someone had thrown a bucket of paint at it and hung it out to dry. He had a liking for traditional art, figures, scenery, flowers, that sort of thing. One painting caught his eye, hung on a column in the center of the room. It showed a Tuscan villa set in the middle of rows of grapevines on a rolling hill. The yellows creams and browns took him straight back to his last visit to Italy.

"I see you like the vine house," a voice said.

They all turned to see a very slender, but attractive Chinese lady in her early twenties standing in a doorway that was a part of the exhibit wall.

"Yes, this is a work of art whoever did this really captured the character of the Tuscan house, I presume that's what it is?" said the Don.

"Yes, it is. I am glad you like it. The sister painting is on the other side of the column." She walked around the column, pointing towards the second painting.

"So, this shows the rear view of the house, clever stuff." The Don said as he saw the picture.

"So, glad you like them," she replied.

"A talented person, whoever did this," said the Don.

"Thanks, they are my work," she said.

"This way please," a male voice said. The Don turned and saw a Chinese man standing in the doorway the young lady had come out of. Benny and Angelo had already noticed the man.

The don walked through the door into a room that was scattered with paintings, easels and partly-finished paintings on canvas. In the corner, sat Jimmy with his son standing behind him.

Jimmy held his hand out, palm up indicating the Don should sit down. "Let's get down to business, Jimmy. You are a busy man as I am." The Don didn't want to waste any time.

"Leave us," Jimmy said to his son and the other man in the room.

The Don waved at Benny and Angelo to leave also.

"So, you want to find these men?" Jimmy was making a statement more than asking a question. In his mid-fifties and only five feet six inches tall, he still looked younger and fitter than most men in their late thirties. He practiced the martial art of Ai Kido twice a day, sometimes as much as two hours at a time. His son had followed his father's ways and was a black belt in four different styles of martial arts, Kendo being his favorite.

The Don admired the little man with his fit physique and healthy looks. Above all, though, he respected him as he was old school and had honor as one of his greatest attributes, something they both felt the young men of today were losing.

"Yes, I could use some help in finding those responsible for the murders of two of my men. These people have no honor and they are trying to break into both of our areas of operation. They operate like animals with no care for the consequences. You and I both know that if they continue to operate this way the attention of the police and the FBI will increase." The Don knew that he would relate to the honor comment.

"Yes, they are spreading their wings like the small hawk but they only cast a little shadow on the ground. They are not a problem."
The Don was used to him using these kinds of Chinese ways to describe things.

"Ah, but when the small hawk gets closer to the ground the Shadow gets bigger by then its prey is trapped and he attacks and devours it." The Don was proud of his version.

Jimmy smiled like the Don had never seen before. "You are learning our ways, you give a good picture." Jimmy was impressed.

"Are you willing to help?" the Don asked.

Jimmy paused deliberately, "The FBI is already watching you. Why should I worry?"

"They watch you as well, Jimmy and you know it." The Don showed no signs of emotion.

"Yes, you are aware of what is going on in my territory, as always. I'll help but only to stop them from bringing the unwanted attention of the FBI you talk of. I'll put the word out." Jimmy stood up.

The Don did the same and for some reason unknown to himself, he stuck his hand out offering it to Jimmy. This had not happened on previous meetings and Jimmy was equally surprised, but he shook his hand heartily.

"You like the paintings outside of the Italian villa," Jimmy said.

"Yes, she is very talented, your daughter." The Don replied.

"It would be a great honor to know that it hung in your home." He returned the honor comment the Don had made earlier.

"Yes, I'll talk to her on the way out," he replied.

They walked into the gallery together.

"Goodbye, Jimmy." The Don said and walked towards the exit, "Goodbye to you, miss."

Jimmy could feel the anger swell up inside. The Don was going to walk out without even discussing the painting. He watched as the mafia boss got to the door.

The Don knew exactly what he was doing he wanted to agitate Jimmy just a little by saying goodbye and not even discussing the painting with his daughter. He turned suddenly at the door.

"I almost forgot. Young lady, how much is that painting?" he pointed to the one he'd been admiring.

"Fifteen thousand," she said, expecting to have to come down in the price.

"It has to be bought as a pair," said Jimmy smiling.

The Don grinned and thought "touché, Jimmy."

"Ask your father for my address. I'll send you a check for $30,000 in the morning. I think this one would look nice in your new restaurant you are building, Jimmy." He turned and left pointing at the very large painting hanging from the ceiling.

The two guards were still waiting outside either side of the door.

"Good little soldiers," the Don said, with sarcasm.

A uniformed police officer was talking to Pete, his driver.

"Look at that boss. They even have Arab looking cops in New York."

As this was said, alarm bells went off in their heads. A garbage truck half a block down the street accelerated suddenly towards them. Hanging off the back was a man in coveralls holding a back pack.

"Inside," shouted the Don, at the top of his voice. They charged back inside the gallery, quickly followed by the two Chinese guards.

Jimmy's son was in the middle of the gallery. He immediately started to run towards the Don and his men, thinking they had come back to fight.

The Don saw this and thought fast "Jimmy, get down, get down," he shouted at the top of his voice as he dove to the floor.

Jimmy's son quickly changed direction towards his father, realizing something was wrong. Jimmy was already at the door with his daughter. He pulled her to the floor and tripped his son all in one motion.

The police officer saw that they had suspected something was wrong and drew his side arm to shoot Pete. Pete was already suspicious of the police officer. He saw him going for his side arm and quickly pulled his sawn-off shotgun out from its hiding place next to the seat. He fired both barrels in the policeman's direction, the pellets tearing into his neck and face, destroying it. The policeman dropped to the ground dead.

The man on the back of the garbage truck leaned back, getting ready to hurl the backpack full of explosives into the gallery.

The driver of the truck saw his friend in police uniform step back and his face and side of his head explode. The body fell back into the path of the truck and he instinctively braked.

The backpack thrower was slammed against the back of the vehicle as it suddenly braked. He lost his grip on the backpack as it shot forward into the road and under Pete's car, closely followed by his own body. He rolled in the road and jumped up all in one motion, his training paying off. He looked at his right hand the trigger mechanism had broken away from the bomb, it was live. That was his last thought as the backpack erupted in a ball of flames.

Pete was now on full alert. As he shot the cop and saw the garbage truck coming down the street, he pressed the window button on the door and watched as it quickly closed. A bag of some kind was flying towards his car. Pete quickly dropped down across the two front seats. Three seconds after the bag landed in the road, the bomb inside exploded. Windows shattered in cars and buildings, sending glass flying in all directions. The armor on the Don's car had suppressed a lot of the explosion. The shock wave was causing most of the damage to the property in the area. The driver of the garbage truck was hit by flying glass and the ball bearings that were packed in the bomb. He was knocked unconscious and would slowly bleed to death before help got to him.

Inside the gallery, they all heard the explosion and the sound of breaking glass. It wasn't as bad as Jimmy had thought a bomb would sound, but he didn't realize how lucky he was.

"Jimmy, you OK?" the Don shouted.

"Yes," he replied, as he checked his daughter.

They all slowly got to their feet. Dust was everywhere. The floor had glass on it from the windows of the studio and several of the paintings were strewn about the room. Jimmy shouted something in Chinese and the two security guards went outside. His son came out with his sister as Jimmy checked her for injuries. He was saying things in Chinese that the Don didn't understand. It was a miracle nobody was injured. Jimmy walked over to the Don and bowed deeply before he straightened. His son followed suit.

"I owe you a great debt, you saved the lives of my children." He bowed again.

"Stand up, Jimmy, you owe me nothing." He gave him a big hug.

Jimmy was surprised by the hug but realized they had both a renewed respect for each other.

"Oh! No check on Pete," the Don shouted to Angelo and Benny. They ran outside. The car was engulfed in smoke from the bomb. The tires were all blown out as the vehicle sat on the rims. The driver's door opened and out staggered a stunned Pete.

"He's alive," shouted Angelo. He ran over to the car, closely followed by Benny. They both helped Pete to the sidewalk. They could see that he was in shock and badly shaken by the explosion.

"In here," said Jimmy's son, waving them towards the gallery entrance.

They all scrambled to get him inside the gallery where Jimmy's son quickly checked him over. He'd taken paramedic lessons in case he ever needed the skills should his father become ill or injured. He'd qualified with flying colors.

Pete was mumbling something they couldn't understand. The Don got down on one knee.

"Pete, you O.K.?" he asked.

He mumbled again in Italian.

The Don burst out laughing to the shock of everyone.

"What is it?" asked Benny.

"He said 'I told you the armor plating would work'." He realized he was laughing somewhat out of relief.

Everyone else started to laugh nervously, not sure what to do.

"Armor plating, very smart," said Jimmy.

"Yes, it was his idea," said the Don. It had taken Pete over a year to convince the Don that he needed an armored car to protect against a bomb. Little did he know that he would save his own life when the Don agreed to purchase the new armored car.

"We will find these people and remove them from our lives," Jimmy said.

"Yes, we will, but I have a friend that will need to talk to them before they go to Allah or whatever they call their God," said the Don.

"We will try to give your friend the chance, now I must go as there's a lot of work to be done," Jimmy headed towards the back of the building, they could hear police sirens in the distance.

"Time to leave. Get Pete to his feet. We will leave the same way as Jimmy and get one of the boys to pick us up," the Don started walking.

"I'll take you wherever you want to go," said Jimmy's son.

"O.K.," replied the Don.

The newspapers reported the bombing the next day as an attempted assassination of the Don by a rival gang, the prime suspect being one of the Chinese triad leaders. This suited Jimmy and the Don because nobody would ever suspect them of working together.

When the news broke, the attempt on the Dons life didn't surprise Strain. He knew that it wasn't the Chinese gangs after he found out that it took place outside Jimmy Chu's daughter's art gallery.

On the way to the little Italy area of New York, the Don made several calls, the most important to the Capodecina's or Capo's to have all family members taken to a safe place. The second was to have their soldiers on site when he arrived, at least those that were not protecting family.

The number of soldiers or Soldati each Capo had was normally at least ten. By the time the Don got to the safe house close to Little Italy, there were forty soldiers ready to do his bidding.

The news of the attempt on the Don's life spread quickly through the Mafia underworld. The Don received many calls offering assistance and man power if he needed it. When he arrived at the safe house, he received some good news on a possible location that was being used by Arabs. He would pass the information on to Strain, even though he wanted to go there and blast them all to pieces.

169

CHAPTER 22

CALIFORNIA

Musaad was walking into the mosque to pray when he saw Matthews standing by the door. "How are you doing?" he asked.

"I am well. I need to speak to you."

"I am going in for prayer maybe we can meet tomorrow." He thought that his friend looked rather happy and upbeat for a change.

"No, I need to talk to you now. It's very important." He almost pleaded with Musaad.

"Can we meet after prayer?"

"Yes, I'll see you at the same café we met at last time." He walked away, leaving Musaad very confused.

After prayer, Musaad walked into the café where Matthews had suggested they meet. He was already waiting for him. He had two cups of coffee in front of him.

"Thank you for coming, I have already bought you a coffee." He said pushing the coffee cup across the table.

Musaad sat down, "Is there a problem? Are you in trouble?" He wasn't concerned, just curious.

"No, I am fine, but I have something that I need to discuss with you. It's very important." He was getting nervous.

"What is it?" Musaad was now very interested. He could see that his friend was very anxious about something.

Matthews leaned across the table and whispered to Musaad, "I want your help. I want to get revenge and salvage some honor for Numa."

"Yes, whatever I can do, I'll help. Tell me what I have to do and it's done."

"I want to take the item I told you about last time we met."

MICHAEL J BENSON

Musaad had to play it cool and made it look like he'd forgotten their last conversation. "What item are you talking about?"

"You know I told you about it, the thing that I am escorting the special weapons system."

Musaad's couldn't believe what he was hearing. He showed surprise and a sudden recollection of their last discussion. "Yes, I remember now. I completely forgot about it. You really want to steal it or are you just going to drop it off a cliff like you said?"

"Yes, I am going to steal it, but as I said I need your help and your brothers'. I can't do it alone. I must tell you there is one complication."

"What is it?" he replied.

"We have to do it by the end of next week because they are going to move me to another base soon." He didn't want to tell him about the fight or that the Colonel thought that he was losing his mind.

"Next week that is too soon, we have to plan such a thing it is impossible." This time he wasn't faking his surprise, they had less than ten days to plan and execute.

"No I think I know of a way to do it but it's dangerous."

Musaad acted like he was getting nervous, "You didn't say it was going to be dangerous before, I thought that I would drive you somewhere or something like that."

Matthews was at a loss what to say next. He really thought that his friend was going to be fully on board with the idea.

"What is it? That is dangerous?"

"You or one of your brothers will have to cut the brake pipes of the truck that follows me."

"What is so dangerous about that?" He smiled at Matthews.

"You will be doing it when you are lying on your luge board."

"On my board? Why don't I just crawl under the truck and cut them?" Again, he was playing dumb.

"You will be traveling down a steep road behind the military truck on your luge board," replied Matthews.

Musaad couldn't help but laugh out loud, "You are mad, my friend. You have lost your mind." He continued to laugh.

"No, it can be done. I have seen you on those boards. It will be a matter of catching up to the truck and then cutting the brake pipes. Once the pipes are cut, you can stop the board and your brother can pick you up in his car. I'll take care of the rest."

He could see that he was deadly serious and stopped laughing. "I can't just roll under a truck and cut the brakes. It is impossible." He had to hear the rest of his plan.

"Please, Musaad, it can be done. I need your help."

"OK but I need to talk to my brothers and you will have to tell us the complete plan and then we will make a decision," replied Musaad.

"No problem. When can we meet? It has to be soon."

"I'll call you, do you have a cell phone?" he asked.

"No, I don't. Call me at the apartment I'll wait for your call," replied Matthews.

Musaad had him hooked, "OK give me an hour."

They both shook hands and left the café.

Musaad called the Imam at the mosque with the news. "I have excellent news the soldier I told you about wants to exact his revenge, we need our friend to be there."

"Do not say anymore. I'll meet you in the morning at the mosque, ten o'clock with your brothers. Arrange for him to be there at eleven, goodbye." The Imam knew that Musaad meant Mohammed Ali Ghahi when he said "their friend."

Musaad was excited as he knew this would elevate him in the eyes of the Imam and hopefully, the great Mohammed Ali Ghahi. He called Matthews thirty minutes later and gave him the time and location for the meeting.

CHAPTER 23

Mohammed was very interested in the story that Musaad had to tell. He saw a great opportunity to get his hands on a very valuable piece of US military equipment. He would listen to the plan but he knew that he needed more men. He was standing out of sight inside the doorway of the mosque when Musaad arrived.

Musaad entered the mosque and was immediately confronted by Mohammed.

"Where are your brothers?" he was concerned.

"They are coming, do not worry."

"When this man comes, you will take him into the room at the back of the mosque through that door on the right." He pointed it out. "Have your brothers meet him and get him to tell you what the plan is and make a lot of notes. I'll be in the room next to you. When he has told you what his plans are, you give him this cell phone and tell him to wait for your call." He handed a small phone to Musaad.

"What do we say about helping him?"

"That is why you are giving him the phone. Tell him that you need to discuss it with your brothers alone before you can decide. Ask him go home while you stay with your brothers to talk, he will leave without any questions."

"Good. I'll do this," he replied.

Mohammed rose and left Musaad inside the doorway.

Matthews arrived exactly on time and entered the mosque. Sitting on a wooden bench inside the doorway next to the shoe rack where people left their shoes while they prayed was Musaad.

"Follow me," said Musaad as he walked to the back of the mosque, closely followed by his brothers and Matthews.

The inside of the room had nothing other than a table and four chairs. It was dimly lit with one bare light bulb in the center of the room.

They all sat around the table, "Good to see you again," Matthews said to all three brothers.

Musaad responded first, "We don't get together enough but soon we will convince you to join us when we luge down a nice steep road." The brothers chuckled trying to keep Matthews relaxed.

"No, I am not going to lay down on one of those boards and roar down a mountain road."

"We can talk about that later. You must tell us what your plan is as I know time is against us all." He was straight back to business.

"It's a very simple plan, really, but unfortunately, it involves you and your crazy sport," said Matthews.

"Try us out, maybe we can make some suggestions before we commit to helping you." Musaad was treading very carefully, trying not to spook him.

"OK, here goes. The convoy normally involves two escort vehicles, usually Humvees, one at the front and one at the rear. Then there are the two trucks that transport the weapons system, I'll be driving one of them. We are in radio communication with each other at all times. All the soldiers guarding and transporting the weapons system are armed. When we leave the range, we can't take many detours as we have to eventually take Pine Hills Road for the last eight miles down to the interstate back to the base. Pine hills Road is very steep in places with many bends and turns. Some of these turns are extremely dangerous if you are going too fast. We therefore must go very slow as we negotiate them. This is where you will be able to catch up to the truck and slide quietly underneath and cut the brake pipes."

Musaad interrupted him, "We can't slide under a Humvee." He saw that this wasn't going to work.

"Wait. I am just trying to give you an idea of what the convoy does. Before we leave the test range, I'll tell the other soldiers to get a drink while I watch the vehicles. When they are gone, I'll disable one of the Humvees so that when we leave, they won't be able to follow. I'll instruct the remaining Humvee to lead the convoy and I'll follow with the weapons systems in the back of my truck. The second truck is normally for emergency breakdown purposes anyway." He put his hand inside his jacket and pulled out a map that was neatly folded up.

"You have come prepared," said one of the brothers, but Matthews didn't say anything in return he was too focused on the details of the plan.

He spread the map out across the table, pressing it flat with the palms of his hands. "This is where the test site is and this is the route we will take to go back to the military base. I have highlighted it in yellow." He followed the yellow line with his finger. "This is where the first set of very bad bends are we have to slow right down. Next to this bend is an old driveway. This is where you could be ready to follow on the luge boards after we pass. The next half mile is very slow going and you will have no problem catching up to us. Here, half way down Pine Hills Road is where the road is the most dangerous, this is where you can cut the brake pipes. After you cut the pipes, you stop yourself at this bend and the trucks will carry on down the hill. We will start the steepest part of the decent at this point and braking is pretty much continuous. The vehicle behind me will soon its fluid and be forced to pull over to the side of the road. The emergency procedure is that he will radio me to tell me that they have a problem. I'll instruct him to fix the vehicle and follow on or, if the vehicle can't be fixed, he will radio the base for assistance. Our instructions are not to stop for vehicles that break down unless the vehicle is carrying weapons or sensitive equipment. I'll obey this directive and tell the lead security vehicle to continue. They also know this directive and won't question my decision." He paused slightly, following the map with his finger. The eyes of the al-Saleem brothers didn't leave the map, they were fascinated.

"What will we do with the security vehicle?" asked Musaad.

"I am about to tell you. Here is another extremely bad bend with a sheer drop on one side. On the other side is a cliff face about one hundred feet tall, it's not unusual to have rocks fall off the cliff into the road. Here is where your other brother comes in. He can place several rocks in the road right on the bend. As we come down the hill, the security vehicle will see the rocks and realize that the truck can't get past them, he will have to stop. He and the other soldier with him will push the rocks gently out of the way with his truck so that we have enough room to get past. As they maneuver the rocks out of the way I'll stop my vehicle close behind them. When their truck gets close to the edge, I'll ram it knocking it off the road and down the steep cliff. They will be killed. The weapons system is then ours." He sat back and stared at the map.

Musaad looked at his brothers. They both shrugged their shoulders wondering what to say.

"Won't you have someone in the vehicle with you?" asked Musaad.

"Yes, do not worry about him. I'll take care of him when the others are moving the rocks out of the way." He knew that he would have to kill him.

"Are you not concerned about killing the soldiers in the vehicle?"

"No, because I believe that they may be responsible for Numa's death."

"How do you know this?" he was surprised at this news, but it now made sense why the soldier had decided to steal the weapons system.

"I don't, but I am sure they took part." He could feel the emotions building in his body.

"Can you give us some time to discuss this plan and we will call you?" Musaad followed Mohammed's instructions.

"Yes, time is against us, do not wait too long," he replied and stood up to leave.

"Here take this cell phone. I'll call you soon, maybe within the hour," Musaad gave him a phone.

Matthews didn't think twice about taking the phone he wanted to move on with the plan. He left the mosque and walked back to his apartment, grasping the cell phone tightly the whole way. He kept going through the plan in his mind, trying to find ways of improving it. There wasn't enough time to make drastic changes and he knew it.

Unknown to Musaad and his brothers, Mohammed had installed a hidden camera in the room and he'd recorded the whole conversation. He intended to keep the video a secret and to possibly use it at some time in the future.

Mohammed walked into the room where Musaad and his brothers were busily discussing the information that they had just been given. They all stood up when he entered.

"You have something very valuable in this soldier Musaad, you have done a good thing befriending him." Mohammed walked over to him and hugged him, kissing him in the traditional Arabic way on both cheeks.

"Thank you," he replied. A personal congratulation from Mohammed himself was great praise indeed.

"We will have to change the plan slightly but it seems reasonable. Do any of you know this road he talks about?" asked Mohammed.

"No, but we still have the map that he brought and it wouldn't take long to get to know the road and the area that it covers." Musaad's eldest brother Fadi spoke for the first time.

"It's a long road." He questioned whether they could get to know it in such a short time.

"We do this all the time when we are looking for new hill roads to use for our Luge races. When we do this, we must know the road like we know our own street where we live. We have to know all of the turns and bends, junctions, surface conditions, just about everything about the road." Out of the three brothers, Fadi was the best at this. He had a knack for quickly memorizing the luge runs, closely followed by Ghaazi.

"Yes. I heard him talk about this board that you lay down on. I thought that a luge was something used on ice in Switzerland or somewhere like that, not California." Mohammed really had heard of street luge when he'd been checking on the brothers to make sure that they were still loyal followers. He didn't know much more than it was a street sport popular with the brothers.

"Yes, it is, but the ice sport gave birth to the idea that if you used a skateboard type vehicle you could run down steep roads. You use the bends and turns of the steep mountain and hill roads just like the bends and turns on the conventional ice luge. It's very exciting but it can also be dangerous if you do not take it seriously." Musaad said.

"That is one reason why you have to memorize the bends and turns in the road that you race on. The surface conditions of the road can be equally as dangerous especially if you hit a pothole. This is why I think it will be easy for us to get to know the road, we do it all the time." Fadi was trying to impress Mohammed as he was a huge idol to him.

"We need to see the road he is talking about. Call him and tell him that you agree to take part and ask him to meet you here in the morning at seven. He must not know of my involvement, it's just you three." Mohammed protected his identity again.

"He won't know anything about you," replied Musaad.

"Good. Meet me in the lobby of my hotel at one o'clock this afternoon. It's the Holiday Inn on 34th street. Do not be late," he warned.

"We will be on time," replied Fadi.

CHAPTER 24

THE WHITEHOUSE

Strain was totally pissed off with the actions of the US government agencies that had been not only following the team but hindering them. He was reasonably sure that Thorn wasn't involved but he had to be certain, the meeting was going to be tense. Strain had George and Chalky sweep his hotel room for the second time before Thorn arrived. They had also installed hidden cameras in the corridors on the floors where the team members' rooms were.

Thorn had a good idea what the meeting was about and had already called the White House to set up an urgent meeting with the President. He was still waiting for a reply when he arrived at Strain's hotel room.

Strain heard the knock on the door and knew it was Thorn, as Chalky had just called him to let him know Thorn had just exited the elevator.

He opened the door, "Come in."

"Well, do I need to ask why the sudden meeting?" Thorn could still hear Strain on the phone saying, "I don't know what the fuck is going on, but you need to meet me now at the hotel."

"I guess not, seeing as my whole team is being fucked about by your government." Strain was in no mood for small talk.

"Well, I didn't expect us to have problems with our own agencies. I am as upset as you about it, so much so I have already requested an urgent meeting with the President."

"Good, because I am ready to pack our stuff and the team and I'll get on the Gulfstream and fly back to the UK."

"I don't want you to do that and nor will the President, we have too much important work to do here."

"I understand that but when we have people running surveillance on us and you, we can't operate properly. It won't be long before one of those following us blows the job and exposes us to the terrorists. I'll not put my team at risk when we have fucking idiots out there playing games with them." Strain picked up two glasses from the cabinet and poured out some whiskey.

"I know who the agencies are. I have requested that when I meet with the President, I have an additional meeting with him and the Directors of the four Federal departments. I know that they have had me under surveillance because I have seen them and found listening devices in my apartment. I am now living in a safe house which none of the agencies know about. The President gave us an open budget and I am using it in safe houses, vehicles and equipment." He took a sip of the whiskey.

"That's all well and good, Thorn, but what if the President wants them involved?" This was Strain's biggest fear as he knew that the team couldn't operate properly with other agencies involved.

Thorn's cell phone rang, "It's the White House," he said to Strain.

"Hello," said Thorn.

"Can you hold for the President please Mr. Thorn?" It was the President's assistant.

"Thorn, what is this meeting about and yes this call is being scrambled." The President was in no mood for time wasting meetings.

"Sir, our overseas team and I are having problems. We are getting interference from our intelligence and law enforcement agencies." The President cut in very quickly before he could continue.

"What are you talking about interference, which agencies?"

"We have been under surveillance, had equipment damaged and a physical confrontation which didn't work out well for our agency people." Thorn waited for the President to tell him he was talking through his ass.

"Can you make it to my office in two hours? I must leave this evening. Which agencies are we talking about?"

"I think if all four directors are present it would be best, not that we think that they are all involved. It would help smooth things along if they were all there."

"I hope you are wrong about this, Thorn, but I don't think you would have made the call if you were." The President hung up the phone.

"Wow, he is not in a good mood. We see him in two hours."

"It won't make his mood any better when I tell him the lengths we have gone to avoid being followed or listened to. Just so you know I don't intend holding back in the meeting. If he believes us great, if he doesn't I'll call the Prime Minister and let him know we are on our way home." Strain was in no mood for games.

"Understood, say what you have to because I intend to. We are on the same team, Strain and they need to know it. I won't have a career in the secret service after this job anyway, the Director will see to that. He has already made it clear through the agent in charge of my old office. He's not involved in the problems we are experiencing he just feels he can't trust me anymore." Thorn wasn't bothered, as he'd heard the President had other things planned for him if this mission went well.

"Sorry you will be shut out of the secret service. Who is involved? My guess is the FBI and CIA," said Strain.

"Yes, and the director of the FBI is going to explode when he gets in the President's office."

"I always did like fireworks," replied Strain.

The White House seemed particularly quiet to Thorn when they arrived. The calm before the storm he thought.

Strain was looking forward to moving on with the job but not without laying down a few ground rules first.

As they waited to be called into the Oval Office, the Directors started to arrive. First was Dan Pierro, NSA, closely followed by Butch Shattuck, CIA. What was unusual to Strain and Thorn was Dan Pierro gave them both a smile and a wink when he walked into the room. They didn't expect any warm welcome from any of the Directors. It would be five more minutes before Victor Corinth, head of the Secret Service, arrived. The atmosphere in the room was electric after formal greetings were exchanged but it went up ten notches when Randolph Atkins, of the FBI, arrived. No smiles or greetings were coming from him when he entered, he didn't even acknowledge the other Directors.

"What's up Thorn you and your buddies from Blight fucked the job up already?" He was bright red in the face everyone could see he made the comments to cover up his nerves.

"No, we haven't but you certainly may have," replied Strain.

"I wasn't talking to you," Atkins said, as he stepped towards Strain.

"Well, I was talking to you and I suggest you step back before you fall over in the shit you dragged in with you." Strain stood his ground and seriously wanted to head butt the Director.

"I have eaten bigger than you for breakfast. You're fucking with the wrong man." He pushed his body up against Strain's.

Atkins was baiting Strain in the hope that he would hit him. He knew this was the only way to get him thrown out of the country and off the operation. If he succeeded his department would take over the operation against the terrorists.

"Good to see that you are in one of your better moods, Randolph," said Dan Pierro as he stepped between the two men.

"Get the fuck out of my face," replied Atkins.

"You really need to do something about that bad breath of yours it smells like a burst sewer line," said Strain.

It took a lot for the other three directors not to laugh as Atkins' halitosis was famous in D.C., but nobody had talked about it, until now.

"Strain," Thorn gave Strain's arm a gentle tug to pull him away.

"It's OK, Thorn, nothing's going to happen but I am rather enjoying myself." He smiled at Thorn, as the other directors looked on with some amusement.

A female voice sounded, "Mr. Thorn and Mr. Strain, this way please." The President's assistant escorted them down the corridor.

"You seem to have upset Mr. Atkins," she said to Strain.

"Well, I had to let some air out of the old windbag before he burst," he replied.

She opened the door to the Oval Office, trying not to laugh and let them in.

The President was already walking towards them as they entered, "Take a seat and tell me what this is about."

Thorn and Strain could see that the President's mood had not changed.

"Sir, when the team arrived from the UK, I made arrangements for them to clear the usual immigration and customs channels quickly. Two members of the team had certain equipment with them that was handled by what I thought was ground crew. It turns out after some investigation that they worked for the FBI. By the time the equipment was placed into the vehicle that I had provided some of the equipment was damaged."

"What do you mean damaged? That could have happened on route," replied the President.

"Sir, if I may, the equipment we are talking about was in solid metal cases wrapped in foam molds. The cases weren't damaged therefore someone must have opened the case and damaged the items inside. We know it didn't happen at the UK end as the cases were taken to the plane and handed over to agents who immediately loaded them into a specified location in the plane's cargo area," said Strain.

"I see, so you think somebody, namely the FBI by your previous comment, has damaged the equipment. Why would they do that?" The President wasn't convinced that the FBI was involved.

"There is more. Since our last meeting, I personally have been under surveillance by members of the FBI, so have Strain and his team." Thorn saw the surprise in the President's face.

"I am finding this hard to believe. You really think that the FBI is involved?"

"Yes sir. They are involved, not just in surveillance on the street, but electronically in our hotel rooms. They have even tried to push two of my team into a fight," said Strain.

"Again, why would they start a fight?" asked the President.

"There can be only one reason. The team members involved would be arrested for assaulting government agents and they would then be thrown out of the country. They are trying to disrupt our operation by showing we are incompetent," replied Strain.

"Sir, I honestly believe that what Strain has said is the only reason for them to interfere with us. The FBI has lost some face over Strain's team being brought in and they have also recruited certain sources from the CIA in the surveillance. I honestly don't think that Director Shattuck knows his department is involved, I may be wrong." Thorn had it from a good source in the CIA that the request for the CIA satellite surveillance was from Atkins to an old friend in the CIA.

"When you say, they tried to push them into a fight, did they or didn't they?" asked the President.

"Yes, they did in a bar in the city, but they were taught a lesson in manners," replied Strain.

"A lesson in manners." The President gave a laugh at the thought, more of a laugh than he meant to.

"Yes, sorry sir," replied Strain.

"Sorry, I would have liked to have seen that lesson in manners, were your men injured?"

"No, sir but I can't say the same for the other side. We would have had the cops knocking on our hotel doors if it weren't for Thorn here and his contacts."

When Thorn got the call from Strain about bar incident, he'd called the Chief of Police for D.C. and told him it would be handled internally. The chief agreed not to send officers to investigate the incident and cleared the report as false at the dispatch end.

"Anything else?" asked the President.

"I think that's enough, sir, I hope we have already proven our point." Thorn didn't see the point in mentioning the incident at the harbor restaurant.

"Sounds like there is more, but you're right let's get them in and the Directors can explain themselves. I don't think the Secret Service or NSA need to be in here. I'll let them go about their business. I'll have a quiet word with them this evening they'll be at an event I'm attending." He walked over to his desk and pressed the intercom button, "Please send in Atkins and Shattuck. Tell the other Directors I'll see them tonight."

The President rejoined Strain and Thorn carrying a folder, but this time he sat on a chair next to them. A sign to the incoming Directors which side he was on.

"Sit down," said the President when the Directors entered the room.

"Yes, sir," replied Pierro.

"I'll make this as short as possible. When we met and I introduced you to these gentlemen in this very room, I told you to give them full cooperation and not to interfere or obstruct them."

"I haven't, sir," said Pierro in surprise.

"Let me finish, Dan. It's very clear that the opposite has happened and members of your agency, Director Atkins, have gone against my orders. I have proof that the team has been under surveillance since the minute they set foot on US soil. They have had equipment damaged and have been set upon by members of the FBI. What have you got to say for yourself and your department Director Atkins?" The President was calling him by his surname to let him know how official he was making this.

"These claims I take it are from those two and they are outrageous and false."

Atkins' face was getting red again, as it had been in the anteroom when he tried to bait Strain.

"Yes, they are making these claims and you are saying they are liars, a strong accusation." The President knew that what he'd been told by Strain and Thorn was true, he could already see it in the Atkin's face and by his fidgeting in the chair.

"I would say mistaken. They are running around the streets of this country like a couple of cowboys doing God knows what." Atkins pulled at his tie as he could feel the room getting hotter.

"They must be a lot better than the fucking cowboys you employ because they caught your people in the act and chastised them for it. Maybe we need to rethink how we train the FBI agents in surveillance and from what I hear hand-to-hand combat," replied the President.

"Sir," Atkins replied knowing not to push it further.

Strain and Thorn both looked at each other and gave a victory smile.

"Let me be clear one more time. Nobody is to interfere, obstruct or investigate these men and their team as long as they work for ME." The President shouted the last word so loudly it even startled Strain and Thorn.

"Sir, these two are not what we need," said Atkins.

The President cut him off, "For once in your life, Randolph, know when to shut the fuck up and listen, do you understand my directive?" The President kept his voice at a much higher level for emphasis and a little out of frustration.

"Yes, sir," replied Atkins.

"Butch, I suggest that you do an internal enquiry as to who is responsible for providing satellite surveillance for the FBI without your consent. Director Atkins would be a good place to start with your questions. Let me know the results within the week, please." He was letting Atkins know that he had to give up his CIA contact.

"Right away, sir," Shattuck was relieved nothing else came from his department.

"That's all except we will talk further, Director Atkins, when you give me a full report about your department's involvement within the week also. No bullshit in there either as it had better match up this very extensive report I have in my hand. Photographs, video tapes, voice recordings need I go on?" He waived the folder at Atkins.

"No, sir," Atkins replied.

Atkins left the office with his head down, he'd well and truly been found out. What made it worse was that the agents had been caught keeping surveillance.

Strain and Thorn now knew what the folder was for, a little bit of deception for effect by the President.

"Give them fifteen minutes to leave, gentlemen and then go about your business," said the President.

"Yes, sir," Strain and Thorn said at the same time.

They went straight to the anteroom to give the Directors time to leave.

"What a crafty move that was with the folder," said Strain.

"The old man didn't become President without getting to know a few tricks. We have a clear road now, John, we just have to get results," replied Thorn.

CHAPTER 25

NEW YORK CITY

Strain arrived at Newark airport to be greeted by the same Mafia driver who had met him the first time and assisted the team to the apartment.

Thorn was due to arrive about two hours later, as he was arranging an assortment of vehicles and surveillance equipment for the team to use.

After several dry runs around parts of the city performing counter surveillance, they arrived at the apartment where the rest of the team was waiting. Strain liked the look of the old buildings, he could imagine that they looked much different when the Italian immigrants arrived at the turn of the 20th century. The streets would have been bustling with people, washing lines full of drying clothes hanging outside tiny apartment windows. Hawkers would have been in the streets selling goods and trying to offer services to the local residents. He thought that it was amazing that over four and half million Italians arrived in the US in a fifty-year period. A third of the total population of Italy had left their homeland, the vast majority of them impressionable young men.

"I have something for you in the trunk," said the driver, as he pulled into the enormous underground parking garage attached to the apartment.

Strain got out of the car just as the driver was opening the trunk, there was a giant cooler inside and he passed it to Strain.

"Thanks, what is it?" he asked.

"A food parcel from the boss," he replied.

Strain put it on the floor and opened it. He knew straight away by the smell it was meatballs. A large chunk of cheese, two Italian bread sticks and a couple of bottles of wine were also inside.

"Tell him thanks."

The cooler weighed a lot and Strain was glad it had wheels on one end.

Strain arrived in the apartment to the calls from the team of, "Where have you been? It's about time you got here," the usual banter from the team.

"I have been busy in the kitchen making food for you fat bastards," he opened the cooler.

"Oh, get that on the table," said George.

"Are we clear here, George?" Strain was asking if they had swept the apartment for listening devices.

"Yes, and running interference," he replied.

George and Chalky had set up some technical equipment that sent out electronic noise into the apartment. The noise was above the hearing capabilities of the human ear but really screwed up any device that was trying to listen in from inside or outside.

Thirty minutes later, they all sat down at the kitchen table for an early lunch.

Strain had cooked up some spaghetti and put it in a giant bowl he then poured the meatballs and sauce on top, decorated it with a generous helping of Parmigiano Reggiano cheese. The two bottles of red wine were already open when he placed the bowl in the center of the table. Steam drifted to the ceiling from the meatballs and pasta as the room filled with the smell of the sauce.

"Bloody hell, that smells good," said Wheels.

"Thank you, mother," Bulldog said to Strain.

"If you don't eat it all, you will have it for your breakfast," replied Strain something his mother used to say when he was a child.

The freshly cut bread didn't last long and they managed to clean out the bowl of pasta between them.

"Right lads, down to business," said Strain.

A very loud belch erupted from Chalky White's throat.

"Bloody hell, Chalky, it's a wonder you didn't throw up," said Shadow.

They all complained to him at once, wafting the air to break up the stench of his belch.

"Yeah! Yeah! Stop whining," said Chalky.

Strain continued, "We have the assistance of two of the local organized crime gangs based here in New York City. One is the local Italian mafia and the other is a Chinese Triad family. They are both trying to locate the Muslim extremists responsible for the bombings. One is Don Caputo. He controls most of this part of the city and business entities regarding organized crime. The other is Jimmy Chu, the biggest triad boss on the North-East coast of the US. The bomb that went off in the Village area of the city was targeting both of them. Obviously, someone had one or both under surveillance and it almost paid off." Strain took a drink of wine.

"Do they know what we are here for?" asked Bulldog.

"Yes and no. They know that we want information from the terrorists, but I declined to tell them that we would kill the terrorists whenever we had chance. If we don't get them, I don't think we will need to worry about them living long once those two find out where they are. We are going to have to work with them, no matter what, or at least until they find Mohammed and his people. There is a slight problem with Don Caputo," Strain had paused long enough for a question from Shadow.

"Would that problem involve the law enforcement agencies?" he asked.

"Yes, it would The Don is under constant surveillance from the FBI. We need to try to disrupt the surveillance long enough for him to get the information for us." Strain knew that they would enjoy this.

"Well we can certainly screw up their electronic surveillance," said Chalky.

"We could sweep the Don's place for him and remove any bugs they may have placed inside," George was excited at the thought of seeing the inside of a real Don's home.

"We will need to have his phones scrambled as well," said Chalky.

"Whatever you two think needs doing, do it, just don't get caught by the Feds. Shadow, figure out where they are keeping surveillance from and what cars they are using. Wheels work with Thorn, see what kind of cars we will need to outrun

the Feds if we have to and figure out a blocking strategy." By"
blocking strategy," Strain was telling him to arrange for vehicles
to be available to block roads if they are followed.

"When do we meet the Don?" asked George.

"All in good time. Work on your equipment and put a list
together of anything you may need." Strain could see the
excitement building in his team.

"What about firearms and stuff?" asked Bulldog.

"We will have them tonight. Thorn is having them
delivered to the Gulfstream."

"You think we can trust him?" asked Shadow.

"As sure as I can be. He and I had a meeting with the
President about the FBI keeping us under surveillance,
tampering with our equipment and Bulldog and Shadow's little
fight," he replied.

"What did he have to say about the fight?" Bulldog
didn't care, but he didn't want the team to be sent home because
of it.

"Well, I told him that my team members taught the
attackers some manners which he found to be rather funny. The
president was OK where we are concerned, for now anyway.
Thorn backed us up one hundred percent we will finish what we
came here to do. The FBI Director has had his rear end chewed
off by the President, so watch out for the Feds they may want
some payback. To change the mood, how about some music?"
said Strain as he stood up and turned on the CD player. It was a
track from the Band of Gypsy's album by Jimi Hendrix called,
"Machine Gun."

"How great is that machine gun and we are going to do
work with the Mafia," said Shadow.

"A toast to success," said Bulldog raising his glass.

"Success," they all shouted and drank to the toast.

Strain's phone rang. He looked at the caller ID and saw
the code he'd put in for the Don's number.

"Hello," he said.

"Are you in New York?" asked the Don.

"Yes."

"Remember where we met the first time? Be there one hour from now, urgent." The Don said no more.

"I'll return soon. Lads stay here until I get back," said Strain.

Nobody asked why, they knew he would ask them to be with him if they were needed.

It didn't take Strain long to get to the meeting location. He was walking towards the building when a car pulled alongside him.

"Get in," said the driver.

Strain recognized the driver as the one that met him at the airport and got into the back of the car.

"Hello John," said the Don.

"What's the problem?"

"Those Arab bastards tried to blow me and Jimmy Chu up when we met at his daughter's art gallery."

"I heard are you OK, was anyone hurt?"

"Yes, my driver got a little shaken up but none of our side was hurt. I got this address from one of our longshoreman today," he handed Strain the address.

"I hope to have further information for you soon. I have a lot of people searching for the terrorists and it looks like we may have found at least this one location. I have given instructions that the warehouse is to be left untouched and nobody is to approach them or ask questions. I look forward to killing the bastard that killed my men and tried to kill me. Once we know where he is, I'll take care of him personally."

Strain knew he meant it and had to tread carefully so as not to upset him.

"I understand, but I do need to obtain information from them first. It's crucial that they talk about the terrorist attacks they are planning and who is involved."

"Yes, yes, you will have your time. The address is in Port Newark, a very busy container terminal. This is a basic map of the port with the warehouse you are looking for marked in red."

"I'll have my team put surveillance on the warehouse, with some luck we might be able to get in quickly. Obviously, the hope is we will be able to catch them planning operations or giving up names of accomplices, safe houses you know the usual stuff." Strain sat back as he could see that this didn't go down well with the Don for some reason.

"You say quickly. What do you mean by that?"

"We will look at it tonight." Strain was hoping that the Don wouldn't jump the gun and send some of his men to kill the occupants.

"Here are eight passes for the dock if you need them, they will get you anywhere you need to go."

"OK and here is something for you." Strain handed the Don a small grey box with a button type switch on the side. On the top of the box was a line of green lights going backwards and forwards.

"What's this?" asked the Don.

"You use this in your car and it will interfere with anyone trying to listen in to a conversation you are having. One of my mad tech guys made it and we have tested it many times. It really works don't ask me how it just does. All you have to do is press that button on the side and the lights will show Green. If they show Red, someone is trying to listen in but they won't be able to hear or record. It just shows you that someone is trying to listen to you and this little gadget lets you know about it."

"I'll keep this in the car it will mess with the Feds," replied the Don with pleasure.

"It won't work inside a building too many bricks and concrete."

"OK, get those Arab bastards quick because if they strike again, I won't wait for you or anyone else," said the Don.

"I'll let you know when we find out something." Strain got out of the car.

CHAPTER 26

Strain arrived back at the safe house where the team members were waiting for him after his short meeting with the Don. As he was entering the parking garage, a vehicle pulled in behind him and flashed its lights. Strain pulled his handgun out of his center console just as he heard Thorn's voice.

"I'll follow you in, John," shouted Thorn.

Thorn put his interior light on inside the car so that Strain could see that it was him.

Both men drove into the underground parking garage, Thorn closed the roller garage doors behind them.

"Have you seen the news?" said Thorn.

"No, I have just had a meeting with Don Caputo," replied Strain.

"Well, it looks like our terrorists are already moving things along. There was an explosion today outside the art gallery that Jimmy Chu's daughter owns."

"Yes, the Don mentioned it and is ready to start cutting heads off."

"These fuckers must be crazy or delusional to think they can attack Caputo or Chu without them retaliating. The news is saying it's a Chinese gang warfare situation but one of the dead is possibly Arabic."

"Let's go upstairs the team is waiting we can discuss it there," replied Strain.

"Roger that," he replied.

In the apartment, the team was gathered around the television set watching the news. They had seen the same report repeatedly about an explosion outside an art gallery. They all looked for telltale signs of what kind of bomb it may have been by the extent and design of damage that was committed.

"OK, lads this is special agent Thorn with the President's office. I just realized I don't remember your first name off the file I read on you." Strain lied, the file showed his name as Benjamin Franklin Thorn.

"Thorn is fine," he replied.

"Come on now, we would all like to know your full name, what is it?"

"As I said Thorn is fine," he said, smiling back at Strain.

The team shook hands with Thorn and they got down to business.

Thorn went through what surveillance equipment he'd acquired and the weapons he had in the trunk of his car downstairs. The surveillance equipment was in one of two vans at a secure parking garage that he would take them to.

"OK, now we know what equipment we have, we need to go straight to work. Don Caputo has given me information that there may be an Arab group of men operating on a dock in the Newark area. Thorn, do you know anything about the Newark container terminal?" asked Strain.

"Nothing other than where it is," he replied.

"I have a satellite picture of the site," said Chalky,

"Wow! He didn't hang around getting that," said Thorn.

"That's what Chalky lives for, computers and geek stuff, so does George. I won't leave you out, George," replied Shadow.

They all gathered around the computer monitor and looked at the satellite image.

"That's the one we want, according to this map the Don gave me," said Strain, pointing at a building.

"It looks like there are a lot of possible eyes and ears around there. Look at all of the warehouse type buildings and there are hundreds of containers," said Thorn.

"That's why they chose it, the perfect location lots of people and vehicles going in and out twenty-four hours a day," said Shadow.

"Let's have your thoughts," said Strain to the team.

A lot of suggestions were thrown out by the team and a plan was formulated.

They left the apartment to get the vehicles and equipment Thorn had sourced for them.

An hour later, they arrived at the dock area where the team split into four units. Strain and Thorn went to the building next to the target. Shadow was given the job of finding a way in and to see if anyone was inside. George and Chalky stayed in a surveillance van a block away, waiting for Shadow to return. Bulldog and Wheels kept surveillance on the east side of the building while Sleepy and L.B. watched the West side.

It took Shadow three minutes to find a way in through a ground floor window. There didn't appear to be any lights on inside, so he climbed through the window. Shadow crept around inside the warehouse, the only light inside was coming in from the street, he came out after ten minutes and called Strain on the radio.

"All clear inside. I suggest Chalky comes in with me. He can set up some listening devices and cameras."

"Roger that. Chalky, did you get that?" asked Strain.

"Yes, on my way," he replied.

"Come due south you will see me leaning on the corner of the building," said Shadow.

"Thorn and I'll meet you when you are inside, which side of the building are you?" asked Strain.

"East," Shadow replied.

Shadow and Chalky entered the building through the window.

Once inside, Shadow gave everyone a running commentary of the layout of the building over the radio.

"At the far end is an office, not much inside just a desk, chairs and a filing cabinet. When you come in, you will see there is a big rig with a container on a trailer, a flatbed truck with a mobile crane on the back. On the other side are several cars, one has a cover over it. At the end, closest to the office are several work benches with tools, blow torches and welding machines."

"OK, you and Chalky put listening devices and cameras wherever you think they should be, we will join you in a few minutes," replied Strain.

Shadow and Chalky worked their way around the warehouse, planting the bugs and cameras. Chalky placed the first bug and camera in the office then moved into the warehouse.

Strain and Thorn performed a check of the building next door to see if anyone was working. The place was in darkness but occupied by a shipping company. They were hoping that it was vacant as it would have made an excellent observation point. After twenty minutes, they had checked all the buildings around the target and all had occupants. There didn't seem to be any good surveillance point for them to watch the building. The only good thing was there was only one road in and out and that would help monitor vehicles.

"Let's look at that warehouse,' said Strain.

Sleepy and L.B. were watching the road that led to the warehouse area from the parking lot of a factory a block away. There were about twelve cars parked around them, owned by the night shift workers in the factory.

A car approached from the main road and they watched it as it drove past.

"One incoming towards your location, one male on board," said Sleepy.

Everyone became a little more alert at the news and waited for an update.

"Clear," said Sleepy, as the car turned down a side road.

Shadow was curious what car was under the cover in the corner but was busy planting devices with Chalky. He would wait until they had finished before he looked under the sheet. He started to put tracking devices on the vehicles when he heard Sleepy in his ear piece.

"Another vehicle coming your way, two males aboard."

As the car got level with them the street light lit up the faces of the men inside. Sleepy couldn't believe it they looked like they were Arabic. The car passed the side road and turned towards the parking area at the front of the building where Shadow and Chalky were.

"Everybody clear out, repeat, clear out," he said.

Strain and Thorn had just walked around the corner of the building to get in through the window when they heard the news.

"Chalky, come on, that's enough, we got to go," said Shadow when he heard Sleepy's voice. Both moved quickly towards the window and started to climb out. Chalky was first to go through, just as he heard a car pulling up to the front of the building. Strain and Thorn were waiting outside the window, as it was on the opposite side of the building to where the car was. Chalky jumped out of his skin when he saw them standing there before he realized who it was.

Shadow wanted to know what car was under the sheet and ran back to it as Strain helped Chalky through the window. He had one more tracking device left. He lifted the side of the sheet and placed the tracking device inside the wheel arch. He had just a glimpse of the back-door panel of the car when he heard voices by the front door. He heard the key being rattled into the door lock and quietly ran back the far side of the building. Thankfully, he heard the person with the keys opening a second lock as he started to climb through the window. The two men entered the warehouse and slammed the door shut just as Shadow closed the window.

George rolled up to the building in the surveillance van without any lights on and all four men got inside.

"Holy shit! You guys have balls of steal or you're just fucking crazy. You cut it so close. You had my heart pumping a little too fast, but it was fucking enjoyable," said Thorn.

"Welcome to the team," said Shadow as he sat on the floor of the van sweat running down his face.

"That's nothing - wait until they get crazy," said George laughing.

"Sounds like we are going to have some fun together," replied Thorn.

"That's all we need, another nut job," said Chalky, as he dodged a friendly slap from Strain.

"Did you get everything in place?" Strain asked Chalky.

"Not as many as I would have liked but enough in the main areas of the building."

"Well done," replied Strain.

CHAPTER 27

NEW YORK CITY

Shaady had been in the US for two years, his sister Karida had recently joined him by being granted a student visa to attend university. This was exactly the way in which he'd entered the US, but he was there for a different reason than his sister. She genuinely wanted to try and earn a degree. Shaady had been recruited for the greater Muslim cause, to eventually perform a duty on behalf of his brothers, as he saw them.

Shaady had worked for Sammy as a summer intern in his company for the two previous summers. Sammy had him working on several company projects that were sensitive, not only to his business but also for Mohammed, their spiritual leader and mentor. Sammy slowly gave Shaady tests of his loyalty and so far, he was passing in every aspect.

Sammy was looking forward to interrogating the brother and sister. He would to use it as an opportunity to gain information and to rape the sister. Rape was something he'd done in the past before he came to America. Women in the Middle East are much more submissive than women of the Western world. Sammy kept them in place whenever he could.

He'd met Karida on three or four occasions when he was with Shaady. He'd fantasized about her several times. She was to be his one day, he would make it happen.

Sammy put his ear to the apartment door. He could hear music inside, he knocked on the door. Keeping his ear to the door, he listened for movement inside. He could hear somebody walking towards the door. He stood back from the door slightly so that whoever was inside could see him clearly through the door viewer.

Karida danced towards the door when she heard the knock, she was thinking only of the dinner that evening. She stopped suddenly at the door, remembering her brother's words, "Always look to see who is at the door"'.

Karida slid the cover back on the door viewer and looked through the glass peep hole. She recognized Sammy straight away and wondered why he was here. She didn't like him he gave her the creeps. She put the door chain on and opened the door slightly to talk to him.

Sammy watched the door viewer, the glass was black and then a sudden flash of light and then black again. He knew that someone was looking through the viewer at him. He heard the door chain being slid into place and smiled, the chain wouldn't keep him out. He gave the corridor a quick look to make sure nobody was around just as the door opened.

"Hello, Sammy, I'm sorry Shaady is not home yet," she said.

"He said he would be here, in fact I am fifteen minutes late," he replied.

"I don't expect him for another hour."

Sammy saw a chance to con her into opening the door, if she didn't he would kick it open. "Not to worry, I'll come back, ah! Here he is. Shaady, how are you?" He was lying, as he walked away from the door. Karida, hearing Sammy say that Shaady was there, slid the chain off to open it for her brother.

Sammy smiled to himself, proud of his deception, as he heard the door chain being removed. He stepped back to the door and as Karida opened it, burst in, knocking her backwards off her feet. He was on her in a split second and put his hand over her mouth as she was about to scream. He punched her in the jaw, not quite knocking her out, as he kicked the door to close it. The door chain swung and jammed in the door frame, stopping it from closing completely. Sammy didn't see that the door was still slightly open and didn't care as he dragged the subdued Karida into the bedroom. He threw her on the bed and took his jacket off and placed his gun on a chair with it. He had an hour with the girl until her brother came home, he relished the thought as he tore at her clothes.

Karida tried to fight him and he punched her again, this time knocking her out. "Wake up, wake up," he said slapping her face. Karida was unconscious thankfully for her.

Sammy cursed that she was unconscious, as he liked his rape victims to struggle while he abused them. It wasn't going to be easy to wake her up so he carried on regardless. He would rape her a second time when she woke up.

Karida started to gain consciousness and realized something was weighing her down, she was struggling to breathe. As she opened her eyes she saw the fat face of Sammy a few inches away from hers, he was raping her. She came to very quickly when she realized what was happening. She screamed like she had never screamed before and thrashed out at the fat man.

As Shaady walked up the stairs in his apartment block, he couldn't help but look around and compare the squalid surroundings of the apartment building with his family home in Fez, Morocco. His father had worked hard all his life in the tourist industry, catering to the needs of foreigners on vacation who were living a life of luxury. His father would return home cursing the tourists after he'd spent many hours driving them around for a mere pittance of a wage. On the odd occasion, he would praise someone because they had made him feel that what he did was important. Those days however were few and far between. He always told his children that tourists were essential for the survival of the country and its economy and for the food on the table.

Shaady smiled to himself there were many fond memories of his childhood particularly with his sister Karida, his favorite sibling. She was dating Tony Caputo, the son of Don Caputo, the local mafia Godfather. Shaady was looking forward to going out to dinner with them as Karida had set him up with a blind date. She had told him that his date was very beautiful and was in one of her classes at the university. He managed to get off work a little early so that he had plenty of time to prepare for the dinner. He took the key out of his pocket and went to put it in the door lock when he saw that it was very slightly open. Karida must be home, he thought, but it wasn't like her to leave the door unlocked. He opened the door and entered the apartment taking his jacket off as he walked into the lounge which was also the kitchen. Karida's bedroom door was open. As he walked towards it he heard her scream out, it was a cry of pain. He grabbed a carving knife from the kitchen counter and instinctively shouted out her name as he ran into the bedroom, "Karida."

He saw his sister lying on the bed naked, other than a blouse that was pulled down her arms and around her back. He saw Sammy, naked from the waist down, climbing off her, blood around his crotch and fat belly. He couldn't believe what he was seeing. He looked back at his sister on the bed. There was blood on the bed and around the tops of her legs, Sammy had raped his beautiful virgin sister.

He screamed with all his might and lunged towards Sammy with the knife.

Shaady's pause to take in the scene of Sammy and his sister had given Sammy the opportunity he needed to get to his gun.

He heard the scream from Shaady and knew that Shaady was going to attack him. Sammy was fast for a man of his overweight size. Sammy jumped off the screaming wretch of a girl and rolled onto the floor, grabbing his 9mm revolver off the chair as he did so. As always, the safety wasn't set on the weapon and as he rolled over for a second time he had a clear, but very close, shot of Shaady. He fired twice, both bullets hitting their intended target one struck in the right side of Shaady's abdomen and the other went into his right hip, smashing the bone and exited through the right buttock, tearing it away as the bullet left the body.

Shaady didn't see the gun he just thought that his sister's rapist was scurrying out of the way. The loud bangs from the gun startled him. When he felt something knock him backwards off his feet, he knew he'd been shot.

Sammy got to his feet and picked up the knife that Shaady had dropped. He was looking down at Shaady when Karida jumped on his back. Karida was clawing at Sammy's head and punching him as hard as she could, screaming the whole time. He tossed her off his back onto the bed and lashed out with the knife as she fell. The blade caught her across the face opening a huge wound across her jaw and nose, blood sprayed out over the bed and curtains. Sammy gave Shaady a swift kick to the ribs as he lay on the floor in a pool of blood.

"I am going to finish what I came here to do and fuck your whore of a sister again for going out with that Italian dog," he said.

The kick was brutal and Shaady coughed up blood, it trickled down his cheek as he fought against losing consciousness. He heard his sister. She had not given up the fight she was attacking Sammy again. He couldn't help think what a brave soul she was. Their father would be proud. He tried to go to his sister's aid only to see Sammy attacking her with the knife, stabbing away at her body as she lay on the bed. He could hear Sammy saying something to his sister.

Karida fell backwards onto the bed with the force of the blow from the knife. She put her hand to her face it was covered in blood. Shock was her initial reaction then anger welled up in her like she had never felt before. She was up on her knees and throwing her arms around Sammy's neck, she dragged him backwards. She put her right arm around the fat man's chest and dug her nails into his skin dragging her hand back up towards her. She left four long deep scratches in his flesh. She heard her rapist scream out in pain as she clawed at him for the second time with the same hand.

Sammy felt the nails dig into his skin and tear away the flesh. A searing pain shot through his chest from the wound inflicted by his attacker. She was on his back when he threw his head back into the girl's face as hard as he could to get her off him. It worked, she lost her grip. He spun around with the knife and plunged it into her body. He had lost control and went into a frenzied attack that lasted several seconds. He would inflict over twenty deep stab wounds to her body. Blood was squirting everywhere as he stabbed the unconscious body. His brain went into overdrive, how dare a woman attack him? He was shouting at the already dead girl as he stabbed away.

"You fucking whore. I'll teach you to fight me, you and your mafia boyfriend. I'll enjoy killing the Italian shit and his father. Then we will see how big the great Don Caputo is."

He didn't even know that he'd shouted at the body, he was so incensed that she would dare attack him. She was a woman and she needed to learn the old ways and know her place. He plunged the knife into the body for the last time. He turned towards Shaady he was going to make sure that he was also dead, when he heard people running up the stairs. Sammy couldn't afford to get caught. He grabbed his jacket, trousers and gun and ran into the bathroom, locking the door behind him. This bought him enough time to put his trousers on and quickly wash some of the blood off his face and hands. People were in the apartment he could hear their shocked voices and screams as they discovered the two bodies. Sammy climbed out through the bathroom window onto the fire escape outside and made good his escape.

He ran down the alley at the side of the building, tearing his shirt off as he did so and putting on his jacket. He wiped the handle of the knife and his face with the shirt, removing the blood splatters. He threw the shirt and the knife into two separate dumpsters in the alley as he ran. He wanted to get as much distance as possible between him and the apartment. He knew that he had to make it to a safe haven, he had already run two blocks. The sounds of police sirens could be heard in the distance, arriving at the apartment where he'd left the bloodied bodies of Shaady and Karina. He was nearing the Italian quarter of the city and saw that there was washing hanging from one of the fire escapes a block ahead of him. He ran faster to the fire escape and climbed it.

Sammy sat on the fire escape for a minute to compose himself, trying to get his breath back. He pulled a blue shirt off the washing line on the fire escape and put it on. It was still partially damp, but it didn't matter, as he was sweating profusely. He now noticed that there was still blood on his hands and wrists. He had to clean them and reached to the washing line again for a towel. He used it to wipe his hands and face. A woman appeared at the window and he threw himself backwards against the wall so she wouldn't see him. She stayed by the window cleaning something inside. Sammy slid away down the fire escape unnoticed.

He already had a story formulated in his head for Mohammed. When he stopped at the apartment to ask the brother and sister questions, they both attacked him and they gave him no choice but to kill them. He knew Mohammed wouldn't care about their deaths, as they were just collateral damage. All Mohammed would care about would be whether they had talked about what they were planning. Sammy would tell him that he believed they didn't that they only attacked him when he asked Shaady to leave with him. They obviously thought that Sammy didn't believe their story and that Shaady was going to be punished. He kept telling himself that it was a good story, as if he wanted to believe it himself.

CHAPTER 28

The morning came around fast and with just a few hours' sleep, the team was already awake and eating breakfast in the apartment. In front of them on the large dining table, was a map of the warehouse they were in the night before. Chalky had marked where each listening device and camera was located. He was frustrated because he'd only just started putting the cameras in place when they had to leave.

"Here are the listening devices marked in Red and the two cameras marked in Green," said Chalky.

"We only had time for two cameras one in the office and one just outside looking at the vehicles inside," said Shadow.

"Well, it looks like you have enough ears in the place to pick up what everyone is saying," replied Thorn.

"Here is a road map showing all of the roads for a four-block radius." George had printed out twenty-four sheets of paper and made one street plan by taping them together.

"Christ, George, it looks like a jigsaw puzzle," said Bulldog.

"If it's too taxing for your tiny brain don't worry," replied George sarcastically.

"OK, lads, let's focus a minute, especially you, Bulldog and your brain," replied Strain.

"Bloody hell even Animal is having a go at me," said Bulldog.

"Animal?" questioned Thorn.

"A long story," replied Strain.

"I'll look forward to hearing it." Thorn didn't remember that in his file.

"When are you going to give Thorn a nickname?" asked Sleepy.

"In time," Strain smiled, he wanted to move on with the plans.

Nicknames were something that Strain gave all the team members in time and they had all stuck.

"How close do you need to be to get a good signal off the listening devices?" asked Strain.

"Two blocks is close enough. They are great cameras Thorn gave us," said George.

"OK, let's find a place for you to park in the van, or somewhere that may be available to rent. Which one of you wants to do the first twelve hours?" asked Strain.

"I will. The vans are like mini mobile homes, got a crapper and everything" said Chalky just beating George to the punch.

"OK, Sleepy, you stay with him make sure you have plenty of water, coffee, food, the usual."

"There's a building on the main road a half a block from the junction with the road leading into the area where the warehouse is. On one of the upstairs windows there's a sign saying "office for lease." This is too far away for Chalky in the van but it would be a great place to set up a camera to monitor traffic." Thorn didn't remember the phone number on the sign, but he did the name of the real estate company.

"See what you can do to get us in there, Thorn, as quickly as possible," said Strain.

"On it," he said walking away with his cell phone in hand.

"If we get in the office space, you take control of it, George and set up the electronics. Bulldog, will you stick with George until we find out if we can get into the vacant office?"

"Will do," he replied.

"The real estate office does not open until 8am," shouted Thorn from the other side of the room.

"Let's get things rolling anyway, Chalky and Sleepy, you head out now. As soon as Thorn gets through to the real estate agents, he can go to the office space and get George and Bulldog inside. There isn't much else we can do right now, so the rest of you just chill for a while." Strain didn't like sitting around.

"I'm going over to the office space that is for rent, just in case they have a janitor or someone that can let me in," said Thorn.

"We will follow Thorn that way we are in place as soon as he gets us in," said Bulldog.

"Sounds good. I'll call Don Caputo and let him know we have the warehouse under surveillance. Hopefully, once he knows we are already inside with ears he will keep his mob away.

Strain dialed the Don's phone number, not really thinking about how early it was.

The Don's phone rang four times and he answered, "Can't you sleep?" he said.

"Well, about as much as you, because you sound wide awake," he replied.

"I don't sleep much past six in the morning anymore, you know what they say the older you get, the earlier you wake up. What can I do for you?" He sipped on a hot coffee.

"Just letting you know that we are settled into the address you gave us," said Strain.

"You move fast, I'll give you that. Hold on my other phone is ringing,"

Strain could hear what sounded like another cell phone ringing in the background. The Don must have answered as the ringing stopped. He could hear the Don's voice in the background, but couldn't tell what he was saying.

"I'll call you back. It's our friend on the other phone," said the Don.

"Speak to you later." Strain knew he was talking about Jimmy Chu.

"Don't get tied up on anything we will be done in twenty minutes. Meet me at the last location, walk two blocks."

"Will do," replied Strain.

"Anything new?" asked L.B.

"Yes, we're going out. Wheels you are driving me, L.B., stay with us at a distance. Watch out for anyone keeping surveillance."

As always, they checked their weapons as they went down to the garage for the cars.

The drive to meet the Don took longer than usual due to the rush hour traffic. Wheels dropped Strain off as planned, two blocks from the Don's safe house. Strain saw the Don's car parked in a side street on the opposite side of the road, he ignored it and kept walking.

Strain heard Wheels in his ear piece, "You have company, black Lincoln, one driver, passenger windows blacked out in the back."

Strain knew the description was the same as the Don's car. He'd walked another half block when the Lincoln pulled up a little ahead of him. As he got within ten feet, the rear door opened and the driver's window came down. Strain could see that it was the Don's driver and he got into the rear of the car.

"Follow us," said Strain, as he got into the car.

Wheels voice confirmed in Strain's ear piece.

"We got company?" asked the Don.

"Yes, just one of my men driving me."

"Grey Camaro?" asked the driver.

"Yes, that's him," Strain replied.

"Drive," said the don.

"How was your meeting?" asked Strain.

"Possible interest for you, he gave me two names, Tony and Rudy Hoffman. They have done some work for our friend in the past in Detroit, just muscle stuff. He tells me that they have also been doing work for an Arab type goes by the name of Hamed. He visits a lot of gun shows around Michigan and knows a lot of the dealers. He buys a lot of firearms, rifles handguns etc. but plays it off as just a hobby. He has bought too many weapons for a private collection, unless he is a total gun nut. More recently, he has tried to purchase high end sniper rifles from a dealer in Flint, Michigan. The dealer was overheard by an undercover cop telling this Hamed guy to meet him at the next gun show in Flint and he would help him. The next day, the dealer's place was raided by ATF agents and he is sitting in jail."

"Why the hell didn't they wait to get the dealer in the act selling stuff to this Hamed guy?" said Strain.

"That's what I said, apparently, the undercover cop thinks that his cover was blown."

Strain was curious if the Hamed he was talking about was Hamed Drig, a longtime friend and supporter of Samir al

Bahrani. If it was him they were really onto something. Samir or Sammy as he is known was closely connected to Mohammed Ali Ghahi.

"This is good information your friend has good contacts," said Strain.

"Well, he thinks that he can get more information on the movements of the Hoffman brothers," said Don Caputo.

"Thanks again and we will be visiting your homes and a select eating establishment as soon as we can. As promised, we will sweep for bugs that may have been put in by the Feds and help you run some interference. It will really piss off the Feds listening in, if they are there." Strain smiled at the Don, hoping this would cheer him up.

"Good, I look forward to it."

They shook hands and Strain got out of the car.

Strain had walked a couple of blocks when he heard wheels in his ear piece, "Next side street, I am parked forty yards down.

"All clear in the street," said L.B.

Thirty minutes later, they arrived back at the apartment. Thorn called Strain on the Cell phone.

"We are in the office," he said.

"Is it any good?" asked Strain.

"Yes, perfect in fact, on the third-floor corner overlooking the main road. I have spoken to the real estate agent and she is meeting me here in about fifteen minutes. It looks like we can rent the place for a minimum six-month period, first and last month up front."

"That's great news. I have just had a meeting with our Italian catering company and they have some really good items for us, when will you be back here?"

"The realtor called the maintenance man and he let us in for a review and I told her we would take it. I told the realtor to bring the contract with her for signing, so I hope to be back in about an hour and a half," replied Thorn.

"See you soon." Strain was excited as things seemed to be slowly working out.

CHAPTER 29

THE BRONX, NEW YORK

Ehab and Idrees were sitting in the small living room of the apartment when the doorbell rang. The noise surprised both of them, as they were not expecting any visitors.

"Who could that be?" Idrees said nervously.

"I don't know, ignore it." Ehab replied.

This time whoever it was banged on the door and rang the bell at the same time.

"Hide the vests under the bed I'll see who it is." Ehab said, as he slowly walked to the door.

Idrees picked up both bomb vests and ran into the bedroom with them. In his rush, he banged one of the vests hard against the bedroom door frame. He froze for a brief second as he looked down at the vests, expecting them to blow up. He gave a sigh of relief and pushed them under the bed out of sight. He was shaking badly and sweat started to form on his forehead. He left the bedroom and stared at Ehab who was standing by the front door.

"Go inside," Ehab said waiving his hand at Idrees.

He did as he was told and returned to the living room and sat on the tattered sofa, his eyes focused on the front door.

Again, the doorbell rang, followed by a bang on the door.

"Who is it? He said.

"Open the door, Ehab," was the reply.

He recognized the voice, it was Mohammed. He'd spoken to him twice on the Imam's cell phone he opened the door quickly.

"Mohammed, what are you doing here?" He didn't reply but stepped into the apartment, closely followed by Sammy.

Ehab closed the door behind them, still very surprised at the visit.

"I am here to see my brave soldiers and wish them well," Mohammed said.

"Yes, we wanted to wish you well before you leave on your mission to see Allah," said Sammy.

Idrees walked out of the bedroom he too was shocked to see Mohammed.

"Idrees how are you?" Mohammed asked.

"I'm fine thank you," he replied nervously.

"I smell coffee," said Mohammed.

"Yes, in the kitchen, please join us." Ehab was now as nervous as Idrees, the great Mohammed very rarely showed himself.

"Are you ready for your mission?" asked Sammy.

"Yes," replied Idrees.

"And where are your vests? I do not see them," asked Mohammed.

"They are under the bed. I hid them there when you rang the bell."

"Cautious, very commendable, did you take the photographs as instructed?" said Mohammed.

"Yes, we did about ten minutes ago."

"Good. I have come for the camera chip. We will be sending the photographs to many people to make them realize what brave soldiers we have and that we have more to follow in your footsteps."

"I'll get it for you," Ehab left the room and quickly returned with the envelope containing the camera chip.

"When is your vest being collected?" asked Mohammed.

"In about thirty minutes," replied Ehab.

The vest Ehab was to wear would be collected by one of the young fundamentalists that had been groomed at the mosque. The young man was working as a janitor at the court. He would place the vest in the trash can at the back of the court house. Just after he arrived at work, he would take the trash out through the rear employee door, as he did every day. He would then smuggle the bomb vest back into the court house and keep it hidden in the janitor's closet until Ehab arrived.

Mohammed sat and talked for ten minutes all the time he was evaluating Idrees.

"Where is the toilet?" asked Mohammed.

"Next to the bedroom," replied Idrees.

He left the room, as they poured another coffee out for Sammy.

They talked for another ten minutes and then left, leaving Ehab on a high and Idrees even more nervous than he was before.

Now that Mohammed had left, it was time for them to put the bomb vest on Idrees for the last time. Neither one said anything as they secured the vest tightly around his body.

Idrees picked up his CD player and put in a Green Day CD, one of his favorite artists and listened to it through his ear buds. Five minutes later, they were putting on heavy outdoor coats. They had both been given the money to buy the coats by the Imam to cover the vest's bulk. They hugged each other and said their goodbyes and left the apartment.

Their target was the local courthouse where two members of their group had been found guilty of planning terrorist acts and sentenced to ten years in prison. They had only been in prison for two days when the warning of retribution was sent to the federal authorities. The warning wasn't taken very seriously, as t it was believed to be a hoax. Security at the courthouse was very basic, with the cheapest kind of metal detection available. A police officer performed bag searches at each of the two main doors, but that was as far as the security check went. No special security was provided to the judges until they entered the courtroom itself, where a uniformed officer was on duty always.

The target for Ehab was the judge who had sentenced the two men to prison. Ehab would kill him in his own courtroom. He was to walk into the courtroom as a member of the public, to listen to a case being presented.

Idrees was to wait outside the courthouse main doors until he heard Ehab's bomb go off. When he heard the panic inside, he was to make his way inside, as everyone was running towards the exit. He would then detonate himself.

Ehab walked calmly up to the courthouse doors and entered. He gave the policeman his folder full of papers, all very legal looking and the policeman waved him on inside.

As he walked towards the back of the court building, he watched the people standing in the hallways. There were a lot of attorneys with clients going through their cases before they entered court, other people just sat on benches looking very nervous, waiting to find out the result of their case.

The restroom was directly next to the janitor's closet and next to that was a set of stairs which led down to the boiler room. Ehab knocked on the door to the janitor's closet three times and walked into the restroom. There was one man standing by the urinal and one of the four toilet stall doors was closed, with the engaged sign showing on the door lock. Ehab went into the last stall and closed the door. He had only waited two minutes when he heard the door in the stall next to him close. A roll of toilet paper rolled under the wall into his stall. He said nothing and rolled it back. He heard some shuffling, like someone was getting something out of a bag. The bomb vest slid under the wall to him, he then heard the stall door next to him open as the person left.

It took Ehab five minutes to check that all the wires on the vest were connected as they should be. He put the vest on and clipped the three plastic buckles across the front that held it in place and tightened the straps. Next, he put the heavy outdoor coat back on, feeding the wire with the detonator button on the end down the sleeve of the coat. He opened the stall door and looked at himself in the mirror. The coat covered the vest perfectly he was ready now.

He went to the second floor to Judge Dressler's court room and sat on a bench outside. He would wait until a small group of people entered and he would go in with them. A police officer passing him thought that he looked suspicious and approached him.

"Can I help you?" he said.

"No, I am just waiting to go into Judge Dressler's court room."

"Then why don't you go in?" asked the officer.

"I will soon. Courtrooms make me nervous," he replied.

The officer took this as a good reason, as he'd seen many nervous people parading up and down the court corridors.

MICHAEL J BENSON

"OK," he replied and walked away, still a little curious. This would save his life.

Ehab had his finger on the trigger device the whole time, in case the officer tried to make him leave. He could feel the sweat start to run down the middle of his back. He got up off the bench and followed a man and woman into the courtroom.

The courtroom wasn't very big and there were only about twelve people inside. It looked just like a courtroom he'd seen on television programs, rows of wooden benches and a table on either side at the front. The judge's bench at the head of the room looked ominous, with a large black leather chair behind it for the judge.

He was standing in the aisle, looking around the room, when someone tapped him on the shoulder.

"You need to take a seat," said the police officer behind him.

He cleared his throat and said, "Yes, I will."

Ehab moved to the front of the court and sat in the row reserved for the defense attorney's staff.

The policeman at the back of the room tutted to himself and walked down to him. "Sir, you need to move back a row or two. That is for the defense team."

Ehab stood up quickly, apologizing to the policeman, "Sorry, I am new to all this."

The policeman put his hand on Ehab's back to usher him to the seat, as the judge was due in the court room at any moment. He felt something unusual under the man's coat.

"Sir, what do you have under your coat?" he asked.

"Nothing," he replied and tried to push past the policeman.

"I would like you to step outside the court room for a moment, please," the policeman said.

"No, I have to be here when the judge comes in." He didn't realize that he'd blurted this out.

"Sir, you will be back in one minute," he said, holding Ehab by the arm.

Ehab panicked and turned to run towards the back of the courtroom where he thought the judge would be.

The big policeman was quick and grabbed him by the coat and pulled Ehab back towards him.

Ehab fell backwards and accidentally pressed the trigger, the bomb detonated.

The explosion was tremendous a giant roar and fiery light filled the courtroom. The explosion ripped the court benches from the floor, sending shattered pieces of timber and metal in all directions. Large pieces of the broken benches rocketed through the air like giant wooden javelins. Some pieces embedded themselves into the courtroom walls as others found human targets. There were no survivors in the courtroom all of them killed quickly and mercifully by the blast. The old solid wood doors on the courtroom saved several people outside from serious injury, as most of the shrapnel didn't make it through. The blast had split one of the doors in two and the second hung precariously by one hinge. Clouds of thick black smoke filled the room, as flames licked the ceiling scorching the concrete. The damaged courtroom doors were allowing the smoke to spill out into the hallway outside, creating more panic for people trying to find the exit. The sprinkler system activated, raining water down on the dead bodies and the devastation. It wouldn't take long for the water to do its duty and put out the flames.

Outside, panic and screams started almost immediately following the explosion, people began running towards the exit doors. Some of the court building staff and visitors assisted colleagues and people they didn't know, while others ploughed into whoever got in their way, knocking them down. These people had only one thing on their mind and that was self-preservation.

Mohammed was two blocks away on the roof of an office building that he'd gained entry to. He was watching the courthouse through binoculars, waiting to see what would happen when the bombs were detonated. He also wanted to make sure that Idrees carried through with the mission. Idrees was much too nervous in the apartment and Mohammed didn't think that he would go through with his part of the plan. He scanned the front of the court house for a second time trying to find Idrees.

"Where are you?" he said in a whisper.

That's when he saw Idrees standing next to a giant stone column in front of the courthouse doors, he still looked very nervous.

Even though Idrees was expecting the explosion from inside the court house, when it came, the sound still made him jump. He was now sweating profusely and couldn't control the shakes that rattled through his body. He gathered himself together and decided that he would go through with his part. He turned to look at the sky and said a quick prayer for additional courage. He was ready to go to his glory. As he looked down from the top of the steps, he saw a group of school children and what was obviously their teacher walking up towards him. He had to stop them entering the courthouse, he wouldn't have them on his conscience. He ran down the steps to send them away, planning to return to the court house and detonate himself inside the building.

Mohammed watched from the roof of the office building and saw Idrees run down the courthouse steps away from the building.

"You coward," he said out loud to himself.

He was ready for this and had booby trapped the back pack when he visited the apartment. He reached into his pocket and took out a remote-control device. Without hesitation or thought for Idrees, he pressed the button to detonate the bomb attached to Idrees' body. Mohammed looked through his binoculars so that he could see the bomb explode as it destroyed the coward's body.

Idrees ran down the steps screaming at the children to go away, waving his arms in the air as he ran. He looked like a deranged lunatic as he headed towards the school group. The teacher stepped forward to protect the children, not knowing what this mad man was going to do. Her bravery would be rewarded in her death, along with that of her sixteen pupils.

Mohammed watched the whole gruesome scene as a bright ball of red death erupted on the steps of the courthouse. The explosion threw the torn and tattered bodies of the children and teacher into the road. Car alarms were set off by the shock wave and a large plume of smoke was rising into the air above the deadly scene.

Mohammed was pleased that the bomb detonated but was angry that it didn't go off inside the courthouse as planned. The coward was dead they would still make the news headlines. He didn't need to see anymore, he left the area quickly.

CHAPTER 30

NEWARK, NEW YORK

Chalky and George had set up all the equipment for the surveillance of the warehouse. The room looked like any other computer-based office with a lot of monitors and electronic equipment. If the realtor came back, which they hoped she wouldn't, all she would see would be the backs of the monitors and screens.

Chalky was setting up two cameras that were on a continuous recording feed to one of the computers. One camera faced the main road and the other the side road that led to the warehouse. George had a facial recognition system loaded into the computer system. He hoped to get lucky and have a good identification of the people driving to and from the warehouse. The only downside to the surveillance, they couldn't see the entrance to the warehouse because a truck had parked across the street blocking their view. They had a camera on the door inside the warehouse so neither of them was too concerned.

All the hidden cameras and listening devices had been tested and were working well, as were the tracking devices.

"We are ready when they arrive," said Chalky, as he tested the second camera covering the road outside.

"I have put the camp bed and coffee equipment in the other room where it can't be seen," replied George.

The camp bed was so that they could take turns sleeping as they would possibly be in the office for several days. One of the team was due to arrive with supplies of food and water. They had asked for a small fridge to keep some of the food and drink cold.

"Here's our first car," said George.

Chalky went over to the monitor where George was and saw a dark blue car parking outside the warehouse. They both watched as two men got out of the car and walked out of sight towards the front warehouse door.

One of the listening devices inside the warehouse was picking up a faint metallic sound. They knew it had to be a key opening the door lock. The camera covering the door on the inside of the warehouse showed the door opening and the two men from the car entered. "I'll make coffee before the others arrive," came from one of the listening devices.

Chalky called Strain. "We have just had two arrive at the warehouse," he said to Strain when he answered the call.

"Good. Let me know if anything significant happens, at least we know they are there now."

"Will do," Chalky ended the call.

Within thirty minutes, four other men arrived at the warehouse and the place was getting very active. One man arrived on his own, dressed a little smarter than the rest and appeared to be the boss, as everyone stopped what they were doing and greeted him.

George could hear the conversation clearly and thought that he recognized the man's face.

"Chalky, take a look at this man, tell me if you know him?"

Chalky had a great talent for remembering faces and names.

"The picture is a bit bright because of that light in the ceiling," He stared at the man moving around the vehicles.

When they had put the cameras inside in the dark, they didn't know how they would be affected by the positioning of the lights.

"He is moving towards the office area. The picture is better in there," replied George.

Sammy was pleased that everyone was on time, as he hoped that they could complete the container work by the end of the day. He walked amongst the vehicles in the warehouse, giving everything a quick check. He could smell coffee and walked towards the office in the corner.

Fadi had grease on his hands from moving one of the tool boxes and went to the office to pick up some grease remover. As he was about to enter the office, Sammy walked inside. Fadi stopped, resting his greasy hands on the top of the door frame.

As the others entered the office, Sammy's phone rang. He walked out of the office onto the warehouse floor. The rest of the men sat sipping on the hot coffee as he talked.

"Stay in the office," he shouted to the rest of the men.

He walked to the warehouse door where he had come in and waited on the inside, Mohammed was on his way.

"Holy shit, one of them just put his hand on one of the cameras," said George, out loud.

Chalky ran over to the computer and saw that one of the cameras wasn't showing a clear picture. The camera inside the office showed four, possibly five men inside, one man was off the camera shot. The man in the doorway with his hands resting on the door frame walked inside.

"He has left dirt or something on the camera, it's useless," said George.

"Let's be thankful he didn't knock it down," replied Chalky.

"What's that guy doing in the warehouse, the one who just told the rest to stay in the office?"

"Looks like he is waiting for someone," replied Chalky.

"If he takes another step forward we will see his face clearly," said George hopefully.

The door to the warehouse opened and another man walked inside. The face of the man waiting inside was made clear by the daylight flooding in from the opened door.

Chalky stood back in surprise, "Fuck me! It's Samir al Bahrani, get Strain on the phone quick," he said, as he focused on the face.

George was on the phone straight away, as he now knew who this was, one of Mohammed's hierarchy.

Mohammed was quietly confident that his plan to hijack an armored truck would go smoothly. But he also knew that even the best plans had faults and that something unforeseen could happen. This played on his mind continuously and made him over-cautious in other people's minds.

As he approached the security gate at the entrance to the Port Newark dock, he took his false pass from the sun visor above his head. This was a very good fake, certainly good enough to fool the security guard at the entrance to the dock area.

The Port Police were his main problem anyway, not the hired security guard on the gate. The Port Police were always sniffing around the dock, especially when a ship came in from the Middle East or South America. Drugs were the prominent contraband from South America and guns from the Middle East. The Port Police even had a dive team that sometimes searched the bottoms of ships for hidden cargo.

He called the warehouse on his cell phone and spoke to Sammy.

"Is everything clear there?" he asked.

"Yes, everything is ready."

Mohammed easily passed the security check and parked his car by one of the warehouse buildings where the dock workers parked and walked over to the warehouse. The warehouse was on the opposite side of the container dock perimeter fence. He walked behind a tall stack of containers out of sight of the dock. The perimeter fence was made of chain link he'd already cut a part of the fence to make a quick hole to squeeze through.

Mohammed entered the warehouse through the main door and was greeted by Sammy.

"Good to see you again, how are you?" he asked.

"I am well," Sammy replied.

Chalky and George were glued to the computer monitors as they waited for the second man who had entered the warehouse to come into view.

"Come on, Strain, answer the fucking phone," said George.

"I have answered. What are you two chirping about," said Strain.

"We have eyes on Samir al Bahrani in the warehouse," George replied.

"That's very interesting, who else?" asked Strain curiously.

"Another man has just walked into the warehouse and he is talking to Bahrani. He has his back to the camera. I'll put you on speaker,"

"I can't see the other man yet, ah! He is moving," said Chalky.

As Strain waited he could hear the two techs talking to the computer monitor, telling the man to move.

"It's Ghahi, Mohammed Ali Ghahi," said Chalky louder than he realized.

"Chalky, are you sure," said Strain as he waved at Thorn and the other team members to get ready to leave

"Yes, it's him," Chalky couldn't believe it.

"We are on our way. Keep us up to date on the phone, we will switch to radio when we get close," replied Strain.

"Roger that," said a very excited Chalky.

The team members were on their feet by the time Strain finished the call.

"Chalky and George have just identified Mohammed Ali Ghahi and Samir al Bahrani at the warehouse. Thorn, you and I go together, the rest of you split up into three cars. Let's get the bastards," said Strain.

Strain and the Mask Team had dealt Mohammed a series of terrible blows to his terrorist campaign in the UK where he was responsible for several terrorist attacks. The team had disrupted his plans and killed several of his followers in targeted attacks. Mohammed had sworn to avenge the deaths of his followers and kill Strain. Mohammed had eluded Strain and his team in England.

Mohammed stopped to look around the warehouse. At the far end of the building was a large shipping container on the back of a trailer. A flatbed truck with a large mobile crane on the back was parked on the same side as the container vehicle. There were several cars and vans scattered around and what looked like a vehicle underneath a large dust cover. He walked towards it.

Sammy saw Mohammed taking in everything around the warehouse and followed him as he started to walk towards the covered vehicle.

"That is the special car," he said to Mohammed.

"I thought that it must be, as it's the only vehicle that is covered," he replied.

Sammy ran ahead of him and lifted the corner of the sheet, revealing just enough of the car to show Mohammed that it was a marked police vehicle.

"What do you think?" he smiled.

"It looks very good, very professional." Mohammed knew that Sammy had worked hard to get the vehicle to look as authentic as possible and it had paid off.

"We will start work on the shipping container this afternoon. It will be complete in two days." The timetable for getting the shipping container completed was getting tight and he knew it.

"Are you sure we will be ready to go by Friday?" Mohammed was disappointed that the work had not already been started.

"Yes, we have an extra day for any unforeseen problems. I have several our people working on the project and they all know that I want the shipping container and trailer ready to go on Friday. They are in the office waiting to meet you and start the briefing." He pointed to a corner of the warehouse where there was a set of stairs leading up to an office.

"Lead the way," Mohammed said.

At the top of the staircase, they entered an office. The office had windows that overlooked the entire warehouse, a good vantage point.

"As you can see I'll be able to watch over all the work from here." Sammy wanted Mohammed to know that he was, as always, in control of his troops.

"Yes, you have a good view from here. Where is the rest of your group?" he was anxious to get on with the meeting.

"Inside the next room," Sammy pointed to a door in the corner.

"Bring them in here."

Mohammed watched as five young men walked into the office. He greeted each one of them with the cultural kiss on each cheek.

"Tell me what you have planned?" He said to Sammy.

"As I said before, we will have the shipping container modification completed in two days. I want each of the group to tell you their part and what they have arranged for the smooth running of the operation. You know these men and they are eager to get started. Fadi will be the first followed by his brothers and so on."

Fadi stepped forward, "As you can see we have acquired a shipping container," he pointed to the warehouse below.

"The shipping container is called a forty-foot cube which is larger than the average shipping container. Its eight feet nine inches high and seven feet eight inches wide and forty feet long.

Modification on the bottom of the shipping container will start as soon as we finish here. We have obtained a US customs seal and the necessary paperwork for the shipping container to leave the dock when we are ready. The seal and paperwork will prevent any potential inspection by the security guard at the gate, as well as any policeman on the street. The trailer is the strongest we could find and it will be able to take the load we are going to put on it without a problem. I'll be the one to drive the trailer and Ghaazi my brother will drive the police car. We will be in position ready to follow the armored car as soon as it finishes collecting the cash from the last bank on his route. Ghaazi will drop in behind the armored car and I'll follow in the tractor trailer." He opened a map and laid it out on the table in the middle of the room. "This is where the last bank pick up is and this is where we will be waiting," he pointed out several red dots on the map. "I'll overtake the armored car before it gets to this area where it goes through a small disused industrial complex and then out past a park on the other side." He again pointed to the map. "This is where the diversion sign will be and Younis will be wearing the local electrical company uniform and holding a red flag. This is where the armored truck crew will get nervous and call the control room in their HQ if we do not act fast. As planned, on the other side of the diversion barrier in plain sight of the armored truck crew will be an electric power pole lying partly across the road, looking like it fell over. Next to the pole there will be an electric company vehicle. The police car will give them some comfort as they will see the police car stop and the policeman, Ghaazi, talk to the flag man. When they see the policeman drive on as directed by the flag man, they will follow the police car. Hopefully at this point they won't call their headquarters. They will follow the directions given by Younis as he waves his flag closely followed by myself in the tractor trailer. As soon as I pass Younis he will press a remote-control button which will operate a winch on the back of the truck that is parked next to the fallen electric pole. The winch has a cable that is attached to the pole and it will drag the pole out of the road into the ditch. Younis will then move the diversion barrier to block the road the armored car has entered. He will waive any other vehicles down the previously blocked road." He was interrupted by Mohammed.

"What is the size and weight of the armored car?" He asked.

"The armored car is just over seven feet wide and eight feet high. It has a gross weight of twenty-five thousand pounds and a pay load capacity of fifteen thousand pounds. We must do something with the wing mirrors as they will get in the way."

"Good, what next?" Mohammed was impressed with them as they had done everything that he'd asked and memorized their parts.

"Musaad will tell you the next part." In some ways Fadi was glad to hand over to his brother, Mohammed made him nervous.

"There is a bend in the road just three hundred yards from the junction where they meet the diversion this is where we will hijack them. I'll leave a very large electric company truck on the side of the road in such a position that the police car and armored truck will have to go over to one side of the road. I'll be in a crane on the other side of the road and it will look like we are working on the power lines over the road. We have everything ready to disable the armored truck and hijack it. We have two other men who will help with the hijack that Sammy has arranged plus he has four more at the location where we will take the armored car."

Mohammed had another question, "What does the armored truck have in the way of communications, panic alarms that sought of thing?" He was only asking a question to make sure that they knew their business.

"The armored truck has radio and satellite communications with the headquarters as well as a panic alarm which transmits a signal also. At manufacture, they install a guidance positioning system in the vehicle also. There is a ten thousand pound towing hitch on the rear fender of the vehicle, we will use to our advantage. We have someone operating inside the electrical company control room if enquiries are made the electrical company system will show that a crew is working at that location. The main power generation control room will also know that a crew is working there and won't be suspicious of any requests we make of them. The armored truck will be transported to the location that you give to Fadi once we have hijacked it." They didn't know where it was going Mohammed wouldn't tell them until the last minute.

Thorn drove the car with the other team members following closely behind. They were thirty minutes out from the warehouse and would cut it down to twenty at the speed they were driving. Thorn had taken one of the spare dodge chargers that had been fitted with a police siren and flashing police lights in the grille. New Yorkers had become accustomed to unmarked vehicles with flashing lights and sirens and were mainly obliging about getting out of the way.

Strain was on the phone to George and Chalky through the hands-free system in the car, "We are on the way, what's happening?"

"They are in the office area talking to a small group of men. It looks like they are planning something with a shipping container they are just starting to go into the details now."

"Can you put their conversation through to the cell phone so we can listen in?" asked Strain.

"Yes, here goes."

As soon as he said this the lights and computers in the office lost power.

"Shit we have just lost power in the office," said George.

"Lock the office door and wedge a chair under the handle. There is a wall ladder in the corner of the second office it leads to the roof, get the fuck out," shouted Thorn.

"You think they have been discovered," said Strain.

"I don't know but we need to play it safe I don't think those two are fighters," Thorn replied.

"No and they aren't armed, what the fuck is going on?" Strain was genuinely scared for George and Chalky.

George was wedging a chair under the door handle when he heard footsteps outside. He ran towards the room where Chalky was and scrambled up the ladder as Chalky was opening the hatch above. He could hear someone banging on the office door whoever it was they were shouting something.

George froze on the ladder as he heard the man shouting again.

"If you can hear me the breaker box in the basement has blown, I'll get it working soon."

George got down the ladder and stopped at the bottom listening for any further noise.

"What are you doing?" asked Chalky as he held open the hatch to the roof.

"I think it was a power cut in the building," he replied.

"Stay there I'll go on the roof," Chalky replied.

Chalky walked to the edge of the roof keeping far enough back that he couldn't be seen from the street. The traffic lights in the road were working and so where the lights in the building across the street. He ran to the back side of the building and looked over the edge carefully. There were two men and a woman standing by one of the fire exit doors smoking cigarettes. He went back to the roof hatch and climbed down into the office.

"George there are three people out back smoking cigarettes, I am going to shout to them from the window."

"Be careful," he replied.

Chalky looked around through the windows to see if there was anyone outside watching them, there wasn't. He opened one of the office windows and immediately got the smell of cigarette smoke. He looked outside quickly and bobbed his head back again. They were still there talking about lunch, he was going to shout down to them.

"Hey is your power out down there?" he said the smokers with his head and shoulders outside the window.

"Yeah happens every couple of weeks in this place, it will take him about forty-five minutes to an hour to fix it," replied one of the men.

"Thanks," replied Chalky.

George was on the phone to Strain again, "Panic over it's a power cut in the building."

"As long as you two are OK," replied Strain.

"Yeah we're OK but we don't have any visual or sound until the power returns."

"We are still heading your way about twelve minutes out now."

"Wow that was scary for a minute, at least they are safe," said Thorn.

For once the power came on in record time in the building it only took twenty-five minutes.

George and Chalky quickly worked to bring the camera and sound receivers back up.

"We are live again," said Chalky.

They both looked at the screens and could see Mohammed and Samir in the warehouse by the door. The sound kicked in just as Mohammed was walking out of the door.

"Shit Mohammed is leaving," said George as he dialed Strain's phone again.

Chalky took one of the surveillance cameras that was watching the road and aimed it at the parking area of the warehouse building.

"Mohammed is leaving we are waiting to see which car he is in," George said to Strain.

"OK keep the line open while you are watching him," replied Strain.

Chalky zoomed in to the parking lot trying to see if Mohammed had walked from another parking area.

"Samir is leaving," said George as he watched the monitors.

"I see a maroon car driving away from the parking area maybe Mohammed is in the car with him." Chalky zoomed the camera lens in on the front seat of the car.

"Anything?" asked George.

"There isn't anyone in the car with him," replied Chalky.

"He could be lying down in the back," said Thorn.

Chalky stood up from the camera and looked towards the warehouse. He couldn't see him in any of the streets leading from the warehouse. Chalky was frustrated how could they miss him? He watched him leave. Then in the container yard behind the warehouse he saw someone walking across the huge area where the shipping containers were stored. He picked up the video camera and zoomed in it was Mohammed he was disappearing behind a building.

"I see him he must have gone through the container terminal fence. He is on the container base dock area but I don't have a visual." Chalky was somewhat pleased that they didn't miss him.

"That sneaky bastard has always got another exit," said Strain.

"I don't think there is any point in racing there now as both of them have gone. We will only blow the operation if we go to the warehouse now," said Thorn.

"Yes, I agree, let's head back, did you get that George?" asked Strain.

"Got it, we will send you the license plate number of Samir's car," he replied.

CHAPTER 31

CALIFORNIA

Hakeem Ali Shamoun, he was named after his father but also because Hakeem meant, 'wise one', in the Muslim world. Meanings in Arabic names normally embody beauty or kindness and on the Day of Judgment it's believed that you will be called by your name. Ironically Arabic names are sometimes sourced from the Old Testament not just the Qur'an, with the most popular name in the world being Mohammed after the prophet and founder of Islam, a name which has numerous spellings. His father had thought long and hard about calling him Mohammed but thought that this was too great a name to bestow on his son. Some Western people who switch to Islam change their born name for an Islamic name, people like Cassius Clay changed to Muhammad Ali and the singer Cat Stevens changed to Yusuf Islam.

Hakeem had been living in America for seven years, the first four as a student at the Southern University of California. He kept to himself most of the time, socializing whenever it was needed so that he didn't bring attention to himself as being a loner. He was popular with the small group of friends once again not standing out just a nice ordinary guy. He didn't get involved in any political or religious debates with his friends or as part of his curriculum. He obtained a degree in Business Management with honors finishing second in his class. He could have done much better but his remit wasn't to stand out just be a good student.

Fortune had shone upon him in the early years in America and it all seemed too good to him. To his shock and amazement only a month after he submitted his application for permanent residency his name was pulled out of the Immigration lottery giving him an instant green card. He saw this as a sign from Allah that it was his destiny to fulfill the wishes of his masters in the future. Of course, he had to get through all the usual background checks by the immigration authorities and the FBI. He knew that they wouldn't find anything in the way of a criminal record or anything else for that matter that would obstruct his application for a Green card. His hidden life of radical Muslim support and terrorist training wouldn't be discovered by any of the authorities.

The Green card meant that he would be a permanent resident with the ability to apply for Citizenship later if he wished. Hakeem had been working for Aloha airlines as a flight attendant for a little over a year. He was an exceptional employee and showed no signs of radicalism or interest in the Muslim faith.

It was time for him to check the PO Box he had set up to receive any potential mail from his leaders, as always, he did this on a week day. The post office was always busy during the week this gave him more cover and nobody would remember him. He opened the PO Box and as usual didn't expect to find anything, this time he was wrong. Inside he saw a plain white envelope facing him on the front of which he could see his name and PO address neatly typed. He stirred at the envelope inside the grey metal box for what seemed like an eternity he then quickly snatched it out of its hiding place. As he closed and locked the PO Box he put the envelope in the inside pocket of his jacket and quickly walked away.

As he approached the doors of the post office he realized he was rushing he could feel his heart beating and he slowed himself down. He walked slowly to his car performing his usual discreet surveillance of the parking lot and surrounding area. He had been trained well he couldn't see any obvious signs of a surveillance team the area appeared to be safe. He took his car keys out of his pocket and pressed the unlock button on the remote control he heard the doors unlock. The grey Toyota he owned had been chosen deliberately so as not to bring any undue attention to him. As he opened the door someone placed a heavy hand on his left shoulder and a deep male voice said, "Excuse me."

Hakeem visibly jumped with surprise as he didn't see the person come up behind him.

"Sorry I didn't mean to startle you," the man said.

Hakeem was looking at him his eyes wide open with surprise and his mind was going wild as to what he should do. Should I knock this man down, should I get in the car and drive away how did I not see him? All these things raced through his mind.

"Can you tell me where Sonoma Drive is, I am trying to find Toll Technologies?"

A weak smile came over Hakeem's face as he replied, "Yes turn right out of here and go to the third traffic light, turn left and that will lead you into Sonoma Drive."

"Thanks," the man said as he turned and walked away to a red Ford vehicle that was double parked with the engine running.

Hakeem got into his car and gave a big sigh of relief he could feel the sweat running down his back and realized that he was more nervous than he would have expected to be. His days as a terrorist sleeper where soon to come to an end and his first set of instructions in the envelope in his pocket would make him active.

As he drove out of the post office he saw the red Ford ahead of him he questioned whether this man was really looking for Toll Technologies maybe he was under surveillance or maybe now he was becoming paranoid. Again, he put his training into effect and followed the Ford at a safe distance. He could see the driver was looking around at street signs and had the appearance of someone that didn't know where he was. Five minutes later he saw the car turn into Sonoma Drive and then turn into the parking lot of Toll Technologies. Hakeem started to relax and drove home to his condo on the south side of San Diego.

Once safely inside his condominium he removed the envelope from his jacket and opened it. Inside was a small key and a PO Box address and nothing else, no instructions, no information, no contact, his stomach turned over as he swallowed deeply.

He checked his watch it was 5.15 in the afternoon he had fourteen hours before he had to report for his morning flight to

Maui. He had time to find the PO Box address on the computer. As always, his lap top was on the breakfast table in the corner of the room, he switched it on and sat down while it booted up. It only took him two minutes and he had a map printed out giving the exact driving directions from his condo to the PO Box location forty-five miles away. The PO Box was in a store and not a US post office, the telephone number was on the internet sight, he called only to be told that they would close at seven pm and open at seven in the morning.

He didn't sleep very well the thought of what was in the PO Box and what he would be asked to do keep him awake most of the night. Five o'clock in the morning and he finally gave up trying to sleep and made a pot of strong coffee. After a shower, he dressed in his flight attendant uniform. He looked at himself in the mirror knowing he looked handsome in his uniform and much younger than his twenty-five years of age. He used his good looks to his advantage when attracting his female counterparts on the flights. He left early for work as the PO Box location was only ten miles from the airport. The Mail Boxes etc. store was in the middle of a long strip mall with very limited parking. Hakeem followed another car through the small parking lot as they both searched for a vacant space. This was perfect for Hakeem as it gave him time to perform his counter surveillance. A car reversed out of a space ahead of him and he drove forward and parked in the vacated slot. He locked the car and walked in the shade of the front of the strip mall again performing a discreet appraisal of the area.

When he entered the store, he saw that the right-hand wall was a mass of PO Boxes. The left-hand wall hand various things for sale on shelves. The customer service desk was at the far end of the room. The was a customer being served and two others waiting in line, this would give him the opportunity to locate the PO Box he needed without the staff or customers realizing that he didn't know where it was. Box 121 was in the center of the wall about two feet off the ground he wasted no time and opened it. Inside was a small cardboard box he removed it, locked the box and quietly left the store.

He drove all the way to the airport with the box on the front seat. He occasionally looked down at it wondering what was inside.

At the employee parking lot, he swiped his I.D. card in the reader at the security gate and it slid open with a rusty metallic sound as the iron wheels rolled along the rusting track. He drove inside and found a parking space in amongst the other vehicles. He picked up the box from the front seat and opened it carefully as he didn't want to damage the contents. Inside was a small silver cell phone, a charger, a plastic bag containing three sim cards and three pre-paid phone cards. At the bottom of the box was an instruction booklet on how to use the phone. He didn't need the book to know how to turn the phone on and did so immediately. It came to life with a green light on the display panel this was closely followed by a welcome message from Verizon Telephone Company. He was about to put the phone in his jacket when it gave a single beep and an envelope appeared on the display indicating that he had a message. He now realized why he needed the instruction booklet and quickly scanned through to find out how to obtain his messages. He followed the instructions and listened to the message that had been left for him. It was an electronically disguised voice that told him that he would receive another message soon and that he would have eight hours to respond. Eight hours to respond he thought to himself, that was ok as his flights to and from Maui were only just over five hours. He would leave the phone switched on until the last minute when he boarded the aircraft.

CHAPTER 32

NEW YORK CITY

Thorn obtained the name and address details for the car that Samir was using at the warehouse.

"Strain that car that Samir or Sammy as I believe he is called is registered to a company called, 'Computer Parts US' out of New York. The registered owner is one Sammy Barn I guess our guy wanted to use some of the letters in his own name. I have the address where the office is supposed to be I'm going over there," said Thorn.

"Hold on I'll go with you. Shadow do me a favor and give Chalky a call let's see what he can find out about this company?" replied Strain.

"On it," he replied.

"It will be quicker if we take the subway, the traffic will be horrendous getting there," said Thorn.

"You know the place much better than me, let's do it."

Whenever Strain was in New York he rode the subways a lot not just for the convenience but they reminded him of the subway system in London. They walked past the usual street beggars as they went down the steps to the platform below. There were people hurrying and scurrying everywhere with no regard for others or awareness of their surroundings. Strain could see just about everyone was talking, texting or just looking at the screen on their cell phone. There were tourists standing in front of the subway map on the wall trying to figure out which way they had to go. It was no wonder so many people were robbed or mugged on the subway system, he felt like screaming out, pay attention to what's around you.

Thorn bought two passes for the subway that were good for one week anywhere on the subway system. He handed one to Strain and walked to the ticket machine that opened the turnstile to allow you onto the platform.

After a short run down some steps they were on the platform waiting for the train. The dark and musty smell of the subway was somewhat pleasant to Strain but he didn't know why. The wind picked up on the platform as the approaching train pushed the air out of the tunnel. He could see the lights on the front of the train now as the people on the platform took a slight step back. They didn't step back too far for fear of losing that spot they had already designated for themselves.

It took no time at all and they reached their final subway destination only one block from the business address.

"We can do a quick circle of the block that the building is on to get an idea what it looks like on all sides. With luck, it will have a side or rear fire escape like most of the other buildings in this area," said Thorn.

"Sounds good," replied Strain.

They walked past a woman who was sat on the subway floor playing a guitar and singing, 'Cry Baby,' by Janice Joplin. Strain was amazed how good she was and the acoustics of the subway tunnel only made her sound better. He bent down and dropped a ten-dollar bill into the open guitar case. She gave him a nod to acknowledge the money but would be surprised when she looked later and found out how much it was. People in the subway that gave money to the musicians normally threw down loose change or a dollar bill this was excessive by most people's terms.

As they came out of the subway into the light of day it was blinding after the darkness of the subway.

"This way," said Thorn.

"Have you been here before?" Strain asked.

"In this area, yes but not to the building that we are going to, this is a great area for restaurants and bars it's being revived by developers," he replied.

After a fifteen-minute walk around the block where Sammy's office building was located they decided to have a look inside.

The building looked very clean on the outside as though it had recently been power washed. At the front was a sign that said, 'Style' a ladies and men's hairdresser, there was an arrow pointing down some steps towards the basement. At the double door entrance to the main building was a list of companies that occupied the building, there were six altogether. Sammy's company name was the only one on the top floor of the four-floor building. The lobby inside had been modernized with an attempt to try to keep some of the old features. On the right-hand side was a glass office door with a for rent sign on it. Strain was looking through the glass to see what it looked like inside when he heard someone speaking.

"Can I help you?"

"Yes, we are looking for an office," said Thorn.

"The realtor is in the third building down, I am the super for all three buildings," the man said wiping his hand on a cloth.

"Pleased to meet you super, my name is Steve this is my business partner Joe," Thorn threw out two names that he knew he would remember.

Strain shook the man's hand, "You keep this place looking great super," said Strain in an attempt to get on the man's good side.

"Thanks, I don't get too many people saying that around here," he whispered.

"My father was a super in an office building in London for twenty years, so I know what you mean," replied Strain.

"A Brit, tell your dad I've been a super for twenty-two years as well." The man was warming to Strain and felt he had some kind of kinship with him.

"I'll we are looking for an office on a top floor just to try to avoid a least some of the street noise."

Thorn was leaving the talking to Strain as he could see he had the super where he wanted him, a friend.

"Well you won't get that in this building," the super replied.

Strain leaned forward as a sign of discretion, "What do you mean?"

The super looked around to make sure nobody was listening, "You got a minute?"

"Sure," replied Strain.

"Follow me," he replied.

"Super do you mind if I look around while you and Joe talk?" He could see politeness was working with the super, something he wasn't used to receiving.

"No go ahead," he replied.

Strain followed the super down the stairs to a small room in the basement. As they went in Strain could tell that this was his workshop and by the looks of it a place to take a nap. The room was immaculate tools in special places on the walls, a bench that you could have eaten your breakfast off. He had a kettle in the corner for boiling water and a small fridge that had seen better days.

"Here sit down," the super said pushing an old office chair on wheels towards him.

"You know you remind me so much of my father, you keep this room very clean and the tools have their own place." Strain wasn't lying this time like he did when he said his father was a super.

"Sounds like his is old school like me, that's what's wrong these days' things come too easy for today's kids."

"I have to agree with that, so what's the problem with getting a top floor space?" Strain replied.

"Do you drink tea?" asked the super.

"Yes, absolutely," he replied.

The super filled the kettle from a faucet that was over a small sink in the corner.

Strain watched the man and could tell that he didn't get visitors very often and he was going to be his captive for a short while. He didn't mind as he felt quite at home sitting in the little room, something he knew his father would have enjoyed.

"The top floor in this building is taken by one of those Arab looking types. He is a total pig, treats everyone like he owns them, he thinks I'm his servant or something. He won't even talk to me when he wants something he gets his assistant to call. When I go to the office to fix something he tells his assistant while I am standing there what he wants doing, he doesn't even look at me. That sort of thing may work where he comes from but it doesn't work here, I feel like shit when I leave that office."

Strain could see that the man had been humiliated and belittled by Sammy.

"You know people like that get what's coming to them eventually," replied Strain.

"Yeah well his can't come soon enough sorry I didn't mean to bore you with the ranting of an old man."

"No, you are not boring me at all, it's good to get to know who your neighbors might be. We like this area and may have to take the bottom office if we can't get a top one. I'll go see the realtor for a look around, I like the idea of having a good super looking after my office space."

"Well I hope you get what you want but it would be nice to have a friendly face around here. The only people that are friendly and speak to me with kindness are the girls in the hairdresser's downstairs they are crazy in a fun way. They know what that Arab guy is like he goes down there to get his hair cut he treats them like shit and is always making lewd comments to them. The girls say that he gives them the creeps, he has even offered one of them money to go out with him like she is a hooker or something." He poured hot water into two cups that had tea bags in them.

"I could do with a haircut, are they any good?" Strain knew this was going to be another good source of information.

"Yeah, their good, mind you they give me a haircut for free because I look after them when they have a problem. I would pay for it anyway, which I have tried to do but they won't let me."

Strain could see the Super was enjoying his new-found company, "I'll tell them you referred me them, it lets them know that you are trying to pay them back," Strain replied.

"You're a kind guy, but watch out they will eat you for lunch with that Brit accent," he handed Strain a mug of tea.

"So, what does the Arab guy do for a living to make him so nasty?"

"His company does something with computers but I have never seen any computers in there other than the one in his office. There's only him and his secretary on the whole floor which has six rooms. He uses one of the rooms as storage but there isn't much in there. He could be a terrorist for all I know he has had other Arabs types up there recently. I had to come in one evening last week when I had left my ticket to the ball game on my bench and four of them were walking into the building as I arrived."

Strain didn't want to push this point and made small talk for fifteen minutes with the super to change the subject.

"Sorry super but I have to go or Steve will wonder where I have gone, it was truly nice to meet you," said Strain.

"Thanks for spending some time with a rambling old man," he replied humbly.

"You know something I'll try to get that office space, you're a good man."

"Look if you ever want to come back and see it after office hours give me a call and I'll let you in, just don't tell anyone," he handed Strain a card with his name and cell phone number on it.

"Thanks, you take care and look after yourself," Strain shook his hand and left.

Thorn had used the time to have a look at the inside of the building and had located all the fire exits that were in the common areas of the stairwells.

He was standing outside the front of the building when Strain came out.

"That was an interesting conversation," Strain said.

"Super's know everything that goes on in their buildings," replied Thorn.

"That guy does and so might the ladies in the hairdresser's downstairs. He tells me that our man upstairs gets his hair cut by them and he has propositioned one or more of them a few times. Apparently, he gives the ladies the creeps and they don't like him. I am going to get a haircut to find out what else they know about him."

"Good idea, hairdressers get to know more about their clients than bar tenders, I'll be in that café across the street when you're done." Thorn pointed to what looked like a rundown café that most probably served good coffee and food.

"See you over there," Strain replied.

The hairdressing salon looked very modern inside with pictures on the walls of headshots of men and women. Hair products and ladies' jewelry lined one of the walls for sale to customers.

"Put your name down we will be with you in a minute," said one of the women without even looking away from the customer, Strain did as instructed and put down Joe as his name.

There were six hairdressing chairs in the room three on each side with only three ladies working. It looked like the two women customers were close to being finished and the one male customer was checking his hair out in a mirror. The chatter from the women customers and the hairdressers was constant making Strain smile, exchange of information he thought.

The male customer was paying at the desk as the floor was being swept of the hair cuttings around the chair he'd occupied.

The hairdresser picked up the board that Strain had signed his name on, "OK Joe your next, I'm Jean," she said to Strain sticking her hand out for it to be shaken.

"Thank you," he said shaking her hand.

As he walked to the chair he could see the hairdresser in the mirror waiving at the other ladies to get their attention, she had picked up the accent.

"What do you want today," she said running her fingers through his hair feeling how thick or thin it was.

"I would just like a trim please."

"OMG have you heard this guy's accent, girls ooh! I got the winner," she said to the other ladies in the room.

"Go on, let's hear you talk then," shouted one of them.

"What do you want me to say? I can tell you the super upstairs referred me to you ladies if that helps," he replied.

"Wow, referred you to us," said his hairdresser in a sexy voice.

Strain smiled as the banter from the ladies picked up.

"Trust you to get the sexy voice Jean, watch her she goes out with dirty men," said a voice from across the room.

"I am sure that is untrue about this lovely young lady," Strain replied.

"Lovely young lady? You obviously don't know her, now if you want lovely come see me," said one of the customers.

"It looks like the customers are also against you and not just your colleagues."

"With that voice, gorgeous, I would like to be against you right now," replied one of the hairdressers to which all the ladies laughed.

"He sounds like Sean Connery when he talks, go on say something else I am getting horny just listening to you," said his hairdresser.

The banter went on for five more minutes as he had he haircut, he was waiting for a break when he could try to open the discussion of Sammy and it came.

"Well you ladies may see more of me as I might be renting the office space upstairs."

"I would like to see more of you, if you know what I mean," said the lady cutting his hair.

"You dirty bitch," said one of the other ladies.

"Yeah dirty lucky bitch he's my customer," she replied.

Strain smiled and the door was open, "So what are the other tenants like in the building?" he asked.

"Most of them are OK not too friendly, you know busy with work when they come in here."

"Except for that fat bastard at the top," said one of the other ladies with venom.

"I assume that is the Arab businessman?" he replied.

"Yes, that's him, dirty bastard," the same voice said.

By now both lady customers had left and Strain was the only customer in the salon.

The other two hairdressers came over and sat in the chairs either side of Strain, stroking his hair playfully.

"Hey, hey hands off he's mine," said his hairdresser.

"How do you know about him?" asked one of the ladies.

"I met the super and he was telling me who was on what floor and he described the Arab man."

"Yeah, he is a real piece of work, comes in here trying to get one or all of us to go out to the clubs with him. He even put his hand on my ass one time and I almost called the cops on him."

"I think Arabs like the club scene?" said Strain.

"That dirty bastard does, he goes to one of the clubs we like sometimes and he has a couple of hookers with him every time."

Strain kept the interest of the ladies for the next fifteen minutes obtaining as much information on Sammy from them as he could. He left after a torrent of playful offers from the ladies and joined Thorn but not before he called at the florists next to the café and sent three bouquets of roses to the salon, one for each of the ladies.

Strain and Thorn returned to the safe house with the new information on Sammy in hand.

CHAPTER 33

SAN FRANCISCO

Sammy had taken his time driving from the airport to Downtown San Francisco in the rental car. He was running counter-surveillance and when he was sure he wasn't being followed he made his way to meet Adel.

Adel had been working with Sammy for three years and had gained a certain amount of trust. He had performed minor tasks such as delivering explosives to operatives, at the same time he didn't know what he was delivering. He wanted to move up in Sammy's organization and he'd been promised that this new job was the one that would do that.

His cell phone rang, "Hello, he said.

"Where are you?" asked Sammy.

"Where you told me to be at home," replied Adel

"Good, leave and walk to the Starbucks down the street and order a coffee," Sammy hung up.

Adel did as he was told and walked two blocks to the Starbucks and went inside. He was halfway through his coffee when Sammy walked in with a newspaper under his arm. Sammy ordered a coffee and sat on the table next to Adel, neither one acknowledged the other.

Sammy sipped on his coffee for ten minutes as he read the newspaper. He finished reading and put the newspaper on the table and left with his coffee.

As soon as Sammy left Adel picked up the newspaper and started to read it. Inside the newspaper, he found a note from Sammy, he took his time with his coffee before leaving.

Sammy waited for fifteen minutes and drove to the rear of the cinema a block away from the Starbucks he'd just been in. As he turned the corner he saw Adel standing in the fire exit doorway of the cinema.

He stopped the car and Adel got into the front seat, Sammy drove away.

"Is everything OK?" asked Sammy.

"Yes," Adel was a little nervous and it showed.

"You seem nervous," replied Sammy.

"Yes, I am a little I want to prove to you that I am ready to do greater things," he replied.

"Good, there's a large hiker's backpack on the back seat. I want you to take it with you on your next trip to the islands. Do you still sail to the islands to join the ship you work on?"

"Yes, we work on the ship that leaves the mainland and then transfer to the island cruise ship."

"Can you get the backpack onboard when you board the mainland ship without it being inspected?" This was the part that Sammy was very concerned about.

"Yes, I'll board in the early hours of the morning well before everyone else. The security guard knows me and he never searches me when I am on my own." Adel was very confident about this as he also gave a bottle of rum to the security guard whenever he saw him.

"Good, are you still on the ship that stops in Maui on this date?" Sammy showed him the cruise ship brochure timetable.

"Yes, that is my ship we are there overnight and leave at noon the next day."

"When you get there, you will receive a phone call, you will be given an address to go to. The person that calls you will also be working with you, do whatever he says, do you understand?" Sammy was staring hard into Adel's eyes.

"Yes, yes, I understand, I'll do whatever he says."

"Good, do not open the bag under any circumstance until you give it to the man you are meeting. You will work with him and then return to your ship, very simple." Sammy stopped the car.

"I won't let you down," Adel said as he got out of the car.

CHAPTER 34

NEW YORK CITY

The safe house was buzzing with activity as the team members went through a stack of paperwork that Thorn had obtained on possible terrorists. The information they had at their initial meeting at the White House plus new information that had come in since. They had given some of the information to George and Chalky who were running a computer analysis program they had developed. The program was very sophisticated but the simple description was put names, addresses, times, flights and other similar details into the program and it would spit out any patterns and affiliations.

"I have just received information from homeland security that Sammy has just boarded a flight to San Francisco. He has several flights and cars that he has hired charged to one of four credit cards in his name. It looks like he parties a lot especially here in New York and Atlantic City. All of the cards are in his alias but he has somehow obtained a driver's license in that name." Thorn was reading the information on his laptop.

"So, the lady's in the hairdressers were right he frequents the local clubs. Any unusual activity on the cards, purchases from gun stores or electronics shops?" Strain asked.

"No nothing like that. If he is out of town now it may be a good time to search his office and plant some listening devices," said Thorn.

"Is there a return flight for his itinerary to San Francisco?" asked Strain.

"Yes, he comes back on the first flight in the morning."

"Let's go to his office to see if his assistant is there, maybe we can distract her long enough to plant the devices," said Strain.

It only took forty-five minutes to get to the building armed with a pocket full of listening devices.

As they both made their way up the stairs to Sammy's office they walked right into the super who was walking down.

"Hey good to see you back so soon, does this mean I have a new tenant?" the super asked as he saw Strain.

"We hope so but I really wanted to see the top floor office, you know the Arabs place," Strain whispered the last part. "We thought that he may want to do a switch with us for the downstairs office."

"He won't do that son he is too nasty to help anyone," replied the super.

"That's a shame maybe he or his assistant will let us look at the space anyway, you never know."

"Neither of them are in the office I was just in there fixing one of the lights. Come with me I'll let you see the place but be quick I don't want anyone to know."

They both followed the super up the stairs and straight to the office where he unlocked the door.

"You go in I'll watch just in case they come back, we don't want the super to get in trouble because of us," said Thorn.

"Hell, no you go in I'll watch, I don't like the bastard anyway," replied the super.

Thorn was hoping that he would say that and followed Strain who was already putting the devices in place.

Thorn went to work quickly trying file cabinet draws to see what there was of interest.

Two minutes had gone very quickly as they finished snooping around.

"OK let's go no need to make him suspicious," said Strain.

"Thanks," said Thorn to the super as they left the office.

"I think you're right, I don't want to deal with that guy, besides I like the space downstairs better," said Strain.

"Yeah you won't regret it, he's nasty," replied the super.

They said their goodbye's and headed to the real estate office to get more information on the ground floor office. After a short meeting with the realtor and a viewing of the office space they rented it for the minimum six months. The office already had two desks and file cabinets that the previous tenant had left and they come to an agreement to rent them also. The realtor agreed that they could move their office equipment in the next day when they could finish signing documents and pay the rent and security deposit. The realtor also arranged for the super to open the office for them at 8am the next morning to move their computers and small office items in. She was at a showing until noon and agreed to do it providing they went to the realty office to sign the documents when it opened at 9am.

The next morning the super was waiting on guard by the front door when Strain and Thorn showed up. He let them into the office and said his goodbyes as he had a water leak in one of the other buildings to tend to.

Shadow and Bulldog arrived at 8.15am the next day with a van carrying two computers and an array of electronic equipment. They had everything set up within an hour ready for when Sammy or his assistant arrived.

Sammy's assistant arrived at 10 am she made a few calls and was heard to say that her boss wouldn't be in the office until two in the afternoon. He had taken the last flight out of San Francisco to New York the night before instead of flying out the following morning.

Just after one in the afternoon Shadow heard the voices of two men talking to Sammy's assistant on the hidden microphones, they had arrived for a meeting with him. She told them to take a seat as Sammy wouldn't be in the office for almost an hour.

Shadow decided to go upstairs with a hidden camera in a parcel to try and get a photograph of them. First, he walked to the building next door and went to the top floor and saw the name of a business, 'Amber Attorneys' on one of the office doors.

He went back the rental office and put on his grey jacket and a baseball cap he had in his bag. Shadow always had an array of disguises in his bag. After a quick test of the camera in the parcel to make sure you couldn't hear it taking photographs he went upstairs.

The door to Sammy's office was closed and he knocked once and walked straight in without waiting for an answer.

"Hi, I have a delivery Ambrose attorneys can you sign for it please?" he said in a very passable New York accent to the young woman sat behind the desk.

To shadow's left sitting in chairs next to each other were two men who looked to be Middle Eastern.

"Sorry you have the wrong building they are in the next one down," replied the lady politely.

"Sorry these places all look the same, that building next door," he replied pointing to the window on his right.

"Yes," she replied.

Shadow turned slowly to leave the office keeping his head down as if he was reading the address on the parcel.

He'd taken at least a dozen photographs in the short time it took for him to turn towards the door. He could feel the eyes of the two men on him and he paid them no attention.

Sammy didn't arrive until two thirty and the two men were still waiting for him.

"Go get three sandwiches' anything will do," Sammy commanded his assistant without so much as a hello.

"Yes," she replied with fear in her voice.

The assistant only worked for Sammy because her father told her he was a powerful client and she did as she was told. The girl was still under the male influence of her family and hadn't learnt the more Western ways of an independent woman. Her father was secretly trying to get Sammy interested in marrying his daughter. She was only eighteen, slim and very timid, a perfect mix for Sammy's perversion. He often ran his hands over her body when she was making coffee or bringing papers into his office. She had complained to him once and was beaten by her father when she got home that evening.

"Come," Sammy said to the two men waiting for him.

The two men followed him into his office.

"She is quiet," said one of the men.

"Keep your eyes off she is mine," said Sammy.

"Yes," the man replied.

"I want you to go to Allentown, Pennsylvania the day after tomorrow, no sooner. There's a self-storage building at 1800 South 4th Street, I want you to keep the place under surveillance until you see Hamed Drig. He will arrive late at night in a car and drop off several firearms and explosives in unit 101. Here is a small motion detector that you can fit above the frame of the unit facing 101. The frame is recessed and eight feet off the ground so you will need ladder. The detector will be hidden from view by anyone walking in and out of the units but you must aim it at the top of the roller door on 101. When Hamed arrives and opens the door it will sense the movement of the door and a signal will be sent to this receiver. When he leaves wait one hour and then go in and take everything out of the unit. This key will open the gate at the storage building and this one will open the unit. There are a lot of items already in the unit, take everything. Wear gloves so that you do not leave finger prints and no smoking inside the storage building, they have smoke detectors I don't want any accidental activation of them. I have a van parked in the garage at the back of this building ready for you to use, here is the key to the van. This key opens the padlock on the garage door the garage door number is on the key. Take the van now and store it somewhere safe for the next two days until you are ready to leave for Allentown. There's a private security guard that patrols these buildings and garages between 7pm and 7am we don't need him watching us. You will bring everything back here and store it in the garage, then take the van somewhere and set fire to it."

"Why aren't we meeting Hamed to take the weapons from the storage place?" asked one of the men.

"Because Mohammed is not sure if Hamed can be trusted, you are not to mention this to anyone especially Mohammed. If you do he will see that you question his methods and he won't trust you. As you both know people he does not trust do not stay alive very long."

Sammy was lying about the whole thing Mohammed had no knowledge of what he was doing. Sammy was going to kill the two men after they had taken the weapons and explosives. He would then blame the theft on them and tell Mohammed he had no choice but to kill them because he discovered their deception.

Sammy already had a buyer for the weapons and explosives it was a Colombian drug cartel that had moved into the Atlantic City area. Sammy met the head of the cartel at the casino when they were playing poker at the same table. They had become friends and shared the same luxuries of life, especially women.

"We will do as you say you can tell Mohammed that nobody will hear about this from us. We are loyal to him and you Sammy you can trust us," replied one of the men.

Shadow and Bulldog couldn't believe their luck when they heard what was being said.

"I have a tracking device in my bag I'll get into that garage and put it on the van. Keep me up to speed if they move out I have my radio with me," said Shadow as he was putting his earpiece in his ear.

"I suppose you're going to guess which garage it is then?" said Bulldog.

"I am hoping there aren't too many," replied Shadow as he left carrying his bag.

Bulldog sat listening to the three men talking when he heard the assistant's voice, she had returned with the sandwich and was told to leave by Sammy.

Shadow walked down the narrow street at the back of the building, he could see a row of about ten garages. On the opposite side of the road was a mirror image of the building he'd just left. There were office windows all along the back of the building and he was on full view, this was too risky in daylight.

"Too many eyes out there," he said to Bulldog as he walked back into the office.

"Why don't you wait until they leave and try to put it on the vehicle then, it sounds like they are going to take it straight away," replied Bulldog.

"Yeah that's what I was hoping to do now that I can't risk getting into the garage."

They listened for thirty minutes to the three men as they discussed nothing much of interest.

"I must go, take to van out of garage 211 now and don't make a mistake Hamed can't know you are around," said Sammy.

Shadow was already heading out the door to locate which garage was 211. In the side road, he saw the garage and they could drive out in either direction. Coming down the street was a garbage truck if he could stall them the men could only drive in one direction.

"Bulldog, get out here quick before they arrive," he said on his hidden microphone.

Bulldog was out before the men as he could hear them talking as they came down the stairs.

The garbage truck was getting close when Bulldog arrived.

"Stall that garbage truck and they will have to drive down the street that way. I'll be able to put the tracker on the van at the junction," said Shadow.

Bulldog was standing on the step of the garbage truck next to the driver's window when the two men entered the street he looked like one of the workers. The two men walked along looking at the numbers on the doors until they found the one they wanted. One minute later the van was being driven out by one man while the other locked the garage door. The second man got into the van and they left down the street towards the junction where Shadow lay in wait.

As the van stopped at the busy main road Shadow walked around the back of the van as did several other pedestrians. As he passed the rear of the van he bent down to tie a shoe lace and put the tracker under the fender and carried on walking.

Bulldog thanked the garbage truck driver for directions to the best local pizza place and left. He'd made out that he was on vacation in the city and he also worked on the garbage trucks in the UK. It gave him the three minutes that Shadow needed.

Shadow contacted Strain about the new information they had gained from Sammy's office. It wasn't long before they were on the road to the safe house to pick up some equipment and a change of clothing.

Sleepy and L.B. took over surveillance of Sammy's office.

CHAPTER 35

MAUI THEFT OF HANG GLIDER

The flight to Maui was smooth but for some reason it seemed to take much longer than usual, he knew this was because he wanted to turn the phone back on. He was getting tired of the flights to Maui dealing with the same kind of passenger's day in, day out. Over excited, boring people wearing their flowery Hawaiian style outfits all chattering away about their holiday and what they were going to do.

As usual he and the rest of the crew left the airport quickly and got onto the bus provided by the hotel. When they arrived at the hotel he went straight to his room. Once inside he took the telephone out of his pocket and lay it down on the bedside cabinet, "Ring," he said to the phone.

Hakeem was an accomplished hang glider pilot and loved to drive up Haleakala, at the top of which was an extinct volcano. He would normally stop around six thousand feet up and spend hours watching the locals ride the thermals. This time however he wouldn't hire the car and drive up to the viewing spot as he knew that he wouldn't get a signal on the phone. He'd been hang gliding for almost five years and had achieved the highest pilot rating with the US Hang gliding and Paragliding Association (USHPA). As a student, he excelled and his instructor told him that he had the makings of a top quality competitive pilot. The thought of competing appealed to him but he knew that this meant unnecessary exposure. Keep a low profile and do not bring undue attention to yourself, maintain a modest lifestyle he'd been told in his training.

To be on the safe side, he connected the charger to the phone and then plugged it into the wall socket next to the bed.

He lay on the bed thinking about the drive through Paia town where he would normally stop at a restaurant called, 'The Fish Market'. He always had the same thing an Ono fish burger to go, it was the best sandwich he'd ever had.

The phone rang and he snatched it up quickly, "Hello."

"Are you on the island?" the electronic voice said.

"Yes," he replied, wondering who had to disguise his voice.

"I want you to make some preparations for the future it involves you going to the top of the extinct volcano on the island. You need to know how long it takes you to come down the volcano. Time will be against you when I ask you to take on this job." Mohammed said into the device that changed his voice.

Hakeem was wondering what the caller was up to, "Am I to use a car or motorcycle or will I need something bigger, like a van?" he really didn't know what to use.

"Whatever you choose will be fine. You will have help on the way up but you will come down alone, do you understand what I am asking?"

"Yes," Hakeem didn't hesitate in replying he had to kill his accomplice, whoever he was.

"I may make the request of you very soon or in a few weeks, be prepared. When I call, you won't have any time to rent vehicles, find one now and store it." Mohammed pressed the end button on his phone.

"Hello, are you there?" asked Hakeem, the caller had gone.

He lay on the bed for almost an hour running questions through his mind about the call. The caller called it a mountain but it was a volcano, so there is a reason he kept saying mountain. He had to steal a vehicle and hide it until it was needed. There were plenty of storage facilities on the island and he could easily steal a car. He planned to steal one that afternoon and a motorcycle just in case he needed one. It would be easier and faster to use a motorcycle to come down the volcano. Then it hit him that he may be getting prepared for something on the Mainland, some other mountainous road.

Hakeem went to a storage rental building just outside of Kahului and rented a storage unit for three months. As with everything else, he paid cash and showed a false I.D. He could now go into the town of Paia and watch cars being parked by tourists in the public parking lot. He had an off-road motorcycle in the lockup already that he'd stolen from the back of the storage facility office. It obviously belonged to the young man running the office and he didn't even have to start it up, he just wheeled it away. He took a taxi into Paia town for a fish sandwich as he felt he'd earned one before he stole a car.

This was the first time he'd sat in the restaurant to eat his sandwich. Eating in the restaurant gave him the opportunity to enjoy the unique décor of fish pictures, surfing and fresh cut Hawaiian flowers. The tables were all wooden as where the bench seats that people sat on to eat. On the table was a container that held cutlery, napkins and an assortment of condiments. It was a little reminder of home in many ways as people ordered their food and sat at a table wherever there was a space. Everyone mingled with each other to eat, no individual seats here.

He was just finishing his sandwich when two men in their early twenties walked in, he recognized one of them. Josh Pale was the US hang gliding champion he was featured in the Hang Gliding association magazine almost every month. Josh and his friend ordered their food and sat at the table behind Hakeem. He wanted to ask him so many questions about hang gliding but he had to keep his profile low. As Josh and his friend waited for their food they talked about the hang gliding they had done that day on the side of Haleakala.

Hakeem watched another man enter the restaurant, he walked straight to Josh, "Hey man do you have my backpack I left it on the grass where everyone was landing?" he asked.

"Yeah I picked it up just after you had gone it's in the back of my Jeep. I parked it behind Charlie's," Josh replied.

Charlie's was a local bar and restaurant on the next block favored by locals and tourists.

"Thanks man, see you tomorrow," the man said as he left.

Hakeem sat there listening as an idea formed in his mind, he knew how he was going to get down off the volcano quickly. He finished his sandwich and walked over to where Josh had said he parked his Jeep. The parking lot behind Charlie's was full and there were many cars but only three Jeeps and there was Josh's, it had to be, there was a hang glider in its long PVC Cover tied to the roll bar of the Jeep. Within a minute, Hakeem was driving the Jeep out of the parking lot and up the winding road towards Haleakala.

Hakeem didn't want go all the way to the top of the volcano but found a good spot to hide the hang glider around eight and a half thousand feet. He carried it through some heavy ground cover and slid it under the overhang of an old laver flow.

Hakeem drove the long way around back to the storage facility as he couldn't drive back through Paia for fear of being seen in the stolen Jeep. He loaded the stolen motorcycle into the Jeep and drove back to Haleakala. At around two thousand feet there was a field with Eucalyptus trees on either side. Hakeem had landed in this field twice in the past by mistake when he first hang glided down Haleakala. It resembled the field where the local hang gliders landed a quarter of a mile away on the other side of a small hill. This was a great place to hide the motorcycle as there were plenty of hidden areas in amongst the Eucalyptus trees.

He got back to his hotel room at three am in time to get five hours sleep before he had to leave.

On the way to the airport on the airline crew bus he heard an announcement on the radio about the theft of Josh's Hang Glider. Josh turned out to be a local legend and the theft had stirred up some interest, not what Hakeem wanted. There was a reward being offered for the return of the hang glider, no questions asked. Hakeem had apparently stolen Josh's best competition hang glider, now he relished the thought of possibly flying it one day. It would never be found where he'd hidden it and if it he didn't use it he would leave a message anonymously where it could be located.

CHAPTER 36

CALIFORNIA

Hakeem was religious about keeping the cell phone with him it had been a week and he'd still not received a call, the waiting game was aggravating. He decided to drive up to the hills outside of San Diego to his favorite hang gliding location it was also the favorite of many other Hang Gliding enthusiasts. As he drove his car up the winding Californian hillside roads he thought about the effortless glide through the air that he was about to enjoy. He opened the car window and out of habit felt for the hang glider strapped on the roof rack and tugged on it to make sure that it was still secure, it was. This was his third kite and his pride and joy as he was hoping to one day attempt a complete loop the loop. This kite was no ordinary kite it was used by the professionals in competition and he'd seen several of them perform this trick. This was the main reason why he bought this model. It was a glorious sunny day as he looked down into the valley below which was covered by trees and shrubs with the Blue ocean waters in the distance. Ahead he recognized the dirt road that led to the jump site it would take another ten minutes of driving before he got there. As he drove around a bend in the road there in the distance ahead he could see several hang gliders sailing through the sky. He leaned forward over the dash board to get a better look at them and felt his heart start to pick up pace.

Over several years, a rough area of rocks and grass had been turned into a makeshift parking area by the hang gliders and their cars. Hakeem parked his car and practically jumped out with excitement. He walked over to the ridge in front of him fifty feet below on a long downward slope he could see about ten people all watching the gliders. He watched for a few minutes taking in the beauty of the gliders in the sky as they rode the thermals. He was also watching how they responded to the winds, they were very favorable and it was a good day to be in the sky.

Back at the car he opened the trunk and took out a large bag containing his jump suit and harness for the hang glider. It only took him a few minutes to put on the suit he then removed the hang glider in its storage sleeve from the roof rack and hoisted the glider onto his shoulder. Weighing just over seventy pounds it was more cumbersome than heavy, the fourteen-foot length made it difficult to walk down the slope, but he did it safely.

The hang glider was assembled and his thoughts were totally on the jump when he heard the cell phone ringing inside the hold all. It had rung twice before he realized that it was his phone that was ringing. He opened the hold all and took out the phone pressing the green button on the keypad to answer.

"Hello," was all he said.

"You have been patient it's time we met," said the electronic voice on the other end. Mohammed had deliberately disguised his voice as he wanted to keep the mystery going. This wasn't the time to reveal himself that would come later after the test.

"Yes, I agree," he replied calmly.

Mohammed could hear the excitement in the young man's voice even though he was trying to control it. "I'll call you back soon," he replied and hung up.

Hakeem was taken back at first when the caller hung up but he knew that this was to be the first of many calls. He couldn't hang glide now as he dare not miss the next call.

The drive back to San Diego gave him time to think about the future and what it may hold for him. He was passing a sign showing that he was entering the city when the phone rang again.

He answered the call, "Hello."

"A mile down the road is a truck stop, pull in there and wait." The caller hung up again.

How does he know where I am? He must be following me or he has me under surveillance, he thought. He was concerned as he didn't notice anyone following him. He started to doubt himself thinking that he was becoming complacent and that he had let his guard down. This wasn't good he was slowly becoming angry and frustrated with himself.

Two minutes later he was at the truck stop where he waited for the call, he didn't wait long the phone rang again. "Yes," he said.

"Under the seat of your car you will find an envelope, open it and take out the contents." Mohammed was all business.

Hakeem reached under the seat and there it was a large manila envelope. He opened it as instructed and found a picture of a man who looked to be in his late fifties with short brown hair. "OK, I have opened it," he said.

"On the back of the photograph you will see a car key and an address, memorize it and the face of the man. Do you have another phone with you?"

"No, I don't," he replied.

"Good, do you have this man's face and address to memory?" Mohammed knew that this was a big test for the young man but it was something that he'd been trained to do.

"Yes, I do." Hakeem hesitated as he had only a minute to study the face and memorize the address.

"Go into the toilet that is next to the gas pumps and burn the picture and envelope then flush the remains down the toilet. Leave your cell phone on the dashboard of the car where it can be seen. Carry the envelope in plain sight when you leave the car. You will be contacted again you will have one more opportunity to see the face of your victim again." Mohammed hung up the phone and watched Hakeem from his vantage point on the far side of the parking lot.

Now Hakeem knew that he was being watched and realized that whoever this was they had entered his car without his knowledge and placed the envelope inside. He got out of the car and followed the instructions to the letter.

Once he was inside the toilet he set fire to the envelope and its contents as instructed. It gave off a lot of smoke and the small space soon had a lot of smoke in it. He couldn't open the door as this would bring unwanted attention to him. There was an extractor in the ceiling to circulate air out of the toilet, he switched it on. He used these few minutes to look through the space between the door and the frame. He was trying to look outside to see if he could see who was watching him. There was nobody outside all he could see was a large steel dumpster which blocked most of his view of the parking lot. The smoke in the toilet was being sucked out of the room by the extractor as the fire went out. Hakeem carefully picked up burnt remains of the envelope and flushed them down the toilet. He turned on the faucet in the sink and was washing the remainder of the burnt paper down the drain hole when someone banged loudly on the door. The noise startled him.

"Hey how long are you going to be in there?" A male voice said.

"Just finishing, I'll be out in a minute," he shouted.

Hakeem cleaned up as best he could the smell of smoke was still strong but there were no signs of a fire anymore. He unlocked the toilet door and stepped outside. There was a burly looking truck driver stood by the dumpster with his back to him. He ignored the man and quickly returned to his car. As he got to his car he looked over his shoulder and saw the back of the truck driver going into the toilet. He sat in the driver's seat and realized that his clothes stunk of smoke. He picked the phone up off the dashboard and was about to place it in his pocket when it rang.

"Hello," he said.

"Go to your home and wait for me there." Mohammed had no intention of meeting him personally he just wanted to keep him guessing.

Hakeem drove home at a steady pace once again he didn't exceed the speed limit trying not to do anything to bring attention to himself. He took the hang glider off the roof of his car and carried it into his apartment. He wasn't inside more than thirty seconds when the phone rang once more.

"Hello, hello," he said.

"You have the next two days off work, go to the address that was on the back of the photograph. At exactly ten thirty tomorrow night, no sooner, no later, you will find a Blue Toyota SUV parked outside the house. You will disable the car by puncturing the front driver side tire. Keep the car and house under surveillance for four hours and if nobody discovers the flat tire you will use the key to get into the back of the car, this is where the spare tire is located. You will then wait in the back of the car until the owner comes out the next morning. He will see the flat tire and open the back of the car to get to the spare tire when he does you will shoot him twice in the head and return to your apartment. The gun you are to use is under the pillow on your bed. On the way back you will dispose of the gun in the sea." Mohammed didn't wait for any questions and turned off his phone.

Hakeem was somewhat surprised, he had to kill someone in cold blood and the gun was under his pillow. He ran into the bedroom and threw back the pillow on the bed and there it was a Beretta nine-millimeter fitted with a silencer. He picked the gun up and checked it over it had a full clip of bullets. He sat on the bed a little in shock looking at the weapon once again he was dealing with someone very talented and he'd gained access to his personal space, first his car now his apartment. The person on the phone had to be Mohammed, it must be him he thought, but he should at least question in his own mind what was going on. It was becoming obvious that if this is Mohammed he is as good as people say he is but he didn't expect anything else. He had memorized the address in Bakersfield, California and quickly looked it up on Map quest on his computer. He found that the distance between his apartment and the address was just over two hundred and fifty miles. He knew that this was a test and he had to carry out the assassination or he himself would be killed. Why did he have to disable the car at exactly ten thirty, maybe it was another test or maybe they would be watching to see if he could follow orders. He was a little nervous at the thought of killing this man but he knew that he would do it. He didn't know who the man was that he was going to kill but it didn't matter.

To his surprise, Hakeem slept well that night and woke up refreshed ready for the day ahead. By midafternoon he was on the road heading towards Bakersfield. He couldn't help but wonder if the caller the night before had been in his car overnight. He started to check the inside of his car to see if there had been anything left for him then suddenly stopped. If he was under surveillance it would be from a distance and he wouldn't be able to see them anyway. He started to question himself again, what if he was being watched when he searched his car? If he searched the car it would show that he didn't trust Mohammed? If it's him it could be a death sentence. He filled the car full of petrol to get him to his destination and he would do the same when he got closer to the address. He would use cash only and with a full tank he wouldn't have to stop to refuel on the way back. He hadn't been in the car more than twenty minutes when the cell phone rang.

"Yes," he said.

"On the passenger sun visor you will see the picture of the same man he is extremely dangerous so use caution." Mohammed was again brief and to the point.

Hakeem slid his hand between the passenger visor and the roof of the car and found a piece of paper. It was a newspaper clipping with the photograph of the man on it. There wasn't anything to say who he was as the clipping had been cut out of the newspaper very carefully? Written across the bottom of the picture in ink were the words, 'Memorize the face and eat this picture'. He would do as instructed.

"I have it," he said.

Mohammed said no more and hung up.

What Hakeem didn't know was that the man in the picture was Graham Ponting the former head of the FBI counter Terrorism unit. His unit was responsible for freezing over ten million dollars of funds that Mohammed had access to through his business supporters bank accounts. The business entities connected to the accounts were totally false and just a front for money laundering for Mohammed's operations. Mohammed was now running low on money and had to raise more funds quickly, plans for which were already in motion.

CHAPTER 37

BAKERSFIELD, CALIFORNIA

As he drove through Bakersfield Hakeem could smell crude oil in the air. Everything he drove past seemed to be related to the oil industry, it was his first and probably last visit there. He did very well finding the address and past it twice from different directions so that he knew he had the correct address. There wasn't a Toyota outside but it was still only seven thirty. He drove around the area getting to know all the side streets and the quickest way to the freeway heading south which would take him out of the city back towards San Diego. He stopped outside a local supermarket and parked in amongst the rows of shoppers' vehicles. At ten fifteen he drove back towards the targets address.

As Hakeem drove through the neighborhood where the targets house was he wondered what it was like to have a life like theirs. The men go to work each day say goodbye to their families and return home gathering the family around the table for dinner. For a few seconds, he envied them, they had what he saw as a normal life surrounded by a loving family. This wasn't the truth of the modern American family. The vast majority rarely ate together as a family around the evening dinner table.

He was thinking of how hard his father worked but the family always ate together, he yearned for those days of normalcy.

As he approached the targets house he could see the Toyota was parked outside. Hakeem parked two blocks away where had had already identified a place where his vehicle wouldn't stand out.

The street where the targets house was located was very poorly lit and most of the homes were already in complete darkness, the residents retired for the night. He walked along the side walk on the opposite side to the targets house and at the last minute crossed to hide behind the front wheel of the Toyota. He removed the tire valve cap and loosened the valve to let all the air out, then replaced the cap and valve. He then took a rusty old nail out of his pocket, he'd filed the head of the nail until it was shiny. The filed head of the nail made it look just like it would if it had been stuck in the tire and had been worn down by the road. He then pushed the nail into the tire until only the head was visible. It was in the perfect position so that the driver couldn't help but see it in the morning.

Hakeem pleased with his plan so far walked down the street watching all the windows of the homes to make sure that he hadn't been seen. Four hours had past and as instructed he went back to the Toyota carrying a black blanket folded neatly under his arm. All the houses in the street were in darkness and the tire on the Toyota was still flat. He couldn't see anyone around and quickly opened the car with the key he'd received and climbed into the back. Once Hakeem was in the back of the car he unfolded the black blanket and covered himself with it.

Graham Ponting followed his normal morning routine, he put his coffee pot on while he got a shower. When he was dressed, he would take his travel mug and fill it with coffee for the road. As he left the house it was bright sunshine outside and it was only forty minutes after sunrise.

"Going to be a hot one today," he said out loud to himself.

He walked down the short concrete path from his front door to the sidewalk. He looked up and down the street as he always did seeing if there was anything unusual or out of place. As he walked towards the front of his car one of the neighbors was walking his dog on the opposite side of the street.

"Morning Graham," he said.

"Nice day so far," he replied.

"Yes, it is until you see your front tire," replied the neighbor who was walking towards the car.

He walked around the front of his car and saw the flat tire. "Shit," he said.

"Yep, looks like you have had that nail in there for some time," said the neighbor.

"It's worn down pretty good, not the way to start the day changing a tire," said Ponting.

"Well I wouldn't be a good neighbor if I didn't help he tied his dog to the fender on the front of the car."

"No need for you to do that," replied Ponting.

Hakeem lay motionless under the blanket listening to the two men talk he would now have to kill both of them. He heard the lock on the tail gate make the familiar electronic unlocking sound it makes when it's unlocked with a remote key.

"Just give me the jack and I'll put it in place while you start to loosen the wheel nuts," said the neighbor.

"OK thanks," Ponting replied as he pressed the button on the key to unlock the tail gate door and pulled the handle to open it.

Hakeem heard the handle being pulled and the sound of the hydraulic rams pushing the door open. He moved quickly throwing back the blanket he saw the face that was on the photograph.

Ponting jumped in shock as the black blanket in the back of his vehicle jumped in the air exposing a man who was hiding underneath. It all happened at once for him he saw the man's face and the gun with a silencer attachment at the same time. Ponting wouldn't even have time to react. He felt the bullets hit him in the chest and he collapsed to the ground dead.

Hakeem fired two shots straight into the chest of Ponting at point blank range. He saw the look of shock on the man's face next to his victim and shot him twice also as he froze with fear, the man crumpled to the ground. Hakeem calmly got out of the back of the Toyota and shot both men once in the head to be sure they were dead. He walked down the street as he put the gun inside his coat and kept a very casual pace. It wasn't until he got to his car that he realized that he was sweating profusely, he headed home mission accomplished.

CHAPTER 38

MICHIGAN

Several days had passed since the shooting and Rudy was working his way back to full fitness. Hamed had called every other day checking on him and asked continuously if there was anything that he could do. Neither of the brothers had seen this side of him before and it amused them but at the same time it concerned Tony slightly.

What they didn't know was their boss didn't care for either of them he just wanted to finish the job he'd been sent to do by Mohammed and Sammy.

Hamed had spent several months investigating where the next gun shows would be and eventually found the right show that Bill would be attending.

It was time for him to put the final phase of his plan into action. He called the brothers on the telephone. "Tony is that you?" he said.

"Yes, boss it's me," he replied.

"Good, meet me at the Redwood Inn in Lewiston, Michigan at two o'clock tomorrow afternoon. You should both be dressed as if you are going deer hunting lots of hunters up there now you will blend in nicely. I have already booked a room in your name." He hung up the phone without further comment.

It took four hours for the brothers to drive from Detroit to Lewiston, road works on the route slowed them down considerably.

The Redwood Inn was a modest but comfortable hotel that was visited by hunters and weekend tourists from the southern parts of the state. In the winter, it was used more by the winter sports types who raced around the wooded trails on snowmobiles.

Tony and Rudy were both sat in the lounge next to the reception area watching the television when Tony's cell phone rang.

He flipped the phone open, "Hello."

"Meet me outside." Hamed said.

"OK," replied Tony. He nodded for his brother to follow him and they walked out of the hotel into the parking lot outside.

Outside they didn't see their boss at first then suddenly realized that he was also dressed in camouflage clothing stood under a large tree smoking a cigarette.

They both walked over to him. "Didn't recognize you," said Rudy.

"I like to hunt now and again I enjoy the kill," he winked at them and they responded as he expected with weak smiles.

"What are we going to do now?" asked Tony.

"First things first, how are you Rudy, healing I hope?" Again, he sounded like he had a real interest in his welfare.

"Getting back to normal boss and thanks for taking care of the doctor's bill, I know those robbing bastards are not cheap," he replied.

"Thanks, are not necessary you were hurt working for me on a job it was the least I could do. The good news for you both is that there will be a bonus for you at the end of the evening when we will complete our work here. I'll be paying you both double what I had originally told you." He knew that he had them with this comment, their loyalty was set.

"What is our work?" asked Rudy.

"Well Big Bill is at a gun show as we speak, he will be there until seven tonight. It will take him three hours to pack up his stall at the show and return to his home."

"What do you want us to do if he is that far away?" Tony asked.

"We are going to search his home and try to find my property." He replied.

"I think that it's time we knew what the property is or we won't know what to look for." Tony was becoming unusually nervous.

"Yes of course you do. I paid Bill for two antique shotguns, he was supposed to deliver them to me two months ago, and he didn't. Instead he has reneged on our deal stating that he didn't realize how valuable they were. He is holding them until I pay him another fifty percent of the asking price. This gentleman is not fare or good for business, we had an agreement and he should honor that agreement, don't you think?"

"Wait a minute we have been through all of this for two lousy shotguns." Rudy stepped forward as if trying to intimidate Hamed.

"No, no my dear friend," he paused to let that comment sink in, "They are not ordinary shotguns they once belonged to the king of England. Only four were ever made and I have the other two. Can you imagine that the king of England once hunted with those very shotguns," he said?

"The king of England," Tony said out loud. They were both impressed.

"Yes, his majesty himself has hunted with them what a piece of history." The lie continued. "A deal is a deal gentlemen and that man owes me two shotguns. I paid him the money in good faith and he is trying to bleed me."

"Let's go get your guns," said Rudy with renewed loyalty.

"We will meet here at six tonight." Hamed had them back believing that he was just a rich man needing their strong arms to perform his dirty work.

"What about the dogs?" asked Rudy?

"Don't worry about them I have something that will make them sleep."

"What if we do not find the guns?" asked Tony.

"If we do not we will wait until he returns home and you two can do what you do best and bully the information out of him. You do have a score to settle after all he did shot you Rudy."

"Yes, I wouldn't mind putting him in a little pain for a while." He replied.

"I'll see you both later," he said as he dropped his cigarette to the floor and stepped on it.

They watched him walk towards the front of the hotel as they stood under the tree eventually disappearing out of site.

"Those shotguns must be worth a lot of money if he is going to all this trouble to get them," said Rudy.

"I don't know there is still something not quite right about this whole deal, I don't like it," replied Tony.

"You worry too much let's get the job finished and collect our money." He patted his brother on the back trying to reassure him.

Their boss was bang on time as he drove into the parking lot of the hotel. He stopped in a vacant parking space and waved the brothers over to him.

"Get in the car," he said.

They both obeyed Rudy got into the front and Tony in the rear.

"Tony, you will come with me and you can follow in your car Rudy. We will leave my car about a half mile from the entrance to his driveway, I have chosen a place. Rudy, you will then take Tony and myself to the driveway and drop us off there and return to where we leave my car."

Rudy interrupted him, "Wait a minute I am not going to be babysitting your car I want in on this."

Hamed raised his hand for Rudy to be quiet. "Do not worry you will join us before long, besides I need you to keep an eye on the main road just in case Bill comes back early. If he does you call me on my cell phone and then wait for me to call you back, then you will come up to the house to exact your revenge on him." He gave Rudy a reassuring smile that seemed to keep him a little happier.

"I guess so," he replied.

"Good, then let us leave, Tony get in the front," he said.

Rudy followed the car and mumbled to himself the whole way. They parked Hamed's car and Rudy took them the rest of the way dropping them as instructed at the driveway.

As they walked down the dirt driveway Hamed knew that Tony was going to say something he was getting suspicious.

271

"They must mean a lot to you these shotguns," whispered Tony.

"Yes, they do but it's not just that it's the principle of the thing. We had an agreement, we settled on a fair but expensive price. I foolishly let it out that I had the other two from the collection and the man got greedy. He has my money and I'll have my shotguns." He was starting to convince himself that the shotguns really existed which they didn't.

"Surely you didn't just hand over the money on his word that he had the guns, how do you know he has them?"

The suspicion was building and he had to give a credible answer, "I saw both shotguns and inspected them thoroughly, they are the genuine article." He tried to sound excited.

"So why didn't you take them with you?"

"I am not in the habit of carrying around very large quantities of cash especially when I am going to a viewing only. I have no desire to be robbed by someone like Bill. I transferred the money to his bank account the next day. The deal was that when the money transfer cleared he would meet me and hand over the guns. The money did clear into his account and he called me saying the price had changed." He waited for the next question but one didn't come.

CHAPTER 39

CALIFORNIA

Hakeem had earned Mohammed's praise when he'd killed the former head of the FBI. The operation went without a hitch, if you don't count one dead neighbor as a hitch. Mohammed didn't care about the dead Neighbor in fact he relished in the news when he talked to Hakeem about it. The young man had proven to him that he could kill without remorse and nobody would stop him from completing his mission.

Mohammed didn't use the electronic voice changer when he spoke to Hakeem the next time. Hakeem was a little surprised that he was dealing with Mohammed the whole time but grateful for his praise.

An hour before he was due to leave for the airport for his next flight to Maui there was a knock on his apartment door.

Hakeem wasn't expecting anyone as he never took anyone to his apartment, he looked through a gap in the curtains it was Mohammed.

"Come in," he said as he opened the door.

Mohammed stepped into the room quickly not wanting to spend any more time outside than he had to.

"I wasn't expecting you," said Hakeem.

Mohammed placed his hands on both shoulders and kissed him on both sides of the face. "I am proud of you for what you have done for our cause. I can't stay long so let's sit and talk about your next mission."

"Do you want a drink of water or something?" Hakeem asked.

"No, are still going to Maui today?" he asked.

"Yes, I leave for the airport in one hour."

"Good, when you get to your hotel room in Maui I want you to call this number. The man you are calling is called Adel he will be working with you. When you meet, he will have a back pack with him, it contains the explosives you will need.

You are to go to this building I know you have seen it before."
He took a picture out of his pocket.

"Yes, I know it." It was all coming clear now why he
pushed him to get to know the roads on Haleakala.

"This building has operations that are connected to
NASA and we believe the CIA. This circle on the picture is
where you are to place the explosives with a one hour timer.
This will give you enough time to get away before it explodes. If
something happens there will be a remote in the back pack that
you can use to detonate the bomb immediately. Do you have a
problem with what I am asking you here?"

"No," Hakeem answered without hesitation or doubt in
his voice. Mohammed was asking him if he was willing to give
his life if it was needed to complete the mission.

"Good I didn't think you would have a problem with my
request but I know it won't come to that. Adel is not to come
down alive he is a liability, there are some things he has done
that gives me reason to question his loyalty," said Mohammed.

"No I fully understand, I'll take care of him before we
leave the mountain," replied Hakeem.

"I'll go now, you will hear from me as soon as you get
back to the mainland, Allah Ma'ak," he said in Arabic meaning,
God be with you.

"Allah Ma'ak," he replied.

CHAPTER 40

NEWARK, NEW YORK

Chalky and George had listened to the clatter and banging transmitted from the listening device in the warehouse for what seemed like an eternity. On the two cameras that were in the warehouse they saw that the men were cutting the bottom off the container and then they seemed to be welding it back on. This was the only thing that kept their interest for a while but it totally confused them. The men worked until late in the afternoon before they had a break and went into the office for coffee and something to eat.

"We are finished I think Sammy will be pleased," said Fadi.

"Are you going to call him?" asked Ghaazi.

"Yes, I'll do it now." He dialed the number Sammy had given him especially for the job. The phones they used were as always pre-paid cell phones with sim cards that were discarded with regularity. This made it very difficult for anyone to track their calls or phone numbers.

"What," Sammy said.

"Everything is ready," Fadi said.

"I'll call back soon," Sammy replied.

"What did he say," asked Ghaazi.

"He said that he will call back soon, he is not in a good mood," replied Fadi.

"He never is unless he is eating or fucking," replied Younis.

"Be very careful if Sammy hears you talking like that he will have you killed," said Ghaazi.

"Well it's true and you all know it."

"Yes, but we don't say anything about it," replied Fadi.

"He never gets his hands dirty or involved in any of the missions and he expects us to bow every time he walks in the room." Younis didn't hold back which surprised the rest of them.

"Come outside for a few minutes you are tired and have been working very hard," said Fadi.

They both walked outside and sat on the ground with their backs resting against the side of the warehouse.

"I know you have your reasons for hating Sammy but really we all work for Mohammed including him," said Fadi.

"I know but it does not mean that I have to bow down to him whenever he wants. He tried to rape my cousin in the back of her parents' restaurant when they were only a few feet away in the kitchen. What kind of animal is he Fadi, I know women have a different place in our culture but they are human beings and deserve to be treated with respect? He does not treat us with respect never mind the women, I can't help my feelings."

"Here have a cigarette." Fadi had already lit two.

"I am sorry I am not disrespecting you or the others," Younis was settling down again.

"We know just say that when you go in to the others and everything will be OK."

Chalky and George listened with interest as this could be someone that Strain could turn against Sammy in the future.

"Sounds like Sammy is living up to his sick reputation," said Chalky.

"Yeah! We'll wait until Strain gets his hands on him he won't be in charge then," replied George.

"There's a cell phone ringing it could be Sammy calling them back," said Chalky.

Fadi answered his cell phone, "Yes."

"We will go in the morning as planned make sure all of the vehicles are ready. Do not deviate from the plan or the route we will be watching you all. When the vehicle is secured give me a call on this number." Sammy didn't wait for a reply.

"Yes, we will be ready." Fadi realized that Sammy had already gone.

"What did he say?" asked Ghaazi.

"We are to go ahead as planned in the morning, as soon as we get the vehicle I call Sammy he will tell us where to take it," replied Fadi.

They were all excited now and shook hands with each other.

"We need to call Strain whatever they are up to will go down tomorrow," said George.

Chalky dialed Strains number, "It looks like whatever they are doing it's going to happen in the morning. We just heard another phone conversation between one of the men in the warehouse and Sammy. What do you want to do?" asked Chalky.

"Was there no mention of what they are up to?" asked Strain.

"No, they did mention something about a vehicle and when they get it they have to call Sammy.

"That doesn't give us much but we can tail them and find out what they are planning. Any mention of what time they are going to leave?"

"No nothing," replied Chalky.

"OK we will come over there tonight and camp out, I'll call you later."

"What's the news?" asked Thorn.

"It looks like they are moving out in the morning to get a vehicle and when they do they are to call Sammy and he will tell them where to take it."

"Strange what kind of vehicle do you think they need?" asked Thorn.

"I don't know but your guess is as good as mine, I think we will stay at the observation point tonight with Chalky and George. Let's put some stuff together and we can pick up some extra food for them on the way. Wheels why don't you get a car come with us we may need a second vehicle for surveillance on them in the morning."

"Great I am getting bored sitting around here," he replied.

With fresh food and some company to talk to George and Chalky were re-energized and ready for the night time surveillance.

The men in the warehouse had left just before Strain arrived at the observation point and returned at seven the next morning. There wasn't much said between them as they all got to work moving things around in the warehouse.

Ghaazi was twenty minutes behind the rest of the group when he arrived at the warehouse. He was driving a large box van like a U-Haul rental which they had stolen a month before and stored it. A new paint job and license plates for a vehicle the same make and color were now on the vehicle. He pulled up to the warehouse doors and beeped the horn on the van three times. He sat watching as the giant roller door slowly opened.

"We have another vehicle arriving at the warehouse," said George as he watched the building with his camera on zoom.

"Is it going inside?" asked Thorn.

"Looks like it he has pulled up to the doors and stopped but the driver didn't get out," replied George.

On the cameras inside the building they could see one of the men walk to the roller door and press something on the wall, the roller door started to open.

"There it goes inside," said George.

They all watched the vehicle do a three-point turn inside the warehouse and reverse up to the car that was covered. The roller doors were closing again and the driver and one other man stood shaking hands.

Ghaazi was excited at the thought of getting dressed as a police officer and driving the police car. The only thing he was worried about was running into a real cop from the area they were going to.

He got out of the van and shook hands with Fadi, "The day has come," he said.

"Yes, let's get the car into the van," replied Fadi.

They both pulled the sheet off the covered car Ghaazi got into the vehicle and started the engine. The powerful engine fired up first time and roared as Ghaazi revved the engine a couple of times. He tested the lights on the roof and they all worked, he didn't test the siren as he knew it would be heard outside the warehouse. Fadi and Younis opened the back of the van and pulled out two ramps and hooked them onto the rear of the vehicle.

Ghaazi watched as the ramps were put into place and Fadi signaled for him to drive the police car forward. He drove the vehicle slowly forward watching Fadi's hand signals directing him squarely onto the ramps. Two slight increases of engine power and the police car ran up the ramps into the van. Fadi and Musaad his brother unhooked the ramps and slid them under the police car and rolled down the rear door of the van.

As the team watched what was going on in the warehouse they were curious what vehicle was under the sheet. The cameras they had put into the warehouse were now blocked by the van and the covered vehicle wasn't visible. They could see one man pulling the sheet and dropping it to the floor. After a few seconds, they heard the loud noise of a powerful car engine being revved. Then the mystery vehicle was identified as the cameras picked up the flashing lights of a police vehicle on the walls and ceiling of the warehouse.

"It's a fucking police car," said Chalky.

"That just makes it more interesting," said Thorn.

"There is one problem we do not have a tracking device on the van, will the device on the police car still transmit through the skin of the van?" asked Strain.

"To be honest I don't know. What do you think George?" said Chalky.

"I'm with you I'm not sure either," he replied.

"Well it has moved in the warehouse but not enough to register a change in location on the receiver." Chalky had never had to deal with this before one vehicle inside another.

"It's too late to get in there now and put one on the van, we will just have to keep a close eye on it." Strain knew this could really screw the operation up.

"There's a cell phone ringing in the warehouse," said Chalky.

Fadi was pleased that Younis had settled down even more overnight and appeared to be totally focused on the job ahead.

Fadi's cell phone was ringing in his pocket, "Yes," he said as he answered the call.

"The other vehicles are in place, let us know when you are ten minutes away and we will get the diversion signs and traffic cones ready," the voice said on the other end.

"Thanks," he said and hung up.

"Was it Sammy?" asked Musaad.

"No, our colleagues letting me know the electricity vehicles are already in place waiting for us," he replied without thinking.

"What do you think they want electricity vehicles for they can't get money by stealing power?" said George.

"No but if they are going to cut power to a building it would be the ideal cover," replied Thorn.

"They could be robbing a bank but why all these vehicles that doesn't make sense," said Strain.

"We could be guessing all day but I don't think we will wait long to find out, they are opening the doors again," said George.

They could see that the van driver had gotten into his vehicle and as did the drivers of the flatbed with the crane and the big rig towing the container.

"Let's get to the cars, Thorn will be stealing your car George we may have to divide and conquer on this one," said Strain.

"Take these with you there's one each they are the receivers that will let you track all three vehicles. If the signal from the police car does not penetrate the skin of the van it will be active when it leaves the van and will show up on the screen." George handed each of them what looked like a GPS, which is what it basically was with a few Chalky and George modifications.

CHAPTER 41

LONG ISLAND

Charlie was late for the second time in a week and knew that he was going to be chewed out by his supervisor. He'd been working for the security company for three months and didn't want to lose his job but his car had let him down for the third time and by the time he got it started he was already late for work. He was ten minutes late when he drove his car into the parking lot at work, he quickly found an empty parking space. He ran towards the building and saw an armored truck leaving the secured fence area at the opposite end of the building. It wasn't just any truck it was the one he was supposed to be on.

He swiped his identification card through the reader at the employee entrance door he heard the electronic lock buzz, an indication that it was unlocking allowing him to enter. Inside the building, he swiped his identification card again at the door to the changing rooms. The card security system not only allowed or blocked access it was used by the supervisor to monitor employees for their payroll sheets.

Inside the changing room there were rows of metal lockers all painted grey. When he got to his locker it had a piece of paper taped to the door, a message was written on it, 'GO TO THE SUPERVISORS OFFICE' was what it said in bold letters. He put his uniform on quickly all the time praying that they wouldn't fire him. He sat down on the long wooden bench and fastened his boot laces. He stood up pulled down on the bottom of his jacket, an old habit from the military and took a deep breath. "Here goes," he said out loud to himself and turned towards the door, he didn't get chance to take a step.

"Where have you been Charlie?" the voice was that of his supervisor, Captain Dale.

"Sorry Captain but my car wouldn't start again, I." He stopped talking as Captain Dale held up his hand.

"I don't care what your excuse is because there is no excuse, you are late and I had to put another man on your watch riding shotgun. You obviously don't need this job so get changed back into your street clothes and go home. We do not need unreliable people like you in this company." Dale was glaring at him.

Dale had been in the Marines for twenty-five years and he didn't have any patience for slackers as he called them. He liked Charlie a lot as he too had served in the marines with a medal for bravery from his tour of duty in Iraq fighting in Desert Storm. For this the captain had a little more time and respect for Charlie.

"Please captain I need this job bad, my wife is pregnant and only has a couple of weeks to go before the baby is born. It's our first child we need the money." He watched the captains face hoping to find a sign of forgiveness.

"Christ Charlie, I had to put old man Clarke in your place he is two days off retirement and hasn't been late once in thirty years. You show up and give me the old pregnant wife sob story. I don't care if she is giving birth as you leave the house you get that sorry slackers ass of yours to work, on time." He didn't really mean the part about leaving his wife as she gave birth but he had to get his point home. "Get yourself down to the control room and help out with dispatch, go on get out of here before I change my mind."

"Thank you captain I won't let you down again." He quickly walked past the captain and headed out of the changing room. He was quickly followed by the striding military figure of Captain Dale.

CHAPTER 42

Strain, Thorn and Wheels took turns as lead vehicle keeping surveillance on the two target vehicles. The eighteen-wheeler and van stayed on the same route until they got to Long Island at which point they both split up.

"Wheels and Thorn stay with the van and flatbed I'll follow the container," said Strain, he heard them both acknowledge his instruction in his earpiece.

The eighteen-wheeler only went four miles and stopped in a truck stop, the driver and passenger stayed inside the vehicle.

Thorn and Wheels stayed with the Flatbed and van, like the eighteen-wheeler they also only traveled about four miles, they were just two blocks away from Strain's location.

"What are these guys up to?" said Thorn into the microphone hidden inside his sleeve.

"Not sure but my driver and passenger have stayed in the vehicle, what about yours?" asked Strain.

"Yeah! They are staying inside the cab," said Wheels.

Two hours went by before there was movement when the flatbed with the mobile crane drove off.

"I am on the move," said Wheels into his hidden microphone.

"Roger that," said Strain.

"Same here," said Thorn.

Wheels didn't have to stay too close as the tracking device told him where the flatbed was going. The yellow light on the GPS showed the flatbed drove three miles straight down the main road before it did two right turns and stopped. Wheels stopped and gave it a couple of minutes before he carried on. As he did the same first right turn he could see a white commercial vehicle on the grass verge on the right side of the road. At the next right turn where the flatbed had gone was a man with a red flag standing by a wooden barrier that was across the road. As wheels got close to the man he turned his indicator on to turn right. The flagman stepped into the center of the junction by the barrier and waved Wheels on pointing down the road. Wheels slowed down and rolled his window down.

"Sorry sir but we have some utility work going on in this road please take the next right," he said politely to Wheels.

Wheels didn't say anything as his accent would have given him away he just raised his window and drove on. As he drove past the junction he acted like any other driver would and looked down the road. He could see the mobile crane was being driven down ramps off the back of the flatbed. There was another vehicle there that looked like it was a genuine utility company vehicle and a giant crane on the opposite side of the road. He deliberately accelerated slowly to get a look at the vehicle ahead on the grass verge. It also looked like a utility vehicle it had all the markings of a city utility vehicle and a long steal line going across the grass to a telegraph pole that was on the ground.

Wheels called Strain and Thorn on the radio and relayed what he'd seen. He drove to the next right turn and tried to make his way back into the side road where the utility vehicles were, but the end of the road was blocked with wooden barriers.

Thirty minutes later the van drove off in the same direction as the flatbed with Thorn one minute behind.

"The van has stopped at the back of a strip mall I am going to do one pass on the road," said Thorn into the microphone.

Thorn drove slowly behind a school bus in the side street which gave him plenty of time to see the van. He could see the back of the van was open and the ramps were in place as he followed the school bus. There was one man standing by the ramps and he didn't look in Thorn's direction. Thorn drove down the road and made a slow return for another look at the van. As he got level with the back of the strip mall he could see the van driving away and the police car was in the road.

"We have the car on the GPS," said Strain.

"Yes, it's parked at the back of the strip mall but the van is leaving," replied Thorn.

"Stay with the Police car if you can, the eighteen-wheeler is now moving," replied Strain.

Strain followed the eighteen-wheeler on the same route that the flatbed had gone. Like Wheels he was diverted down the side road by the flag man. Strain could see the eighteen-wheeler parked in a road on the right. It was just past where the mobile crane was parked on the grass verge. There were a couple of utility vehicles on the verge just in front of the crane. They could also see a man in what looked like a cherry picker lift working on the power line just above the crane.

"I got the same diversion as you Wheels," he said into the microphone.

"I have moved I am a block away to your east I have a visual of the diversion and the utility vehicle on the grass, I don't have a visual of the eighteen-wheeler or flatbed," Wheels was watching what was going on through his binoculars.

"Stay where you are the police car is on the move," Thorn was watching the light on the GPS.

Thorn didn't want to give it too much room so he made a run down a couple of side streets to get ahead of his path. Thorn parked in a supermarket parking lot across the road from a bank when he saw the police car stop on the main road. There was an armored car leaving the bank and the police car drove off just in time to be in front of it.

Thorn was going to give the police car a minute and would then follow the route the GPS was showing it took. Without any surprise, it was going the same direction as the flatbed and eighteen-wheeler.

"The police car is moving he has an armored car directly behind him," Thorn said into the radio microphone.

"The flag man just waved another car past the side road, very light traffic on that road," said Wheels.

"I have a visual on the opposite end of the road where it's blocked by the barriers," said Strain.

"This looks like they could be targeting the armored car," said Thorn.

"The flagman is moving the wooden barrier and putting it across the road he sent us down. Wait he is pointing something at the vehicle on the grass verge." Wheels watched intently at what was going on.

He could see that the wire attached to the telegraph pole was now dragging the pole into the road. Just as this was done the police car turned into the side road off the main road. The flag man now changed position and waved his flag at the police car as it approached.

"They have changed the diversion they are going to send the police car and the armored car down the side road where the eighteen-wheeler and utility vehicles are," said Wheels.

"Those armored cars are equipped with armor plating, bullet proof glass, panic alarms and GPS. How the hell do they intend getting into it?" said Thorn.

"Wait the flagman is talking to the driver of the police car the officer has one leg out of the car looking down the road." Wheels had a great view of this but not the rest of the side road.

"I'll follow the armored car," said Thorn as he headed for the exit of the supermarket parking lot.

There were two cars blocking the exit Thorn got out of the car to ask them to move. As he started to walk to the two cars he could see that one had run into the back of the other. There was an argument taking place between two women about who was to blame. This was Thorn's only exit and he had to get them to move but he couldn't show his government I.D. as this would only involve him deeper.

"Ladies can I ask you to move the cars so that myself and others can get out of the parking lot?" he gave his best smile.

"I am not moving my car until the police get here, this bitch ran into the back of me, she said it was my fault how in the hell can that be when she ran into the back of my car," one of the women replied.

That really got the other woman fired up and they started screaming at each other again.

Thorn walked back to his car and pressed the hidden microphone in his sleeve.

"I am stuck in a parking lot and can't get to you, accident ahead of me," he said.

"Roger that, get here when you can," replied Strain.

Thorn looked around and saw a car pulling out of a space and looping around the opposite side of the parking lot. He jumped into his car and reversed quickly past the empty space. The space faced the sidewalk and there was only a low concrete stopper to prevent cars driving on to the sidewalk. Thorn fed the vehicle into the space and carefully revved the engine to give it more power to climb over the concrete stopper. The front end cleared with a slight metallic scraping sound and so did the rear wheels. He drove off the sidewalk and onto the road to the annoyed shouts of a couple of pedestrians.

"I am on route," he said into the sleeve microphone, he was at least four minutes behind now.

CHAPTER 43

HIJACK TAKES PLACE

Rogers was driving the armored truck and turning right behind a police car. As the armored truck entered the side road he saw the police car stop. Rogers and old man Clarke were watching what was going on in front of them.

"Looks like a diversion there is a telegraph pole in the road ahead," said Clarke.

"Yeah! The cop is getting out of the car to talk to the flag man," said Rogers.

They watched as the policeman shook hands with the flagman and got back into his car. The police car turned right as directed by the flag man proceeded down the road.

Rogers drove forward and had a clear view of the telegraph pole in the street and some utility vehicles in the side street where the police car had gone. He followed the flag man's direction and went the same way as the police car just as an eighteen-wheeler crawled in behind him.

"Look like they have had some power lines down," said Rogers.

They sat patiently in the armored truck as the police car went on to the opposite side of the road to get past an eighteen-wheeler. As soon as the police car went past the eighteen-wheeler it started to move slowly forward.

"I am going to call this in," said Clarke.

"No look he is waiving us through," said Rogers.

A man in a utility workers outfit had stepped into the road and waved at them to follow the eighteen-wheeler.

"Sorry about this," shouted the utility worker as they got level with him.

They both raised their hands in a thank you motion as they watched the smaller mobile crane ahead extending its arm.

"I'm calling it in," said Clarke.

"You're right they'll see that our route has changed and wonder why we didn't call it in," said Rogers.

The man in the cherry picker swung the platform he was on around toward the top of the armored car. Attached to the side of the cherry picker through an insulated sleeve was the power line with live wires exposed.

He quickly lowered the wire onto the top of the cab of the armored truck and a huge flash of light and melting metal flew into the air.

Rogers and Clarke did now know what had happened as 25,000 volts of electricity surged through the vehicle. The man in the cherry picker hit the vehicle three times with the same resulting flash of light and molten steel.

Rogers out of reaction to the noise pushed his hands out to his sides his left hand went straight onto the door frame. He was dead in seconds as the electricity entered his body burning his left arm and side severely. Rogers didn't do much better as he had a pacemaker in his chest and the electricity had already shut it down, he died clutching his chest.

All the electrical equipment in the armored car was burnt out by the electricity. There was no radio, satellite, GPS or emergency alert system working anymore, the vehicle was electronically invisible.

The flagman was moving his vehicle into the side road and blocked the road with his vehicle. He got out and threw down two smoke grenades into the ditch on each side of the road. He stood guard with an Uzi watching the road in case anyone decided to play hero. The smoke bloomed over the area blocking the sight of the armored truck but leaving the area clear where the hijack was taking place.

What you couldn't see were two men inside the container releasing spring loaded clamps that had been installed at the warehouse. The container had been modified in the warehouse by cutting away the sides and ends of the container from the bottom. Then clamps were welded inside the base with clamp hooks welded on the sides and back in eight places. In addition, four anchor points had been welded onto the outside of the top of the container attached to them were four chains connected to an iron ring in the center.

The mobile cranes arm was now fully extended and one of the men in the eighteen-wheeler was now standing on top of the container. He was holding up the huge iron ring attached to the chains and slipped it onto the hook of the crane arm as it came over the top of the container.

The container shell was lifted off the back of the eighteen-wheeler leaving the base still in place. The giant crane came down with a huge three-pronged claw on it and grabbed the armored truck. The hydraulic claw fingers pierced the skin of the armored car as a man on the ground used a sledge hammer to smash the wing mirror arms into the side of the vehicle to make it a little narrower. The big crane with its huge claws easily lifted the whole armored truck onto the back of the eighteen-wheeler.

Once the claws were released the two men that had traveled to the location inside the container jumped back onto the base by the armored truck. The container shell was lowered over the armored truck back into position on the base as the two men worked on the inside clamping the sides and ends in place. This was to prevent the container shell from being blown off if they encountered strong winds or sudden movement of the truck. The man was back on the roof again and he unhooked the iron ring releasing the mobile cranes grip.

The eighteen-wheeler slowly drove away with its stolen cargo and dead bodies. There was a flurry of activity now from the men in the utility vehicle uniforms as they all jumped into two vehicles and drove off. The whole hijack had taken three and a half minutes from when the armored truck was hit with the first blast of electricity to when the eighteen-wheeler drove away with the cargo.

"Where are, you Thorn?" asked Strain.

"About three minutes if this traffic light changes," he replied.

"They have targeted the armored truck it's going down now, they have set off two smoke grenades and it looks like they are using the cranes for something," said Strain.

He saw the flashes of light from the electricity hitting the vehicle but couldn't see what was happening because of the smoke. Strain watched the GPS to see if any of the vehicles moved that they had trackers on, it seemed like a long time before the eighteen-wheeler started to move.

"They are on the move I'll follow the moving target, Wheels stick with me, Thorn give us an update when you get to the location. Be careful I thought I saw at least one with an Uzi we don't need to tackle them," said Strain.

"With you," replied Wheels.

"Two hundred yards away behind vehicles at another fucking traffic light," said Thorn in frustration.

CHAPTER 44

The dispatch room was behind three security doors in the inner sanctum of the high security building. Next to the dispatch room was the security monitoring center. This whole part of the building was surrounded by a solid concrete walls, ceiling and floor that were three feet thick. The doors that allowed access were solid steel with a double access door system which meant that the inner door couldn't be opened until the outer door was closed and locked. This created a safe room area which was monitored inside by the security team. There were many cameras and electronic security systems in place around the perimeter of the building as well as internally. Everything and everybody was watched and recorded continuously. Alarm systems also protected the building and fences outside which were again monitored from inside.

Charlie knew that the being put in the dispatch room was a punishment but he was happy to accept it. The security surveillance room next door was the prime job in the company. You had to be with the company a minimum of five years before you were even considered. The pay was thirty percent more than you earned riding in the trucks.

The first two hours flew by for Charlie as the crews of the armored cars called in reporting their different positions and what drop or pickup they were about to make. The drop off and pickup locations were given in code so that anyone listening in wouldn't know what they were talking about. All the company vehicles were equipped with guidance positioning systems (GPS) which gave an exact location of the vehicle to within ten feet. On the security monitor, it showed the GPS map location and street address of the vehicle. Once you received the communication you pass it on to the security team in the next room who monitored the vehicles. This was normally very boring as nothing had ever happened to one of their vehicles, until today.

Charlie's truck had made six pickups so far all very large sums of money from different banks, a total more than a million dollars. Charlie was logging his latest communication from one of the vehicles when the red light on the wall started flashing, he'd only seen this happen in a drill when a vehicle was lost or under attack. There was a clock on the wall below the light which showed the time the light started to flash and how long it had been flashing or supposedly how long a vehicle was under duress. Four dispatchers were in the room and one of them had to hit the emergency alert button showing a possible vehicle under distress. The light indicating the vehicles position which came direct from the vehicles GPS had disappeared off the screen.

The door to dispatch burst open captain Dale and the duty manager Bass rushed in, "Situation please," Dale barked.

The dispatcher at the far end spoke, Charlie didn't know him very well, "Unit 609 has disappeared off the screen sir," he said with a little fear in his voice.

Here came the reaction he expected, "What the hell do you mean disappeared?" shouted Bass.

"It was on the map sir at the 2020 block of Carter Rd when it disappeared. I have called them three times on the radio and I am not getting a response."

They all looked at the speakers on the wall as the dispatcher tried again, "609, 609 please respond." Silence was the response.

The duty manager grabbed the microphone from the dispatcher, "609, 609 come in this is the duty manager," he said.

There was no reply.

"Who is in the vehicle?" asked Bass.

"Rogers is driving and old man Clarke is riding shotgun," replied Dale.

"Shit old man Clarke," replied Bass

"Call the police and tell them we may have a vehicle under duress," Captain Dale said to Charlie, "Give them the street address. You keep calling 609 until somebody replies or the police get to their location," he said to the dispatcher.

"Yes captain 2020 block of Carter Street," he didn't know why he repeated the address to Dale.

Dale knew something was wrong he could feel it in his gut, but how could the vehicle disappear off the screen. He hoped that it was a malfunction but he quickly discounted that as all their vehicles had additional power supplies for the vehicle satellite locator and for the communications systems. Why did they not call on the radio if they had a power problem, they had a separate handheld radio that was for emergency backup that was slotted into a charger in the dashboard of the vehicle. This was bad and he couldn't wait to get out to the location to find out what was going on.

"I have the local police on the telephone sir, they want to talk to you," Charlie said to the duty manager.

He took the phone, "Bass here," he said.

Everyone was quiet as he listened to someone on the other end of the phone.

"We have one of our vehicles unit, 609 that has disappeared from our satellite tracking system and we have lost all communication with them." He was listening to the person on the phone again and looked up at the clock on the wall below the light. "The warning system activated one minute forty-five seconds ago."

Dale got a little closer to try to hear what was being said on the phone.

"Christ man can't you get them there any quicker than that?" the frustration was starting to show on the face of Bass. "OK thank you," he said as he put the phone down. "They will have a unit there in four to five minutes they are dealing with a major wreck on the freeway and will pull one of their motorcycle units off that job." His face was bright red with the pressure of the situation.

"I don't like this. How far are they from here?" Dale asked.

"Thirty-one miles' sir," the dispatcher responded.

"Keep trying to contact them I am going to their last known location. I'll call you from my car find the fastest route for me avoiding the freeway." Dale wanted to see firsthand what had happened to his men, they were his responsibility the marine in him came out.

Bass grabbed him by the arm, "You are not going anywhere your job is here in this control room," he snapped at Dale.

"Take your hand off me," he replied as he glared at Bass. "Those men are my responsibility and I am going to see what has happened to them. You can take care of the situation here."

Bass stepped out of his way as he stormed out of the room. They all watched the monitors showing the hallways of the office building there was Dale marching as if he was going to war.

"God help anyone who gets in his way," said Charlie.

"Shut up and get on with your work," Bass shouted as he recovered his courage now that Dale had left.

It had been ten minutes since they called the police and they had not heard anything, Bass was pacing up and down the room continually looking at the clock and speakers on the walls. He couldn't wait any longer he picked up the phone and dialed the police, the operator answered, "Police."

"Give me the dispatch," he rudely commanded.

"One moment sir," was the reply followed by a silent pause.

"Dispatch," a voice said.

"This is Mr. Bass duty manager at Armored Security, we called over ten minutes ago, to report that one of our armored vehicles may be in distress and we still haven't heard anything. What the hell is going on surely your people have reached their location by now." Bass realized that he was being rude but he didn't care he wanted answers and he wanted them now.

"Hold one minute please and I'll find out." The dispatcher put the rude and self-important Mr. Bass on hold.

Bass was going ballistic on the other end of the phone, "What the fuck are they playing at they have put me on hold."

Charlie and the others tried to ignore him.

The dispatcher came back on the line, "Sir, a unit is at the address you gave he states that it's a tree lined country road with no buildings around. Have we got the correct address 2020 block of Carter Road?"

"Yes, yes that is the address. We didn't say that they were at a building we stated that that is the location where we lost contact with the vehicle and crew. The location is given automatically by our GPS system."

"Well maybe your system is faulty there is nothing at that location but trees. Have you checked with the next stop on their route to see if they are there?" The dispatcher realized that this could be a serious situation and was trying to help.

Bass had never even thought of calling the next pick up customer, "Call us if you hear anything," he replied and hung up the telephone. "What was their next pick up?" he shouted at the dispatcher monitoring their movements.

"Interstate Bank at MLK Blvd," he replied.

"Call the bank to see if they have arrived?" Bass continued to pace up and down the floor.

The dispatcher only took seconds to make the call as the number was in an automatic dial system they had for all their customers, they had not arrived. "They haven't been there sir," he meekly said to Bass.

"Get Mr. Stone on his cell phone." Stone was the President and Owner of the company and Bass didn't relish calling him with this news.

Charlie was busy with his dispatch duties and was getting a lot of questions from other armored truck crews as to what had happened to their colleagues, he couldn't give any information over the radio was what he kept telling them. He was beginning to feel guilty about being late for work he hoped nothing bad had happened to his co-workers, especially old man Clarke after he had to stand in for him.

CHAPTER 45

Mohammed and Sammy were sat at the factory they had rented waiting for the arrival of the eighteen-wheeler with the armored car. Mohammed had come up with the hijack idea and the plan for it before he left for the UK to commit terrorist acts over there. He gave the idea and plan to Sammy before he left and let him know that he expected him to locate a suitable target.

Sammy had spent six months planning the hijack with hundreds of hours of surveillance by his team of young recruits. He had lied to Mohammed when he was in the UK that he personally had been on many of the surveillance runs himself following the young recruits.

Mohammed was extremely proud of his plan and he couldn't wait to prove he wasn't just a terrorist mastermind. This armored car hijack would be remembered for many years to come and would rewrite the book on armored car security.

He put tracking devices on the container and the eighteen-wheeler without the knowledge of anyone, including Sammy. If someone decided to get greedy and steal the armored car and contents for themselves, he would give them a surprise. Mohammed had two of his most ruthless soldiers a mile away from the hijack. As planned when the hijack was complete Fadi was to call Sammy for the directions where they were to take the armored car. These would be given to him in three stages so that the final destination wouldn't be known until they were only a few minutes away.

Sammy's cell phone rang, "Yes," he said.

"The target is entering the road," said Fadi and hung up as instructed.

The next call from Fadi was to tell them that they had possession of the armored car.

"It has started the armored car is entering the trap," said Sammy.

"This money is going to help us buy more explosives and weapons. The new campaign I have planned for the USA will shake them to the core. These insular pigs will know that Mohammed is here and a force to be reckoned with. They will see death and destruction nothing and nobody will be safe. The only thing they won't see is me, I'll be like a ghost slipping in and out of this devil's country without their knowledge." Mohammed was walking up and down completely in awe of himself.

Sammy sat watching him he'd seen this before and knew that Mohammed was to embark on a horrific campaign. He would support Mohammed as he had in the past but he had his own agenda for some of the weapons Mohammed wanted. Sammy was enjoying his life in America and had amassed a small fortune without Mohammed's knowledge. His company business that he kept open to Mohammed was doing very well but the profits it earned were nothing compared to his back-door deals.

Sammy wasn't going to let Mohammed or anyone else ruin the luxurious lifestyle he'd become accustomed to. He had a plan in place to give up Mohammed to the CIA when they had finished the latest terrorist campaign. He knew that Mohammed wouldn't name him if he was interrogated he was too loyal and he would want Sammy to take over the terror reigns. The only people that could connect Sammy to Mohammed would all be killed at a bomb factory that Sammy would set up. No matter what the US government did they wouldn't find any credible evidence against him if he was investigated. He was shaken out of his daydream by Mohammed's voice.

"When this is done, I leave for California we have a great chance to get our hands on a new weapon," said Mohammed.

"What is it?" asked Sammy.

"You will find out soon enough."

Fadi was more excited than he'd ever been the hijack went perfectly just like they had planned. Mohammed would be very pleased with him and his brothers. He knew that they wouldn't get much rest before they went back to California on the next job. It was time for him to call Sammy on the cell phone he punched the quick dial he'd set up for Sammy's cell phone number.

Mohammed and Sammy went quiet when they heard Sammy's cell phone ringing, "Yes," said Sammy when he answered.

"We are on the way with the goods secure," said Fadi.

"You know which route to take, call me when you reach the first check point," he replied.

"Yes, it will be around twenty minutes," he finished the call.

Fadi could see the two vehicles tailing him and was sure that they were as excited as him.

He called Sammy as instructed and got the new directions, this happened two more times before they arrived at a factory. As they drove up to the building Sammy was outside signaling them to enter the factory. All three of the vehicles drove inside and parked.

Sammy closed the doors to the factory to keep out prying eyes. Mohammed walked onto the factory floor where the vehicles were parked just as everyone was getting out of them. He watched as they all cheered and congratulated each other. He gave them this moment of joy as he knew they had earned it.

"Enough open the container," he shouted.

"Quickly, quickly," said Sammy.

Fadi cut off the customs seal that was still wrapped around the lock on the container door handle and opened them. They creaked and groaned as he pulled them open revealing the two men inside and the armored truck.

"We did it, we did it," shouted one of the men as the doors opened.

"Shush," said Fadi to the excited young man.

"Open the armored truck," said Sammy.

One of the men still wearing a utility company uniform stepped forward with a blow torch.

"Be careful you do not pierce the metal on the inside we don't want to set fire to the money, Fadi get the fork lift truck," said Sammy.

After several minutes, he'd burnt off most of the lock in the center of the door and the hinges. He jumped down from the truck and Fadi drove the fork lift to the back of the trailer. On the ends of the forks there were four prongs a foot long that looked like arrow heads, he rammed the forks into the doors in the back of the armored car. They went through the doors about two feet and he reversed the fork lift truck quickly. The two doors of the armored truck were ripped off the frame and crashed into the sides of the container as Fadi reversed.

All the men moved forward to look inside at the bags of cash that they had stolen. To their surprise was a man inside the armored car in a company uniform, he was standing there with a shotgun in his hand. Nobody said anything as they were all surprised, including the guard. He was sitting on the bags of money when the truck was hit with the electricity, he was saved.

"Get back all of you," said the guard as he moved the shotgun around from one person to another.

"Everyone back," said Mohammed.

All the men did as they were told and Mohammed stepped forward. He was surprised that the man didn't die from the electric shock like the other two guards.

"Come any closer and I'll shoot," the guard was visibly shaking with fear.

"You need to listen to me before you shoot. You do not have to shoot anyone we will let you go like we did with your colleagues. One of my men will drop you off a few miles from here which will give us time to unload the money and leave before the police arrive when you give them the location," said Mohammed.

"You let Rogers and Clarke go?"

"Yes, they were left at the side of the road where we took the armored car. What is it to be?" asked Mohammed.

"How do I know I can trust you?" said the guard.

"Well you don't have to trust me you are the one with the gun. Fadi go outside with this man and take him close to where the hijack took place. Is that good enough for you?"

"Yes, get back all of you while I get down." The guard slowly got down from the trailer keeping the shotgun pointed at the men.

"Move back," said Mohammed as he stepped towards the man.

"Go with God," said Sammy who was standing across from Mohammed.

"What did you say," said the guard turning towards Sammy.

Mohammed pounced grabbing the barrel of the shotgun, he was on the man before he had chance to react. Mohammed plunged his knife into the guard's right side piercing his lung, a second and third blow found his heart. Mohammed held the man on his feet for a couple of seconds watching the life drain out of the guard's eyes he then dropped him to the floor like a rag doll. The group of men watched Mohammed he had a wild look in his eyes that only Sammy had seen before.

"Get the money bags out," he said quietly as he stared at the dead body.

The group of men didn't hesitate three of them climbed inside the truck and past the bags down to the rest.

Sammy wheeled what looked like a hotel laundry cart over to the pile of bags.

"You two open the bags and empty the money into this cart," he said.

Fifteen minutes later the cart with its load of money was pushed to a van parked on the far side of the factory floor.

"This has been a good day," said Mohammed as he lifted the lid hanging down the side of the cart and placed it over the top hiding the money from view.

Sammy placed a padlock on the lid and locked it. Everyone stood by the cart looking at the money until the lid was closed.

"When do we get our share?" said one of them.

Mohammed pulled out his handgun and shot the man in the side of the head without any warning. Everyone jumped back in shock, Fadi was covered on one side of his face and head with the man's brains and blood.

"Anybody else?" said Mohammed slowly moving his gun from man to man there was a collective group of heads saying no.

"Put the cart into the van," said Sammy.

"Fadi you and your brothers have your instructions, for the next job I'll meet you as arranged. The rest of you this has been the start of a great moment in history for us. This fool on the ground thought that it was for personal financial gain. I have never told any of you that you will be rewarded financially you will be rewarded by Allah when you sit by his side. Now we will eat a feast is waiting follow Sammy," said Mohammed.

Sammy walked to the back of the factory into another section leaving Mohammed with the van. Two minutes later Sammy returned to where he'd left Mohammed.

"Are they all eating?" asked Mohammed.

"Yes, I told them to stay in there until we join them," replied Sammy.

"Good get the other cart," he said.

Sammy brought over another cart identical to the one by the van. They put the second cart in the place where the money cart was standing and wheeled the money cart out of the way. Mohammed pushed the money cart to a small office in the far corner of the factory floor and closed the door.

"When I return, I want six men to support us in an attack I am planning. Talk to the Imam at your mosque he has been helping with the recruits for many years and now it's time to show him we are going to put some of them to work. I only want those that were born here and that have been trained at our camp in Pakistan. I had good reports about the twelve men that went to Pakistan during their college summer break. If something happens to them it will show that we are not just sneaking people in from overseas. These martyrs were born in this devils country and they are American citizens, a powerful message will be sent." Mohammed had that wild look in his eyes again when he finished talking.

"I have such a group of men already in mind, I have met with them recently they are excellent," replied Sammy.

"Let's eat," Mohammed said to Sammy with a huge smile on his face.

They all had their fill of food and sat smoking cigarettes and talking Mohammed watched all of them for signs of a traitor. He knew what money could do to people so he made a decision.

"You have all done well today and I have decided that you will all receive some of the money we stole as a reward. It won't be tens of thousands but it will be enough to enjoy as a small reward. You will get your money when I return to this city," said Mohammed.

"Thank you," said Fadi followed by the thanks from the rest of the men.

Sammy was somewhat bemused by this as he had no intention of sharing the money. He was going to put some of the money to his own good use and not Mohammed's new terrorist plot. Mohammed had confided in Sammy before the robbery that he was to handle the money and hide it in his company. Giving some of the money away just gave Sammy one more reason to hand Mohammed over to the CIA sooner. He wasn't going to share with anyone it was going into an offshore bank account with a Swiss banking group for his own use.

"We will all stay here tonight it will be safer there will be a lot of police activity on the streets now because of the hijack we performed. As you have found out there are toilets down the corridor at the back of this room. Nobody is to go back through this door into the factory area where the vehicles are tonight. In the morning, we will pray together and then we will go our separate ways," said Mohammed.

Mohammed watched for any kind of unusual reaction from the men, there wasn't any.

Sammy was trying not to show that he was shocked that he had to spend the night on the floor like a dog. He was very agitated and went to the toilet so that Mohammed couldn't see his anger. He thought that his days of sleeping on the floor with a group of smelly unwashed men were over. He stood in front of the urinal like he was peeing just in case Mohammed followed him he was gritting his teeth trying not to scream out in frustration. He heard the toilet door open behind him his eyes were going from side to side trying to see who it was.

Fadi walked up to the urinal next to Sammy, "We get to spend time with Mohammed it's a great honor," he said to Sammy.

"Yes," said Sammy as he zipped his pants up and walked away.

CHAPTER 46

Strain and Wheels followed the signal that the tracker was giving on the eighteen-wheeler until it disappeared off the map. The tracker system George and Chalky had designed automatically logged the address and GPS coordinates at the last known location.

They were only three or four minutes behind the vehicle but kept a respectable distance as they didn't know if the terrorists had other vehicles running counter surveillance. They saw the tracker beam die out on the screen in their cars and watched for the address.

Strain pressed the hidden microphone connected to his two-way radio, "I have lost the signal, what about you?" he asked Wheels.

"Yeah same here, but have the address."

"Let's meet before we look at the location," said Strain.

"I am leaving the hijack location it looks a mess here they have just abandoned all of the vehicles including the dummy police car," said Thorn.

"Can you get the tracking units off the flatbed and the police car?" asked Strain.

"Already done, I didn't want the local law enforcement to find them," replied Thorn.

"OK meet us two blocks to the North of the last address that we got on the tracker," replied Strain.

Fifteen minutes later they were sitting in Thorns car which gave them a long-distance view of the road at the front of the factory.

"Wheels already gave the last location a quick once over, tell us what you saw," said Strain.

"It's a massive factory building that has seen better day's lots of broken windows on the back but the rest look intact. There's a parking lot at the side with three cars in it but no sign of anyone around. I managed to get close enough to hear one gunshot, sounded like it came from inside. There was no sign of the eighteen-wheeler so I am assuming that it's inside. The signal we lost has to be this place because there is an overgrown field on either side about two acres in size and nothing but an unused road to the rear," said Wheels.

"Any ideas?" said Strain.

"Well it doesn't look like anyone has left yet so I guess we wait until we see if anyone does. Maybe tonight we can try to have a look inside, we need Shadow for that," said Wheels.

"Yes, we need to know what is in there if they leave they may take the money from the armored car with them. I don't think this place will have an alarm system activated while they are inside, do you?" said Thorn.

"A factory like that would have had motion or some other detectors installed on the inside to cover the windows and work space. An alarm system wouldn't be switched on even if they have a working system, which I doubt it does. Let's split up, Wheels you find a better place to see any vehicles leaving. Try and do a head count and take photos of the occupants of the vehicles. Thorn, see if you can find some high ground where you can cover the fields either side of the factory for tonight. You can watch over Bulldog and Shadow as they will be in the grass in the fields. I'll see how far away Shadow is, if he is not back I'll go into the factory tonight," replied Strain.

Strain really needed Shadow's skills to get into the place they were all good at illegal entries but nothing like Shadow. There wasn't a lock he couldn't pick and he was as quiet as a mouse. The three of them stayed in position for two hours without any signs of life in the building.

Shadow was back at the safe house getting equipment ready for the drive to Allentown the next day. He'd filled the tank of the car with petrol and had just put some extra equipment into his bag. He had additional firearms and ammunition for himself and bulldog plus night vision goggles and binoculars for surveillance. Bulldog was sat a block away from where the two men in Sammy's office had stored the van. He would wait for Shadow to arrive and give him a break for a few hours.

"Shadow," said Strain when he answered his cell phone.

"What's up?" he asked.

"We need you and Bulldog with us I'll explain when you get here," said Strain.

"OK I'll get Sleepy or L.B. to take over for us, we don't expect the van to move until tomorrow anyway," he replied.

"Good I'll text you the location where we are, bring whatever you need for entry into a factory, old style building. We will also need that converted parabolic microphone that George and Chalky made, you know the one," he said.

After speaking to them he called Chalky and George and asked them to get some additional information on the factory. They were very good at finding architect drawings and plans for such properties as well as any modifications that had been approved by the local councils.

Shadow and Bulldog arrived with the equipment Strain had asked for plus fresh tracking devices and assault rifles just in case things went array.

As the daylight faded a light came on in the factory towards the rear section of building that didn't have any broken windows. There wasn't any sign of movement so Strain dispatched Bulldog into the field on the side where the light was showing. He carried with him the parabolic microphone that Chalky had converted to give it the ability to listen through thin walls like those in the factory.

Shadow was in the field on the opposite side wearing night vision goggles looking for a good place to get inside the factory.

Thorn had positioned himself on the roof of a nearby business with his sniper rifle. He was covered in black camouflage so that he couldn't be seen from one of the adjacent properties. He was close enough that the silencer he had on the rifle wouldn't change the trajectory of any bullets that were fired from the weapon.

The area was in complete darkness now that the sun had completely set.

Shadow continued his evaluation of the exterior of the building and after thirty minutes of careful movement he found the place where he could get in.

"I have found a possible way in," he said into his sleeve microphone.

"Roger that wait until we hear from Bulldog," he heard Strain say in his earpiece.

Bulldog was lying in the deep grass resting his upper body on his elbows which also steadied the parabolic microphone. He'd heard the odd cough and mumbling but no real conversation inside the factory. Two hours past when he heard snoring and it was more than one person.

"Sounds like there are at least three people inside, I can hear them snoring," said Bulldog into his sleeve microphone.

"Any signs of movement?" asked Strain.

"Not for the last hour for sure," he replied.

"Time for me to go to work," everyone heard Shadow say in their ear pieces.

Strain wanted to say be careful but it wasn't needed.

Thorn watched Shadow through the night scope on his sniper rifle occasionally sweeping the building for signs of movement.

Shadow went straight to the door he'd identified as a possible way into the factory. He pulled a small bottle out of his pocket and a long thin paint brush no more than half an inch wide but with bristles about three inches long. He squirted some WD40 onto the bristles of the paint brush and inserted it into the key hole of the lock. He twisted the paint brush coating the locking mechanism inside with the lubricant. He did this several times over a period of ten minutes.

Thorn was wondering what he was doing and why it was taking so long as he watched through the scope.

Strain and the other members of the Mask Team knew exactly what he was doing as he'd done this many times in the past.

Shadow inserted two metal rods designed for opening locks into the mechanism and with a couple of twists and turns the lock opened. There was a little metallic noise as it opened and Shadow sat waiting to hear if anyone had heard it. Everything was still quiet inside and he slowly pushed the door open inch by inch squeezing WD40 onto the hinges as it opened.

Five more minutes went by before he could push his body through the gap in between the door and its frame.

Shadow said nothing as he entered the building he gave two clicks on his microphone to the team know he was inside. He put his night vision goggles on and slowly worked his way around the factory floor looking for possible guards, there wasn't any. He made his way over to the container and saw the body of the security guard on the floor. In the back of the container was the armored car with the rear doors ripped off. He continued towards a van which had a large laundry container on wheels standing at the back of it. He saw that the container had a padlock on it and quickly picked the lock opening it. He couldn't believe what was inside it was loaded with old phone books. He re-locked the padlock and carried on his surveillance of the factory. He eventually came to an office and looked through the glass door, inside was another container like the one behind the van. He went into the office and picked the lock on this container, he saw the money from the hijack. He locked it up again and placed a tracking and listening device into the thick material of the cart where it folded over the frame.

Shadow could tell by the placement of the cart that a double cross was going to take place. Someone had switched the cart full of money for the one by the van. He enjoyed the thought of screwing with them and decided to switch them. He squirted WD40 on the wheels of both carts and gave them a slight push to make the wheels turn and oiled them again. He couldn't afford the wheels to make the slightest squeak as it would amplify in the empty factory. It took Shadow almost forty minutes to switch the two carts and just as he got the cart with the money to the back of the van he heard a noise. Someone was coming out of the room where the light was, he crawled under the van and watched the feet of someone walking towards the van.

Shadow lay still with his 9mm in his hand ready to shoot his way out if he had to. The feet walked all the way to the back of the van and stopped. Shadow could smell cigarette smoke, whoever it was they were enjoying a cigarette he hoped that the person wouldn't look inside the cart. In the silence, he could hear the man sucking on the cigarette and blowing the smoke out. The man gave the padlock on the cart a couple of tugs and walked away back towards the room when he found the padlock was still secure.

Shadow lay under the van for five minutes before he slid out, he couldn't see anyone in the factory. He took the opportunity to plant tracking and listening devices on the van and two vehicles that were parked at the back of the factory. He decided that he didn't want to push his luck and left the way he'd gone in and locked the door when he was outside.

Strain saw Shadow coming out as did Thorn.

"What the fuck have you been doing?" he heard Strain say in his earpiece as he crawled through the grass.

"Tell you later, but if the gray van leaves the factory we need to follow," he replied.

It was a long night for the team especially Bulldog who had been in the field the whole time. The darkness of night was starting to fade slightly as the faint glow of the sun rising appeared on the horizon.

Bulldog was just starting to feel the damp of the morning dew when he heard movement inside the factory. After about ten minutes he could hear men talking in Arabic and almost as quickly as they started to talk they stopped. Then there was a new sound, he knew what it was straight away they were performing Salah, the practice of formal prayer in Islam.

"They are all praying?" he said into his sleeve microphone.

"OK everyone except Thorn back to the observation spot where we left the cars, Thorn we will discuss this through the radio so you can hear." said Strain.

They met at the cars where Shadow briefed Strain on what he'd done inside the factory.

"So, you think that someone is going to steal the money from the hijack, why?" asked Strain.

"Same old reason greed," replied Bulldog.

"I agree with Bulldog but there is something bigger going on here," said Thorn into his microphone sleeve.

"They would be sitting ducks if we take them out as they leave in their vehicles, but Thorn is right they are planning something bigger. If Mohammed is involved then it will be for the cause and not money," replied Strain.

"Yeah right now we don't have any idea who they are," said Bulldog.

"I say we let them leave and follow them, there's a good chance we will gain more information that way," said Shadow.

"OK Thorn join us down here and we will follow the vehicles that Shadow has put tracking devices on," said Strain.

Forty minutes later the three cars at the front of the building started to drive away. Five minutes later the van left the factory with one man on board followed by another van and a car two minutes later.

Strain and the team members split up and followed the three vehicles with the trackers on them. Shadow and Bulldog took the van with the real money cart, Strain the car and Thorn took the second van which they assumed had the second cart. The money van went into New York and eventually parked in the garage at the back of Sammy's office.

Shadow called Strain on his cell phone, "The van we followed has been parked in the garage at the back of Sammy's office. The driver locked the garage and walked away, I say we take the cart and store it at the safe house."

"Best do it quick before they come back for the van or move it again," replied Strain.

"Roger that," replied Shadow.

"What did he say?" asked Bulldog?"

"We get to steal the cart before they move it again, let's get the observation van that is at the safe house and come back," said Shadow.

"You go I'll stay here and keep an eye on the garage just in case they do come back," replied Bulldog.

"Looks like we are going in the same direction," said Thorn as he followed the second van. He could see the car Strain was following on the scanner.

"They are staying together so I would say they think that they have the real money," replied Strain.

"They are in for a shock," replied Thorn.

CHAPTER 47

TETERBORO AIRPORT, NEW YORK

Mohammed had left instructions for Sammy to follow him until they got to Industrial Avenue at Teterboro airport. Sammy would keep surveillance to see if they were being followed and once they reached the airport he would return to New York City and dump the car.

Mohammed wanted Sammy to see him go to the airport and believe that he was taking the cart full of money on the plane with him. As he turned into Industrial Avenue he watched Sammy continue driving straight on US Route 46. As soon as he saw Sammy disappear he turned the van around and drove down route 46 in the opposite direction to Sammy. He only went a mile and a half and drove into a housing sub-division to the East of the airport. He'd been renting a house in the neighborhood for almost a year and secured the van in the garage at the house. He didn't worry about the money he knew that it was safe at the house he didn't even check the cart's contents. He started to walk back to the airport as he didn't want to take a cab and have it on a record somewhere. There were a couple of short cuts through the sub-division that led to the road by the airport that he would take. He was going to take a private plane to California.

This use of a small private plane allowed him to sneak in and out of local airports all over the country. Even if homeland security looked at the manifest Mohammed's false ID would stand up to their scrutiny. He was never the pilot but one of his most trusted followers was he was a cousin on his father's side of the family. The plane they used was a twin-engine Piper it didn't have the capability to fly non-stop to California from Teterboro they would have to refuel on route.

It took Shadow over an hour to return in the van but thankfully nobody had gone back to Sammy's garage.

"I'll walk down there and call you on the radio when you can drive down," said Shadow.

Bulldog watched him walking down the narrow road past all the trash cans, even he didn't think that Shadow looked suspicious and he knew what he was about to do. As Shadow got to the garage Bulldog decided to time him to see how long it took him to open the padlock. He watched as his hand touched the padlock and Bulldog looked down at his watch to start the timer.

"OK I'm in," he heard Shadow say in his earpiece.

"How the fuck," he said out loud to himself as it only took Shadow three seconds to open the lock.

Shadow couldn't believe their luck as the van had been driven straight into the garage, the rear doors were looking at him as he raised the garage door. He turned the handle on the rear van door and it opened, they never even locked it.

Bulldog pulled up to the garage doors as Shadow was pulling the cart out he left the back wheels of the cart resting in the van. Bulldog ran around to open their van and ten seconds later he was closing it with the cart inside. Shadow closed and locked the garage door and they drove back to the safe house.

Shadow called Strain again, "We have the cart we will head back to the safe house and then leave for Allentown."

"Good job, stay safe and keep us up to speed on what is happening when you can," said Strain.

"Will do," replied Shadow ending the call.

Thorn called Strain on the cell phone, "Looks like we are heading towards Teterboro airport. If we do the radio's will get some interference from the communication towers around the airport. Let's stick to the cell phones for now."

"Good call, it looks like they have split up the van is going into the airport and the car is heading towards the freeway," replied Strain.

"It's going to be difficult to keep watch on the van as the roads leading into the airport are only two lanes and there are no real places to set up discreet observations," replied Thorn.

"Let's meet on the West side of the airport, do you still have your rifle scope with you?" asked Strain.

"Yes, see you in ten minutes," he replied.

Strain turned onto the highway and headed North past the airport just as he saw the flashing tracker light on the van stop for a few seconds and then go back the way it had come.

He called Thorn, "The van is leaving the airport it didn't even stop."

"Yeah, I see it, I'll head that way how far away are you?" he asked.

"I'm not sure maybe ten minutes as I just entered the freeway, I'll work my way around."

"OK I am closer I'll follow it," said Thorn.

They both watched the flashing light on the tracking receivers in their cars and it wasn't long before the van had stopped again. They both kept an eye on the tracking light as they drove towards it. Thorn was the first to the location and called Strain on the cell phone.

"I am driving into a sub-division where the tracking light showed the van to be. The houses are a real mix of single and two story homes I am close to where the van is. OK I have just past the house where the van is located. It must be in the garage as the tracker is showing it at that location. Meet as planned on the West side of the airport."

"Roger that," Strain replied.

Mohammed had just walked down a footpath in between two houses as Thorn drove into the road where he'd left the van, neither of them had seen each other.

Thorn and Strain found a good location to view the area around the hangers used by private planes.

"The van must have dropped someone off at the airport," said Thorn.

"It looks like it the driver must be in the house. We need to put surveillance on the place it could be a safe house for them," replied Strain.

"I think we should knock on the door and see who answers, door to door salesman type thing," said Thorn.

"Good idea I don't want to waste much time on surveillance we are already getting spread out."

Thorn was watching a small Piper plane that had left one of the hangers. It had taxied over to one of the flight operator's buildings. The pilot didn't get out but someone was walking towards it.

"No, it can't be," he said out loud.

"What?" Strain said dropping the binoculars from his eyes.

"OK, look at the building at one o'clock two red flags flying from one corner. In front is a Piper twin engine plane there is someone walking towards the plane."

"I see the plane and there is the man, fuck its Mohammed Ghahi that's who was dropped off. That bastard is always one step ahead of us. Write down the tail number of the plane. We are definitely looking at that house tonight," said Strain.

"I don't know how he gets so fucking lucky," said Thorn.

"At least we have a tail number to track the plane we are getting close to catching him Thorn I can feel it. Time to use your contacts Thorn and get the flight itinerary, it would be nice to know where they are going. The passenger list will be false names but that doesn't matter to us." replied Strain.

It only took Thorn ten minutes to find the flight information Strain had asked for, "The plane is going to a small airfield outside of Los Angeles with two refueling stops on the way. We could take the Gulfstream and get there ahead of them it will take the Gulfstream about five hours. The Piper will take at least double the time of the Gulfstream with refueling stops."

"Let's do it. I'll call the pilots, we can get L.B., Sleepy and Wheels to join us at the airport." said Strain.

CHAPTER 48

ALLENTOWN, PENNSYLVANIA

Shadow and Bulldog followed the van with the two men in along highway seventy-eight towards Allentown. Thorn had called them on the cell phone telling Shadow he'd run the facial recognition program on the photographs he'd taken in Sammy's office. Unfortunately, neither man showed up in any of the national or international criminal or terrorist data bases.

This made their job even more difficult as they didn't know who or what they were dealing with. Shadow and Bulldog were sent copies of two good facial shots of the men by Thorn.

They had not long driven through the town of Clinton, New Jersey when the highway cut through a heavily wooded area. There were trees on both sides of the road with the occasional break showing a patch of green field.

It was on one of these patches of green field that something caught Bulldogs attention.

"Shadow look at those wild hogs in the field, there must be forty of them."

Alongside the highway was a frontage road and on the other side of that there were the hogs. They were either black or brown many large sows and males with about a dozen or more piglets. Shadow slowed down slightly as they watched them tear up the field with their snouts and hooves.

"I bet that farmer is not too pleased when he finds out what they have done," said Shadow.

They drove for another thirty miles when the indicator on the tracker receiver showed that the van had stopped. Shadow continued driving and turned right in the direction that the van had gone. The town was reasonably big, they drove a block to the east of where the indicator showed the van was and parked.

Bulldog went for a walk to look for the van to see where the two men were. It didn't take long before he saw the van parked in a parking lot off the main street. From his location, he couldn't see anyone inside the vehicle. He walked along the shops as if he was window shopping and picked up a free local newspaper that was on a stand outside a card shop. He continued walking past a diner as he read the newspaper, they weren't inside the diner. He gave the opposite side of the street a quick glance and he saw them sat in the window of a coffee shop on the opposite side of the road.

He pressed his invisible microphone attached to the radio. "Come on down to the main street I'm in the Allentown diner on the west side of the road."

"Roger that," came the reply from shadow.

Bulldog and Shadow both ate a very hearty meal and drank a little water as they didn't want to have to stop for the restroom. The two men they were watching didn't seem to be in any hurry, they had been in the coffee shop for almost an hour.

"Look at this," said Bulldog pushing the local newspaper across the table to Shadow.

On the second page was a story about the vast growth of wild hogs in the State, they were causing millions of dollars of damage to crops and animals on farms in the State. Part of the story was the interview of a farmer who had lost calves and lambs to the hogs. He talked about how they eat everything flesh and bone, even their own kind.

"I didn't realize they were carnivores, did you?" said Shadow.

"No, nasty creatures by the sound of it that farmer says they will attack anyone that comes near them."

"Looks like they are going to have to cull them before too long," replied Shadow.

"The men are on the move," whispered Bulldog.

Shadow left enough money on the table for the food and a healthy tip.

They walked the opposite way to the men and ran back to the car once they were out of sight. The tracker was showing that the van was moving when they got to the car. They sat and waited to give them time to get some distance away before they followed, they only drove for seven minutes and stopped again.

"Looks like they have stopped close to the storage place, they must be putting the motion detector in place," said Shadow.

"Well nothing much we can do not until they get the contents of the storage unit emptied into the van," replied Bulldog.

They had a great vantage point to watch the van. They had parked amongst cars that were in the parking lot of the local cinema. As the light faded and darkness of night set in they used night vision goggles to maintain surveillance.

CHAPTER 49

MICHIGAN

Tony and Hamed kept very quiet as they approached Bills house, Tony wasn't happy with his brother waiting down the road. It was a bright night and they could see that both dogs were lying down outside the dog houses. Both dogs heard them approaching at the same time their ears pricked up and they jumped to their feet. Neither dog barked they just watched the trees as they knew that they had heard something but couldn't see anything. Hamed and Tony watched them sniffing the air as the dogs tried to get a scent but the wind was in the wrong direction.

Hamed produced a plastic bag out of his coat pocket and handed it to Tony.

"Throw them a piece of meat each," he said.

Tony did so without thinking, Hamed was smart Tony didn't have gloves on and his fingerprints were now on the plastic bag. Hamed took the bag off him and threw it into the bushes.

They continued to watch as the dogs walked slowly forward dragging the chains behind them. Tony saw them sniffing at the meat on the ground they didn't waste any time and greedily devoured it.

"Did you poison the meat?" Tony asked.

"I am not a barbarian I injected a sleeping cocktail into it, it will wear off after several hours they will only have a headache in the morning, a doggy hangover." He joked.

Tony was amazed at how fast it started to work as the dog's legs started to give way under them. Both animals fought the effects of the cocktail shaking their heads trying to stay awake. The dogs now knew that someone was in the trees and they had to protect the house but they watched for more meat. With a slight whimper the first dog lay down closely followed by the second, they were asleep.

"Right let's get to work," said Hamed.

Tony followed his boss to the barn the double barn doors were secured by the same padlock as the previous night.

"Did you find a way inside when you came last time?" asked Hamed.

"Yes, there's a window on the side I can open that and climb through," he replied.

"Good." There is no way that I am going to climb through the window thought Hamed.

They walked around to the side of the barn where the window was located. Tony picked up a rock from the ground and punched a small hole in the window. They window was a little too high to get through easily. Tony stood a large log on its end and used it as a step to get a better look at the window. The latch was no problem as he reached in through the hole in the glass lifted the lever securing the window and opened it. Within seconds Tony had hauled himself up through the window and was inside the barn.

The inside of the barn was a shambles there was all kinds of junk piled high on either side with a clear space down the middle for the trailer. He could only just about see his way around and was thankful for the moonlight. He jumped when a loud banging noise coming from the back of the barn.

"Noisy bastard," he said to himself, he knew it was his boss wanting to get inside. At the back of the barn he could make out a door and walked over to it. There was a large bolt at the top and bottom of the door, he slid them both back and swung the door open.

"Thank you," Hamed smiled as he walked into the barn.

"It's a rat's nest," Tony said.

"Yes, it is but like most rats he will have a secret storage place for his stash. Let's see if we can find where he has hidden my guns." He knew that what he was looking for was close by but where would it be?

They spent an hour searching the barn but didn't find anything but a few old revolvers and shotguns that had been used for spare parts.

Hamed kicked a box on the floor that he'd been looking through, "Where are they?" he said angrily.

"Maybe we should look inside the house." Tony wasn't sure what they were really looking for but he was convinced that it wasn't just two old shotguns.

"Yes, let's search the house."

They exited the barn by the rear door and walked around to the front of the house. The dogs were still fast asleep on the floor.

Tony tried to open the door to the house but it was locked. "Soon fix this," he said stepping back. He gave a swift powerful side kick to the door his foot punched a hole in the wood next to the lock. He knew that this powerful kick would impress his boss but he didn't say anything. He reached thought the hole and unlocked the door. He swung the door open and waved his boss inside.

The inside of the house was relatively small they had walked straight into the lounge. There was a fire place directly in front of them with a large armchair either side both of which faced a television that was sitting on a table in the corner. On one side of the fireplace was a door leading into a small kitchen and on the other a door leading into a bedroom.

"Much cleaner than the barn," said Tony.

"You search in here I'll search the kitchen," Hamed was getting frustrated as he stormed off into the kitchen.

Tony performed a systematic search of the lounge trying not to disturb too many items. He could hear his boss in the kitchen slamming doors and making a real noise as he searched the kitchen cupboards. They eventually both ended up in the bedroom and bathroom but they didn't find anything.

Hamed was beside himself with anger and frustration, he vented himself by uncontrollably kicking the bathroom door.

Tony watched as he saw him lose his usual composure, he was surprised. He heard a phone ringing it was his boss's cell phone.

"Boss your cell phone is ringing," he said.

He quickly reached into his pocket not wanting to miss the call and pulled out the cell phone. "Yes," he said.

It was Rudy on the other end, "He is on his way back to the house," he said.

"Wait there until I call you to come up to the house." He hung up on Rudy before he could respond.

"Was it Rudy?" asked Tony.

"Yes, Bill is on his way back here. You stay in the house and turn the lights off I'll wait outside for him," he barked at Tony as he stormed out of the house.

He just shook his head and moved through the house turning the lights off.

Bill was pleased with the gun show he'd exhibited at as he sold more firearms and knives than he had in the previous four shows. He turned his vehicle into the dirt driveway leading to his house once more cursing the tight turn. Once again, he promised himself that he would widen the entrance by removing some of the trees. The truck bounced around as it rolled in and out of the small pot holes kicking up dust behind it. The truck lights lit up the house and the two sleeping dogs on the ground.

"Lazy damn dogs," he shouted out of the window, they didn't move.

He was so focused on the dogs and the fact that they didn't move when he approached that he didn't see the hole in the front door. He stopped the truck and got out to check on the dogs. The headlights on the truck had the front of the house and yard illuminated.

"Get up," he said as he walked towards them.

He looked up at the front of the house and saw the hole in the door, he stopped in his tracks. His shotgun was in the truck he turned and ran back his enormous stomach bouncing around and wobbling side to side as he ran. He made it to the driver's door only to be confronted by Hamed.

"Hello Bill," he said calmly. He was holding a gun with a silencer fitted to the barrel.

"What the fuck is going on, what you are doing here?" he shouted.

"I have come to relieve you of some of your precious firearms namely the rocket propelled grenades and other illegal weapons. Shall we go inside?" He waved the gun at him to move towards the house.

Bill did as he was told he knew that he wasn't fast enough to try something, not yet anyway.

As he walked past the dogs he said, "Did you have to kill my dogs?"

"They are not dead they are sleeping."

Bill was starting to sweat, "I do not have the kinds of weapons you are talking about. I would lose my livelihood if I dealt in those sought of items."

The front door of the house opened as they stepped on the porch, Tony was standing inside.

"Who the fuck are you?" said Bill.

"Never mind who he is go inside," Hamed put the end of the gun into his back pushing him forward.

Tony saw the gun, "Where did you get that?" he said in surprise.

"From the barn," he said.

Bill started to say something, "You didn't," he was hit on the head with the butt of the gun.

"Get inside," he repeated.

"You trashed my house." Bill saw that they had searched the lounge and no doubt had been through the rest of his home. He was getting angrier by the second they had invaded his home, his privacy.

Hamed pushed him in the back again to make him move forward.

Bill turned slowly to face Hamed rubbing his back at the same time. "Can I at least sit down I think I did something to my back when I ran to the truck?" He continued to rub his back as if it was giving him trouble.

"Yes," said Hamed.

Bill walked over to the chair and turned around to sit in it. He slowly bent forward as if he was about to sit down when he suddenly stood up bringing his right arm around from his back. Bill had a large Bowie knife in his hand he expertly threw it at Tony at the same time he lunged at Hamed.

Tony saw the flash of the blade as it whistled towards him he instinctively jumped out of the way. He wasn't quite fast enough as the blade sliced across his forearm as it shot past him and embedded itself in the wall behind him.

Hamed was very calm as the big man came at him, he was expecting him to try something. He quickly dropped the nose of the gun and shot him in the right knee. Bill crashed to the floor immediately screaming in pain.

"The fat bastard cut my arm," said Tony.

"Well he has paid for it now," replied Hamed.

Tony then realized that he'd shot the man in the knee blood was running out onto the floor.

Hamed picked up a wooden chair that was by the wall and placed it next to bill. "Help me get him onto the chair."

They both helped Bill to his feet and Tony shoved the chair under him. He was sweating even more now and growling with pain. He looked a mess with the shattered knee and the sweat oozing through his clothing and dripping down his face.

"What are you going to do with me now?" he snapped.

"Why nothing Bill, all you have to do is tell me where the guns are and we will leave you alone." He gave him a big smile.

Bill had more hatred in him now than he'd ever known and spat a mouthful of blood and saliva into Hamed's face.

Hamed jumped back as the blood spat at him landed on his forehead. He slowly wiped it off with his coat sleeve. "I am sorry that you are not cooperating you could have made this much easier on yourself." He stepped forward and slammed his right foot onto Bill's injured knee.

The man screamed at the top of his lungs as the pain surged through his leg.

Hamed lifted his foot, "Are you ready to tell me now?"

"I don't know what you are talking about," he spluttered his reply as sweat and saliva dripped onto the floor.

Hamed's foot slammed into the knee again once more the screams roared out of the big man.

Tony thought the man had suffered enough and stepped forward to stop the punishment.

In his peripheral vision Hamed saw Tony move towards him and he swung the gun up pointing it at Toni's face. "Do not get involved here this is nothing to do with you, stay out of it."

Tony realized that this was getting out of hand and he wanted out of the whole situation.

"There is no need to do that to his knee he is already in pain," said Tony.

"Stay out of it," was the curt reply.

He backed away again.

"Now then for one last time where are the guns?" He raised his foot again showing Bill that he was going to slam it down again onto the injured knee.

"Fuck you," he replied.

Hamed put the gun up against his left knee. "OK have it your way, say hello to spending the rest of your life in a wheel chair."

Tony moved very slightly forward and to his right, he'd decided to deliver a kick to Hamed's hand to knock the gun away. He took one more step when Hamed took the gun off Bill's knee and pointed it at him.

"I told you to keep out of it now move over to the fireplace where I can see you."

"He doesn't seem to know what you are talking about."

"Really well we are about to find out." He placed the gun back on the knee and started to squeeze the trigger.

"OK stop, stop I'll tell you where they are."

"You see Tony he knew exactly what I was talking about. Now for the very last time, where are they?"

"In the bedroom," he replied.

"We looked there," said Tony. It was more of a plea for him to not play games as he now knew that Hamed would shoot him in the other knee or even possibly kill him.

"They are in a hidden room behind a wall panel at the back of the bed."

"Go and look," he waved the gun at Tony.

"There are four wooden pegs in the wall two at the top and bottom, pull them out and the panel will swing open." Bill didn't have any fight left in him the pain was too much.

Tony was hoping that there would be a gun in the hidden room that he could use to disarm Hamed or kill him if necessary. He stopped in the doorway of the bedroom listening to Bill.

"Go do it," Hamed insisted.

The bed was made of solid wood which made it very heavy. It took several maneuvers to move it far away enough from the wall so that he could get behind it. Just as Bill had described there were four wooden pegs, he pulled them all out. The wall moved inwards slightly as soon as he took the last peg out. He pushed on the panel and the whole section of wall swung inwards revealing a small room full of ammunition boxes and a large variety of weapons.

"Have you found it?" shouted Hamed.

"Yes, it's just as he described." Tony went to step into the room when he heard Hamed's voice behind him.

"I can see that," he said.

"There is an arsenal in here."

"Yes, I am sure, help me with him and then we will leave with my guns." He was playing the game right to the end making out that the shotguns really were the quest. He didn't notice as he left the room that Hamed had taken the knife that Bill had thrown at him out of the wall.

Tony was still a little apprehensive as he walked out of the bedroom.

Hamed had to keep Tony relaxed for a little longer as he knew that he was still very dangerous, he decided to give him a little confidence that it was over. He took the cell phone out of his pocket and called Rudy, he answered immediately.

"Yeah, is that you," he said.

"Yes, come on up we are leaving."

Tony sighed with relief it was over at last, what a mess he thought.

Hamed watched him the whole time and saw that he was suddenly relaxing at the thought that this was at an end.

"Help me get Bill on the floor we can then elevate his leg to slow down the bleeding, then we can apply a dressing."

He couldn't believe what he was hearing now the man wants to help him. He watched as he grabbed a hold of Bill's arm and placed it around his own neck.

"Put your arm around his neck Bill and let us help you up."

He was in no mood to argue and did as he was told. Tony then put one arm on his back and gripped Bill's arm with the other.

Neither man saw what happened next until it was too late. Hamed plunged the bowie knife into Tony's neck he sliced his throat from right to left.

Tony let go of Bill and clutched at his throat with both hands, blood squirted out all over Bill's arm and chest. Tony's eyes were wide open with shock as he looked at Hamed.

Bill was screaming in shock, "Oh your sick bastard, you sick fucking bastard." He could hear Tony gasping for air as the blood flowed over his airway.

Hamed moved behind Tony as he stood upright and removed the silencer from the gun. He held Tony by the collar of his coat and fired two rounds into Bill's chest, the screaming stopped instantly. Hamed saw the shock in Tony's eyes and smiled as his pushed him on top of the fat man. Tony couldn't help himself his hands still clutching at his throat he struggled for air he landed hard on top of the lifeless body of Bill. The wooden chair couldn't hold the weight of both men and collapsed. As the bodies landed on the floor Tony was bounced to one side by the big man's body, he died lying on his side next to Bill.

Hamed placed the gun in Tony's right hand and gently pressed his index finger on the trigger making sure that he had a good fingerprint on it. He then let the hand and gun drop together making it look like it happened naturally.

"You have been very helpful gentlemen." The noise of a car racing up the drive made him refocus he had one last person to take care of, Rudy. He ran into the kitchen and picked up the sawn-off shotgun that was lying on top of the safe and returned to the lounge.

Rudy was driving faster than he should have as he wanted to pay back the fat man for shooting him. He would give him a couple of hard kicks and punches to help him remember who he was in the future.

Rudy saw Hamed appear at the front door as he drove up to the house and stopped the car short of the sleeping dogs, he was still wary of them. He heard him shouting instructions to him.

Hamed went to the front door he didn't want Rudy coming in that way.

"Rudy go in through the back door, quickly hurry." He pointed in the direction that he should go.

Rudy obeyed the instructions without hesitation and ran to the rear of the house. He saw the back door and burst in without thinking, it would be the last thing he would ever do.

Hamed was only eight feet from the inside of the rear door when Rudy burst into the room. He pulled the two triggers on the sawn-off shotgun blasting the man with both barrels. The force of the shotgun blast knocked Rudy backwards against the open door smashing him through the glass panels. His body slid down the door and onto the floor, he was already dead his body had a huge hole in the chest.

Hamed walked back into the lounge and this time put Bill's finger prints on the shotgun and dropped it on the floor in the kitchen.

By the time, he walked to his car and drove back to the house to load the weapons from the secret room, it would take him almost two hours.

As he left the house for the final time he stopped at the front door and turned around to survey the scene that lay before him. "Not a bad day's work," he said to himself.
He drove down the dirt track back towards the main road as it started to rain heavily. "Allah be praised you are washing away my tire tracks and evidence outside the house," he said to himself with a smile on his face.

CHAPTER 50

NEW YORK CITY

On route to Newark airport Strain had George and Chalky leave the container warehouse surveillance and move to Sammy's office building. Strain and Thorn called at the safe house for additional electronic surveillance equipment and weapons. They had plenty of time to make it to California before Mohammed arrived. L.B., Sleepy and Wheels were glad to get out of New York in the hope of catching Mohammed.

The Piper was around two hours behind the Gulfstream as it arrived at Van Nuys, a small public airport in San Fernando Valley, LA.

Thorn had one of his contacts in the military watch the track of Mohammed's plane it had already made one refuel stop and was now less than an hour from Las Vegas. Four vehicles were waiting at Van Nuys when the Gulfstream arrived. Three of the vehicles were the usual high powered engine vehicles and one state of the art surveillance vehicle. They discussed and agreed on a surveillance plan for the team to track Mohammed when he arrived.

The team loaded their weapons and equipment into the respective cars inside a high security hanger used by the military. This hanger looked like any other but was rented by the US military through a private corporation for highly classified military operations. Strain received a call from his military contact to let him know the Piper had just left Las Vegas heading to Van Nuys.

"They are on the way," said Thorn.

"OK everybody you know what to do," said Strain.

Wheels and Sleepy took one car each, L.B. had the observation vehicle while Strain and Thorn stayed together in the third car. The two cars and observation vehicle left the airport and parked at strategic locations close to the airport. Strain and Thorn stayed at the airport where they could see the

Piper arrive. They had moved closer to the hangers where small aircraft parked, this is where the Piper would be parking when it arrived. Thorn had his contact run all the known flights that the Piper had taken in the last two years. When he and Strain had looked at the print out of the flights it was glaringly obvious that the plane wasn't declaring all of its flights. Several times the plane was in Washington D.C. or New York but no history of how it got there.

They watched the Piper arrive with their binoculars and as it taxied they could only see the pilot. The plane eventually stopped a hundred yards from where Strain and Thorn were hiding. The pilot got out of the plane and opened the door on the passenger side. After a couple of minutes of watching the pilot moving things around in the back-seat area of the plane they saw him appear with something in his hand. It was two sets of wooden blocks attached by short ropes they were the chocks that wedge the wheels to stop the plane rolling. The pilot put them in place at the front and back of each of the two plane wheels and returned to the passenger side of the plane. He appeared again with a small brown bag in his hand and walked away from the plane.

"Where the hell is Mohammed?" asked Strain.

"He could still be in the plane it's fairly dark now he may be waiting to see if the area is clear, replied Thorn.

"Possible but unlikely he would have left with the pilot it would be much easier. We need to check the inside of the plane to be sure he is not inside."

"I'll get the airport security guard to check the plane along with a few others so it does not look suspicious," replied Thorn.

Ten minutes later the guard was walking around several planes checking that they were secure. When he got to the Piper he was to point his flashlight towards the floor and give two quick flashers if the plane was empty, which is exactly what he did.

"That son of a bitch must have gotten off the plane in Vegas or the first refueling stop," said Thorn.

"I knew this wasn't going to be easy, that sneaky bastard is one step ahead again, let's get the team back to the hanger," said Strain.

"What about the pilot we could follow him?" asked Thorn.

"We could but I don't see him leading us to Mohammed, he will most probably go home and wait for the next flight instructions. Can your people keep an eye on the Piper indefinitely?" asked Strain.

"Yes, they can and I agree I don't think the pilot will be of use at this point."

"Mohammed is up to something else and I get the feeling it won't be long before we find out what it is," said Strain.

After a long discussion, the team agreed to return to New York in the morning, Thorn had a local team keep the pilot and plane under observation. Thorn's team was all Delta Force members who used the surveillance as training for urban warfare. They would also plant listening devices in the cockpit and passenger areas of the Piper they were connected to a recording device that was attached to the bottom of the pilot's seat. They knew that they couldn't listen in live to the conversation when they were in flight so recording was the best method.

CHAPTER 51

CALIFORNIA

As promised Fadi and his brothers arrived at the Holiday Inn on time and were stood in the lobby of the hotel waiting for Mohammed. Unbeknown to them he had no intention of meeting them at the hotel, the less time he spent with them in public the better. He still wasn't convinced that this soldier Matthews wasn't a government agent working undercover.

He called the hotel and asked for the reception desk, a young lady answered. "Reception desk can I help you?" She said in a well-trained cheery voice.

"Yes, I hope you can. I am meeting three of my colleagues at your hotel and I am stuck in traffic. Can you see them in the lobby one of them his name is Musaad, I would like to speak to him if that is possible?" He was being deliberately nice to gain her cooperation.

"I see three gentlemen standing together please wait a moment." She put him on hold. "Mr. Musaad," she said in a raised voice directed towards the men in the lobby.

Musaad heard his name and turned to see who had called him. "Yes," he replied.

"You have a call sir you can take it on the white house phone on the wall over there." She pointed to three white phones on a wall next to the toilets.

"Thank you," he replied.

"One moment, sir, I'll transfer you," she said to Mohammed.

"Thank you," he replied.

As Musaad approached the telephones one of them rang, he picked it up. "Hello," he said.

"Go out of the hotel via the front doors and turn left. Go three blocks until you see the street market on your left. Walk down the center of the market until it ends and wait there for me." The phone went silent.

Musaad put the telephone down and indicated to his brothers that they were leaving.

Once outside the hotel they followed the directions given by Mohammed and found the market. The street market was very busy it seemed like it was wall to wall people. They were half way down the market when Mohammed walked across in front of them.

"Follow me," he said without even acknowledging them.

He walked down a side street lined with small stores and turned right into another street which had apartments on both sides. Just as they started to wonder where they were going a van stopped next to them and the side door slid open.

"Get in," said Mohammed.

They did as they were told.

Inside was a large heavy set man who didn't look very friendly. "Sit down," he said curtly.

The van drove off with them inside.

"This is Sammy," said Mohammed.

They all nodded as he didn't offer an introduction or hand shake.

"Where are we going?" asked Fadi.

"To look at this road you talked about," replied Mohammed.

It took them two hours to get to the top of Pine Hill Road and another hour of slow driving up and down the section Matthews had described where the attack on the vehicles would take place. They were surprised at the lack of traffic on the road it was very quiet this is why the military used it.

"We have to walk the section of road where we are going to use the luge boards," said Fadi.

"Why is that?" asked Mohammed.

"We can't see the road surface properly from the car we have to walk it and to get a better feel for the road." He took any huge event seriously and this was no different.

"OK we will walk it." Mohammed was very impressed with their attention to detail and felt that the soldiers plan would work. What the soldier wouldn't know would be that Mohammed would have a few changes to the plan.

"Fadi and I will walk the road, Ghaazi you can follow us in the car." Ghaazi was the youngest brother and the one with the least experience in street luge.

"I'll walk with you," said Mohammed.

They got out of the car where they would start the luge run and checked the old driveway.

"This looks like a pretty good surface we have to brush away some of these stones that are loose on the road." Fadi didn't want any of them to get caught up in the wheels of the board.

"These bushes along the side of the road will help hide you from the view of the military vehicles. You are looking down on the road below and that will give us an observation advantage," said Mohammed.

"You can push me to get me going." Musaad said to Fadi.

"Ha! You assume that you are the one to have the fun of chasing the trucks, I am the one with the most experience." Fadi automatically thought that he would be the one to have the honor of chasing down the hill after the military vehicles and cutting the brake pipes. The thought excited him.

"No, no I'll be the one to follow the trucks," replied Musaad.

"We will decide later," said Mohammed. He didn't want any petty family argument to sour the plans and he'd to cut it off before it started.

"OK let's walk down the road." Musaad was a little angry at his brother but he would do whatever Mohammed said.

Mohammed didn't say anything as he walked along with the two brothers he just listened to their conversation. He thought that they were talking about breakfast at one point when he heard the brothers discussing scrambled eggs and bacon. He was concerned that they weren't paying full attention.

"Why are you talking about eggs and bacon?" he asked.

"Oh, sorry we are talking about the road surface. In street luge, there are certain words that are used to describe different things in the sport, a sort of slang or street luge talk. Scrambled eggs and bacon describe the condition of the road surface. I'll show you what we mean." Fadi stopped at the side of the road and squatted down.

"These names describe a road surface?" Mohammed was a little bemused.

"Yes, you see that section of road here that is a little rough and worn away by the continuous use by vehicles."

"Yes." Mohammed squatted next to him, now interested again.

"This is what we would call scrambled eggs because it's rough but not too rough. Now look on the other side of the road up against the rock face that is very rough and has a lot of holes, we would describe that surface as bacon." Fadi smiled at Mohammed.

"Why don't you just say that it's rough or very rough?" He didn't see the sense in this creation of words to describe something this way.

"It's just the way athletes in the sport talk," said Musaad.
"I see," he said.

They continued down the hill closely followed by Mohammed who didn't want to ask any more questions about the language they were using. They got to the area that would hopefully mark the end of their run on the board and by now the vehicle would be way ahead of them.

"I am a little concerned that if we do not get the chance to stop here we would continue on around the next bend and hit the steepest part of the hill. This could be dangerous as we may puke a wheel." Fadi saw the expression on Mohammed's face when he said this.

"He means that a wheel may come off the board," said Musaad.

"Hopefully this won't happen." Fadi knew that losing one of the Urethane wheels on one of the bends could result in disaster. On a conventional luge course, they would have barriers or hay bales to stop them going over the edge, this wasn't going to be the case here. Sometimes when they get to high speeds the wheels would also melt or catch fire, this was also called puking a wheel or flame.

"What is that steep gravel road for?" said Mohammed.

"I am not sure but we can look at it," replied Fadi.

They walked up the gravel road as the main road went into a sweeping bend.

Mohammed studied the road below and the steep gravel road they had walked up.

"This is where the soldier will come with his truck after you cut the brake pipes in the truck following him. As the second truck comes around that bend that you can see in the distance he will run off the road. Tell the soldier that the plan has changed and instruct him to drive up this gravel road there is nothing up here. You have your vehicle ready to transfer the weapon from the military truck and two cars parked here. You are happy that you can use your boards to get under the truck to cut the brakes?" said Mohammed.

"Yes, we can do it," replied Fadi with confidence.

"Good then we will go back to the mosque and talk about the plan before you meet with the soldier tonight. Are you all ready for your trip to the East Coast?" asked Mohammed.

"Yes, we are ready," replied Fadi.

"We have a very busy time ahead of us it's important to stay focused," said Mohammed.

"We will," replied the brothers.

He knew that he'd already put these young men through a lot but they had earned his respect. The brothers were a true asset as he'd never had three brothers so committed to him before. In the past, he had brothers working for him operating in Pakistan and Afghanistan but not in the West. They were proving him to be right, the Imam's he had talked to didn't think that they would find US born Muslims that would be so dedicated. It had taken five years to get them to this level and there were many more being trained behind them. They were recruiting the trainees from Universities, colleges and mosques all over the USA and Canada. Different Muslim extremist groups based in Europe were doing the same type of recruitment drives.

Mohammed was operating his a little differently by selecting some men with the looks of Central or South Americans. He had several recruits already training in the North-

Eastern region of Argentina and others living in Mexico to learn the language fluently. By doing this he believed they could hide amongst the Mexican and South American communities in the US until they were called upon.

CHAPTER 52

ALLENTOWN, PENNSYLVANIA

People started to leave the cinema after the midnight movie special.

"We need to move soon the cinema is emptying out and our car will be the only one in the parking lot," said Shadow.

"You're right let's have a look around," replied Bulldog.

They drove around a couple of blocks being careful not to pass the van with Sammy's men in it. The only place they found was at the side of a local bar they could only see the passenger door of the van but had a full view of the storage facility.

The bar had been closed a couple of hours now and the streets were dark and quiet. This was the hardest time for any surveillance as the early hours of the morning the body wants to rest and sleep. They had taken turns to sleep for an hour at a time but only managed the odd ten-minute cat nap. It was now four thirty in the morning and there wasn't any sign of movement at the storage building. Shadow was giving up hope when he saw the light from a vehicle coming down the street. The car went passed their position and the storage building, five minutes later it was back. Shadow and Bulldog were staying low in the car seats both using the night vision goggles.

They watched as a man got out of the car and unlocked the gate leading into the yard where the storage units were. Within a couple of minutes, they saw a dim light appear inside the storage building. The next twenty minutes went very slowly as they kept eyes on the storage building.

"The light has gone off inside," said Shadow.

They watched as the car left the yard and the driver locked the gate again.

"Well if they stick to the plan they will wait an hour," said Bulldog.

Sammy's men didn't wait for an hour as instructed their van drove up to the storage yard thirty minutes after Hamed had left. They watched as Sammy's men repeated what Hamed had done with the gate and the lights inside.

"OK time for us to make a move," said Shadow.

They had formulated a plan as they sat in the car keeping surveillance, disable the car and the two men. They could then steal the van and weapons returning to New York with both.

They climbed the gate to the storage yard and split up Shadow went straight to the van. He carefully opened the driver's door and pulled out one of the ignition wires so that the engine wouldn't start. Bulldog was covering him with his 9mm Browning from about twenty yards away.

The side door to the building burst open and a faint light came out into the yard from inside the building. Shadow dropped and crept to the front of the van with his sidearm in his hand. The man opened both doors to the back of the van and threw in some rifles. This went on for about twenty minutes one after another the men loaded the van with rifles, handguns, two rocket propelled grenades and over a dozen military style wooden boxes of ammunition. The final two boxes they brought out were full of plastic explosive, fifty pounds in each box.

Shadow and Bulldog came out of hiding as the two men closed the door to the building.

"Stand still," said Bulldog.

The two men did as they were told for a split second and then turned to the sound of the voice. One man had an Uzi sub machine gun under his coat and the other came around with a handgun at the ready. As the Uzi was raised towards Bulldog he fired off two rounds at the man, both struck him in the chest.

Shadow was moving into the open and fired twice at the second man who managed to get a shot off at him. Shadow was on target and hit the man in the torso one was a little low and went straight through his body missing the vital organs. He fell to the floor blood oozing through his clothing.

Shadow and Bulldog both walked quickly towards the men keeping them covered with their weapons. The man with the Uzi was dead and the second man was bleeding badly. They tied the hands and feet of the two men and threw their bodies into the back of the van on top of the weapons. Shadow took electronic copies of the finger prints of the two men and sent them straight to George and Chalky to run. Bulldog took some DNA samples from them and kept this for when they returned for Thorn. Five minutes had gone by since the first shots were fired and they we

re now heading for the highway. Shadow drove the van after reconnecting the ignition and Bulldog drove their car.

On the outside of town Shadow called Strain, "John we have two packages with us, one is beyond repair the other is going to be rotten by the time we get home."

"What about the rest of the consignment was it there?" Strain asked.

"Yes, we have a lot more than we expected and I sent information to the techs for analysis."

"OK you can throw away the goods that are rotten if you find a trash location I'll speak to the techs." Strain didn't need them to bring the bodies to New York, you can't interrogate the dead.

"Understood," replied Shadow.

It only took Chalky ten minutes to run the fingerprints and he contacted Shadow.

"The first one is negative the second is positive he made the vest for the recent court appearance." Chalky was referring to the two suicide bombers at the court house where the school girls were killed.

"Thanks for the information pass it on to the boss," replied Shadow.

"Already have he says to continue as planned."

Shadow hung up the call with Chalky and called bulldog, "The second came up as the court house vest maker," he said when Bulldog answered his cell phone.

"I have an idea follow me," he said and drove past Shadow.

After ten more miles Bulldog eventually left the highway and drove onto the frontage road, he went about two miles and turned the lights off on his car. He travelled a further half a mile in the dark turning into a dirt road leading towards some trees.

Bulldog parked the car and walked towards Shadow in the van.

Shadow got out of the van and said, "I hope you're not going to do what I think you are?"

"Yeah! Feed these two fuckers to the hogs, at least they won't kill any more innocent school kids, hold these for me." He handed Shadow his night vision goggles.

They drove two hundred yards and in the field to their right they could see the herd of hogs feeding. They kept as quiet as they could as they were upwind of the animals and they didn't want to spook them or make them attack.

Shadow opened the rear doors to the van and they both pulled out the dead body of the man Bulldog had shot. They stripped the body down to his underwear and carried the dead man by the arms and legs into the field alongside the tree line. They returned to the van and did the same with the second man again keeping out of the sight of the hogs.

"Keep an eye on the hogs," said Bulldog.

Shadow watched them with the night vision goggles and looked towards Bulldog to see what he was doing. In the night vision goggles he could see bulldog standing over the body of the man he'd shot. He then realized what he was doing he was cutting his stomach open the smell would attract the hogs faster.

Keeping in the shadow of the trees they started to walk away back towards the van when they heard a noise. It was the second man Shadow had shot he gave out a low moan.

"Fuck he is still alive," said Shadow.

"I think that was him dying, he won't make any more bomb vests, look the hogs are walking this way they have the scent, we have got to go," replied Bulldog.

They made it back to the van and drove off slowly so as not to scare the hogs off. As Shadow looked back towards where they had left the two bodies he could see the hogs were only a few feet away from them. At the car, they washed their hands with water from a bottle and drove back to New York with their stolen cache of weapons and explosives.

CHAPTER 53

CALIFORNIA

The meeting at the Mosque between Fadi and his brother's and Matthews went well. They had given him the plan just as Mohammed had instructed them to do. Mohammed sat in one of the back rooms of the Mosque watching the whole meeting. They had discussed the option of Matthews cutting the brake pipes of the tail vehicle while it was parked during the weapons testing. Matthews stated that if he had the opportunity he would do it but the soldiers normally sat at the back of the vehicle playing cards or smoking. The plan was simple in discussion but dangerous for the brother that would be on the Luge board.

The hijack of the military truck was set for the next day late in the afternoon after the weapon was tested.

Matthews had a very restless night his mind jumped from pictures of Numa to the soldiers and their disgusting comments of having sex with the Iraqi women. He ran through the plan time after time looking for problems and couldn't think of one. He left the barracks and checked out the three vehicles that were to take the new weapon system to the test site.

An hour later the weapons system was loaded into the canvas backed vehicle he was driving and the two escort vehicles were front and back of him. As he drove up the winding hills leading up to the test site he was looking for Fadi and his brothers but couldn't see them. He knew that it was too early for them to be in place but he had to look for them. They arrived at the test site and as he'd predicted the soldiers sat at the back of the tail escort vehicle out of the sun playing cards. The vehicle was identical to his with a canvas back and lots of storage room inside. This was the vehicle that they would use to transfer the weapon if Matthew's vehicle broke down. At the front of the mini convoy would be a Humvee with a driver and two armed soldiers as security.

The weapons system had a fifty-caliber sniper rifle mounted on it for the days testing. Everything went as scheduled with the tests and three hours later the new weapon system was being loaded into the back of Matthew's vehicle. He sent a text to Fadi letting him know that they were leaving, which meant they were twenty minutes away from his location.

Mohammed was on the top of one of the hills covered in a desert camouflage cloth with a sniper rifle trained on the road below. He could see Fadi and his brother Ghaazi on the hill across from him which had an old tarmac drive that once led to a house. Ghaazi was wearing what looked like a motorcycle helmet and a black leather suit. To stop the fighting about who was going to ride the board and cut the brakes the brothers drew straws and Ghaazi won. Mohammed could see Ghaazi sit on the luge board as Fadi watched the road above them through binoculars. Well below his position around a couple of bends was the steep gravel road which Matthews was to take. At the top of the road was a truck and two cars with Musaad the third brother standing guard.

"They are coming," said Fadi into the radio.

Matthews watched the road ahead anticipating one of the brothers to appear on the luge board. As he followed the lead vehicle around the next steep downhill hairpin bend he pressed his brakes slightly to slow the big truck down. Up and to his left is where they were supposed to be but he couldn't see due to the steepness of the hill. As the tail vehicle passed the old tarmac drive Fadi pushed his brother who was lying down like a stiff plank on the luge board. He ran as fast as he could and with enough speed going he let go of his brother as he shot down the hill on the luge board.

Matthews had three more major bends to negotiate and before he would take the steep uphill gravel road to where Musaad was waiting. He looked in his rear-view mirror and saw a flash of black as the luge board shot into position behind the tail vehicle.

Ghaazi almost lost the board from under him as he went from the tarmac surface to the concrete road. The wheels on the board slid slightly as they tried to grip the concrete surface. He shifted his body weight slightly to the left side correcting the board by putting downward pressure on those wheels. He was now catching up to the tail vehicle as it entered a very steep down ward drop in the road. Ghaazi let the board run shifting his weight again to turn the board keeping it in the center of the road. The driver of the tail vehicle braked gently to slow it down as they went into the next turn. Ghaazi was now under the back end of the truck holding on to the axle. He pulled the cutters out of the pocket on the chest of his suit and cut the right-hand brake pipe. Carefully changing hands, he switched the cutters to his left as he held on to the axle, he cut the left side. Ghaazi waited for the next bend which was a series of three very bad downward curves. He let go of the truck as it came out of the first bend just as brake fluid squirted out of the pipes he'd cut. He was slowing himself down gradually by using his feet, he had two more bends and he would be at the uphill gravel road. He watched the tail truck staring to swerve with the loss of brakes as the vehicle picked up speed. The driver was losing control and getting dangerously close to Matthews vehicle. As the tail vehicle was in the middle of the third bend the driver was trying to drop the gears down to slow the vehicle down.

Mohammed watched the tail vehicle going through the bends and saw Ghaazi on the board close behind, he must have cut the brake pipes. He had the cross hairs of the sniper rifles scope trained on the head of the driver of the tail vehicle as it started to negotiate the last bend in the series. He slowly inhaled and held his breath as he squeezed the rifles trigger he fired one round at the driver. Through the scope, he could see the drivers head lurch back violently with the impact of the bullet. The vehicle went straight instead of following the bend of the road and shot off the cliff. The soldier who was the passenger bounced around the cab of the vehicle as it rolled over and over, before it came to a sudden and crushing stop killing him.

Matthews saw the tail vehicle go off the cliff but the lead vehicle was already around the next bend out of sight. The gravel road was now in front of him and he let the truck run up the steep incline. The soldier with him wasn't paying attention to what was going on as he was reading a book. He looked up as the noise of the gravel road caught his attention.

"Hey where are you going?" he said to Matthews.

"The follow vehicle is not behind us, can you see him?" said Matthews.

The soldier bent down and was looking into the rear-view mirror on his side when Matthews hit him in the back of the head with the butt of his sidearm knocking him unconscious. He could see the truck and two cars at the top as he came to a grinding halt on the loose gravel.

Mohammed watched the tail vehicle go off the cliff and smiled as he could see Matthews was driving towards the gravel road. He refocused the scope of the rifle on the soldier in the passenger seat of the Humvee and fired one round at his chest. He moved the scope slightly and fired again this time at the driver killing him instantly. The Humvee followed the fate of the tail vehicle and flew into open air as it left the road and crashed down the side of the mountain. He folded the bi-pod rest on the rifle against the bottom of the barrel and ran down to where Matthew's vehicle had stopped. He stayed in the brush waiting for the arrival of Fadi and his brother who were only seconds away. Mohammed didn't want his identity to be revealed to Matthews yet.

Fadi, his brothers and Matthews moved the two-hundred-pound weapon system from the military truck to the one Fadi was going to drive. Matthews got into a vehicle with Ghaazi and they drove off behind Fadi. Mohammed was walking to the vehicle that the brothers had left for him to use when he saw movement in the cab of the military vehicle. He opened the passenger door of the military truck that Matthews had been driving and saw a soldier sitting up holding the back of his head. Without a second thought Mohammed shot the soldier four times in the head and closed the door. He walked to the car and drove to the meeting place where they would hide the weapons system.

The weapons system was unloaded at the back of a strip mall close to Van Nuys airport. Matthews went to work on the computer that controlled the weapons system. He had to configure the computer attached to the system so that it would recognize the laptop that he was using. This allowed the operator of the laptop to remotely access the computer on the weapons system from anywhere in the world. Once this was done any computer could be cloned to the weapons system with the security codes required. The weapons system had a battery system that would keep it fully operational for up to twelve hours. If no commands were sent to the systems computer in a fifteen minutes' period it would go into sleep mode to save the battery life.

The frame of the weapons system was unique in that it could hold one of over thirty weapons that were registered in the systems computer. The operator entered the make and model of the weapon he wanted to use and the system would electronically move several arms and clamps. These arms and clamps would go to a position where the weapon of choice would be placed into the cradle and locked into place.

The fifty-caliber sniper rifle that was already in the system was a perfect example of how the system worked. It could fire two rounds per second and in between each round the system would recalibrate the scope to the exact location of the target. The added feature was that the weapon could be controlled by the operator without any assistance from the computer other than reloading. He could move the weapon to change to a different target that he wanted to shoot at.

Matthews had taken the weapons system out of the travelling crate and was ready for a demonstration in the back of the store in the strip mall when Mohammed arrived. Matthews didn't know Mohammed and just thought that he was another one of Fadi's friends. After an hour of demonstrating the weapons system and showing the brothers how you changed from one weapon to another Mohammed was comfortable that they could handle it. He did several practice runs on how to change from one weapon to another and how to control the system. It was so simple he couldn't believe it, he was elated.

"Put it back into the wooden crate and load into the truck," Mohammed said to Fadi.

"Where are you going to take it?" asked Matthews.

Mohammed didn't reply he pointed a handgun with a silencer on the end at Matthews head and pulled the trigger. Matthew's body dropped to the floor as the brothers looked on in shock. Mohammed stepped up to the body and shot it three more times in the head. The brothers said nothing as they had learned enough not to ask questions of Mohammed.

"Quickly load it into the truck," Mohammed said to the brothers.

Mohammed had already called his pilot and told him to meet him at the airport. The crate caused a slight problem when they got to the Piper aircraft as it was too big to go inside. After thirty minutes the pilot had removed two of the seats and the crate fitted inside easily, they left for the east coast.

CHAPTER 54

MAUI, HAWAII

He'd only just arrived at his hotel room in Maui when the cell phone rang.

"Yes," he said when he answered.

"I am to meet you, where will it be?" asked the caller.

"What is your name?" Hakeem asked.

"Adel."

"Go to the Maui Beach hotel at eight o'clock this evening, wait outside in the parking lot, carry the back pack on your left shoulder," replied Hakeem.

"See you there."

Adel had been waiting for thirty minutes and there was no sign of the man he was supposed to meet. He'd waited long enough and started to walk towards the hotel entrance to get a taxi.

Hakeem had watched Adel since he was dropped off by the taxi and it didn't appear that he was being followed. There was some reason for Mohammed wanting him dead and he hoped it wasn't that he was an informer. He saw Adel walking towards the hotel entrance he had given up waiting, he cut him off.

He called out to him, but not loud enough to call attention to himself, "Adel over here."

Adel heard his name being called and saw a man standing under a Plumeria tree.

"Follow me," Hakeem said as he got closer.

Once they were inside his hotel room Hakeem felt a little more relaxed. He had to change his plan as the Jeep he'd stolen from the hang gliding champion was too high profile. He would get Adel to hire a car from one of the airport locations and they would go to the top of Haleakala in that. It wouldn't matter if the authorities find out that Adel was involved in the explosion as he would be dead and couldn't talk. He sent Adel out straight away to collect the hire car he wanted him to get a four-wheel drive Jeep. This was a typical choice of tourists and there were many running around the roads of Maui.

Hakeem's plan was to leave at one in the morning and leave the bomb in place by four am, just an hour and forty minutes before sunrise. Now the tourists waiting to see the sunrise would witness the explosion and see a sunrise of a different sort.

While Adel was out getting the car, Hakeem opened the back pack and checked the bomb mechanism and timers. There were three bombs in all but they were connected to each other by three feet of wire. The plastic explosive looked stable and wasn't sweating which gave him a little comfort. In a small pocket inside next to the bombs was a paper bag with a remote detonator and two batteries. He would leave the batteries out as he didn't want any accidental detonation of the bombs.

Everything was going well so far and Hakeem had kept the talking down to a minimum telling Adel it was best that way. They were on the Haleakala highway when the Jeep suddenly lurched to the right Hakeem knew straight away that it was a flat tire. He pulled the Jeep over to the side of the road and they both got out. The tire wasn't just flat it looked like it had lost the whole tread and burst open.

Hakeem was calm but a little frustrated this was going to slow them down.

"Get the spare tire and I'll get the jack and wheel brace," he said to Adel.

Adel spent several minutes getting the spare tire off only to find that it was also flat.

"This one is flat as well," he said.

"You didn't check it when you rented it?" Hakeem was now at boiling point he could see why Mohammed wanted this incompetent erased.

"I'm sorry I'll call the company," he was already looking for the number on the rental paperwork.

They sat at the side of the road for over an hour before a breakdown vehicle showed up.

The driver was a very heavy set man and looked like he was a local.

"You got a flat bro?" he asked as he walked towards Adel.

"Yes, the one on the Jeep blew out and the spare is flat," Adel replied.

Hakeem had walked onto the grass bank a little further along the road and sat down. He didn't want the breakdown man to be able to describe him to the police later if he was asked any questions by them.

The breakdown man did a quick inspection of the spare and took it to the back of his truck. He started an air compressor and started to fill the tire with air, he kept banging the tire with his fist as it filled.

"I am sorry bro' but this tire is not holding the air, I'll have to go to the car hire place later when they open and get you a couple of wheels."

"Can't you fix that tire?" asked Adel.

"Not right now because you won't get a tire shop open this time of the morning."

"I'll pay you double if you can fix the tire?" replied Adel.

The breakdown man smelt money and was going to make him an offer, "I'll take it back to my garage and try to fix it that means me missing calls and I'll lose money."

"I'll pay you two hundred dollars if you fix it and return within an hour." Adel was getting very scared that he would be responsible for the mission failing. If it did fail he knew that he would be killed for it.

Hakeem watched from the grass bank as the breakdown truck drove away. He was trying to stay calm but he was madder than he'd ever been with anyone.

"What is happening?" he asked.

"He has taken the spare tire to his garage to fix it, he will be back soon," replied Adel.

"If he is more than forty-five minutes we must abort the mission."

"I know we can make it if he gets back soon," Adel replied.

Thirty minutes' past and the breakdown vehicle arrived.

"You are in luck bro', my friend has a place here in Pukulani and I fixed the tire." He bounced the newly repaired tire towards the Jeep and fitted it to the vehicle.

Two hundred dollars lighter they headed up the road to Haleakala, they were well behind time. Hakeem was bordering on cancelling the mission as they wouldn't have the benefit of complete darkness to fulfill the mission. He knew that the sun would be rising soon he originally wanted to be an hour away before it rose.

They parked the car in the public parking area next to the steps that led up to the viewing area where the tourists would go to watch the sunset. Hakeem had brought two coats with him to protect them from the near freezing temperatures at the ten thousand foot elevation.

Hakeem put the back pack on and they both walked towards the observatory away from the parking lot and public observation point.

They were only a hundred yards from the observatory and stepped off the road. They were going to make their way around to the main building where the largest telescope was located. As they started to walk down a slight drop off a car pulled up on the road above them.

"Excuse me," the woman driver shouted.

"Yes," replied Hakeem.

"You can't walk in this area it's restricted, please keep to the road areas until the sun comes up. Once the sun rises you can see the main trails that you can walk on."

"Sorry we will go back to the parking area," said Hakeem.

"Thank you," she closed her window and drove on to the observatory parking area.

Hakeem and Adel made it look like they were walking back but turned around as soon as she disappeared.

CHAPTER 55

NEW YORK CITY

Chalky and George were sitting in the safe house with the rest of the team going through the events of the last several days. Chalky and George had installed hidden cameras inside Sammy's office and in the entrance to the office building. All the monitoring was now being recorded for Sammy's office and the Newark container location from the safe house. The roads leading to the container warehouse were also being recorded through the city's traffic light system that Chalky had hacked into.

Strain and the rest of the team were in the garage area of the safe house going through the weapons and explosives that Shadow and Bulldog had brought back from Allentown.

"You really left those two in the field for the wild hogs?" asked Thorn.

"Yep they were dead anyway and we didn't have time to bury them," replied Bulldog.

"Wow kind of wild but they won't blow up any more kids," said Thorn.

None of the team could get the images of the courthouse steps out of their heads. The media were showing it on TV over and over for several days blurring out the parts of the screen that showed bodies or body parts. Typical media they wanted the bad news screened but blocked certain parts of the carnage like they were doing the viewers a service.

Thorn had received a call about the murder of the US soldiers in California and the theft of the experimental weapon system. The military and government were keeping the deaths and weapons system out of the news. There was a full-scale investigation taking place in California with every federal department and military investigation team involved.

The team believed that this had Mohammed's fingerprints all over it that's why they believe he went to California on the Piper aircraft.

Thorn's cell phone rang, "Hello," he said answering the call.

Everyone kept quiet as he took the call.

"Keep me up to speed with the planes progress," said Thorn to the caller.

Thorn put the phone back into his pocket, "The Piper left LA ten minutes ago, with the pilot, one passenger and a large wooden crate. The photos of the pilot, passenger and crate are being sent to me now. The pilot has given the final destination as Montgomery County Airpark, Gaithersburg, Maryland."

"What's the bet the crate contains the weapons system that was stolen," said Strain.

"I wouldn't bet against it but why are they taking it to Gaithersburg," said Bulldog.

"It wouldn't take long to drive to D.C. from Gaithersburg. There would be a lot of potential targets for that kind of weapon in D.C.," said Thorn.

"Too many let's go look at the photos on the computer," said Strain.

The photographs sent through to Thorn by the Delta Team were very clear and one of them had a full facial shot of Mohammed Ali Ghahi. Facial recognition had already been run by George and the pilot was known to be a cousin of Mohammed but he had no record of criminal or terrorist activity.

"We can get him this time it will take them several hours to get to Gaithersburg, let's go through the plan," said Strain.

After almost an hour of multiple suggestions for a plan the team came to an agreement on how to handle Mohammed. It was obvious that he had a target in mind very possibly in D.C. They had decided to cut their losses and take Mohammed just after he'd left the airport grounds. They couldn't afford for the weapon to be on the streets and a possible high profile assassination take place because they wanted to see what he was doing with it. The team would deal with the known associates of

Mohammed's after they had taken him out this wasn't going to be an arrest. All the team except for Chalky and George left for Gaithersburg in four separate vehicles. They decided to drive as they would need vehicles when they got there anyway, it would take about four hours.

Chalky and George took the Gulfstream to D.C. along with all their counter surveillance equipment.

CHAPTER 56

HALEAKALA, MAUI, HAWAII

Lolani and Judd had become National Park Rangers the same week and had just completed their first year. Being Park Rangers in the Haleakala National Park was a dream for both of them for different reasons.

Lolani loved the diversity of plant and wildlife in the park and as a native Hawaiian was dedicated to help preserve it. To her native Hawaiian people Haleakala Crater is known as the 'House of the Sun' and is sacred ground to them. It has been a place of worship and meditation by ancient priests known in Hawaiian as, 'na Kahuna Po'o' for well over a thousand years. The summit of the extinct volcano stands at 10,023 feet and has an observatory at the summit operated by the University of Hawaii.

The observatory and the continued growth of the site had been contested by native Hawaiians for decades. Native Hawaiian's and their supporters held many peaceful protests over the years to try to protect the land and give free access to the mountain to all people.

Judd joined the Park Rangers for a different reason he was looking for a kind of solitude or calm in his life he didn't really know which he wanted. His parents had moved to Maui when he was only eight years old, it was the only true home he knew. He'd returned to Maui after serving twelve years in the military as a marine. His latest tour in Iraq was the bloodiest and his last he got out alive and decided not to sign on for another six years.

They both had a day off and Lolani told Judd that she was going to trek on part of Haleakala that was closed to the public. She was hoping to find some ancient Hawaiian petroglyphs, one of her favorite pastimes. Finding and reading petroglyphs made her feel much closer to her ancestors, it also helped her make another contribution to her culture.

They were to meet in the parking lot of the Observatory which was a short distance from the public parking area. The sun was due to rise in less than an hour and the cold of the night was still hugging the ground. There was a frosty feel in the gentle breeze blowing through the parking lot as Judd got out of his car. Lolani's car was already there but he couldn't see her. He decided to walk over to the high point that was on the East side, he thought she may be getting ready to see the sun rising. This was a favorite place of hers to greet them morning sun, she had shown it to him on one of their patrols. It was about a half mile trek around a couple of small rock peaks and valleys. He started the walk using a small flash light to see where he was going.

As he walked over the crumbling lava rock he could see the headlights of cars arriving in the public parking area. This was a favorite time for tourists to visit Haleakala to watch the sun rise after a long dark two hour drive up the winding road leading to the volcano crater. Judd had seen the sunrise many times from the top of the volcano and it never looked the same twice. He always knew that one day he would meet the girl of his dreams and propose to her as the sun rose over Haleakala.

As he rounded the side of the peak facing the sun he saw Lolani, she was standing with her arms stretched out towards the East. The sun was starting to give off a yellow glow on the horizon it was the start of a new day. He could see that Lolani had some native clothing on and what looked like a water bowl and food offerings at her feet. She started to speak in her native tongue just as the sun peeked over the horizon. He sat on a rock as he watched and listened to her voice sail on the wind as she chanted.

Judd was in struck by the beauty of the sight and finally gave in to the thought that he was falling in love with Lolani. For the first time in his life he felt like there really was peace surrounding him. His body gave a slight shiver and he tried to put it down to the chill in the air but it was different and he knew it. Could the spirits of God's and former Hawaiian priests be here, he didn't disbelieve it?

Lolani finished her chant and turned towards Judd, "Aloha," she said.

"Aloha," he replied.

Lolani walked down to Judd and gave him a hug, "Let me put these clothes in the car."

"Sure," he replied.

Lolani put her heavy coat on as the wind on the North side of the volcano was always colder and it took a lot longer for the sun to get high enough to warm that area.

"I thought that we could start on the other side of the observatory and hike over the top of the small peak and head down into the valley from there. The tourists will come in from the other side but don't get to go on this side of the ridge that we will take." She was excited.

"OK you're the boss lead the way," he replied.

They had only been walking a couple of minutes when Lolani stopped by a line of Silverswords and bent down to inspect them.

Silverswords are an endangered succulent leafed plant that grows above 6000 feet in the volcanic soil of the extinct volcano. The species can grow to be over fifty years old and flowers once and then dies. This delicate plant was one of the many reasons that Lolani had become a National Park Ranger.

"Young plants, that's a good sign they are spreading," she said.

"Have you seen them on this side before?" asked Judd.

"Yes, but not a line of them like this let's go over that ridge that may be where the mother plant was," she pointed to a small ridge to her right.

It didn't take them long to get to the top of the ridge as they scanned the slope leading down into the small valley on the other side. The wind had picked up and was blowing directly into their faces.

"There it is the dead mother plant," said Lolani.

Half way down the slope was the brown remains of what was once a beautiful and elegant plant.

Judd was staring at something at the far end of the small valley just behind the observatory.

"That looks like two people in a hollow at the back of the observatory, can you see them?

From their elevated position, he could see the whole of one side of the observatory.

"I can't see anyone, where are you looking," she replied.

The sun was rising fast now and it was shining straight down the small valley creating deep black Shadows below them.

"I think I see them, two huddled together. We have to tell them to move, they might be the two men I spoke to when I arrived they were going the wrong way then."

"Let's do it and then we can get on with our day," replied Judd.

"Why don't we go straight down the lava flow and up the other side it will be quicker than walking around the rock face?" she said.

"OK but the wind is picking up so we had best move," said Judd.

They cautiously worked their way down the slope on the blind side of the observatory into the small valley below.

The loose lava rock posed a problem when you walked on it and the fact it was covering the steep slopes leading into the valley made it even more precarious. The strong walking boots they wore helped handle the lava rock and their dark green park ranger clothes covered with a heavy weatherproof coat helped keep out the mist and cold of the early morning.

As they moved into the bottom of the valley the wind had picked up again. Due to the shape of the valley the wind was forced towards them creating a wind tunnel effect. Lolani and Judd leaned into the wind as they walked to help try and keep them stable. Lolani pulled the hood of her coat over her head to keep the bitter cold from her ears. Judd was a little surprised that the wind had picked up so quickly but then that wasn't that unusual at this 10,000 ft. elevation. He gave thumbs up sign to Lolani checking that she was OK, she replied with the same sign indicating that she was fine.

"Come on follow me," he shouted and waved his arm for her to follow.

Lolani couldn't hear him because of the noise created by the wind but understood his signal. She knew that when they got on the other side of the valley and over the rock face the wind would ease up.

Judd had set a very fast pace but Lolani was extremely fit and used to the conditions and kept up with him. A few minutes had passed as they came to a sharp drop in the lava of about twenty feet. They stood together looking down the lava flow.

"We will have to go over the ridge to our right and make our way around."

Judd wasn't happy with this as it was costing them time but he knew they had no choice. He made his way up the side of the valley thankfully it was a lot shallower from where they had started. They scrambled up side by side sometimes using their hands to steady themselves as they negotiated the steep slope.

Lolani was starting to enjoy this as they were out of the wind and decided that this was about to become a competition. She practically bounded past Judd and quickly outpaced him. Judd looked up as she went past him and smiled realizing what she was doing and he wasn't to be outdone. There was no way he could let her beat him up the side of the slope as she would have bragging rights when they go back to the ranger station. His 6ft 3 in height gave him long arms and legs and he used them to his advantage.

Lolani pushed her 5ft 2in slim frame harder her hands stretching out above her finding solid rocks to grip while her feet below her searched for equally safe footholds. They were now fully into a climbing contest as the valley wall became steeper. Lolani looked down and saw Judd quickly gaining on her they continued the competition. Five minutes of furious climbing had taken place they were now side by side, neck and neck sweating profusely under their clothes. They reached the top of the valley wall at the same time and both jumped up to claim the win and of course the bragging rights.

"I'm the winner," claimed Lolani as she looked across to Judd.

"I think this was a dead heat," he replied.

They stood staring at each other both breathing heavily and laughing.

"O.K. next time I won't let you beat me." She had not seen this side of him and was truly enjoying his company, maybe a little too much.

They walked across the ridge moving a little slower as the wind was forced over the ridge into their faces again.

"They will be on the other side of that large outcrop," he said pointing to a huge black lava rock formation.

The sun had risen above the clouds and the chill in the air was slowly starting to disappear. They had several small peaks and valleys in the mountainside to negotiate and wasted no time in doing so. They walked over the first rise to find a cloud had settled in the shallow valley below them. As they waded through the mist of the cloud they could see the observatory buildings slightly above them. The large round domed roofs seemed to shine like miniature planets in the early morning light. As they appeared out of the cloud on the other side Lolani put up her hand to stop Judd. "I hear voices," she said.

"You're right that must be them, we are down wind," he replied.

Lolani knew that sometimes you could hear voices in the valleys of the volcano as they were carried along by the wind. It didn't necessarily mean that the people where close by as she had heard people talking over a mile away in the past due to the boxed in canyon effect.

"I wonder who it is?" said Judd.

"It's most probably those walkers I told you about," she replied.

When they reached the top of the slope Judd looked over the other side. He couldn't believe what he was seeing, he waved at Lolani to get down and put his fingers to his lips indicating for her to stay quiet.

The men had not seen them and they couldn't hear them from their position as the wind was blowing on their side of the ridge. Judd used his former military training and moved slowly peering over the rocks in front of him he looked back down to where the men were sitting. On the ground around the men were three packages all of which were wrapped in black tape and coming out of the side of each he could see what looked like wires. Judd could also see the red glow of the numbers of a digital clock. He slid back down behind the rock to where Lolani was lying still.

"The voices we heard belong to two men on the other side of this ridge, it looks to me like they have several bombs that are attached to a digital timing device," he said.

"How do you know they are bombs," she asked.

"When I was in the military serving in the Middle East we saw plenty of bombs like this when we were locating weapons and ammunition storage houses."

"What are we going to do?" she asked.

Hakeem and Adel were giving the bombs a second quick check to make sure that everything was OK. Adel was surprised when he saw the bombs when Hakeem opened the back pack. He was nervous but excited at the same time he was finally joining the movement as a real member not just a message boy.

"Everything looks good I have set them to explode in one hour, I'll put them back inside the back pack. I want you to go up that ladder and place the back pack against that slop of the dome. When you get on the roof you will be able to see the parking lot, I'll turn my flashlight on and off twice, this means that it's clear for you to come down. Then meet me in the parking lot and we will go back to my hotel." Hakeem headed towards the parking lot.

Judd watched the two men, "You go down the slope towards the road, check that it's clear and run across to the observatory. Tell them what is going on and call the police I'll try to stop them from this side."

"What do mean stop them, you can't go down there on your own." She was scared he was going to be hurt.

"You forget I used to do this sort of thing in the military, I'll be careful, you do the same." He gave her a kiss on the cheek and made his way around the ridge.

Hakeem was moving quickly along the edge of the road staying in the shadows of the ridge. He was pleased with how the mission was going. He was still very angry as they should have left an hour and a half earlier. Adel would pay with his life for his stupidity he was going to die anyway.

He heard movement on the rocks to his left and he quickly put his back against the rocks keeping his body in the shadows. He put his hand on a knife that he had on his belt. A woman came bounding over the loose lava cinders only four feet away from him. She was startled to see him standing against the rock face.

"What are you doing?" she said.

Hakeem didn't wait and plunged the knife into her chest twice covering her mouth with his other hand.

Lolani was startled to see the man as he lunged at her, she felt him punch her twice in the chest. As she clutched her chest she felt the warm wetness of blood on her clothing as she fell backwards.

Hakeem let the woman drop and walked quickly to the Jeep, he had to get away.

Adel was on the roof and watching for the signal from Hakeem, he was relieved that it was soon to be over.

Judd tried to be as quiet as he could as he made his way around the ridge towards the observatory. He had to catch the men off guard to be able to defeat both of them. He came around the lava rock expecting to see them about forty feet away, they had moved.

He ran across to the observatory building and worked his way around towards the ladder that led to the roof. He knew they had to be on the roof as there was no other way into the facility on that side of the building.

Hakeem sat in the Jeep and started the engine he looked towards the observatory where he knew Adel was waiting for the signal to come down. He put the Jeep in gear and started to drive at the same time he detonated the bombs.

Adel's body was torn to pieces by the explosion spreading bits of him over the roof and on the road below. A huge whole appeared in the roof as parts of the building started to collapse.

Judd had just put his right foot on the bottom rung of the ladder when the explosion took place. He instinctively dropped to the ground and pressed his body against the building for protection. Debris was landing on the road and the ridge he and

Lolani had just been on. Lolani he wondered if she had made it inside before the explosion.

Judd stood up as the early morning sky was lit with a red glow from the explosion. As he moved around towards the front entrance of the building in the light of the fire he saw Lolani's body lying on the rocks by the side of the road.

"Lolani," he shouted at the top of his voice.

When he got to her he could see the front of her coat was soaked in blood.

"Lolani wake up, please wake up," he tapped her face lightly.

He checked for a pulse on her neck and it was there but very faint, he had to stop the bleeding. He tore open her coat and shirt below exposing her bra and bare body. There appeared to be two puncture wounds just below her heart. He took off his coat and shirt applying pressure to the wounds, the blood loss was slowing down. He knew he couldn't carry her into the observatory as she would lose too much blood on the way.

He could hear voices coming from the observatory, "Hey over here we need help," he shouted.

A rather dazed man in a white coat came running over.

"Keep pressure on this here like this," he grabbed the man's hands and placed them on the blood-soaked shirt. "Is there a first aid kit inside?"

"Yes, inside the door as you go in, we have already called 911 for police and ambulance." The man returned his concentration to Lolani.

Hakeem felt a slight shock wave as he drove out of the parking lot he took no notice of the screaming tourists as he left.

He drove down the twisting and winding road a little faster than he would normally but he had to get away before the police arrived. It would be at least an hour before the first one's arrived so he would be well gone. All he had to do now was make it back to his hotel and join the rest of the flight crew for the afternoon flight to the mainland.

Hakeem had been driving for five minutes and suddenly realized that there were no cars going up to the volcano crater. This was unusual because by now he would have expected the local bicycle tours to be heading up to the top. They would be loaded with tourists who were going to ride bicycles back down on the road. He saw an observation point ahead and pulled into one of the allocated parking spots. He got out of the Jeep and walked across the road to the observation point like many tourists had done before. He scanned the road leading down to the ranger station below where vehicles stopped to pay the entry fee into the area. There were a lot of vehicles lined up at the entrance as if they were waiting to drive in. He could see a Park Rangers vehicle had been parked across the road blocking any vehicles from exiting the volcano area. He didn't expect them to have a contingency plan for emergencies at the observatory other than the usual injured or sick tourist. This wasn't good but he had a contingency plan of his own, it would mean him leaving the Jeep where it was. He started walking to where he'd hidden the hang glider he'd stolen.

It took Hakeem over two hours to hike to where he'd left the hang glider. He stayed off the road as much as possible using the low-lying foliage to conceal him. By the time he got to the lava over hang he was soaked in sweat. The hang glider was still there where he'd left it he was pleased that one thing was going right. He looked at his watch it was seven am he'd to wait for the sun to burn off some of the clouds before he could use the hang glider. He knew that if he tried to go through the clouds below him he could be in serious trouble. The turbulence created in the cloud may make him lose control and he would fall to his death. He couldn't see anything below him due to the clouds but the sky was a clear Blue above him. He'd heard several sirens from either police or ambulances but from his position he couldn't see the road. He had to get his wet clothes off as he was starting to shiver with the cold. He put the coat, shirt and trousers in a slight gap in the overhang where the wind could get to them, held down with a rock he would wait for them to dry. He opened the PVC cover on the hang glider and crawled inside his own body would keep it warm inside for a short time.

Hakeem checked every thirty minutes to see if the cloud had gone but it showed no signs of moving. It was now 8.30 and he kept reassuring himself that it would thin out soon with the sun rising in the sky. Without realizing it he fell asleep and woke startled as he realized what had happened. He looked at his watch it was 10.30 five hours before he was due to join the rest of the flight crew. He waited another hour and there was a slight break in the clouds appearing. He felt the clothes he'd hung out and they were mostly dry. Once he was dressed Hakeem assembled the hang glider and walked with it to the short sloping ground ahead where he could take off. As he looked to the west he could see that there were no clouds, he cursed he could have left sooner.

Hakeem held the tubular triangle frame of the hang glider on the sides and lifted it off the ground. As he steadied the kite he started to run, it only took ten paces and he was airborne, the kite lifted him gently into the sky. He felt the cold immediately as he only had the harness to hold his body in place on the frame of the kite. At these altitudes or on colder days he would have had more layers of clothing, today he had no choice. As he hit the lower altitudes it would warm up considerably. Hakeem sailed under the last layer of cloud and relaxed as he enjoyed the view of the island and the West Maui Mountains in the distance.

Josh and his friends were setting up their hang gliders on the side of Haleakala. This was their usual spot just above the 6000 feet elevation point which had a smooth grassy take off point. Josh had already assembled his hang glider and was sitting talking to his friends as they finished assembling theirs ready for flying.

One of Josh's friends came running across the grassy slope pointing into the sky, "Josh isn't that your kite that was stolen?" he said.

Everyone looked up and about 1500 hundred feet above them they saw a hang glider in the distance just under the clouds.

"Fuck that's it, the bastard," replied Josh.

He was up on his feet and clipped his harness onto his hang glider, within thirty seconds he was flying. He could still see his stolen hang glider it was slowly losing altitude and he knew from this angle the pilot couldn't see him.

Josh used the thermals to bring his hang glider higher in the sky as he closed in on the unsuspecting thief. He was behind him now and only a quarter of a mile away from him.

"You're going to get the surprise of your life, mother fucker." He was talking to himself constantly feeling the thermals and wind.

He chose another thermal that lifted him as he shifted his weight to make the hang glider turn to the right. He was ready as he pulled the bar under his body he pushed the hang glider into a dive. At the last minute, he shifted his weight again this time forcing the hang glider into a sharp left turn as he crossed under the stolen kite.

Hakeem didn't see the other hang glider he was relaxed and heading towards his landing point. The sudden change of air and the speed at which the hang glider flew underneath scared him. He watched as the pilot drove his hang glider into the sky and was turning for another dive on him. He was sure that this had to be Josh the man whose hang glider he'd stolen. He steadied the hang glider as Josh came in from behind him he turned to avoid being blindsided.

Josh was attacking again this time he was going to confront the thief and sail alongside him.

"That's my kite you fucking thief," he yelled at Hakeem.

"I don't know what you are talking about I bought it yesterday," Hakeem shouted back trying to bluff.

"Fucking liar everyone on this island knows my kite was stolen and they wouldn't sell it." He swung his hang glider in to bump the thief.

Hakeem saw the move coming as he pulled the bar under him and dived out of the way. Almost immediately he pushed the bar forward and right to lift and turn he was going to try and make Josh crash. He felt the rush of the wind on his face and felt the cloth of his jacket flapping in the wind. He couldn't feel the cold anymore as adrenalin had taken over his body.

Josh followed Hakeem and came up on him again before he could respond. He came in a little higher than Hakeem and put his foot under the end of the wing flipping it.

Hakeem didn't see how he could have gotten back on him so quickly he felt something lift the wing almost throwing him out of control. Hakeem got angry and tried to attack again he was going to teach this guy a lesson. He came in from the side swooping down on Josh, then it happened something he'd never seen in real life.

Josh watched the thief and was getting to know his moves, he was skilled but not in the same league as himself. The thief was coming in to attack him again he pulled the tubular frame towards him put his hands on the side of the frame and his feet on the bottom bar. At the last minute, he forced his arms and legs forward holding them stiffly with every ounce of strength he had. The kite shot upwards at high speed and performing a complete 360 turn or loop de loop. He could almost hear his friends cheering the move as he came down again towards the thief.

The aerial battle went on for ten minutes, one dive bombing the other, but Josh always had the upper hand. Hakeem had to do something as he could see three other hang gliders heading towards them. He would try to reason with Josh at the same time he would make his move.

Josh came at the thief again and saw that he was waiving at him to stop. He slowed his kite down enough to where he could shout to the thief to land.

As Hakeem waived, he took the knife out of his pocket, the same one he'd stabbed Lolani with. At the last minute as Josh came in alongside him, Hakeem pushed the tubular frame forward and lifted over Josh. He hung on with one arm and leaned down towards Josh's kite with the other. He slashed at the top of the kite, putting a twelve-inch tear in the wing material and severing one of the support lines.

Josh felt the kite tip slightly and he looked up to see the tear in the wing. He knew this was dangerous and he had to fly gently now or he risked the wing tearing completely.

"I'll get you, you fucking coward," he yelled.

Hakeem was pushing the hang glider into a steep dive now so that Josh couldn't follow him. Josh could see that

Hakeem was heading towards the side of the mountain, looking for a place to land.

Hakeem was sweating profusely for the second time that day as he landed the hang glider in the field, just five minutes after the battle with Josh. He unclipped the harness from the hang glider and ran to the tree where he'd hidden the motorcycle. An hour later, he dumped the motorcycle and was in his hotel room taking a shower.

Judd was pacing up and down outside the operating room in the hospital. He'd called Lolani's family and they were on the way. He kept wondering if there was something else he should have done, told her to stay behind the rocks or something. He knew that Lolani wouldn't have done it anyway, she was too independent.

Her family arrived and he sat with them in the waiting room explaining what had happened. There were a lot of tears and some angry threats from her brothers that he should have protected her.

The doctor came out of the operating room, pulling the mask off his face. The family stood and waited for the news.

"Are you Lolani's family?" he asked.

"Yes," her mother replied.

"She is going to be fine, she had two serious stab wounds and lost a lot of blood. Whoever kept the pressure on the wound when she was stabbed most probably saved her life. Give her some time in the recovery room and the nurse will let you know when you can see her."

"Mahalo, mahalo," said her mother, thanking him.

Judd was already walking through the doors to leave the family alone, this wasn't the place for him to be.

CHAPTER 57

MANASSAS REGIONAL AIRPORT, MD

The pilot called the tower at Manassas airport for clearance to land, stating he had a problem with the oil pressure in one of his engines. The tower didn't question him and gave him the landing coordinates.

After the plane landed, he was cleared to taxi to the Manassas aviation hanger, which he did. At the hanger, the pilot had a word with one of the mechanics who brought a van that the pilot had arranged for Mohammed around to the plane. The three of them loaded the wooden crate into the van and Mohammed drove off with his cargo. Thirty minutes after Mohammed left, the plane was cleared for take-off to its destination, Gaithersburg.

The team kept a close eye on the plane as it landed in Gaithersburg and taxied straight to a small hanger at the side of the runway. Once again, they watched the pilot get out of the plane but there was no passenger, he secured the plane and walked to the hanger.

"This bullshit is not happening again," said Thorn into his sleeve microphone.

"Let's pick him up. Bulldog and Thorn check out the plane," said Strain.

As the pilot walked along the outside of the hanger towards the parking lot, Strain and Shadow pulled up next to him in a car. Shadow was the first out with an HK53 sub machine gun pointed at the man. Wheels stopped his car directly behind Strain and they bundled the pilot into the back seat.

"Where is Mohammed?" asked Strain.

"Mohammed who?" smiled the pilot.

"Well, I guess we are going to make you talk a different way," said Strain.

Shadow stuck a needle into the pilot's neck before he could react. The syringe contained a strong dose of Halothane.

The pilot was fast asleep in seconds as the drug entered his bloodstream.

Thorn quickly picked the lock on the door of the plane and removed the recording device the Delta Team had put under the seat. Thorn, Shadow and Strain rejoined the rest of the team and found a place in the parking lot to listen to the recording. The quality was very poor due to the sound and vibration of the plane engine.

"We need to get the recording and the pilot back to Chalky and George. They will be able to clean up the recording," said Strain.

"They will be at the safe house I arranged for them by now. We can go straight there," replied Thorn.

It wasn't long before they were pulling into the garage at the safe house where Chalky and George were waiting. Strain had called them on the way to tell them the problem. They had a software package that would be able to take out the background noises and isolate the voices. Strain gave George the recording device while the team pulled the pilot out of the car. He was awake and his eyes were the size of saucers.

"He doesn't look very happy," said George.

"He'll be less so in a few minutes," said Thorn.

Strain and Thorn walked the weak-legged pilot into a room at the back of the garage. The room was empty except for a couple of chairs and a workbench that had a tool box on it. They sat the pilot on the chair and tied his arms and feet to it and tore off the tape that was covering his mouth.

The pilot was terrified and screamed at the top of his voice, "Help, help!"

Thorn laughed at him and imitated him, "Help, help! You see nobody can hear you in here. Scream all you want because that is what you are going to be doing if you don't tell me what I want to know."

"Please. I don't know anything. I am just a pilot with a plane for rent," he replied.

"Is that right? Then who was your passenger today?" asked Thorn.

"I didn't have a passenger. I just flew in from Atlantic City."

"I don't like to be lied to. We had a recording device in your plane and your conversation with Mohammed Ali Ghahi is on it." He stepped back to let this sink in a little.

"We'll let you go if you tell us the truth," said Strain.

"I don't know what you are talking about," replied the pilot.

"Do you have any of that truth serum with you?" asked Strain.

"Yes, upstairs," replied Thorn.

"Let's use it, we don't have time to fuck around with this bastard, inject him and he will answer our questions."

"What drug? What are you talking about?" asked the pilot in fear.

"Just a little something to make you talk and then I'll kill you because you didn't cooperate," said Strain.

Thorn left the room and returned a few minutes later the syringe in hand.

"Wait! Please don't inject me. I'll tell you what you need to know," said the scared pilot.

"OK, where is Mohammed?" asked Strain, as Thorn stood over the man with the syringe.

"I landed at Manassas Regional airport and dropped him off," replied the pilot.

"What else did you drop off?" asked Strain.

"A wooden box, a big one. He didn't tell me what was inside," he replied.

"Where is he going with it?"

"I don't know, he didn't tell me," said the pilot.

They questioned him for another thirty minutes before George came into the room.

"We have clear voices on the recording, he knows where Mohammed is going," said George.

"You lied to me. Shoot him," said Strain.

"Wait, wait. I may know where he is going," said the pilot.

"You have ten seconds to start talking or I am leaving the room and he is going to go to work on you," Strain pointed at Thorn.

"About nine months ago, Mohammed asked me to rent a small factory or workshop close to Washington D.C. I found one in Waldorf just south of the city. He got me to rent it for twelve months."

"What is he using it for?" asked Strain.

"I don't know. I paid the rent for one year upfront and gave Mohammed the keys," said the pilot.

"What's the address?"

"I don't remember the road number but it's just off Leonardtown Road in a small industrial area of Waldorf. It's a large brown building set back from the road. On the main road, there's a steakhouse and a McDonald's the drive that leads to the building is between them. The main door of the building has a sign on it from the previous tenant, Waldorf Enterprise is the name."

"What am I going to hear on the tape, what terrorist attacks are you two talking about?" asked Thorn.

"We didn't talk about anything, really. He slept for the first three hours. I don't get involved in his terrorism business. I just fly him around whenever he needs it."

"You are involved, don't kid yourself," said Strain.

"You go listen to the recording, leave this one to me," said Thorn as he stuck the syringe into the man's neck.

The pilot was telling the truth about the tape. They hadn't discussed anything about Mohammed's operations. Chalky found the building on satellite and printed images for the team to review.

Thorn joined them after thirty minutes of interrogating the drugged pilot.

"He didn't have much else to offer except that he didn't rent the whole building just a part of it. It is split into four very large units, each occupied by different companies. The one we want is the third one along. He says the end unit was vacant when he rented the unit for Mohammed," said Thorn.

"Time we went down there for a look at the place," said Strain.

"What about trying to bug the place if we can get in?" said Thorn.

"Yes, we will. Chalky, you come with me and Thorn, Wheels and Sleepy bring along a surveillance van. Shadow, Bulldog and L.B., see if you can locate Sammy at his office, maybe it's time we brought him in," said Strain.

It didn't take the team long to find the building, it was exactly where the pilot told them it was.

In the parking lot of McDonald's Thorn switched to the observation van and put on a baseball cap. He drove to the unit where they believed Mohammed was with a parcel addressed to Waldorf Enterprise.

Thorn was banging on the door with the Waldorf Enterprise name on it. He could hear the sound echoing inside the building, it sounded empty. He was banging on the door for a third time when a small door in the second unit opened.

"There's no one in there," said a man in dirty coveralls, wiping his hands on a rag.

"I have a delivery for Waldorf Enterprise," said Thorn, holding the package up.

"Sorry, buddy, they left about a year ago. Some Arab looking guy has it now," he replied.

"Was the Arab guy part of the company before?" asked Thorn.

"No, I only saw him a few hours ago for the first time when he arrived in a van. I said hello and tried to introduce myself and he practically growled at me, not very pleasant," replied the man.

"Maybe that's why he won't answer the door," replied Thorn.

"No, he left about ten minutes ago in the van."

"What about the unit on the end, would he be in there?" asked Thorn.

"No. Until I saw the Arab guy I was the only one in the whole building."

"OK, thanks for your help. I'll send the package back," Thorn said as he walked back to the observation van.

The team kept the building under surveillance for the next two hours until the sun set. They saw the man Thorn had been talking to leave his unit and drive away.

Strain, Thorn and Chalky drove up to the door that Thorn had been banging on earlier and went to work on the lock. It took no time at all for them to get inside, Strain and Thorn entered ahead of Chalky, sweeping the building with their weapons as they walked. The building was empty apart from a large wooden crate in the center of the floor. Chalky brought a crow bar from the van and worked the top of the crate loose. With their flashlights, they could see inside the crate. There it was the weapons system with the fifty-caliber sniper rifle still mounted.

"Let's open the crate properly," said Chalky.

"Let's just take it with us," said Thorn.

"If we do we won't know what Mohammed intends to do with the weapon," replied Strain.

They carefully opened the crate leaving no marks on the wood. Chalky took an electronic gadget out of his bag and was connecting it to a computer screen on the side of the weapons system.

"What are you doing?" asked Thorn.

"Seeing if this baby is alive," replied Chalky. As he punched codes into his gadget numbers flashed faster than the eye could see on the computer screen on the weapon system.

"Got it," Chalky said out loud.

"What do you have?" asked Strain.

"Access to the computer control system, give me a minute," replied Chalky.

Strain and Thorn watched as he went to work for a couple of minutes, punching buttons on his gadget again.

"OK, this is cool. I have accessed the systems computer panel that controls everything it does. Watch this."

Chalky punched a code into his gadget and the weapons system computer came on. There was a display on the tiny computer screen showing a line of numbers and letters. He was now connecting a laptop to the system and getting more animated as he assessed the equipment.

"Look, this mini-computer works the movement of the weapon and calibrates distance, wind speed, etc. to the target. The mini-computer is then connected wirelessly to another computer and the camera on the front allows the computer operator to see what he is shooting at. As long as you have a signal to a cell phone or SATCOM, you can operate this from anywhere. It is fascinating because it has a built in hacking system that helps the operator search for a wireless signal wherever the weapon is located. Once he has hacked into the wireless system, he can operate the weapon from his laptop," said Chalky.

"We can't leave this here then. Let's get the van," said Thorn.

Strain was watching Chalky and recognized the look on his face, "What are you thinking, Chalky?" he said.

"Well, if we leave this here, I can modify the computer software on the mother board and be able to override any actions by the operator. This would allow you to see who his target is but we would have control of the weapon. I can even disable the firing capability without them knowing."

"You can really do that?" asked Thorn.

"Yes. It will take me thirty minutes or so but I can do it. I'll need my other laptop."

"I'll get it," said Strain.

Thirty-five minutes later, Chalky was finished, "OK. I'll go to the van and you stay here for a minute," he said to Strain and Thorn.

"What is he doing now?" asked Thorn.

"Sometimes with Chalky and George it's best not to ask," replied Strain.

They were waiting by the weapons system for Chalky to return when suddenly, the machine started to turn. The rifle was moving up and down and side to side in its cradle. Strain and Thorn jumped backwards, not expecting this to happen.

"Chalky, you little bastard," said Strain out loud.

"Is that him operating it?" asked Thorn.

"I wouldn't bet against it," replied Strain.

"Well, what do you think?" said Chalky, as he walked back into the building.

"Fucking amazing," replied Thorn.

"Yeah, didn't know you two could jump so high," laughed Chalky.

"Right, let's box this back up before he comes back," said Strain.

"I have already planted an electronic tracking and listening device on the computer system that is connected to the weapon. Even when the computer itself is switched off, the devices operate through the battery in silent mode," said Chalky.

They closed the building and left, taking up positions to keep surveillance on the building.

CHAPTER 58

DOWNTOWN, D.C.

Mohammed had given Sammy a task to find a location in Washington D.C. where he could place a sniper on the roof of a building within an eight-block radius of the White House. Sammy flew into D.C. and met with the Pakistani Ambassador for some help. The Ambassador had the perfect place for them it was an apartment he rented to spend time with a prostitute he liked. The prostitute was on vacation for ten days and she wouldn't be at home.

Mohammed arrived at the apartment building on H Street NW where Fadi was waiting for him.

"Where is Sammy and why are we going to an apartment? I asked for a roof," said Mohammed.

"Please, let me show you what Sammy has found we can still use the roof if you don't like the apartment," Fadi replied.

"Go," said Mohammed as the elevator opened.

The elevator went straight to the top floor. When the doors opened, they walked to a door at the end of the corridor and Fadi opened it with a key. The inside of the apartment was huge with twelve foot ceilings and ornate crown moldings.

"Over here," said Fadi.

Mohammed followed him across the room to a set of double French doors that were ten feet tall. Fadi opened the doors and there was a clear view over the buildings outside and the White House in the distance. Mohammed took the scene in for a moment then stepped onto the balcony outside. He was pleased that Sammy had not only found a good location, the weapons system would be placed slightly inside the doorway where it couldn't be seen by anyone outside.

"This is good Fadi, very good," said Mohammed.

"Thank you," he replied.

"Did you rent the place?" he asked.

"No. Sammy organized it but he didn't say how he got it."

There was a knock on the apartment door and Mohammed pulled a handgun out from under his jacket. He said nothing but waved Fadi towards the door to see who was outside.

Fadi looked through the door viewer and could see Sammy's face on the other side.

"It's Sammy, he's alone," said Fadi.

"Let him in," replied Mohammed.

"What do you think?" said Sammy, as he entered the apartment.

"It's good, who owns it?" asked Mohammed.

"A friend, it will be empty for the next ten days," he replied.

"Do you have the six men I asked for?" asked Mohammed.

"Yes, they are close," he replied.

"Send them to this address here is the key to get in. There is a large crate inside the building. Tell them to bring it here, but not under any circumstance to open it." Mohammed handed him a key and a note with an address on it.

Four hours later the men arrived at the apartment with the wooden crate they placed it in the center of the living area.

"All of you wait outside in the vehicles until I call you back up here," said Sammy.

"Help me open the crate," said Mohammed to Sammy.

After a couple of minutes, they had the crate open and the weapons system exposed. Sammy was amazed and couldn't help but think that he could sell this to the Colombians for a small fortune.

"Tomorrow morning, the President will be leaving for a tour of Europe. He always takes the helicopter from the White House lawn to Air Force One. This machine will shoot down the helicopter when it takes off, killing the President when it crashes. I'll operate the machine with this computer and watch it perform a great duty for us," said Mohammed.

"This will be a great day. What do we do with the machine afterwards?" asked Sammy.

"If they do not find this place within a week, we will transport it back to the building and wait a couple of more weeks before we fly it out of here."

"Who is to stay with the machine?" asked Sammy.

"The six men you have brought, they will protect it until the job is done and then they can leave."

Sammy and Mohammed placed the weapons system right up to the double French doors ready for the next morning. The six men were briefed that they were to stay with the weapon and open the French doors at exactly six in the morning. They were to then stay clear of the doors and the weapon, but protect the apartment against anyone that might try to get in.

"What about Fadi and his brothers, should they come here?" asked Sammy.

"No, I have put them through a lot and we will need them fresh for the next operation. They are here in D.C. with Hakeem from California, he did well in Bakersfield and Maui. Young men like him are our future. Bring your men in and tell them what to do. I'll call them on this phone before I arrive," said Mohammed.

"I'll tell them to wait for your call," replied Sammy, as Mohammed left.

Mohammed wasn't going to the apartment. He just wanted to call to make sure none of his men were in front of the weapon when he was in position.

CHAPTER 59

The team had tried to find a good observation point to watch the door to the building where the weapons system was located, but there wasn't one. They parked the surveillance van a block away, with George and Chalky inside. The remainder of the team parked in different locations covering the main road. It had been quiet all night with no signs of movement when the tracking signal started to beep in the van. George called the team to let them know that the tracking device had activated, the crate was on the move.

Strain and Thorn drove into the parking lot of McDonald's, Wheels was further up the main road with a view of the road leading to the building. A dirty white van drove to the main road, followed closely by a car with three men in it.

The team stayed well back and waited for the van to gain a little distance from them. Wheels made one run past the van to see where the car was with the three men in it. As suspected, they were about six vehicles behind the van, keeping surveillance. The team followed the tracking signal into the capital until it stopped on H Street NW. Shadow parked around the corner from the building and walked to where the van was parked. He saw the back was open and the wooden crate was being removed. There was a man holding the door open to the building. Shadow wasted no time and walked past the man and through the door straight to the elevator. Shadow didn't look back as he knew that the man at the door was watching him. The elevator arrived and he got in. He pressed the button inside the elevator for the first floor and looked up to see the men carrying the crate.

Shadow got out of the elevator and waited, looking at the numbers on the floor indicator above to see which floor the elevator would stop at next. It went straight to the ground floor and Shadow put his ear to the doors. He could hear the men struggling to get the crate into the elevator and then the doors closed. He stepped back again and watched as the elevator went straight to the top floor. He took the fire stairwell down to the lobby. It was clear so he returned to his car.

All members of the team were listening to the conversation between Mohammed and Sammy in the apartment through the device Chalky had set up in the computer.

"The President is the target. We need to tell him to delay his trip," said Thorn.

"No. Chalky has fixed that weapon it won't fire even if they try. I think we should pay them a visit in the morning when Mohammed returns. We can get into the building tonight and find out exactly which apartment they are in. Chalky and George can get the floor plans of the building for us. I don't think we should take a chance on Mohammed getting away this time," said Strain.

"Sounds good, we hit them in the morning just before the President is due to leave," replied Thorn.

"It doesn't sound like Sammy will be there but we know where he goes. It won't take long to catch up to him," said Strain.

"Shadow, see if you can follow Mohammed when he comes out," said Strain into his sleeve microphone.

"Will do," he replied.

They waited for fifteen minutes but there was no sign of Mohammed. Shadow went into the building and did a quick search of the ground floor. At the back of the building was a fire exit door that was partly open, this was the way Mohammed had left.

CHAPTER 60

The next morning Mohammed drove around the apartment building three times, working his way inwards from a three-block circle. He noticed a van parked in a small park n pay area two blocks from the apartment. He was sure that he'd seen it the day before.

He went to the building that he'd chosen to watch the weapon do its work when he activated it. The roof of the building was easy to access and there was a small alcove between two air conditioning units and a wall where he could hide. He had a clear view of the trees above the White House from this position and turned on the laptop computer. It was seven in the morning and he knew that the helicopter would leave sometime in the next two hours. He activated the weapon system and moved it around a little, using a joy stick that he'd plugged into the USB port. He was fascinated by the machine as the picture moved on the screen, it was just like playing a video game. He tested the scope on the rifle next the camera that was sighted into the scope gave a very clear picture. He could see the leaves on the trees by the White House. He was ready for the greatest day of his life.

Thorn had arranged for a cleanup crew to be on hand in the hope that the apartment assault went smoothly. The crew was only four blocks away waiting for the signal to go. They would clean up any bodies and mess in the apartment. One of them would be in a police officer's uniform to calm any excited residents. All calls through the building's telephone switch would be diverted for the period of the assault in case anyone called 911. The callers would think it was a genuine operator if they made the call and the uniformed officer would visit them to say it was being handled.

Shadow and the team had put on bullet proof vests before they left the safe house and double checked their weapons. Each man had the latest Heckler and Koch carbines, side arms and additional ammunition clips for both, plus gas masks. Shadow and Bulldog had flashbangs and smoke grenades, as they would be the first on the floor to the apartment.

Strain and Thorn were in one stairwell as L.B. and Wheels took the other. Sleepy was in position in the lobby, which covered the corridor to the rear fire exit where the team would come in.

Everyone was in position when Shadow and Bulldog took the elevator to the top floor. They had large raincoats on which they threw off once they were inside the elevator. They put the gas masks on and stood to one side of the elevator as it arrived on the floor and the doors opened.

From the apartment door, the two men on guard couldn't see the elevator doors as they were on the side wall. They heard the ping from the elevator bell and the doors open, nobody came out. The two men walked slowly towards the elevator, hands on their weapons.

Strain and Thorn heard Shadow in their earpiece say the men were going to the elevator. Strain slid a snake camera under the tight-fitting fire escape door and could see the two men as they walked towards the elevator. As the men got level with the fire escape door, Strain pulled it open and Thorn shot both men in the head. The silencer on the weapon cut the noise from the shots down to almost nothing.

"Clear," Strain said, giving the signal for Shadow and Bulldog to come out of the elevator.

Shadow left the key in the door control in the elevator so that nobody could use it. L.B. and Wheels were now making their way down the corridor towards the apartment.

Thorn held up one of Mohammed's men and turned his head to the side slightly so that he could be seen through the door viewer. Strain knocked twice on the door and they waited for an answer. Shadow and Bulldog were to the side of the door, out of sight, ready with a flash bang each. They heard the slide on the door viewer inside being opened and the door lock was next.

The flash bangs were thrown into the room the minute that Shadow and Bulldog could get their hands through the opening. The men burst into the room, sweeping left and right, with Strain and Thorn on their shoulders. Shadow and Bulldog fired two shots each at the first two targets, killing them, as Strain and Thorn shot and killed two more. From Mohammed's conversation, there were supposed to be six and they had killed all of them.

They quickly checked the bodies, but Mohammed wasn't amongst them. They immediately secured the apartment and left down the fire escape without anyone seeing them.

As they went out the back, Thorn called in the cleaning crew. He knew that some of the residents will have heard the gunfire.

Mohammed called the apartment from his roof top location to make sure they kept away from the weapon. He didn't want one of the men getting in the way of the weapon or machine and ruining his opportunity to kill the President. The phone rang several times but nobody answered, he called again with the same result.

He called Sammy, "Did you give them the phone?" he said angrily.

"Yes of course I did, why?"

"They are not answering," replied Mohammed.

"Wait. I have another number for them stay on the line," replied Sammy.

He had the same response as Mohammed and knew something was wrong, he reconnected to Mohammed.

"They never answered my call either," he said.

"Go to the bakery, now," shouted Mohammed.

Mohammed called Fadi and told him to pick him up, which he did within two minutes. They drove past the apartment building and saw two black vans parked outside with a man standing by each vehicle wearing black coveralls.

"Drive around the next corner," Mohammed said.

Fadi did as he was told. Without warning Mohammed started punching the dashboard of the van with his fists. Eight, nine ten blows Fadi lost count as Mohammed took his rage out on the dashboard. Fadi kept driving saying nothing as he was now scared of what Mohammed might do to him. Something had gone terribly wrong and he wasn't going to ask what.

Mohammed stopped beating the dashboard and sat back. Breathing heavily, he asked, "Where are your brothers?"

"They are waiting where you told them to in the other van with Hakeem," replied Fadi.

"Good, get them to meet us there at that parking lot," Mohammed pointed to the location ahead of them.

When the brothers arrived, Mohammed pointed out a van in a parking lot on the opposite side of the street.

"See if there is anyone in that van. If there is, put them in your vehicle and take them to the bakery."

"Yes," replied Ghaazi.

Mohammed watched as Ghaazi drove his van out of the parking lot and onto the one on the opposite side of the road. Hakeem was first out of the van and plunged a spike on the end of a long tube into the lock on the rear door handle. He pulled the tube hard, ripped out the lock in the door handle and opened the doors. Musaad joined him.

Chalky and George turned in surprise when the rear doors of the van opened. Chalky had the presence of mind to hit the alarm signal in the van which alerted the team that they were under duress.

"This way," said the man next to Chalky and grabbed him by the collar pulling him out of the van quickly followed by George.

George was pushed in the back by his gunman, "Move," he said.

"OK, no need to push," replied George.

He turned as if he was about to do as he was told and did what he thought was his only option, he quickly spun around and pushed both of his hands into the gunman's chest knocking him backwards.

"Run," he shouted to Chalky.

It was too late for Chalky as his gunman saw what was happening and quickly hit him in the back of the head with the butt of his gun, Chalky was knocked out. Mohammed watched as one of the men pushed Musaad to the ground and ran.

George ran as fast as he could to the corner of the side street where he could see the traffic on the main road. Just as he thought that he was going to make it, he heard a loud gunshot and felt a burning sensation in his back. George collapsed to his knees on the road. He heard a second gunshot and felt like someone had punched him in the right arm. George fell to the ground, face down, just as a group of men walked around the corner.

The gunman saw the men come around the corner and jumped into the back of the van with his partner and their victim Chalky. The van sped off as they closed the rear doors to the shouts of the men in the street.

The group of four men ran to where George was lying, "You OK, pal?" asked one of them to George but he didn't respond.

"I'm calling 911" said another.

CHAPTER 61

When the team got the alarm signal on their phones, they raced to where Chalky and George were supposed to be in the van. The first to arrive was Wheels. He called the team to let them know that Chalky was missing and George was in an ambulance on route to the hospital with gunshot wounds.

"Who the hell is behind this? Do you think it's Mohammed?" Thorn asked.

"Yes, I would bet money on it. You know he has to be pissed that we stopped his attack on the President," Strain replied.

"I'll get a protection team to the hospital to watch over George. We should call the rest of your team and get them to meet us at another safe house I have. It will only take five minutes to get there from here."

"OK," Strain said.

Strain sat thinking of what Mohammed was going to do next as Thorn made the calls.

"They are going to split up and make their way to the safe house. I have warned them that they may be under surveillance. I have also given them the access code to enter the safe house when they get there." Thorn was convinced that they were also under surveillance.

They had to regroup and plan for the next possible attack.

Whoever it was that had attacked Chalky and George they were very good.

The teams biggest concern was for Chalky. Where had the abductors taken him and why? Chalky had a world of intelligence and knowledge of the team in his head. To break him for this information wouldn't take much as he wasn't trained in how to handle an interrogation.

Chalky could also be very helpful to any terrorist organization. His technical skills with surveillance and counter surveillance equipment was second to none. He built many of the pieces the team used himself.

George was also very much in their thoughts as they didn't know how bad the gunshot wounds were.

CHAPTER 62

SHAW NEIGHBORHOOD, WASHINGTON D.C.

It took almost forty minutes for Mohammed and Ghaazi to get to the bakery with their captive. Mohammed asked Chalky for the phone number of his boss. As soon as he heard Chalky's English accent, he knew that it was Strain hunting him again. Chalky held out for twenty minutes before the beating became too much and he gave them Strain's cell phone number.

Mohammed was pacing the warehouse floor hard, deep in thought. He stopped pacing and dialed Strain's number on his cell phone. He waited as he listened to the ringing. It seemed to go on forever and then a woman's recorded voice answered.

"I'm sorry but the number you are calling is not available at this time, please try again later."

Mohammed's eyes were wide with rage, his fists clenched, as he spat out some Arabic curse words. Chalky was the only person that didn't understand what he was saying. Mohammed's voice bounced off the walls and echoed in the rafters above.

Chalky watched with pleasure it was obvious things weren't going smoothly for the Terrorists. He didn't realize it but he had a slight smile on his face.

Mohammed looked at Chalky and could see the smile. "Is something amusing you?" He said as he walked over to where Chalky was sat.

"Well, it doesn't look like things are going to plan," replied Chalky.

The blood vessels in Mohammed's eyes became bright red as they expanded with the pressure of blood. His hands went into fists as he rained down blow after blow on Chalky's face and Chest.

Sammy stepped in but not before several punches landed on the defenseless man in the chair. He grabbed Mohammed from behind in a bear hug and lifted him away.

"Get off me. I'll teach that pig a lesson," Mohammed screamed at the top of his voice.

Sammy held on for a few seconds more and let go. He positioned himself between Mohammed and Chalky, who was now thankfully unconscious from the attack.

Mohammed pulled a nine-millimeter handgun out of his waistband and pointed it at Sammy.

"You will die for putting your hands on me," he screamed.

"Mohammed, my leader you cannot kill this man. Not yet, we need him. The man Strain will want to know if he is alive and he will ask to speak to him. This man is no good to us dead if we are to trade him for Strain." He could see Mohammed's finger hesitating on the trigger.

Mohammed was frozen with anger. He glared at his old friend and realized that he was speaking truthfully. He lowered his weapon and put it back in the waistband of his trousers. Dripping with sweat, he walked over to a table at the side of the warehouse and picked up a bottle of water, drinking it in one go. He wiped his head, neck and face with a towel and turned towards Sammy.

"You ever touch me again like that in front of my men and I'll kill you. We will keep him alive for now but I'll finish what I have started with my bare hands when we get Strain." He walked into an empty room that used to be an office space to regain his composure.

CHAPTER 63

SAFE HOUSE, WASHINGTON, D.C

The Mask Team members had arrived at the safe house and were anxiously awaiting the arrival of Strain and Thorn. The safe house was more than any of them had expected it was an old office building that had been renovated on the inside. Once inside the front door there was an old service elevator with metal gates as doors and nowhere else to go. There were only two buttons in the elevator, one for up and one for down. The safe house took up the entire third floor. There were four bedrooms, a massive lounge with a TV and a bank of computers and screens. On the back wall was an expansive kitchen with two fridge freezers and enough food to sustain an army. It even had a floor-to-ceiling bookcase with cookery books and all manner of reading material, fiction and non-fiction.

Thorn slid back the metal gate on the elevator and Strain and Thorn stepped out into the giant floor of the safe house.

"What happened?" asked Bulldog.

"Well, we know Chalky has been taken and George is in the hospital with two gunshot wounds," replied Strain.

"No prizes for guessing who did it," stated Shadow.

"I expect its Mohammed, but we don't know yet. Thorn here thought that it was a good idea for me to turn the phone off to give us a little time to strategize. It won't be long before Mohammed calls me about Chalky."

"We can't afford to leave it off too long. In the meantime, we need to get ourselves kitted out with weapons, surveillance gear, etc." Thorn said.

"That's good but what are we going to do about vehicles? They may know which ones we are using if they have had us under surveillance." replied Wheels.

"That's where we are going now, right after I turn these computer screens on." Thorn flicked a couple of switches and the computers and monitors came out of sleep mode filling the room with light. Thorn waved at the team to follow him as he walked into the kitchen.

"Intriguing," said Shadow.

Thorn pulled a book off the third shelf of the bookcase and then took a small wooden panel out of the back, revealing another keypad. He punched in a series of numbers into the keypad and the bookcase opened inwards. Thorn walked through the opening followed by the Mask Team. There was a narrow corridor about twenty feet long at the end of which was an elevator exactly like the one they came up in at the front door.

The elevator was larger than the first one and fitted all the men in easily. Thorn closed the gate and punched in another code on a keypad next to him. The elevator was much faster than the first one and reached the bottom in seconds. Thorn slid the gate open and turned to his right where he flipped a series of light switches.

When the lights came on, they flooded the room in bright light. The team couldn't believe what they were seeing. The room was the length and width of a full city block. Directly in front of them, about fifty feet away, was a row of ten vehicles all in different shades of Grey or dull silver. There were vans, sedans and what looked like a couple of very high powered sports cars. The team fanned out to look around.

"Three of the four vans are complete mobile surveillance units, the fourth is for carrying goods or should I say 'guests'." He meant people that needed to be abducted. "The two sports cars you see have been modified and are most probably two of the fastest road cars in the US. Two of the sedans are armored and the other two are standard factory models with turbo engines." Thorn watched as they admired the vehicles.

"I'd love to take one of the sports cars out for a spin," said Wheels.

"Over here, please," Thorn shouted. "We don't have much time so I'll open up the whole store to you and we can decide what we need for support." Thorn then stuck his index finger onto a small box on the wall. A small green light came on just above his finger and they could all hear electric motors kicking in, as half of the wall by the elevator started to slide open. The wall slid backwards about eight inches and then sideways. The next part of the wall did the same and the next until over one hundred feet of wall had opened revealing a shallow room. The back wall of the room was covered in an array of weapons.

"Fuck me," said Bulldog out loud.

"These weapons are at our disposal. On the bottom shelf, you will find Kevlar vests of varying sizes. In the draws, directly below each set of weapons are ammunition and clips for those weapons. On the far left is a tall cabinet with grenades, flash bangs and tear gas canisters. In front of us is a cabinet full of electronic surveillance equipment including the latest microwave slash infrared camera that can pick up infrared images through walls. On this screen, here it shows the heat signature of people in the building you are scanning."

"Let's sit down and put something together before I switch this phone back on," said Strain.

The team walked through who was going to drive what vehicle and who was going to take charge of sniper duty, which came down to Thorn and Shadow. They discussed the weapons needed and agreed to regroup if needed after Strain talked to Mohammed.

Strain turned the cell phone on and made sure that there was a good signal. The team was organizing the communications equipment that they were all going to wear. Thorn pulled out several tracking devices in case it involved a payoff.

The phone had been only on three minutes when it rang.

"Quiet everyone all equipment down, phones off," said Strain.

Everyone put down anything they were holding so as not to make a noise and checked their cell phones. They were all so focused on Strain that they didn't notice Thorn standing by the armory with an electronic gadget in his hand.

Strain answered the phone, "Hello."

"You play a very dangerous game Mr. Strain, ignoring my first call," said Mohammed.

Strain had to think on his feet now, "You should know that signals get blocked in some areas of this city because of the number of government communications."

"Is that the best excuse you can come up with? You are a disappointment."

"Enough of the chit chat Mohammed. I presume that I am speaking to Mohammed Ali Ghahi?" said Strain.

"Yes, you are. Let's get down to business, as the Americans say. I have one of your men here Mr. White and we will let him go in a trade for you."

Strain didn't think this was going to be a trade situation but they had to deal with it. "I need to talk to him," said Strain.

"Ah! Proof of life I think they call it in your world." Mohammed walked into the warehouse and put the phone up to Chalky's ear. "Speak."

"Hello," said Chalky.

"How you doing?" said Strain.

"I have had better days this fuck head gave me a beating though."

Mohammed took the phone away. "This is what you will do if you want him to go free. Go to the corner of M Street and 14th St and wait for my call. You have twenty minutes be sure the phone is switched on this time."

Thorn was waving his hand in front of Strain he was holding up three fingers and mouthing thirty.

"I am at least thirty minutes from that location," Strain tried to buy time, as he didn't know exactly where that was.

"Then you need to hurry and if we see anyone with you or following you he dies."

Before Strain could say anything, the phone went dead.

Strain turned to the team, "Mohammed wants me in exchange for Chalky."

"He will kill both of you he isn't going to trade," replied Bulldog.

"I know, but we have to go through with this in the hope that we can get Chalky back safe. It sounds like he has had a beating already."

"That Mohammed is a gutless bastard, poor old Chalky couldn't fight his way out of a paper bag." Bulldog was angry.

"OK. It will only take about ten minutes to get there from here. I know exactly where that is. Wheels can drive in one of the fast cars. I'll sit up front and direct him. We will stop one block away in a side street where you can continue on foot." Thorn's mind was working overtime.

"What about putting a tracking device on John?" asked Shadow.

"I think we should put two on me. Let's put one on my belt and another into the lining of my jacket."

"I like it, we have a new miniature one that will be helpful. This is a quarter the size of a matchstick and the signal can be detected up to five miles away. If these guys are switched on and we know Mohammed is, they will run a scanner over you to find bugs. This one can only be detected by a scanner after we activate it, but there is a slight downside." Thorn had gotten to know Strain well and knew that the downside wouldn't be a problem for him.

"OK, what is the downside?" asked Strain.

"We normally insert these just under the skin."

"I presume you can do it," replied Strain.

"Yes."

"Can we do it somewhere in my hair line, that way the cut will be hidden?" Strain said.

"Yes." Thorn got to work while the rest of the team chose weapons and other items from the supplies available.

"Fifteen minutes to go," said Shadow.

Thorn's cell phone rang breaking the silence of preparation. "Go," said Thorn when he answered.

The team watched as Thorn listened with a smile on his face the call took thirty seconds.

"What was that about?" asked Strain.

"I'll explain on the way." Thorn knew time was getting tight.

Sleepy and Bulldog took one of the surveillance vans with a stack of equipment, Shadow went alone in one of the sports cars and L.B. took a sedan.

Wheels, Thorn and Strain took the second sports car. They were all now kitted out with a mass of firearms, technical equipment and the latest in high tech communications. Strain would remove his when they got to the drop-off point. All the vehicles left at the same time but took different routes to the drop-off area. The Mask Team plotted their routes on the vehicles' GPS. During the drive, they all talked and agreed to points where they would all arrive, no closer than two blocks from the drop-off but covering all exit routes. Their comms' or communications devices, would now stay live throughout the mission so that everyone could hear what was being said. Nobody would cut in unless it was a matter of urgency.

"Well we are as ready as we will ever be, so what was the phone call about?" Strain asked Thorn.

Everyone's ears pricked up.

"We have a Guardian Angel flying above us as we speak. They will stay with us throughout this and will be the key to giving us the go signal to turn on your tracking device. The chopper is the latest in stealth technology at the height he is flying, he can't be heard. There is thick cloud cover tonight also, so if anybody looks up they won't be able to see them. It's manned by the best pilot and co-pilot I know, as well as a four-man Delta Team, should we need them to drop in on the party. All on board the chopper are fluent in four Arabic dialects and three of them speak fluent Farsi. They are also listening in on our comms' so that they know what is happening. The second locating device we put into your belt is also an active microphone. Once you dispose of the comms' when we drop you off the chopper will switch on your belt tracking device. We will hear what your belt microphone is picking up and know what is happening to you, until they discover it of course. Then they will switch on the device in your hairline." Thorn was pleased that no questions came from the team.

"Impressive," replied Strain.

CHAPTER 64

Wheels made good time and dropped Strain off two and half blocks away from the rendezvous point in an alley. "Take this. If they put you in a vehicle, try to put it on the roof. If you can't before you get in, dump it, it won't work inside a vehicle." Thorn put a small black disc in Strain's hand. It was only the size of a casino chip and half as thick. Another piece of tracking technology, but this one would be invaluable to the guardian angel above them.

"OK." Strain didn't have to ask what it was.

"I know I speak for everyone when I say good luck, John," Thorn said.

"No need for luck when I have all of your ugly asses watching me," Strain got out of the car and started walking.

Strain passed one of the team vehicles on route and was very pleased that he couldn't tell if anyone was inside. His senses were on overload. As he walked, he scanned the streets and doorways, looking for people keeping him under surveillance. He fully expected someone to suddenly pull up at the side of the road and snatch him. As he approached the corner of the road where Mohammed had told him to go, the phone rang.

"Yes," Strain said.

"Keep walking east on M Street until I call you again," Mohammed said no more.

Strain kept a steady walking pace, not too fast, not too slow. He could almost feel his team running the streets parallel to his position, performing counter surveillance as they drove.

He'd walked almost a mile when a black van pulled up to the curb next to him and a sliding door opened. A man jumped out and grabbed Strain by the arm, pulling him towards the van.

As they were getting into the van, Strain saw an opportunity, "Get the fuck off me, I can get in without your help," he growled at the man, as he climbed in through the sliding door, using the roof to pull himself inside.

The van pulled away from the curb without too much speed so as not to attract attention.

Strain couldn't see much inside the van but could certainly smell the stench of body odor.

"Take all of your clothes off," said the man who put him in the van.

"Why? You going to fuck me up the ass? I hear you guys like that sort of thing but normally with little boys." Strain baited the man perfectly.

The man took a swing at Strain and missed only to receive a huge head butt from Strain. It landed on the bridge of his nose, breaking it. The nose now looked like a seasoned boxer's, it was totally flat at the top and pouring with blood. Strain was getting control of the situation. The man pulled out a gun in anger only to be screamed at by the driver in Arabic to put the gun away. "Mohammed told us no violence. Tie his hands together but not his feet he will need to walk soon. If he tries to escape, we can kill him and Mohammed will kill the other man" referring to Chalky. Strain held his hands together in front of him and couldn't believe it when his captor tied them together. Strain had him so flustered he wasn't thinking straight or he would have put Strain's hands behind his back.

Strain smiled at the man and said, "I would listen to your friend if I were you because if ANYTHING happens to me before we get to Mohammed he will butcher you. You know he wants me for his enjoyment, not yours." Strain started to undress.

Once Strain was naked, the man looked over his body with a flashlight looking for listening or tracking devices. "Open your mouth," he said to Strain.

Strain did as he was told, opening his mouth wide and moving his tongue around so that his abductor could see he had nothing hidden.

The man threw a pair of coveralls in Strain's face and said, "Put them on."

Strain did as he was told he saw no further reason to aggravate him.

The man went through Strain's clothes with a detector piece by piece including his underwear. It didn't take long for the two tracking devices to be found.

"You must think we are as stupid as you," he said, holding up the two tracking devices. They went two more blocks and stopped by a group of homeless people who were sitting on the corner, drinking. As the van stopped, the homeless men got up and approached the van with their hands out, expecting money, but all they got was Strain's clothes thrown at them.

"You're giving all of my clothes to homeless people? Well, at least they can put them to good use," Strain said. He knew that the team and Guardian Angel were listening and would know it was safe to turn on the tracking device Thorn had inserted under the skin in his head.

"Shut up and lie face down," said the driver.

The van drove off again and wandered the streets for thirty minutes. Although he couldn't see, Strain knew they were performing counter surveillance and were most probably good at it, but not as good as the people following them. He had to buy some time for his team but didn't see an opportunity yet. Strain knew that even two minutes in these situations was a lot of time for the team to get in place.

The van finally stopped and the side door was opened by the driver.

"Get out," said the man in the back with Strain, as he pulled on the collar of Strain's coveralls.

"I keep telling you to keep your hands off me," Strain said, pulling back from the man. This gave him an idea.

The silence on the team's comms' system was broken.

"This is Guardian Angel. The target has stopped in an alley on the north side of an old bakery building at 641 S Street NW in the Shaw Neighborhood. Our system shows this building has been empty for almost twenty years and is in a very poor state, but is huge. The west side of the building is two floors and the east is three. I am sending you the schematic of the building."

One by one, the team acknowledged the information received. As they reviewed the building schematic, they could see there were doors on all four sides and dozens of windows. This wouldn't be an easy place to sneak up on.

The building had been used for many decades as a bread factory, dating as far back as 1878. The building went through many changes over the decades including expansion into the adjoining properties to increase the bakery's business. The most famous of the bakeries to occupy the building was most probably the Continental Baking Company whose products included the well known and loved Hostess cakes and Wonder bread.

"This is Guardian Angel. Your man is exiting the vehicle."

Thorn spoke, "Guardian Angel, be ready for my go, then deploy your team onto the roof."

"Roger that."

"Shadow, can you choose a vantage point to keep an eye on the van and building from that side?" Thorn said.

"Consider it done."

As they had driven around keeping surveillance on the van Strain was in, the team had come up with a very flexible plan. They knew that Chalky would have been held either somewhere remote or in an area where there were a lot of business properties and little or no houses. The old bread building fell into the latter category but was much larger than they had expected. Thorn deployed the Mask Team, Bulldog and L.B. went to the East side, Sleepy and L.B. to the West, Thorn and Wheels took up the front of the building.

Strain climbed out of the van and was walked around the corner to the east side of the building. Strain deliberately walked slowly, trying to buy time, his bare feet feeling every stone in the road. The two men following closely behind both had their weapons pointed at Strain's back.

Mohammed was watching the side street from a window when he saw his two men and Strain walk around from the rear of the building. He saw one of the men push Strain hard in the back.

Perfect thought Strain. He spun around, "What is wrong with you, fuck head? Keep your hands off me?" He stepped right up to the man, keeping his arms down so that he wouldn't think he was a threat.

"Keep moving," he snarled at Strain and pushed him again.

"Ibn Himar?" Strain said to the man in Arabic.

This was a huge insult in Arabic it meant, 'son of a donkey'. It got the reaction Strain wanted.

The man immediately lost control and raised his gun hand to strike Strain on the head. Strain anticipated the move. Taking a half step back, he threw his bound hands over the man's head and pulled it towards him head butting him once again. At almost the same time he brought his left knee up as hard as he could and buried it into the man's balls. As his colleague went down the driver shot at Strain, the gunshot strangely quiet almost like it had a silencer. Standing still in an attack stance Strain suddenly realized he wasn't hit and his attacker was falling backwards. As the man crumpled to the ground, Strain saw a small red dot of blood in the middle of his forehead. He turned to see Mohammed standing there his right arm outstretched with a nine millimeter in his hand with a silencer on the end.

"This is Guardian Angel. We have audio and visual on Strain. He is walking towards the building. Standby, something is happening." The pilot and Delta Team watched what was happening on their monitors and listened intently to what was being said.

"This is Guardian Angel. Strain is fighting with the van driver and you won't believe it, but a man who looks very much like Mohammed has come out of the building and shot the driver."

Shadow had just got into position behind a trash dumpster down the side street where Strain was and saw Mohammed shoot one of his own. Through the scope of the high-powered sniper rifle he also saw another lying on the ground. Shadow slowly squeezed the trigger on the rifle he had a perfect head shot on Mohammed. As he was about to shoot Mohammed moved towards Strain, this blocked the shot as

Strain was in the way. He waited and could see them both standing as if they were having a conversation.

Strain was pleased with his delaying tactics but it didn't work out quite as he'd expected as he was now staring down the barrel of Mohammed's gun.

"You are still creating problems for me, Mr. Strain," said Mohammed.

"Well, I don't know if I should thank you for shooting him or have I just delayed the inevitable?" Strain played for more time.

"Oh! I'll deal with you but not as quickly as that we have a lot to talk about." Mohammed intended to torture Strain to get information from him about Strain's organization. He also wanted to punish him for the deaths of his followers and failed terrorist attacks.

"I presume that won't include tea and biscuits," Strain smiled.

"Only if you can eat the biscuits through a straw. I intend pulling your teeth out one by one." Mohammed was trying to strike early fear into Strain.

"I guess we can leave the biscuits out then." Strain smiled.

"This way and no tricks or I'll shoot you in the leg." Mohammed heard his man on the floor spitting. "Get up and drag his body into the building," he told him. Mohammed was going to kill the man later for failing him.

The radio silence was broken as everyone confirmed that they were in position. Shadow moved down the alley towards the van, sweeping the building with his rifle scope as he went. He got to the van that had carried Strain and tested the handle on the driver's door, it was unlocked.

Bulldog and Sleepy were the first to enter the front of the building as they went through an old door that had been badly boarded up.

"We are in the front," said Bulldog.

L.B. covered the west side of the building in such a position he could also see the front.

Shadow was operating the body imager that saw through walls. He could make out the heat signatures of nine people standing and one sitting. Two were walking towards the one sitting. He knew the one sitting down had to be Chalky. They were all in the north-east corner of the building just behind the wall where the van was parked. He relayed this to everyone.

Shadow was curious why there wasn't anyone keeping observations from the building when he saw a body falling from the roof.

The chopper was hovering overhead, picking up a clear visual of the building and audio from the inside.

"We have two on the roof. The one on the north side is looking over the edge of the building into the street below where the van is," said the pilot.

"Not anymore," said the Delta sniper, "And there goes number two off the roof."

His shots were perfect the bullets tearing into the tops of the heads of the two men dropping them like stones.

"Heads up below, there are people are falling from the sky." said the Delta sniper.

"Roger that," said Shadow.

"We are in," said Thorn.

Mohammed walked Strain into a giant square room that was an old factory floor. Strain gave the room a quick scan, looking for exits and safe points. On the second floor, was a square gallery of vandalized office windows looking down on the room they were in. He could imagine this was a busy factory floor at one time with all the office staff looking down on the real workers on the shop floor. He was taking his time again as he stood still taking it all in. He focused on Chalky sitting on a chair in the middle of the factory floor, he headed straight for him. Strain could see that Chalky had taken one hell of a beating, both eyes were badly swollen and he had a nasty split above the left eyebrow and a bloody nose.

"Hang in there," Strain said.

"No problems here just got a little slap around by that big girl over there." Chalky gave a weak smile, showing his blood-soaked teeth and gums.

"I suppose this is your handiwork, is it?" He glared at Mohammed. Beating up a man tied to a chair? You're nothing but a coward. Why don't you take this rope off my hands and fight me, fight like a man? Or are you scared to show your terrorist followers how fucking weak you really are?"

"Nice speech, Mr. Strain, but you don't know anything about me." Mohammed was cursing him inside but had to show that he was remaining calm.

"This is what I know you kill and maim innocent men, women and children, ripping their families' lives and souls apart. This power you think you have is all in that sick mind of yours. The only power you have is fear over these mindless bastards. It feeds your sad fucking ego, just like it does to have these zombies follow you around like you are God. Well you aren't, you weak fuck." Strain swung his arm around pointing at the men in the room. "Why don't you strap a bomb to yourself and prove to your followers that you are willing to give your life? It's what you and your kind ask women, children and weak minded young men to do every day. You and the likes of that fat bastard behind you are too scared to do it. You're the scum of the earth and an insult to your religion." Strain was trying hard to get a rise from one of them, trying to get into their heads and buying more time.

"Be quiet, infidel," shouted Hamed stepping towards Strain.

Mohammed raised his hand in Hamed's direction for him to say no more. Sammy also hushed him. He knew it was fatal to interrupt Mohammed when his anger was building. Sammy could see Mohammed was holding it together, keeping his anger in check.

As Thorn slowly moved through the old bakery, he heard voices towards the back of the building. A few yards away were concrete stairs leading up to the next floor. He quietly went up the flight of stairs in the hope of getting a better vantage point. Wheels was working his way around to the west side of the second floor. Bulldog and Sleepy were in position in the room next to where Strain and Chalky were being held prisoner. They had positioned themselves either side of a huge opening that used to be a giant factory door. Light flooded into their location from the next room.

"You and you check the side and front entrance," said Mohammed, dispatching two of the terrorists in the room. The men left the room in different directions to perform a security check.

Shadow had moved position a little further back down the side street to give him a larger view of the building. He was watching the heat signatures of the team members and terrorists on the scanner. Although Shadow couldn't tell who was who, he knew where each team member was because of the discussions on route. He noticed two of the heat signatures in the room were leaving in different directions. One was heading straight for Bulldog's position he was going to walk right into him.

"Bulldog, one incoming," said Shadow.

Bulldog heard Shadow's warning but didn't reply he was too close to the terrorists. He heard footsteps coming towards him and he slipped quietly up against the wall. Sleepy was on the opposite side of the huge doorway. A man walked past, not three feet from where Bulldog was standing. He was carrying an AK47. Bulldog waited for him to pass then made his move. In a swift and silent motion, he stepped behind the man. Reaching around, he put his hand over his mouth lifting him into the darkness. Before the man could react in any way, Bulldog plunged his knife into his throat, twisting it as it entered the windpipe. He grabbed the AK47 as it slipped towards the floor and held onto the man with his other hand until he drowned in his own blood and stopped struggling. Bulldog lay the man down quietly on the floor. Although this only took about thirty seconds, it seemed like it was forever to Sleepy as he watched from the other side of the room. He had Bulldog covered the whole time with his MK53 submachine gun. Bulldog gave him thumbs up to let him know all was OK.

Mohammed was ready to leave the building and take Strain somewhere else where nobody would hear his screams as he was tortured. "It's time to go," he said.

"Wait, you let him go first," Strain said pointing to Chalky.

"I lied, he will die here. You however will die somewhere else." Mohammed waved

Hamed walked towards Chalky, it was his signal to kill him.

"Don't I get chance to say a prayer first?" asked Chalky. He was really praying that the team would arrive, but there wasn't any sign of them.

"Make it quick," said Mohammed. He was happy to let the man make peace with his God.

Strain was protesting and cursing Mohammed for his betrayal of trust, the words were wasted but he knew that.

Thorn was on the floor above Strain, but with a partial view of the room, could only see Chalky and one of the terrorists. He was about to move to better vantage point when he heard the conversation between Strain and Mohammed and hit his microphone, "Now, Guardian Angel," he said.

The pilot took the chopper off silent mode and quickly lowered it to within fifteen feet of the roof. The Delta Team rappelled down in practiced fashion.

The whole team heard him, but didn't know what to expect until they heard the noise of the chopper above in the down draft as from the blades blew debris off the roof to the street below. The noise of the helicopter was perfect. They all looked up at the ceiling, all except Strain who was making a move on Mohammed.

"Go, you know what to do," said Mohammed to his team of followers.

The terrorists scattered towards different parts of the building. Hakeem jumped through a hole in the wall behind Mohammed and disappeared.

Hamed was standing over Chalky and raised his gun to shoot him in the head.

Thorn waited for the noise of the helicopter to distract everyone in the room, he knew that they would all instinctively look up. He kept his rifle scope trained on Hamed's head and fired once.

Chalky looked into the eyes of Hamed, showing no fear, ready to accept his fate. He still had faith in the team even in what could be the dying seconds of his life. As Hamed raised his weapon towards Chalky, Thorn snapped off a single shot to the center of Hamed's head. The bullet slammed into the skull just above his right ear and exited the left side with a mass of skull fragments and brain matter. Blood and brains spreading over Chalky's face made him jump in his chair, not that he could jump far being tied down like he was. The team arrived, he thought. Turning his head, he saw Strain shoulder-charging Mohammed.

Mohammed looked at the ceiling above when he heard the chopper and was caught off guard when Strain slammed his shoulder into his right rib cage. Both men went crashing to the floor as a cloud of dust enveloped them.

Bulldog and Sleepy entered the room their HK53's raised sweeping the factory floor ready to pick off any terrorist targets. Sleepy was first to fire as one of the terrorists almost run straight into him. Two quick shots into the chest and he was dead. Bulldog took out another running towards the far side of the room.

"One heading up the stairs towards you, Wheels." Shadow loved the scanner.

Wheels didn't wait and pulled out a flashbang, tossing it towards the top of the stairs. He stepped back into a room, covering his ears protecting them from the imminent bang. As soon as it detonated, he would partially enter the hallway and shoot the terrorist.

The terrorist reached the landing and was just sticking his head around the corner, with his AK47 aimed down the hallway, when the flashbang exploded. The flashbang did what it was designed to do as the blinding light and sound totally disorientated the terrorist. He dropped on the landing. He didn't realize at first what had happened and began firing blindly down the hallway in Wheel's direction, just a reaction on his part.

Wheels was about to take his position to shoot the terrorist when a hail of bullets came screaming down the walls and ceiling of the hallway. He took cover, but not before one of the bullets ricocheted off the ceiling and down into his upper back behind his Kevlar vest. Wheels felt the bullet thump into his back. "I'm hit," he said over the comm.

The shooting had stopped and he could hear the terrorist cursing in Arabic. Wheels dropped his head and shoulders out onto the floor of the hallway and through the smoke and dust from the flashbang he saw a faint image of the terrorist writhing on the floor at the top of the stairs. He fired three short bursts from his HK53 at the terrorist. All but one round met the target and he died instantly.

Thorn heard Wheels say he was hit and ran through the second floor, sweeping doors and windows with his sniper rifle as he went. He heard more shooting and recognized the sound of the HK53. At least you're not dead, he thought to himself as he heard Wheels shooting. Thorn came around the corner to the landing where Wheels was laying on the floor still in his shooting position. "Right behind you, Wheels," he said.

"Where are you hit?" he asked Wheels.

"Top of my back, behind the vest," he replied.

Thorn pulled at the top of the vest to get a look as Wheels kept watch.

"You are one lucky son of a bitch the bullet stuck in the top of the vest. It looks like it grazed you right before it hit the vest, just a flesh wound." They both headed towards the stairs to continue the sweep and join the rest of the team.

Mohammed's gun flew across the floor towards the hole in the wall as Strain tackled him. Mohammed interlocked his fingers and brought them down into the middle of Strain's back right between the shoulder blades.

Strain felt the blow to his back and arched up just as Mohammed kicked him in the face.

Mohammed felt good kicking Strain in the head and dove for his gun. With the weapon in his right hand, he rolled over, firing three shots in Strain's direction and slammed through the hole in the wall that Hakeem had gone through.

Bulldog saw Mohammed firing at Strain, "Stay down, John," he shouted and fired more than a dozen rounds at Mohammed. He was too late Mohammed was disappearing through the hole in the wall to safety.

Shadow, still watching the events inside on the scanner, saw one thermal image running towards the back wall at the opposite end to where the van was parked. He lowered the scanner and looked at the building, it was solid brick. Even the old delivery bay doors had been bricked up. One thermal image running nowhere, he thought. He raised the scanner again and saw the thermal images going all over the place now. He heard Wheels saying he'd been hit and then Bulldog telling Strain to stay down. Another thermal image was going in the same direction that Hakeem had gone he was in a corner of the building.

"Hiding like a coward," Shadow said to himself.

Shadow could hear the team members checking in with each other, clearing areas. There was a window on the west corner of the building but the two terrorists who ran into the room didn't attempt to go through it. He wished they had because L.B. would have cut them down. He couldn't understand why they would run to an area where there wasn't anything but a bricked-up wall.

Shadow felt something was wrong. He decided to make his way towards the van and then to the northwest corner of the building. As he was about to move, the helicopter started to gain altitude and switched back to stealth mode. Shadow gave it the briefest of glances as it went over his head.

"There are two in the northwest corner of the building. Do you see any movement, L.B.?" said Shadow.

"Nothing here," he replied.

The Delta Force Team was now sweeping the inside of the building from the top down for terrorists. They would only find those that had already been killed.

Sammy couldn't believe that they had been found by Strain's team. As the shooting started, he ran away from Mohammed towards a back room. He cursed as he trod on something and twisted his ankle. As he fell to the floor, he dropped his gun. He heard it rattle on the concrete before it disappeared in a trash pile in the corner. He dragged himself towards a small cupboard under the stairs, crawled into it and closed the door. He was sure nobody had seen him as he sat in the darkness, trying not to breathe too loud.

Bulldog was covering the hole in the wall that Mohammed had gone through in case he came back.

Strain was back on his feet and untying Chalky, "You OK?" he said.

"Better now, but could they cut it a bit closer next time?" Chalky was joking, mostly out of nerves.

Mohammed felt a couple of the bullets flying past him as he ran through the hole in the wall, others where burrowing into the brick. He made his way to where he'd arranged to meet Hakeem if things went wrong and they had.

"Everything is ready," said Hakeem.

"You take the van when we get out, now do it," said Mohammed.

Hakeem nodded and they both stood around the corner of the room. Hakeem had a trigger mechanism in his hand and pressed a button on it. The old delivery bay doorway that had been bricked up blew out into the street outside.

Strain and everyone else heard an explosion coming from the direction in which Mohammed had run.

Outside the chopper was rising but still monitoring the building when they saw the explosion as did Shadow. No one asked any questions in order to keep the lines of communication open.

Two of the Delta Team were half-way through sweeping the ground floor when they saw a tiny red light on the wall in one of the side rooms. One of them checked it out, it was a box with wires running from it to a large military style canvas bag against the inner wall.

"Everybody out, this place is rigged to blow," he said into his microphone.

Nobody needed to be told twice they all ran towards the front of the building where Bulldog had come in. Strain threw Chalky over his shoulder like a sack of potatoes and started to run with the rest of the team. He knew Chalky wouldn't be able to walk, let alone run, as he'd been tied to the chair for several hours. The beating he took didn't help either.

"Has he blown himself up?" said Thorn. Just as Thorn had asked the question, they heard a motorcycle starting.

Two days earlier, Hakeem had put a ring of plastic explosive on the wall the size of a doorway. Hakeem had also put plastic explosives in four other locations in the building, all of which could be detonated remotely. This and another location on the opposite side of the building had been planned as possible escape routes. The explosion wasn't very big, just enough to blow out that section of wall.

Mohammed on the motorcycle started it as the explosion took place. He didn't wait for dust to settle. He carefully worked the bike over the rubble and out into the street and accelerated down the opposite side street.

"This is Guardian Angel. We have a motorcycle coming out of the building."

Shadow saw the motorcycle come out of the building but couldn't get a shot off before it disappeared behind the building on the other side. He watched as Hakeem ran to the van and got in. The van started up and reversed quickly towards the side street where Shadow was located.

Hakeem knew that he might not make it to the van but he had to try. He bolted out of the hole made by the explosion just as Mohammed sped out over the rubble. Hakeem was amazed he'd gotten this far. At the same time, he started the van, he pressed the second button on his detonator.

Mask and Delta Teams cleared the front of the building and were diving for cover behind cars on the opposite side of the street. All the men had their hands over their ears as protection from the effects of the bomb shockwave. When the explosions came, they were immense. The ground shook underfoot and the men were showered with glass and wood from the windows at the front of the building. Car and building alarms all around were activated by the shock wave, creating a cacophony of noise.

Most of the blast was designed to go inward to eliminate anyone inside the building. Walls and floors collapsed inwards in a mass of concrete and steel rebar. The team had a lucky escape as they would have all been killed by the explosion or by the concrete and steel that was sent flying through the building by the blast.

Everyone again checked in to see that they were all accounted for. Nobody had any injuries from the blast, everyone was OK.

"Guardian Angel, keep eyes on that motorcycle," said Thorn.

"Already on it," was the reply.

"Come on, Wheels, let's get after the bastard." Strain knew that if anyone could catch up to Mohammed it would be Wheels in the high-powered sports car he was driving.

Shadow couldn't believe the size of the explosion inside the building and was relieved when he heard everyone checking in O.K.

"The van is leaving," said Shadow.

"Can you stop him?" said Strain as he ran to the sports car.

"That's affirmative, need to give him a bit more distance first," Shadow replied.

"What's he up to?" asked Bulldog.

"Don't know, but I am sure he has something in store and I don't think that terrorist will like it," replied Strain.

As the Delta Team listened they were a little bemused by the casual attitude of Shadow. They had been warned by Thorn that these guys were unorthodox but this seemed more than unreal.

Hakeem reversed the van into the side street and pushed the automatic shift into drive. The van's wheels gave a slight spin on the road surface before they gripped and jumped the van forward. He kept his foot down hard on the accelerator and held his head and shoulders down towards the steering wheel. He was trying to make himself as small a target as possible in case somebody shot at him. As Hakeem looked ahead he could see the side street he was going to take about a hundred yards away. He was almost delirious with relief and excitement he'd escaped, he was banging the steering wheel in delight.

Shadow watched as the van was about eighty yards down the side street running parallel to the one Mohammed had taken.

"Here goes," said Shadow for all to hear.

The van rocked and lit up inside with a super white light as it ran into a dumpster. Earlier Shadow placed a phosphorous grenade rigged up to a small amount of plastic explosive under the dashboard of the vehicle. He wired it to the ignition switch so that when the engine was started it set off a fifteen second timer.

The explosion inside the van wasn't big but it was devastating. The plastic explosive and phosphorous grenade tore through the dashboard and into the cab and engine compartment of the van. The explosion blew off the lower half of Hakeem's legs and engulfed him in white hot phosphorous that was burning at 5000 degrees Fahrenheit. The choking smoke that followed filled the van, swallowing up Hakeem and the inside of the vehicle. Hakeem wouldn't suffer long, as his heart gave out with the shock of the burning phosphorous.

Shadow watched the van through his sniper scope. If the bomb didn't go off, he would send a volley of bullets into Hakeem. He didn't have to worry as he saw the blast of white light and watched the van crashed into a dumpster. For a split second, he saw Hakeem's arms flailing around and then all he could see was smoke billowing out of the vehicle, covering it in a grey and black shroud.

The team heard the explosion even though it wasn't that big.

"Shadow, you OK?" asked Strain.

"Yes, they are down another man this side," he replied.

He turned the scanner towards the old bakery one more time. He could see the heat signatures of the remaining team members, all heading for the exits.

Mohammed couldn't hear the helicopter anymore and thought that he'd escaped before they could react. At least this part of his escape plan was working. He knew that if they were found that the van would be under surveillance. He'd used Hakeem and the van as bait to aid his escape and left him to detonate the explosives in the old bakery building. In the distance, he heard the explosion and smiled to himself, hoping that he had at least killed Strain. He reduced his speed now so that he wouldn't bring attention to himself, he didn't want to get pulled over by the police. He was heading east and soon he would change back towards the north. Once he was sure he wasn't being followed, he would head to Hwy 500, then west on the East-West Hwy 410 and finally north again on Hwy 201.

Strain got into the back of the sports car with Thorn in the front, acting as the navigator for Wheels.

"Guardian Angel, can you guide us to him," said Thorn.

"He has been all over the map but he is now on Hwy 500 crossing Chillum Road," replied the pilot.

"We will take Rhode Island Avenue North East there are several roads we can cut across to Hwy 500." Thorn knew D.C. like the back of his hand and didn't need a road map to know where he was going.

Wheels followed the directions given by Thorn, driving down Rhode Island Avenue.

"Where does Hwy 500 lead?" asked Strain.

"Nowhere really, it cuts across Hwy 410." Thorn was mentally running the route to see where Mohammed could possibly be going.

Wheels was putting the sports car to the test and it was responding beautifully. He was doing eighty miles an hour and so far, hadn't seen a police car or had a red light.

"Guardian Angel. He has turned right onto Hwy 410 heading east, repeat heading East on Hwy 410."

Wheels had finally found a red light with a line of cars ahead waiting for it to turn green. He didn't hesitate and went into the oncoming lane, causing the drivers to swerve out of the way beeping their horns in annoyance. The traffic light was still red as he reached the junction. With a quick right and left tweak of the steering wheel he barely missed the back of a Metro bus. Wheels slammed the accelerator to the floor again.

"You were right, John, this fucking maniac can drive," Thorn was truly impressed.

"Easy there, I resemble that remark," replied Wheels.

"Holy shit, I know where he is going," said Thorn.

Before he could tell Strain and Wheels, Guardian Angel transmitted again.

"Guardian Angel. He has turned north on Hwy 201."

Before they could continue Thorn cut in, "He is going to College Park Airport."

College Park Airport had a long and distinguished history dating back to 1909 when it was visited by Wilbur Wright, one of the fathers of aviation. It's also the oldest operated airport in the world with its own museum on the premises.

"The bastards got a plane," said Strain.

"Turn right here, turn right," Thorn pointed at the junction just thirty yards.

Wheels hit the brakes hard and in a controlled slide he turned the car right into Decatur Road.

"In a minute, you will come to Hwy 201, you need to go left," Thorn said.

"Thanks for the warning," said Wheels, with a huge smile.

"You are enjoying this way too much," said Strain.

"Guardian Angel. Looks like you are right. He has turned left on Paint Branch Road."

"I knew it he won't get away this time." Thorn was convinced this would be the end of Mohammed.

Wheels was doing over a hundred miles an hour when he saw the sign for Paint Branch Road one mile ahead. At the junction, he took the left turn in perfect sliding fashion again and accelerated hard as he came out of the slide.

"Easy there's a turning ahead on the right for the airport. There it is," Thorn was pointing at Corporal Frank Scott Drive.

Mohammed rode the motorcycle into the parking lot of the airport and parked it by a grass island in the center of the parking lot. As he got off the motorcycle, two men got out of a car that was parked just twenty yards away and walked over to Mohammed. The two men were observing what was around them as they walked. One of them was carrying a large black bag.

"Good to see you again," the man with the bag said.

"Is everything in there?" Mohammed asked, foregoing the pleasantries of shaking hands.

"Yes, everything you asked for."

"Guardian Angel. He has stopped at the front of the building and is talking to two men."

On hearing this, Wheels slowed the car down as he turned into the airport approach road that Mohammed had taken earlier. Thorn was checking his sidearm and past one to Strain who was still in the coveralls that he put on in the van.

"There are two MK53's under my seat," said Wheels.

Strain reached down and placed one on the center console for Wheels.

As they drove towards the airport entrance Thorn said, "Slow down and take the next right into College Avenue."

Wheels never questioned why he just did it.

"Pull over on the left just before the junction. If we drive straight in, we are sitting ducks especially now Mohammed has additional support. Drop me off here and I'll go down the side of that factory building. As you can see there are trees all the way down. I can pick a position at the end where I can see Mohammed and give you cover with my sniper rifle." Thorn got out of the car.

"Thorn, if you can kill him do it. He is not the kind that's going to come quietly anyway," said Strain.

Thorn gave him a nod of acknowledgment and ran off between the factory building and the trees.

Strain climbed into the front seat and dropped down onto the floor out of sight. "Let's go, Wheels, but take it easy - give Thorn time to get into position," said Strain.

Wheels turned left behind a large truck driving slowly in the direction he needed to go.

Strain turn on the car radio and quickly tuned from one station to another.

"Odd time for music, John," Wheels pressed a couple of preset buttons on the radio.

"Lower the windows all the way down," Strain said.

Wheels pushed the window buttons on the door and they lowered automatically all the way down.

"They won't expect someone driving and playing loud music to attack them," said Strain.

416

He quickly found what he was looking for, a rock music station. It was playing, Reaction to Action by Foreigner. Strain turned the volume up loud but not quite to deafening level.

Thorn could hear the music as he stood in amongst the group of trees, totally hidden from anyone. A truck went past in front of him and then there was Wheels driving with the radio on, blasting out music. He could see Wheels' head bobbing up and down to the beat of the music. These guys are crazy, he thought to himself. The truck had moved on and Thorn could now see the parking lot.

Mohammed was about to leave the two men and walk into the airport building when a car drove into the parking lot. All three watched it, their hidden weapons at the ready should it be an ambush. At the same time, a car went past on the road playing very loud music. Mohammed could see the driver was alone. Americans and their loud music, Mohammed thought, as he watched the driver shaking his head to the sound of the music.

The car had entered the airport parking lot was parking across from Mohammed and the two men. The two men faced the car while Mohammed focused on the car playing the music as it also entered the parking lot on the far side. The two cars coming in at the same time made them nervous. A man got out of the first car dressed in a pilot's uniform, walked around to the rear of the car and opened the trunk.

"Keep watch on the other car," Mohammed said to the two men as he marched quickly over to where the pilot was standing. He wanted to make sure this wasn't a trap and that Strain had not found him.

Thorn could see Mohammed clearly through the scope and per Strain's instructions was ready to shoot him. He had to wait until Strain and Wheels were out of the line of fire and in a position where they could get safely out of the car. If he shot Mohammed now, the other two terrorists would start shooting at anyone close by and that included vehicles.

Wheels saw Mohammed and his two men as he drove past the parking lot but ignored them. He turned right into the parking lot, staying on the far side away from Mohammed and reversed the vehicle into an open space at an angle so the passenger door wasn't visible to Mohammed and his men. He also didn't want to be in the line of fire if Thorn started shooting.

Thorn was ready to shoot Mohammed when he moved but the man in the pilot's uniform was blocking his shot, "Get out of the way," he muttered.

The pilot was bent over in his trunk when Mohammed got to him.

"Do you have a light?" asked Mohammed. He had a cigarette in one hand and a gun in the other inside his coat pocket. He had the gun pointed directly at the man's spine, ready to shoot.

The pilot straightened up with a dark brown leather bag in his hand, "Sorry, I don't smoke but they will have matches inside the building, if you're going in," he replied.

"You flying this morning?" asked Mohammed.

"Yes, I have two flights today but only short ones. Maybe I am your pilot." He smiled at Mohammed.

"No, I am with a friend who is taking me up in his Cessna. He just bought it." Mohammed still wasn't convinced this guy was genuine.

"Really, I have a book on the Cessna in my bag, if you want to read it." Before Mohammed could say anything, the man closed the trunk of the car and opened the bag.

Mohammed was about to shoot him when he saw that the inside of the bag was full of papers and a couple of books.

"This is it, a great little book."

"No, thanks, I won't have time." Mohammed walked off.

The pilot put the book back in his bag and started to rummage through it, looking for something else.

Wheels closed the windows and got out of the car and walked around to the passenger side. Even though he didn't look, he could feel the terrorists watching him. He opened the passenger door and Strain rolled out onto the asphalt.

Mohammed watched the driver of the second car take a jacket out of the passenger side of the vehicle and walk towards the airport building. Nothing seemed out of place. He would let the man enter the building and then he would do the same. The pilot was still going through papers, some of which were now on the trunk of his vehicle.

Thorn had no shot because of the pilot. He swung the weapon to his left and could see Wheels opening the passenger door of his car. He heard someone shouting and looked to the sound, there were three men walking towards him from the factory.

"Hey, in the trees, what the fuck are you doing?" One of the men shouted out loud.

Now all three men were shouting things at Thorn as they approached him.

"You a fucking pervert or something?" another man said.

"I got trouble over here - factory workers found me hiding in the trees," Thorn said into his microphone, then turned so the men could see him and his sniper rifle.

"Holy fuck, he has a rifle," one man said and they all ran back towards the factory.

Mohammed could hear shouting across the street and saw three men walking towards some trees by a factory. He heard one of them say something about a rifle and then the men were running back towards the building, He started firing shots towards the trees, as did his two men. Mohammed let them continue shooting as he jumped back on the motorcycle.

Wheels turned as he heard the shouting and saw Mohammed shooting in Thorn's direction. Wheels wanted to shoot at Mohammed and his men but the three men running were in the line of fire. He ran towards the building to get a better shooting position.

Strain heard the shots and saw Mohammed racing off on the motorcycle towards the parking lot entrance. He stepped out from behind the cover of the car and fired four shots at Mohammed. Three bullets hit the motorcycle and one grazed Mohammed in the right forearm. The motorcycle was now out of control and Mohammed came flying off, landing hard on the road.

Thorn heard bullets hitting the trees around him as he threw himself to the ground. He could also hear a motorcycle and worried that Mohammed was escaping. The bullets stopped hitting the trees but he could still hear shots. He got to one knee and saw Wheels crouched behind a parked car, taking cover from the hail of bullets from the two terrorists. He reacted without thought and fired the rifle. One terrorist's head turned into mush as his body fell to the ground. The second terrorist had taken cover when he saw his colleague fall.

Wheels couldn't believe how many bullets were being fired at him, he could feel them punching holes in the car. He moved again just as he heard a rifle shot. He could now see one of the terrorists running in a crouched position between cars. Wheels took careful aim following the man's track and fired two rounds as the man lost cover between two cars. The first bullet found its target entering the man's shoulder, the second struck the base of his skull taking out the top of his spinal column.

Strain ran towards Mohammed as he flew off the motorcycle. He could see Mohammed's gun skidding down the road.

Mohammed expertly rolled twice as he came off the motorcycle at the end of the parking lot and landed on his feet. His gun was lying near him, next to a parked car. He ran for the gun as he saw Strain coming from behind a car.

Thorn and Wheels both broke cover and headed towards the two terrorists they had shot to check that they were both dead. Both men had their weapons up in the firing position should one of them appear to be alive.

"This one's dead," said Wheels.

"Yes, so is this one," replied Thorn.

"Look, Strain's after Mohammed," Wheels said as he started to run in Strain's direction closely followed by Thorn.

Strain could see that Mohammed was going for the gun and jumped onto the trunk of a car and started to run jumping from one car to the next. He saw Mohammed standing up and launched his body at him. In midair Strain, could see the gun in Mohammed's hand.

Mohammed turned. It looked like Strain was flying at him, his arms were outstretched and he had the face of the devil. Mohammed raised his gun and pulled the trigger twice when

Strain's chest was only a foot from him, but the gun didn't fire, it was out of bullets.

Strain crashed down on top of Mohammed knocking him backwards, taking the wind out of him at the same time.

Mohammed jumped up. He was filled with anger when he saw Strain standing in front of him. His gun still wouldn't fire.

Strain swung his right foot into Mohammed's kidney and followed with a right fist to Mohammed's face. Undaunted, Mohammed hit Strain with two left jabs to his face and then a savage punch to his ribs.

Strain felt one of his ribs break from the punch Mohammed gave him but the adrenaline was pumping hard and he ignored the pain. Mohammed struck again with a karate kick to his right hip quickly followed by a second one to his right knee.

Strain saw the second kick coming and grabbed Mohammed's right leg. With his left leg, he swept Mohammed's left leg, knocking him to the ground. In one motion, Strain was on top of Mohammed, giving him no chance to regroup. He threw his right elbow into Mohammed's face four, five times he couldn't tell how many blows he hit him with.

Mohammed put both of his feet on Strain's stomach and grasping Strain's coveralls, he lifted him over the top of his head crashing him onto his back. Mohammed's face was covered in blood, his nose broken in two places and he had a gash three inches long on his forehead. Strain was already up on his feet, he was also covered in blood.

Thorn raised his rifle to shoot Mohammed and Wheels put his hand up, "Strain will finish this," he said.

They watched as both men exchanged blows.

Mohammed gave as good as he got but could feel Strain getting the better of him. He reached into a pocket on the side of his pants and pulled out a six-inch knife.

Strain saw the knife come out and raised both of his hands in front of him to block it. Mohammed took several wild swipes at Strain, slashing left and right. Then he faked a slashing motion and punched Strain in the temple with his left fist, but immediately slashed with the knife catching Strain on his left side. Strain instinctively putting his hand on the burning wound created by the knife. Mohammed attacked again he'd found renewed energy. Strain kicked his knife hand with a high swinging left foot, sending the knife into the air. Mohammed lost control and lunged at Strain, only to be hit in the throat with a straight fingered right hand jab. Mohammed gasped for air. His windpipe was crushed and he collapsed to the ground. Strain knelt over Mohammed as he lay on his back holding his throat trying to suck air in. Strain considered Mohammed's cold eyes.

"You won't be able to kill anymore," said Strain. He stood over Mohammed and smashed the heel of his boot into Mohammed's throat, crushing his spine where it joined his skull.

Thorn and Wheels walked over to Strain. "Time to go," said Thorn as they heard the police sirens in the distance.

"OK, leave this scum where he is," said Strain.

As the three of them drove off in the sports car, they could see people peering out of the factory windows and doorways wondering what the hell just happened.

Thorn called the incident in so that the Feds would take control of the scene and no record would appear of Strain or himself. He also called for a cleaning crew to go to the bread factory, they would make the bodies disappear and the burnt-out van would be covered and towed away.

CHAPTER 65

THE WHITE HOUSE

The President had heard about the shooting at the airport and knew it had to be Strain and Thorn. It had only happened two hours earlier and they had requested a meeting with him in private.

"That wasn't as discreet as we would have liked, but at least the bastards are dead," said Thorn, as they sat in the waiting area close to the Oval Office.

"I guess it could have been worse - it could have been one of us," replied Strain.

"The President is ready for you now," said the aide sitting at her desk.

Both men stood without saying a word and walked into the Oval Office. The President was sitting at his desk signing something and didn't look up.

"Sit," the President said and carried on signing papers.

It was the longest minute and a half either of them had experienced.

He finally looked up from the papers, as he slung them into a tray on the corner of his desk.

"Well, you two have caused quite a mess out there. The media are all over the airport, thankfully after our people had arrived. The local PD is still out there taking statements from some of the witnesses. How do you suggest we explain this one?" He stared down both men.

"Sir," that was all Strain got to say.

"Not you, Thorn, let's hear it."

"It looks like two drug gangs got into a fight with each other. They were waiting for a shipment to come into the airport when one tried to rip the other off. As the public knows, these drug gangs are heavily armed and are always fighting with each other. The secrecy of the police and Federal authorities at the scene would be totally normal in this type of situation." Thorn waited for the ass-chewing of his career.

There was total silence for about ten seconds until the President burst out laughing. Strain and Thorn looked at each other wondering what the hell just happened.

The President walked around the desk to them, still chuckling away to himself. They stood as he shook hands with both and returned to his desk.

"You think fast on your feet, Thorn and I am sure that you would have given just as good a story, John. My God, do you two really understand what you have done for this country? I don't give a damn what the press says about the incident, your story is very plausible and that is the one we will go with. You, John, have also done a great service for me and I won't forget it. By the look of your face, you have paid a painful price. I think that you should both know that Khurram Al Khan, the Pakistan Ambassador, is moving to a new post in Dubai. He called thirty minutes ago, asking to see me here. It is protocol for an Ambassador to inform the President in person, I found out through another source before he called. So, I am expecting him here in thirty minutes to make things official." He paused to take a drink of water.

"Sir, this man is in the middle of all of this and is responsible for several deaths, including Senator Gatts'. We can't just let him walk and continue his support of terrorism in another country." Strain was furious but remained calm.

"Trust me if there was something I could do about it I would, my hands are tied."

"When does he leave sir?" asked Thorn.

"The day after tomorrow. He is throwing a farewell party tomorrow night before he leaves. Stupidly his office sent the party invitation to me before he'd officially told me that he is leaving."

"Where is it being held?" asked Strain.

"I know what you must be thinking but he can't be harmed at his party, too many people. I am also very frustrated by this news he killed a very good friend of mine, he will pay for it one day," he replied.

"I understand sir, just curious." Strain really wanted to know.

"It will be at the St Regis, he is going to be arrogant to the end. I won't be attending, too short notice, but there will be a lot of other Ambassadors and dignitaries there. There will be a lot of security in attendance from many of the Embassies. I have been told that Ali Omarzai, the very wealthy attorney, is flying to London on his private jet. He has offered to take Ambassador Khan as far as London. He is apparently leaving us in style. I want you to make sure that they do leave on his jet and we are not left with any more surprises. Once they leave, I would like to see you both back here in my office. Thank you again for your good work, now I must finish my work before the Ambassador arrives."

Strain and Thorn got up and left, saying nothing until they got outside.

"I didn't see that coming," said Thorn.

"Which the pat on the back or the news of the departure?" asked Strain.

"Neither, shit, look who it is."

Walking towards them was the Pakistan Ambassador and his head of security Ghailani. They carried on walking, trying not to punch the Ambassador in the face.

"Gentlemen, I believe we have never met." The Ambassador stuck his hand out, offering it to them to shake.

"Ambassador," Thorn replied and shook his hand.

"Mr. Ghailani here tells me you are both in security like him. I am sorry we won't get to know each other better, but I have been reassigned. You must come to my farewell party tomorrow night as my guests. Mr. Ghailani, can you put their names on the list. By the way what is your name? I know you are Mr. Thorn, but yours I don't know." He said to Strain.

"John," Strain replied.

"We know that much, it doesn't matter. Mr. John and Mr. Thorn your names will be on the guest list. Mr. Ghailani, can you give them your business card? You can call him on his cell phone if you have trouble getting into the party."

He walked on as Ghailani gave Thorn a business card with just a phone number on it. Ghailani gave them a respectful nod and followed the Ambassador.

"Can you believe that fucker?" said Thorn as they left.

CHAPTER 66

ST REGIS HOTEL, D.C.
AMBASSADOR'S PARTY

Strain and Thorn decided that it would be good to go to the party so that they could see who else was there. It would be interesting to see if there were any of the suspected financial supporters of terrorism attending.

Strain and Thorn briefed the team about the party and took some serious insults as they dressed in their tuxedos at the safe house. After the whistles and cat calls had died down, they left with the final comment from Bulldog, "Aren't you going to hold hands, you look so cute together?"

The response by Strain and Thorn was the one fingered salute as they stepped into the elevator.

The morning of the party, Strain had George and Chalky place some hidden cameras and microphones in the reception area leading into the party area as well as in the main room. They waited until the room had been given a sweep by the diplomatic security group then entered wearing badges showing they were part of the group that had just left. Nobody questioned them. Strain had a room booked upstairs to monitor the cameras and sound.

Strain and Thorn arrived exactly on time at the St. Regis after parking Thorn's sports cars two blocks away. Thorn didn't trust leaving the car at the hotel as it would be all valet parking. If he had to leave in a hurry, it would mean relying on the valet to get the car back to him quickly. He didn't want to leave this to chance.

Ghailani saw them walking towards the hotel through an upstairs window. He gave them enough time to check in and went downstairs, leaving the hotel by a side door. He had every street under surveillance for a three-block radius around the hotel. He knew that they wouldn't park at the hotel and was very pleased with himself when they proved him right.

Because of the good surveillance by his men, Ghailani quickly found where Thorn's car was parked. As he approached the car, he was met by one of his security group carrying a back pack. Ghailani opened the back pack, inside was a large amount of plastic explosive connected to a remote-control receiver, a tracking device and a powerful magnet.

As his security man kept watch, Ghailani slid under the driver's side of Thorn's car. He looked for a flat spot on the underside of the car and found one directly under the driver's seat. He turned the bomb upside down with the magnet on top and clamped it tightly to the steel of the car.

Ghailani brushed himself off and returned to the party, dismissing his security people keeping surveillance. He didn't want Strain and Thorn to see any of them or get suspicious when they returned to the vehicle.

Strain and Thorn mingled with the guests at the party. They had seen the Ambassador but not Ghailani yet. As Thorn was talking to Strain about nothing he saw Ghailani walking from the direction of the restrooms. Thorn hoped he was still suffering from the laxative he'd given him, but it was very unlikely.

"There is Ghailani," he said nudging Strain.

Ghailani saw them they were to one side of the room with their backs to the wall and nodded to acknowledge that he'd seen them.

"Is that all he can do, nod?" said Strain.

"I think he has one or two other tricks up his sleeve. Do you think he is leaving with the Ambassador?" asked Thorn.

"I would put money on it," he replied.

Strain's cell phone vibrated in his pocket he took it out and read the text.

"Everything OK?" asked Thorn.

"Yeah! Fine, it was Shadow, just wanting to know where we are," replied Strain.

"He'd be bored here," replied Thorn.

The party was like most other diplomatic events, all tuxedos and fancy dresses with everyone kissing each other's ass.

"I have seen enough, have you?" said Strain.

They had been at the party two and a half hours. Strain knew they weren't going to gain anything by staying there, besides the hidden cameras were recording everyone and everything going on. He could imagine George and Chalky upstairs in the hotel room, scoffing down food from room service. They were most probably making derogatory comments about people in the party and their dress sense. They both deserved the rest after the beating Chalky took and the bullets only grazing George's right side and shoulder.

"Yep, let's slide out," replied Thorn.

Strain called the number on the card Ghailani had given to him the previous day, it was ringing. He watched as Ghailani took his phone out of his pocket and looked at caller ID. He was about to ignore the caller when he saw Strain waiving his phone at him.

He answered, "Hello."

"We just wanted to thank you for the invitation but we have to leave early," Strain said.

"Thank you for coming," Ghailani replied, as he saved the number to his caller I.D.

Strain could feel the man's eyes on the back of his head as he walked out of the room.

Ghailani tapped the Ambassador on the shoulder and whispered in his ear, "They are leaving."

"Excuse me, please," the Ambassador said to the people he was with and followed Ghailani.

They made their way to where Ghailani had parked the Ambassador's car and Ghailani turned on the tracking device that was attached to Thorn's car. It was a top of the range tracking device showing exactly which street they were driving along to within fifteen feet.

"They have to walk two blocks so we will be in place by the time they get to the car." Ghailani could see the excitement in the Ambassador's eyes.

Ghailani was in no hurry, as he knew he could catch up to them quickly.

They watched for a few minutes until they saw the red dot on the monitor moving.

"We will go one block over and track them until you are ready," said Ghailani.

"Go quickly, I don't want to lose them," the Ambassador replied. He was getting both anxious and excited at the thought of killing them.

"We won't lose them," replied Ghailani.

"This won't be a repeat of the Senator Gatt's explosion that fool Ramzi pressed the button too soon. You have made this bomb you can tell me when it's safe to press the button." He was blaming Ramzi for his mistake but Ghailani knew whose mistake it was and didn't argue. The Ambassador was too much of a self-centered control freak to allow someone else the enjoyment of blowing the Senator up.

Strain and Thorn kept performing counter surveillance as they walked, which wasn't only out of necessity but habit. They didn't see anyone watching or tailing them as they arrived at the car. Thorn drove away glad to be out of the party, he and Strain both undoing their bow ties.

"Putting a tux on is good on the rare occasion that you get to go to an event you like, but that event was pure boredom," said Strain.

"Can't say I disagree with that," replied Thorn.

They drove down Connecticut Ave NW for several blocks and then in and out of side streets. They were again performing counter surveillance as they drove back to the safe house. Thorn could see a car tailing him as he turned onto Beach Drive NW. He'd seen the car a couple of blocks back at one of the intersections when he was driving through the side streets. He was now on headed north towards Whitehaven Park, a heavily tree-lined road.

"They have turned onto Beach Drive heading north. That is a good place for us to detonate the bomb," said Ghailani.

"Good, catch up to them," replied the Ambassador.

Thorn knew this road very well he'd jogged along its trails six days a week just after he left the military. He could see a motorcycle cop ahead with his police lights flashing, he was stopping a pickup truck. The cop was getting off the motorcycle as Thorn went past. The pickup had two men in the front but it was difficult to make out their faces in the dark.

Ghailani was closing in fast now and he, too, saw the motorcycle cop ahead and the tail lights of Thorn's car in the distance, past the cop. He was now driving just a little over the speed limit, bringing his speed down to maintain a reasonable distance from their target.

"We've got company," said Thorn.

"Yes, he joined us a few blocks back. It's the Ambassador's car," replied Strain.

"We are coming to a tunnel soon. It has a long sweeping curve to the right. As I enter. I'll pick up speed and wait for him on the other side." Thorn hit the accelerator and entered the tunnel.

"They are going into the tunnel," said Ghailani.

"It's time," replied the Ambassador.

"No wait, the signal won't penetrate the tunnel we can do it as we come out the other end. The road has a straight stretch just after we come out of the tunnel, you can detonate it then. We will see the whole thing from a safe distance." Ghailani didn't want to take a chance if the signal failed.

"Yes, yes, I can feel my heart pounding with joy," replied the Ambassador.

There was no traffic coming towards them as Thorn came out of the tunnel. He slammed on the brakes, turning the steering wheel just enough to put the car sideways, blocking the road. When the Ambassador's vehicle came out the tunnel, he would have no choice but to stop.

Strain and Thorn both got out of the car and stood on either side of the tunnel entrance, out of sight.

Ghailani saw the car blocking the road as he came towards the end of the tunnel.

"Look," shouted the Ambassador.

Ghailani braked hard stopping, just ten feet from the car.

"Where are they?" said the Ambassador.

Strain and Thorn both stepped out of the darkness and walked up to the Ambassador's car, guns at the ready. Thorn tapped on the driver's window with his hand indicating that Ghailani should lower his window, which he did.

"Good evening, I assume you are following us for a reason?" asked Thorn.

The Ambassador lowered his window as he saw Strain standing by the car.

"I am an Ambassador and you will create holy hell if you shoot us. There will diplomatic ramifications for years." He was terrified and it showed.

"No need to worry Ambassador. We are not here to shoot you, but why are you following us?" Strain kept his gun aimed at the Ambassador's head.

"We aren't you're mistaken," replied Ghailani calmly.

"Then perhaps you should drive on if you're not following us," replied Thorn.

"Your car is in the way," Ghailani had ice in his veins as he stared down Thorn.

"Reverse a little and you can get around by driving on the sidewalk." Thorn had no intention of having his back to these two.

"Goodnight," said Ghailani.

"I'll report this to your superiors in the morning you will be sent to prison for threatening a foreign diplomat." The Ambassador had grown a pair of balls again now that he knew they were not going to shoot him.

Strain and Thorn got back into the car and continued in the direction the Ambassador had gone. They could see his vehicle ahead looking like it was keeping to the speed limit.

"When we get to the next junction, we will be far enough away but you will still see them. If you look around, they are in the distance, plenty of room between us," said Ghailani.

The Ambassador started to laugh quietly with excitement.

"I'll give Ghailani a call, thanks to the Ambassador we have his cell phone number," said Strain.

Ghailani's cell phone rang and was picked up on the car hands free system. He could see that it was the agent, as he knew him, from the party.

"Who is it?" asked the Ambassador.

"It's them," he replied, pointing back over his shoulder.

"Answer it. I want them to hear that I am about to kill them. We are far enough away now, aren't we?" the Ambassador replied.

"Yes." Ghailani pressed the phone symbol on the dashboard of the car.

"Can I help you," said the Ambassador.

Strain's voice filled the car when they answered his call.

"Yes, I have a question for you, Ambassador."

The Ambassador gave Ghailani a quizzical look.

"What is it?" he replied.

"We know you killed Senator Gatts but we couldn't prove it and you are now heading overseas. I would like to hear you say that you are responsible."

"Yes, I killed him. You may be recording this but it doesn't matter as you won't get the opportunity to use the recording as you are about to die." He opened the center console of the car and activated the detonator.

"Is that so and how do you hope to do that?" replied Strain.

"There's a bomb under your car you have five seconds to live."

"Do it now," said Ghailani.

The Ambassador undid his seat belt and having turned around to get a full view of the car exploding, pressed the remote.

Ghailani watched in the rear-view mirror and couldn't believe it when nothing happened.

The Ambassador pressed the detonator again and again, nothing. Then he heard Strain's voice.

"It's you who is going to die. You must think we are as dumb and incompetent as you. We had our team members' switch the bomb to your car and the tracking device stayed on this one. This is for the Senator, his family and the President."

Thorn braked hard to give more distance and saw the brake lights on the Ambassador's car.

"No, no it can't be," said the Ambassador.

The Ambassador's car disappeared in a flash of red, yellow and orange light as it blew up, filling the night sky with white hot heat.

Strain and Thorn watched for thirty seconds as the vehicle burned and gave off a couple smaller explosions. Thorn turned his car around and headed back towards the tunnel.

Strain dialed a number on the phone, "OK, all done, time to go home," he said.

Shadow was sitting on the police motorcycle while Bulldog and Wheels were leaning against the pickup. They were looking in the direction that Strain and Thorn had gone when they passed them earlier. They saw the light from the explosion first and when the sound reached them it was loud even from where they stood.

Shadow's phone rang it was Strain telling them to go home.

"OK, time to go," said Shadow, as they wheeled the motorcycle up the ramp into the back of the pickup.

Shadow called L.B. and Sleepy who were at the junctions of roads north and south of the explosion, blocking access to Beach Drive with police flares and diversion signs. They didn't need any civilians injured in the attack. They picked up the road flares and diversion signs, leaving before the real cops arrived.

The team spent a couple of hours at the safe house with Thorn, enjoying a few drinks to celebrate.

The news of the explosion was already out, with crews trying to get to the site and media helicopters flying overhead, taking videos of the explosion. Thorn had already called in the cleaning crews to take care of the bodies and wreckage. The same crews had the local PD blocking all access to the area of the park where the explosion took place.

It would be released to the media that there was a gas line explosion at the side of the road. Nobody was hurt in the car damaged by fire in the explosion, as it had broken down and the driver left it there.

CHAPTER 67

THE WHITE HOUSE

The next day Strain and Thorn waited outside the Oval office wondering how the President would accept their report. They didn't particularly care if he was pissed off about the Ambassador's death. He would change his view of things when they gave him the news that the Ambassador had murdered Senator Gatts.

The door to the Oval Office opened and the President's assistant came out.

"The President is ready to see you now, gentlemen," she said.

Strain and Thorn gave each other a sideways glance and walked into the room.

The President was already walking around his desk when they went into the office.

"Gentlemen," he said shaking their hands. "Sit down, please."

They both sat on two of the wooden chairs to one side of the sofa they expected the President to sit behind his desk. The President surprisingly brought one of the other wooden chairs over and sat facing them. Thorn didn't know what to expect now as he'd never seen the President do this. He'd been in the Oval office many times over the years and this was totally new.

The President looked them both in the eyes. "What happened last night?" he said.

"There was an attempt on our lives and the bomb that was intended for us ended up on the car of the person that was going to kill us." Thorn watched closely for a reaction from the President.

"I don't need to know how it got on the other car but I am led to believe that it was the Ambassador to Pakistan that was killed, they are using DNA and dental records to find out who they are. The second person in the vehicle may be his driver or head of security. What can you tell me about the occupants of the car?"

"Sir, it was the Ambassador and his head of security. As you know from previous reports, they were heavily involved in recent terrorist attacks on US soil." Strain sat back in the chair and waited for the tirade that was coming.

"There is no doubt in my mind that he deserved to die, but you both seem to do things in a public way. I think a little more discretion could be used next time," the President replied.

"Yes, sir," replied Thorn.

"There is something else you need to know, Mr. President," said Strain.

"What is it?" he replied.

Strain gave Thorn the sign that he should be the one to tell him as he knew the Senator.

"Sir, before the Ambassador died he admitted to killing Senator Gatts."

"What, he had a hand in this personally?" He couldn't believe it as he sat back in the chair in surprise.

"Not only did he have a hand in it, he was the one that detonated the bomb. I'm sorry sir, I know you and Senator Gatts were good friends and that is why we felt you should know," said Thorn.

"He admitted this to you both?"

"Yes, right before the explosion. He thought that we were going to be killed as he'd arranged for the bomb to be put on our vehicle. He bragged about killing Senator Gatts when Thorn asked him outright did he do it. We have it all recorded but have not destroyed it yet." Strain took the recorder out of his pocket to let the President see that he had it with him.

The President was conflicted about listening to the recording but he felt he should.

"Play it," he said.

They all sat quietly as they listened to the short conversation that they had recorded. The President sat quietly for over a minute after Strain had turned the tape off. He and Thorn sat watching him to see what he was going to do next.

"Gentlemen, you have both done this country a great service in ridding us of this scum. I want you to destroy that recording, leaving no chance of it being copied. Agent Thorn, I want you to form a task force like Mr. Strain's here. If you accept, I want you to head such a force and you will be given all latitude to do what you want to fight Terrorism. Mr. Strain, I would like you to work alongside Mr. Thorn here to form the team. You can use your UK team members and if you accept the job. Eventually I want this to develop into a team of sixteen men, which, based on the original Mask Team, means you will have enough manpower for two eight man teams. This will give you the capability to divide and conquer or work together, depending on your evaluation of the situation.

The teams would work under the radar here in the US and possibly overseas. I have already discussed this with your Prime Minister and it has his support.

Like myself he doesn't want a decision today. I want you both to take your time and think this over. I'll be in the UK in two weeks to meet the Prime Minister on a scheduled visit. Mr. Thorn you will be a part of my detail and I believe the Prime Minister will be inviting you Mr. Strain to Number 10 for the meeting.

I can't thank you both and your team for what you have done, may God be with you and protect you." The President stood, shaking both of their hands with vigor and excused them.

Strain and Thorn went straight from the White House to the airport where the team waited on the Gulfstream.

"Thanks for the help, John, your team is exceptional," said Thorn.

"Well, seeing as we are kissing ASS, as you Americans say, you didn't do too badly either."

"Yeah, fuck you too. Do you think you will take the President up on his offer to work over here?" asked Thorn.

"I don't really know. I just want to get back to the UK for a break and think about it later." Strain liked the idea but didn't want to rush into anything.

The team was all standing in the open hanger when Thorn drove in.

"I wonder what the President had to say?" said Bulldog to Shadow.

"I guess we will find out soon enough, he replied.

Once the goodbyes, were over the team boarded the plane and it took off for New York.

CHAPTER 68

NEW YORK CITY

The short flight to New York gave the team chance to debrief and enjoy a drink. Strain had arranged catering for the flight across the Atlantic to the UK, to be delivered when they arrived in New York. The plane taxied into a private hanger and the team got out stretching their bodies.

Don Caputo was waiting by the wall of the hanger as the team came down the steps. With the Don was his son and two of his bodyguards who had been with him since the attempt on his life in the restaurant.

Strain walked over to the Don, "Tony, how are you," he said with a smile.

The Don walked over to Strain and gave him a hug and kiss on the cheek.

The Don had not been very pleased when he received Strain's phone call telling him that Mohammed was dead. The team watched as did the Don's son and bodyguards they didn't know how the Don would react.

"You killed him yourself?" asked the Don.

"Yes, but I couldn't avoid it he was going to kill me. If I could have brought him to you alive I would have, replied Strain.

"Enough, it is done now." The Don patted Strain on the shoulder.

"It's not quite done yet, I have a gift for you." Strain said.

"What is it?" asked the Don.

At the top of the plane steps appeared Shadow with a man wearing a hood over his head. He held onto the man as he gingerly walked down the steps of the plane.

Strain and the Don walked over to him and Strain removed the black hood from his head.

"Let me introduce you to Samir al Bahrani, he was Mohammed's right hand man. He was also with Mohammed when they shot and killed your two soldiers in the alley."

Sammy strained to see as the light was hurting his eyes he'd had the hood over his head for several hours. He still had a gag tightly fastened around his mouth.

"Well, this is a good gift. You are a man of your word, John." The Don was positively glowing with pleasure.

"I owed you one of them at least and he is of no use to us now. We have all the information he has to offer, thanks to modern drugs. If your driver can bring the car into the hanger, you can take him with you." Strain was pleased he could do at least this for the Don.

Sammy heard everything they were saying and was screaming something behind the gag on his mouth.

"Where did you get him?" asked the Don.

"He was hiding in the bakery building when we raided it to release one of our team. I was using a device that shows infrared heat signatures of people inside buildings. As the team was leaving, I could see this piece of shit curled up in a corner. I alerted the team and they snatched him on the way out. He was hiding in a cupboard under some stairs like the rat he is," said Shadow.

Sammy was trying to say something again and shouting as loud as the gag would allow but nobody listened.

"Shout all you want because I'll have you screaming later." The Don got right up to Sammy's face.

"There is one other thing you need to know about Sammy here. When Shaady and his sister Karida were murdered, DNA was taken from her body. I believe you knew Karida, Tony. Her DNA was run through every data base we could find and nothing came back with a positive hit. We take DNA off every one of the terrorists we kill or capture. This DNA is put into a special data base that can't be accessed unless you are cleared at the highest level by the US and UK governments. We take these DNA samples so that we can possibly match them up to previous unsolved terrorist incidents or crimes. When Sammy here was caught, we did the same with him. When we ran his

DNA through all the data bases, we had a match to a crime in the NYPD data base. Sammy here is the one that raped and murdered Karida, a virgin and murdered her brother Shaady."

"You fuck, what did she do to hurt you?" Tony said, kicking Sammy hard in the crutch.

The Don pulled Tony back, "Easy, son, you have plenty of time to make him pay."

Sammy was shaking his head saying no and screaming even louder behind the gag, he knew he was going to be unmercifully tortured.

"Will you be staying in New York? We would like to take you out for dinner, all of you." said the Don, eyeing the rest of the team.

"No, sorry we have to fly straight back to the UK, but next time."

"Next time it is. I'll be busy for a few days with this one, anyway," replied the Don.

"Enjoy his company while you can we have to leave," said Strain.

Both men hugged. The rest of the team and the Don's men shook hands they would indeed meet again in the future.

Made in the USA
Charleston, SC
15 March 2017